# INVESTED

## By

## Iris Bolling

Printed in the United States of America

ISBN- 978-0-9990176-0-9

Library of Congress Control Number: 2017910064

This is a work of fiction. Names, characters, places and incidents are with the product of the author's imagination or are used fictitiously, and any resemblance to actual persons, living or dead, business establishments, events, locales is entirely coincidental.

SIRI AUSTIN ENTERTAINMENT LLC
PO Box 937
Mechanicsville, VIRGINIA 23111
irisb@siriaustin.com
www.siriaustin.com
www.irisbolling.net

# Dedication

**Dahl Olivia Haynes,**

*Lovingly known as Locksie Locks
to authors and readers,
this story is dedicated to you.*

*Sometimes people have no idea how much of an impact they have on your life with just a simple word or phrase or conversation. Locksie is a no hold back, teach you as she scolds you, loving mother with a kick-ass accent. She is a member of ARC INC, a book club that was there to support me early on. SiStar Tea, Debbie Shai Deb, English Ruler, Delonya Conyers, and Locksie Locks all had an impact on me that will never be forgotten. The late night and early morning calls from SiStar Tea, the strikes from Debbie Shai Deb, and the writing challenges from English kept me on my toes during my first series. But it was Locksie Locks' calls that left me in tears at times. However, those calls pushed me to be a better writer. We don't talk as much now, however, I know when I put a book out she is going to read it. I'll wait, biting nails to see if I'm going to get a call from her. LOL. No call is a good thing. I say all of this to tell you all, my way of honoring Locksie Locks is INVESTED. Jonathan Michael is molded from stories Locksie shared with me about her family. Thank you, Locksie for the lessons, the laughter, the tears, nail biting, but most of all for the conversations. It is an honor to put "ARC CERTIFIED" on my list of accomplishments.*

# Prologue

Hepburn Dunning envisioned the last day of his life differently. Lying in his bed with his beautiful wife Winnieford, whom he called Winnie, and his five children standing around with pride, and of course sadness in their eyes. He really did not expect it to look like this.

"Daddy." AnnieMarie stopped her movement on the elliptical machine. She calmly turned towards him.

"Help me to understand. Cainan is a good man. You have him on your board of directors. A board you put him on without a vote from all the members. That demonstrates to me what you think of him. Please, explain why you forbid us to see each other?"

Hepburn turned away from his beautiful baby girl. Seeing the hurt in her eyes tore at his heart. If he had known about the budding romance, he would have put a stop to it sooner. At this point it seems the relationship was more advanced than he thought. To complicate matters, Annie, as he called his youngest child, was right. Cainan Scott was one of the most honorable young men he had the pleasure of knowing.

Under other circumstances he would welcome the man into Annie's life with open arms. However, life isn't always fair. The circumstances are what they are.

He placed the towel capturing the sweat from his run on the treadmill around his shoulder, then glanced out the floor to ceiling windows that surrounded the roof top gym of Dunning Bank & Trust. This was his morning refuge. His get-a-way spot before employees began filing in the room for their morning workouts. Hep had asked AnnieMarie to join him for his routine 7 a.m. workout to discuss Cainan Scott. He did not imagine it would be this difficult. Knowing he had to stand his ground, for giving in could put her life in jeopardy, he took a deep breath.

"Have I ever interfered in your relationships?" he snapped as he turned back to face her.

"No, Daddy, you haven't." AnnieMarie stepped off the machine and wiped her face with a towel. "That is why I don't understand why you are doing it now. What are you not telling me?"

He could hear her anger elevating as she spoke. Her expressive eyes reflecting confusion and hurt could not deter him from what he had to do, no matter how much she looked like her mother with her hair up in a ponytail.

"I'm your father and I am telling you not to see this man socially," he yelled as he walked between the circuit equipment toward her. "I am not going to repeat myself on this, AnnieMarie. You break things off with this man or I will do it for you. Have I made myself clear?"

AnnieMarie took a step back. "No, Daddy. You are damn sure loud enough. However, your clarity seems to be escaping me at the moment. I've never seen you this upset. Well, once, but that was directed at Uncle

Walker. It would be okay if I knew why. It is so unlike you to take such an unyielding stance. You have always listened to reason."

Her eyes narrowed as she took a step toward him. "In case you've forgotten, I'm a grown woman. I can make my own decisions on the man I wish to be involved with. Now..." She stepped back as she stared him directly in his eyes. "I respect you, and in most situations would take your advice. However, we are talking about my heart here. I love this man and I am not willing to walk away from him without you giving me some insight other than your caveman mentality of over protectiveness."

His baby girl was so much like her mother. Hep wanted to laugh at her standing her ground with hands on hips ready to fight for her man. If it were any other man he would be impressed. However, it was Cainan Scott and for her own good he had to put a stop to this relationship. He'd rather have her angry and not speaking to him than dead. Well, he had to think about that for a minute. He did not like when his Annie wasn't speaking to him. It was as if his heart was breaking into small pieces with each passing moment.

"Now you listen to me, AnnieMarie Dunning. You continue to see this man and I will fire him. If you disobey me after that, I will disown you and make the ground both of you walk on a living hell."

AnnieMarie's mouth gaped open. "Do you plan on firing me too? Are you speaking for yourself or the entire family?" She waived him off. "You know, it doesn't matter who you are speaking for, you lose. I would stay with Cainan simply because he would not put me in the impossible position to choose between him and my family. If I have to choose between being with him and speaking to you ever again, I choose him." She turned, walked down the open row, pushed the button to the elevator and waited.

Knowing it was an empty threat, Hepburn walked from the row of elliptical and treadmills as he called out to her.

"AnnieMarie, wait."

The center elevator door opened. She stepped inside, turned back to him then pushed the button.

"Goodbye, Daddy."

"Annie," Hepburn sighed as the doors closed.

Turning towards the shower rooms, Hep shook his head then sat on a weight bench near the elevators. The thought of his daughter's anger ate at him. AnnieMarie was his baby and always had him wrapped around her finger. Hell, she had all of them wrapped around that little finger. Right now he was sure AnnieMarie was going straight to Myles' office to complain about him being unreasonable. In a minute or two he expected Myles to come upstairs to confront him. He sighed and thought. It was time to let Myles, his oldest son, in on the situation. He was certain once Myles knew all the details he would understand that as the father it was his duty to protect AnnieMarie's life. Her being involved with Cainan put her life in jeopardy. He thought he would be able to have a reasonable discussion with her about the man. That's why he approached her first. Now, he would have to go to Cainan and pray he would be more reasonable.

He shook his head, but had to smile at his daughter's stance. She was indeed her mother's child. Standing, he had to laugh at the thought of his wife's response to this when he told her about it. Winnieford would get a good laugh out of her daughter's actions. She would probably cheer on AnnieMarie.

He started walking towards the shower rooms when he heard the elevator bell.

Turning, he briskly retraced his steps to the elevator thinking it was AnnieMarie coming back with Myles. He would simply gather her in his arms and hug her until she could feel how much he loved her. Then he would take Myles aside to tell him the details on Cainan.

The doors opened, but no one stepped out.

"Annie," Hep called out. His steps slowed as he got to the elevator. Pulling the towel from his shoulder he looked inside. Before he could react a gloved hand jabbed a syringe into his chest.

"What the..."

He reached for the person, but his body felt weak. He could feel a warm liquid flowing through his veins. No longer able to support his body, his knees began to buckle. He could feel the movement of the person's thumb against the syringe as more of the substance was pushed through. The sound of the other elevator approaching caused the person to withdraw the syringe, step back into the elevator and push the button.

Hepburn fell to his knees, still unable to hold his body up. His eyes held the eyes of the person as the elevator doors closed. It was in that moment he knew he was going to die. This was that day. Winnie's face appeared in his mind. His children, in different stages of their lives with smiles on their faces, ran through like the credits at the end of a movie. Then the face of the person in the elevator, who was taking all of that away, replaced the smiles of his loved ones.

He heard the doors of the other elevator open.

"You simply have to talk some sense into him, Myles." Hep heard AnnieMarie say as they stepped out.

Maybe, just maybe, Hep thought, but then a pain so fierce gripped his chest that he cried out.

"Dad!" Myles came to his side. "Dad!"

"Daddy," AnnieMarie cried out as she fell to her knees beside him. "Daddy, no....Daddy."

Hepburn grabbed his chest as he watched his oldest son and his baby girl frantic at his side.

"Get the elevator, Annie," Myles ordered as he picked his father up. He carried him to the elevator then laid him on the floor.

AnnieMarie hit the emergency button then knelt down beside her father. "I'm sorry, Daddy, I'm sorry."

Hep reached for her but was unable to speak. She took his hand. Hepburn looked at Myles who was frantically working on him. He tried to move his lips. Nothing came out. He had to tell Myles, raced desperately through his mind.

The security officer's voice came over the speakers. "Is there a problem?"

"This is Myles, Mr. Dunning has collapsed. Call an ambulance. It looks like a heart attack. We are in the center elevator."

"On it, sir," the guard's urgent voice responded.

"Myles, do something," AnnieMarie cried out. "Please don't let this happen."

Hepburn grabbed his son's arm with all the strength he could and pulled him to his lips.

Against his son's cheek he mouthed the name, "Scott, Scott."

Myles took his father's hand in his then held his eyes, nodding. "Hold on, Dad. Hold on."

Hepburn's eyes held his son's for a long moment. He was so proud of the man Myles had become. He knew Myles would now be the head of the family. He needed to know his enemies.

"Son," he mouthed just as the elevator doors opened.

The EMTs were there, as his grip on his son's arm weakened. His eyes were closing. He could feel his mind shutting down. Hep looked to the heavens above. His only request was to see his wife's smiling face one last time.

# Chapter One

"*In financial news, Hepburn Ellington Dunning, the president and CEO of Dunning Bank & Trust, was laid to rest a month ago. In addition to mourning the loss of her husband of thirty-eight years, today, Winnieford Dunning will join the board of directors in naming a predecessor to one of the most prestigious banks in the country. The financial world is watching closely, for today's decision will impact number one ranked Phase International, as well as number two-ranked America's Bank in the country. The question on the table is who will take over the leadership role of the nation's largest African-American owned bank. The predecessor will have large shoes to fill, for Hep Dunning was well on the path of moving Dunning Bank & Trust up the ranks with significant acquisitions on*

*the table. The top two, as deemed by the financial world, are awaiting the decision as Dunning's number three ranking continues to threaten their place as the top financial institutions in the world. Who will be at the helm of Dunning and will the new President and CEO have the tenacity to go up against the ranking top two? This is reporter Robert Tannery for The Financial Review."*

Myles Dunning switched the station on his radio as he drove to work. This was going to be a trying morning for his family, but one that was needed to move forward.

*"This is Lindsey Grant with the Wall Street Review. Dunning Bank & Trust is to name a new President and CEO today. The top two financial institutions in the world shared a sigh of relief that could be heard across the country at the sudden death of Hepburn E. Dunning. Why? Let's be honest here, Dunning Bank & Trust was well on the heels of a historical number two ranking with current acquisitions in the negotiation stage. Never before in this country have we experienced number one Phase International and number two America's Bank sharing anything. Yet, today their collective breaths await the decision to see who Dunning will turn the reins over to. This reporter believes it will stay in the family. My only*

*question on the table is will it revert to
the brother, Walker Dunning Jr., or go
to one of the sons. The decision could
prove to be significant for the world's
financial stability. Back to you, Jim."*

Myles pulled into his parking space in the
underground garage, wondering what the day would
bring. All he knew for certain was the new CEO would
have big shoes to fill. He had no intentions of running
for the position and planned to support whoever is
chosen. However, and it was a big however, he would
not allow William Mitchell, the Vice-President of
Dunning, to succeed in taking over his family's bank.

"Good morning, Mr. Dunning." Chrystina Price,
his Executive Assistant, met him at the elevator. "You
are late. I'm not going to ask why because I can see
from the dirt on your shoes you stopped by your
father's grave site before coming."

Looking down at his shoes, Myles shook his head
at how observant she was. He was reaching for his
handkerchief when she bent down and was wiping his
shoes off with her scarf.

"There." She stood back up and smiled. "You look
good."

"Good morning, Chrystina," he all but laughed. "I
see you are as efficient as ever."

"Only for you, Mr. Dunning. The board meeting is
about to begin. Here is your portfolio. Your reports
are edited and ready for distribution to the directors."
She took his briefcase. "I'll put this in your office." The
elevator doors opened. They stepped out. Myles
turned towards the boardroom as Chrystina walked in
the opposite direction.

"Remember," she whispered loudly as they
separated. "Anyone but Mitch."

Myles put up a hand acknowledging her statement, then continued to the meeting.

#

Today's meeting of the board of directors for Dunning Bank and Trust was certainly out of the ordinary. The historical banner reading "Family Integrity First and Foremost" hung on the back wall as a reminder of what the business was all about. Seated around the oval shaped cherry-wood table, in the conference room on the eighth floor of the downtown Richmond landmark headquarters building, were directors with very solemn faces. No one thought this day would come this soon. After twenty years as President and CEO of DBT, Hepburn Ellington Dunning was not present to lead them.

The tension caused by the effect of Hep's death was felt throughout the room. William Mitchell, Vice-President of the bank, sat in his usual seat on the left at the head of the table, silently scrutinizing the other three non-family members who had voting rights. The members were diverse in nationality and age. Hep always prided himself with the knowledge that he was open to all who worked hard and proved their worth. Mitchell shivered at the thought. It was always his belief to stack the board to ensure his decisions were carried out as he saw fit. Now that Hep was dead and gone, that was no longer a concern. That is, if the vote went his way.

In his estimation, Elaine Jacobson, who had been his sounding board for the last ten years whenever he was displeased with Hep's decisions, would support him as president. His gaze moved on to Preston Long, a young thirty-something Italian or Mexican - William wasn't sure which and didn't care. As long as Preston voted with him, he would give him the promotion he promised. The only one William was not sure of was

Cainan Scott, the newest member. Cainan was a bit of a mystery. Hep had brought him on board about a year ago from Wall Street to head up the Investments department. On paper, he was a very accomplished young man in his late twenties, but investigations were not complete on his personal background and that bothered William. He liked knowing all he could about the people around him, good and bad, that way he could always manipulate at will.

The double doors to the conference room opened interrupting his assessment of his chances and in walked the Dunning family board members. They always came in together giving the vision of a united front. That was one of the first things on his agenda once he became President. Divide and conquer.

Winnieford Dunning walked in on the arm of her second son, Michael Anthony. If anyone had seen them on the street, they could have easily been mistaken as a couple. Looking at least fifteen years younger than her fifty-five years, Winnieford was fashionably dressed in a black shell dress with a thick red belt around her slim waist, black pumps, the usual pearl necklace with matching earrings, accessories complimenting her short haircut and radiant, but sad face. Michael, dressed in an impeccable gray Armani suit, with a pink shirt and matching tie, that only a very secure man would wear, escorted his mother to the head of the table. Gary Hepburn, the youngest and most outspoken of the sons, wore Sean John, navy blue silk, no tie and that confident swagger that seemed to run in the family, walked in behind Grace Heather. The woman, dressed as the ultimate professional, wore her usual navy blue blazer and skirt set with a white blouse and matching pumps. Last, but certainly not the least of all, Myles Davis, the oldest son who was the spitting image of Hep, strolled in dressed in Gucci gray, as if it was made just for his body. This was the man. This was the only person William saw as a threat to him taking over as President and CEO of Dunning. With Winnieford abstaining from the vote and AnnieMarie absent that gave Myles three votes and him three votes. William glared at Cainan Scott. The man representing the tiebreaker had been missing in action all week. Was that an indication? He did not know, but it seemed they were all about to find out.

#

Winnieford took her seat at the right of her now deceased husband's chair, directly across from Mitchell. Doing the one thing she did not feel, she stood, smiled and brought the meeting to order.

"Thank you all for coming to this emergency meeting. As Chairman of the board of directors, I officially call this meeting to order. Our first order of business is the selection of the new president and CEO of Dunning Bank and Trust. To clear up rumors, I would like to say as much as I love this great institution and as much as I respect its rich history, I have no desire to take over where Hep left off. I will remain as Chairman of the board of directors, but I will not take over as President and CEO." She paused, exhaled and then began again. "With that said, the floor is now open for nominations for the position."

Preston Long stood. "May I be heard?"

"You have the floor," Winnieford replied, then took her seat.

"Thank you, Mrs. Dunning. First, I would like to again offer my condolences to the Dunning family. Hep was a great mentor and employer, but a lousy golfer." Winnieford nodded as the group smiled, for they all knew that was true. "Knowing he was at the end of the hall was always a comfort to me. There was never a time in my professional or personal life that Hep wasn't there encouraging me. He will be missed. Now, to the matter at hand, it is important that we show our clientele the tradition of encouraging entrepreneurship; self-dependency and financial stability at Dunning will continue the way that it has over the last few years. I believe the person to do that would be the same person who has been by Hep's side during that time, William Mitchell."

The expected nomination did not take Winnieford by surprise. She reached over and placed her hand on the arm of the chair where Hep would have been seated. Never showing any emotions she silently voiced, *Don't worry, darling. I will not let control out of the family. Your wishes will be carried out.*

Elaine Jacobson stood. "I second the nomination," she stated, as Preston sat, then quickly retook her seat.

Winnieford waited patiently, sending up a silent prayer for someone to step in. A subtle glance down the table showed her eldest son Myles begin to stand and her heart knew he was going to give his backing to William. However, before Myles could speak, Michael stood.

"Before we go further, may I address the board?"

The statement eased Winnieford's fear. "Yes, of course." She sighed then sent a stern look down the table to her oldest son.

"Since its inception in 1840, Dunning Bank and Trust has been led by a Dunning. Mitch, I mean you no disrespect and commend the job you have done for the institution, however, we have two very capable Dunnings on the board, Grace and Myles. I respectfully submit both names for consideration."

Before Winnieford could place the names into the nomination, Grace stood.

"I just as respectfully decline the nomination. I do, however, second the nomination of Myles Davis Dunning." Grinning at her oldest brother, Grace retook her seat.

Silence ensued as all eyes went to Myles. Winnieford closed her eyes for a moment to give her son at least the opportunity to decline. She secretly prayed that he would not. A few beats passed, her heart burst with joy. It took all of her will not to let it show.

"The nomination of Myles Dunning will be added to that of William Mitchell. Are there any others?" She waited. There were none. "William Mitchell and Myles Dunning, as you know the voting of positions are done in private to ensure no retaliation. Will you please step out while we deliberate?"

William stood, adjusted his suit jacket around his protruding abdomen, walked over to the door and opened it waiting for Myles to stand. Winnieford watched as Myles sat there with pen in hand. He first looked to his brother Michael. The smirk on his face was something Myles had to deal with all his life. Myles then looked at Grace, who sat up staring at her brother and had the nerve to smile at him with a mischievous look in her eyes. Winnieford did all she could not to laugh as she continued to observe her oldest son's expressions. Myles looked from Grace to Gary who was grinning like the cat who ate the canary. Then his eyes fell upon her. She was certain he could see the sadness at the loss of her soul mate that was still evident in her eyes. But so was the hope that he would do the right thing.

Her heart jumped with joy the moment Myles placed the pen on top of his tablet and walked out the door. He stopped, turned back and glanced at each of his family members. He shook his head, then stepped out the door. Winnieford closed her eyes and smiled.

#

In the reception area outside the conference door, Myles nodded and smiled at Marie Vazquez, his father's private secretary for the past twelve years. He wondered for a moment why she was sitting outside the conference room. She must have picked up on his confusion.

"You are so like your father." Mrs. Vazquez chuckled at his facial expression. "Some felt I no longer had a place in the board meeting since Mr. Dunning was no longer with us." She glanced at William with a frown then turned back to Myles, smiling. "I see they dragged you in."

"Something like that," Myles said with a tilt of his head.

"Good for them." She nodded. "Your father would be very pleased. I can't tell you how many conversations we've had on you taking over one day."

"Well, the vote isn't in yet. But, son, you know I am here for you no matter how the vote goes," William stated with the right amount of assurance to convince a less observant person of his sincerity.

Looking down at the five nine, two hundred-fifty pound pudgy man for a long minute, Myles always wondered why his father kept him around. Once when he and his father had a disagreement about Mitch, as Myles called him, his father said, 'It is better to keep your enemies close.' With that in mind Myles extended his hand.

"Same here, Mitch." They shook.

Mrs. Vazquez held her smile but Myles could see the contempt the woman had for Mitch. Patting Myles on the back, she cautioned, "We will all be here for you, Myles. Some more so than others have Dunning's future foremost in our minds." She smiled, completely ignoring William.

William was seething inside as he placed his hand back into his pocket. He hated when Hep called him Mitch. Now, if this vote did not go his way he would have to deal with his son calling him that. His name was William, not Mitch. It seemed a norm for these people to shorten each other's name at will. Well, not him. It appeared the only person who respected that was Winnieford. Of course he had to explain it to her in the early days, but she had not forgotten. She always, always, referred to him as William. That was one of the things he loved about her. Well, as much as a White man could love a Black woman, that is.

Back in the day, Winnieford was a beauty. Hell, truth be told she wasn't far from it now. There was just no way he could have her in his life. It was not acceptable back in the day, but if he could, he would have married Winnieford. William knew if he did his family would have disowned him. That notion turned out to be a moot point when he made the mistake of introducing Winnieford to the running back on the football team, Hepburn Dunning.

It was all she wrote at that point. Winnieford was his history tutor. Imagine that...a Black girl tutoring him. But she was smart, pretty and William was hot for her. He invited Winnieford to a game. Afterwards a group of them went for burgers. Hepburn joined them. That was when he realized introducing Hepburn to Winnieford had been a mistake. The two were inseparable from that point on. No matter what he tried, the bond was too damn tight to break. So, he finally gave up. However, the three remained friends on the surface. To William's way of thinking, Hep would eventually screw up and that's when he would step in. The day after Hep graduated, he married

Winnieford. William thought she was lost to him forever. Then Hepburn surprised him. Out of gratitude, Hep offered William a job at his family owned bank. As it turned out, it was the best offer to come his way. He knew it was Winnieford who pushed Hepburn to make the offer. He had confided in her the offers he was receiving were, well, beneath him. William took her actions as a sign that she cared for him. So he took the position knowing that one day he would win Winnieford and take over the business. However, as year after year and child after child came, it seemed the opportunity would never present itself. Until now.

"You know, son, I never got the impression you were interested in running the company. I always saw you as an intellect. With all your outside activities with the education system, I thought one day you would go in that direction."

"Life has a way of stepping in and taking over, Mitch. I'll be wherever my family needs me to be."

Mitch nodded. "I understand. Hepburn's death was a shock to all of us. I have been at his side for over thirty years. It's going to be hard to adjust without him being near."

"Harder more so for his wife and family," Myles stated.

"Of course, of course," William quickly added. "Your mother is a strong woman. You know the board's decision will be fair. Whatever the outcome we will work together to insure Dunning continues to grow."

"Growth is relevant." Myles nodded. "The priority should be the continual dedication to providing ultimate service to our clientele. Growth will be an added bonus."

That was the same way Hepburn thought. William frowned inwardly. If Hepburn had listened to him they would be in the driver's seat of the banking industry in this country instead of chasing after others. There were takeovers on the table he felt they should have done years ago. They could have swallowed up several smaller banks to increase their assets and customer base. But no, what did Hepburn do? He bailed the damn banks out. Instead of taking them over he mentored and financially assisted those in trouble and now some of those banks were trying to take them over. Not him. To him it was time. It was time to change the make up of the board and the Dunning control. It's time to do things his way.

#

Winnieford opened the door to the conference room and asked them to step in. Closing it behind the men as they entered, she walked back to the head of the table to make the announcement.

"The new President and CEO of Dunning Bank & Trust is Myles Davis Dunning." Smiling, Winnieford put her hand on the back of Hep's chair. "Please take your seat at the head of the table."

Thirty years of practice had granted William with the acting ability to appear to be genuinely happy with the results, but inside he was seething. Standing back at his place at the table, William joined the members of the board in applauding their selection. This was a slap in the face as far as he was concerned. Yes, the Dunning family had run the bank since its inception, but it should be about business not the bull crap history sentiment they are always raving about. It's time for that to end. He would be damned if he would let thirty years of his life go down the drain as the second in command...again. He smiled in Winnieford's direction as he thought. He had plans for the unfortunate turn of events and the woman he was certain was behind his defeat.

As the board members retook their seats, Myles remained where he stood. He was not ready to take his father's chair. Unbuttoning the single button on his suit blazer, the handsome, reserved thirty-five-year-old, six-two, two hundred pound, first born of Hepburn and Winnieford Dunning inserted his hands into his pockets and hung his head. It was a humbling feeling. His family and clearly other members of the board felt he was capable of leading them to the next chapter of their history. It was not what he wanted, or sought. He personally believed Grace Heather would be a better candidate. However, when he finally looked up, his heart may have been a little hesitant to take his father's position. He gathered the strength of his resolve, he knew he had to portray that he was ready to accept the responsibility and be at the helm of Dunning Bank & Trust.

"My father once told me that a man's place is determined by his worth. While I accept the position of President and CEO, I will not take his seat at this table until you, the members of this board, declare me worthy." He retook the seat at the far end of the table to continue the meeting.

As Myles took his seat, Winnieford spoke. "It is with honor and pride that I now turn over the control of Dunning Bank and Trust to Mr. Myles Dunning." She pushed her chair under the table.

William stood. "On behalf of the board of directors, we adhere to your declaration and will stand with Myles as he begins his tenure." He looked around. "I am certain no one here will mind this offer. We ask that you remain a voting member of this board as we move forward." He took his seat as others applauded his request.

"Thank you for the kind gesture. I fully relinquish my proxy to Mr. Dunning to vote on my behalf as he sees fit." Her glance turned to Myles. "He knows my and his father's wishes for Dunning. Add that to his vision and I believe he will exceed all our expectations. May God's strength be with him." She then nodded at her son to begin the meeting.

William's eyes narrowed as Myles began to speak. He watched Winnieford carefully. The entire scene increased the anger boiling under William's skin.

"The first line of business will be to assure our employees all is secure and we are ready to move forward," Myles began. "The second will be to assure customers of the same."

She knows that isn't proper, William thought, as Winnieford stopped at Myles' seat, kissed her son on the cheek and then left the room.

He watched as Myles smiled at her actions, then spoke. "Mother, would you ask Mrs. Vazquez to step in to continue in her role as recording secretary?"

Winnieford smiled. "It would be my pleasure, Mr. Dunning." She walked out with a little more pep in her step.

Myles turned back to the members at the table. Before he could continue with his statement, Gary, the prankster of the family, rolled up a sheet of paper and threw it at his oldest brother, hitting him right in the middle of his forehead.

"Momma's boy," he laughed.

Myles froze, disbelief etched on his face. "We are in the middle of a board meeting, Gary."

Another ball of paper hit him next. The culprit was Michael this time. Then one from Grace followed suit. When the ball of paper hit him from Cainan Scott the siblings turned and stared at him.

"Too soon?" Cainan frowned.

The mood softened as another ball of paper hit Myles in the forehead courtesy of Preston then another from Elaine landed just as Mrs. Vazquez entered the room.

As balls of paper flew across the room she put her hands on her hips. "What is going on in here?"

"We are hazing Mr. Dunning, the new President and CEO," Gary explained with a grin.

"Oh." She popped Myles on the head with her tablet, then took her seat. "Continue on."

Laughter erupted in the room.

William joined in with the laughter. The action eased the tension remaining from the vote. Myles looked his way and nodded. William took it as his way of acknowledging the injustice of the vote. For a split second the hatred filled his heart, then William slowly nodded in return, thinking that's right, son, you now have a dangerous enemy.

# Chapter Two

Jonathan Michael dreaded the information he had just received. The call had been expected, however the outcome was not. The short two-minute call changed the tone of his day, if not his life. He knew without a doubt the situation he had dreaded for years was about to unfold.

Jonathan was a man who had done things the right way. The only child to a single parent, Monica Michael, who at times worked three jobs to keep him in school, felt his life was about to come full circle. He had graduated with honors, acquiring an education many only dreamt of gaining. A Bachelor of Science in Economics with a Masters in International Finance, Jonathan was sought after with a vengeance. His decision to join Phase International afforded him the opportunity to travel the world. Excelling at every task the organization threw his way, he moved up in the ranks, becoming one of the highest paid 'Uncle Toms' in the world. Today, Jonathan had been deemed by Wall Street Review as the highest-ranking man of color in the financial industry, as the Senior Vice-

President of Phase International, the largest banking
entity in the world. Yes, he was a long way from
Queens Road in Bounds Green, and Alexandra Park
School where he discovered his love for finance that
led him to where he stood today.

All of that would be in jeopardy the moment he
walked into that office on the thirtieth floor to advise
Richard Dewberry III, CEO and President of Phase,
that Myles Dunning had been named President and
CEO of Dunning Bank & Trust. All he had done in his
35 years of existence was going to be compromised
the moment he revealed the results of the vote. Not
only would he be put in a position to bring down an
institution he admired, he was going to also be asked
to jeopardize a friendship that kept him on the stable
side of sanity as he traveled this incredible journey
known as his career.

The beautiful Grace Heather Dunning stole his
heart when he first met her during college. She was, as
he would call her, a two-sided gold coin. Heather
represented the wild, anything goes woman who
intrigues him, while Grace displayed all the elements
of a queen, with her provocative reserved manner.
Both sides demonstrate the intelligence of a road
scholar. Whichever version of Grace Heather enters
the room, he loves. Though he had never acted on it,
over the years she has never been far from his mind.
They remained casual acquaintances and one day he
hopes they will eventually stop chasing their careers,
run into each other and give meaning to this thing
called life. To do so he knew he had to live up to the
image of her father Hepburn Dunning, whom he'd
had the pleasure of meeting once. Jonathan liked the
man immediately, but knew he had to establish
himself as a man who could care for his daughter in
the same lifestyle she was accustomed. Hepburn

Dunning would settle for nothing less for his oldest daughter. Now that he was in that position, Jonathan may be an unwilling party in the destruction of her family's business.

Jonathan stood at the window to his prestigious office on the 28th floor of PI headquarters, Oxford Circle, London taking a moment to try to reach for something, anything that would change the results of the call. Yet, he knew he was reaching for a needle in a haystack. While the conversation distressed him, deep inside he was proud of the family business that had risen to levels no one saw coming. A family business that started out of desperation had become a source of pride for people of color and a threat to those in control of the financial world. DBT did it by treating their customers like family. Customers were and still are given the utmost respect. DBT worked off the mantra on their banner: Family Integrity, First and Foremost. They worked with the consciousness of the needs of all, never personal gain. The goal of making the American dream of home ownership a reality for everyone was always at the forefront of their policies. DBT did it the right way, battling the evil empires along the way. Somehow the good guys still managed to reach the top.

The Dunnings' rich history of banking started during a time when banks would not accept deposits from African-American organizations or advance loans to people of color. Charles Dunning was a man of talents when it came to building homes. People of all races turned to him to design and build homes. They paid him rather handsomely to do so. Feeling the plight of his neighbors, Charles began by building homes for people of color and allowing them to pay when they could. People would pay him monthly until the cost of the homes was covered. The demand became so great, his wife Carrie began keeping the books on who owed what amounts and when payment would be received. Soon the construction of homes became the secondary means of support, for the income from the loans was substantial. Many of the businessmen in the area of all races supported Charles, because he was a beloved member of their community for many reasons.

On a sunny day in April 1903, the door of Charles Building and Loans was opened. The members of the board of directors, and a few silent progressive businessmen, developed their own network of entrepreneurs who used bartering as a means to grow and develop the African-American community. Loans and services were offered with reasonable interest and sometimes no interest rate at all. The funds were then used to help other families and then the next family, and the next. Business was booming. They had to take it out of the little room off to the side of the kitchen. A two story building in the heart of what came to be known as Charlestown was erected. As with many banks, during the depression, Charles Building and Loans fell into financial trouble; however, thanks to Charles' brothers Clem, Oswald and Oscar, the bank now known as Dunning Bank and Trust consolidated and never closed their doors.

From there Dunning Bank grew from helping people build homes to helping startup businesses, sustaining them until they were in the profit zone. The neighbor helping neighbor theory was expanded to a network of clients helping clients. Contractors who had accounts with DBT were recommended to clients who needed homes or businesses built. Clients who were tailors were recommended to clients who needed suits or gowns made. A network of people helping people became the trademark of DBT. The bank went international when two sisters were granted a loan to start a lemonade stand. Ten years later, the DeSoto sisters opened their first bed and breakfast in England, then a second in Jamaica. Today, DeSoto B&Bs are all over the world. They are raved as the most luxurious accommodations in the world. Any African-American in the banking industry, who knew the history, understood the significance of Dunning Bank and Trust. For them to have grown into the third largest bank in the county is an amazing feat for any organization. For that organization to be continuously owned by the original African-American family, through the struggle of the depression, color barriers, the civil rights movement and the racism of the sixties and today was remarkable.

It was history Jonathan had studied and admired for years. The last thing Jonathan wanted was to be the Brit who worked with the evil empire known as Phase International to bring down the one entity that had served the African-American community and others worldwide, with the same dignity and respect that they began with. If he could see the growing threat of Phase's number one ranking in the financial world, Jonathan was certain Richard Dewberry saw it too. The organization that controlled the purse strings of the financial world carried the power of governments at their will. PI was not going to stand by and watch all that power be swept away. If William Mitchell had been named the new CEO the threat was considerably weakened, for Jonathan knew the man did not have the skill to keep DBT moving in the right direction. However, Myles Dunning was dangerous. He carried the same characteristics as his father and it was certain Dunning Bank & Trust would continue to grow under his leadership. PI executives will take any steps necessary to protect their standings, including the elimination of Hepburn and now Myles Dunning.

The telephone on his desk buzzed. "Bloody hell," he murmured under his breath.

"Michael," he answered and listened. "I'll be right in, Richard," he replied as he disconnected the call. "And so it begins."

This was the beginning of the end of his life as he knew it. There was no way he could be a party to the destruction of Dunning. Yet, he was certain PI was going to try. Now came the time for him to decide what was important in his life. The title, money and prestige afforded to him as the only man of color in a decision making capacity of the most powerful entity in the world, or pride of that same man of color and its rich heritage. It shouldn't be a decision any man would have to make, however, in the real world...the racist world in which he was a part of, the decision would be before him soon. Jonathan stepped out of his office walking towards the elevator to travel to the thirtieth floor thinking, what would Hepburn Dunning do?

## Chapter Three

Myles returned to his office after the meeting and asked his administrative assistant Chrystina to step inside. Chrystina was a 28-year-old curvy powerhouse with an MBA in finance and banking and information technology. She was able to handle anything from researching financial records to putting together a computer network. Myles hired her as an intern during her freshman year at Virginia Union University, then permanently upon graduation. Finally, Myles promoted her to his executive assistant when she earned her Masters at Virginia Commonwealth University. Myles found her to be indispensable and loyal to a fault. Regardless of how late, how many weekends he had to work, she was there when he needed her and sometimes when he did not know he needed her. His concern now was if she would stay with the additional responsibility. A raise and a bonus would be in line, however, he knew for a fact money was not the motivating force for her. That remained a mystery to him.

He would figure it out. At that moment his priority was to determine what direction to take DBT. To the family it was not just a bank; it was a member of the family. To them DBT was a living, breathing entity. When decisions were made, the impact on the bank was taken into consideration. All the members of DBT, business and personal clients, were handled as if they were a part of their family. That was the secret to Dunning's success. When someone attempted to harm DBT, members of the family dealt them with swiftly and decisively. His Uncle Walker Jr. discovered that years ago, when grandfather Walker Sr., who was CEO at the time, stripped him of all shares and voting rights due to his constant gambling. Upon Walker Sr.'s death he turned the controls over to his youngest son, Hepburn. Walker Jr. submitted a request to the board of directors to have him reinstated. His request was denied, citing his continuous gambling issues. Walker Jr. held Hepburn responsible for the decision, causing bad blood between the two brothers.

Myles sighed, thinking Uncle Walker was going to be another issue he would have to address.

Chrystina walked into the office and knew immediately something had happened. To her, Myles was more than just her boss. He was the man she loved, but knew she would never have. He was, in her humble opinion, the finest man to ever walk the earth, with the exception of Jesus, of course.

There was something about the crooked smile that touched her in regions she thought would be best left unsaid. His voice was what she heard first thing in the morning and the last she heard at night. Was she obsessed? No. She was just a woman in love with a fine, generous, kindhearted, intelligent man. Oh, did she say fine? she thought as she glanced his way.

"What's wrong?" she asked as she took a seat in the chair directly in front of his desk, crossing her legs at the ankle.

Myles turned from the view of Marshall Street in downtown Richmond, Virginia with its bumper-to-bumper traffic and exhaled.

"I'm afraid our workload has just become heavier. About an hour ago, I became president and CEO of Dunning. I need you to instruct Nancy to prepare an announcement for the employees. We need to advise the Regulatory Board and make the necessary document changes." He then took a seat at his desk. "I need to see Michael, Heather, and Gary in my office, ASAP. Also, schedule a meeting with William Mitchell for later this afternoon. Make sure it is a time suitable for him."

"The increased work load will only be until all personnel changes are made and you are comfortable delegating responsibilities. Mrs. Vazquez will assist with the transition," Chrystina stated without looking up from her tablet where she was taking notes. "I will set up meetings with the directors, department heads and with AnnieMarie for media announcements."

"Schedule trips to every branch. I want to meet all the managers," Myles added.

Chrystina glanced at him. "It may be easier to bring all the managers here for a meeting or appreciation weekend for the changes they are about to endure." She shrugged her shoulder. "It's a nice way to say thank you before we put them through all the headache." She turned back to her tablet.

Myles nodded. "Take the travel expense and hotel accommodations from my account."

"We have an expense account to cover that, Mr. Dunning." Chrystina shook her head as she continued taking notes. "Even if we did not have the budget to cover it, the CEO's account certainly does," she continued. "I'll coordinate the packing and storing of Mr. Hep's office with Mrs. Vazquez, as well."

Myles hesitated. "There is no rush. I don't plan on moving just yet. Oh, assure Mrs. Vazquez she still has her job. I think Mitch may have insinuated something different."

Chrystina stopped keying on her tablet and stared up at Myles. He has always doubted his ability to take over the family business. But she knew, just as Mr. Hep knew, Myles was more than capable of handling the bank with class and integrity. Just the fact of him thinking to ease Mrs. Vazquez's concern was proof of that. Hell, he had been prepped for this job all his life. However, in the many conversations they've had over the years she knew his passion was with building a private school for under privileged children.

"You know-" She closed her tablet. "-you can still open the school you've been dreaming about. It would be a wonderful community outreach project for the bank. Everything you ever wanted for the school is now within your reach. If you like, I would be happy to continue with the planning."

"You are going to be overwhelmed with the changes here. I can't ask you to do that too."

"You didn't," Chrystina replied, as she quickly stood to carry out the commands from their new chief executive officer. Walking towards the door she could hear her stocking covered thighs rubbing against each other. She hated that sound. Her thighs rubbing were so loud she knew Myles had to hear it too. That just made her more self-conscious about her weight. To stop the noise, she took wider steps to reach the door.

"Oh, Chrystina," Myles called out. "Make sure Nancy's email to the employees is reviewed before it goes out."

Chrystina's laugh was instantaneous. The last time he'd asked Nancy Charles, one of the secretaries who worked in the Risk Management office, to send out correspondence, it was very degrading to the employees. He'd almost fired her and would have if Chrystina had not intervened.

"I will have Mrs. Vazquez review all correspondence. And umm...Mr. Dunning, you may not want to hear this, but the board selected the best man for the job."

"What's with the Mr. Dunning thing? I'm still Myles."

"Oh, no." Chrystina turned to face him. "Let's be very clear. You are now Mr. Dunning. Anyone who has respect for the office, the position and the man will know how to address you. It will be a clear indication of who is with you and who is not. Allow the respect you deserve."

She was giving him her 'don't play with me' look.

"Thank you, Chrystina."

There were a few nice things Myles could say about Chrystina. The most complimentary, in his mind, was her constant infectious smile.

He smiled as she nodded, then closed the door behind her. He could not remember a day when she was not smiling and did not push warmth on everyone around her, including him. Over the last month he had leaned heavily on her to get through the loss of his father. It was her quietly working in the background to keep everything flowing that gave him the time he needed to be there for his family. Her strength more than compensated for his weakness the first few days. Her open arms allowed him to deal with his father's death without his family knowing the full impact it all had on him.

The day his father died, Mrs. Vazquez and Chrystina were at the hospital taking charge. The nurses had all the information on his father, paperwork was ready for signatures, and the doctor was waiting. The immediate attention was what gave them those few precious minutes that allowed his mother to see her husband before he took his last breath. When his mother stepped out of the room and looked at her children, the jolt in his gut caused him to take a step back. It was Chrystina's gentle touch on his back that prompted him towards his mother. It was a time for his hurt to be concealed. He was now the head of the family. It was his job to embrace and console their pain.

The days that followed it seemed Chrystina knew what he needed before he did. The arrangements, announcements, the media inquiries, the flowers, the cards, the calls, none of it ever crossed his path. She handled everything. It wasn't until he received a thank you call from the hospital weeks later for flowers donated to patients that he realized just how thorough Chrystina had been.

During those days and weeks that followed, Mitch attempted to put a few policy changes in place he knew the family was against. Chrystina assembled a coalition of employees to block his actions at every turn. She literally had administrative assistants and secretaries reporting Mitch's every move to ensure nothing major was implemented without the family or board's approval. For him, she had made a serious enemy of Mitch, while trying to protect DBT. That was loyalty. With all she did in the office, it was what she did for him personally that kept him up most nights these days.

The night before the funeral he was drunk. Not a little tipsy, not leaning a little, no...he was wasted, banging on her door. Chrystina took one look at him, pulled him inside by the lapel of his suit that was hanging off of him then proceeded to go off on him.

"You don't have time to breakdown. Your mother needs you, not to mention your brothers and sisters."

"It's too much."

"I know it is." She sat him on the sofa, took off his jacket and shoes, then laid him down. "And it is incredibly unfair. However, your name is Myles Davis Dunning. You are a soldier. Your father prepared you for this moment and so has God. This did not happen by chance. It happened when God knew you were ready to be the man your father raised you to be." She walked away then came back with a wet cloth. She placed it on his forehead.

"It's coffee for you."

She walked off again as she talked. "How did you get like this anyway? One or two drinks and you are usually done. Were you with Michael?"

Myles looked up to see her standing over him with hands on hips and face frowning. "I am not a snitch," he slurred.

"Never mind." She stomped off again. "It doesn't matter. You are a grown man. No one can force you to do anything you did not want to do." She appeared in front of him with a cup of coffee in her hand. "Drink this."

"I don't want to."

"Drink it anyway."

"You just said no one can force me-"

"Drink the coffee, Myles." She glared at him as she shoved the cup into his hand then stomped off again.

Myles sat up, took a sip of the coffee then watched as she came back into view with latex gloves on and a small trash can lined with a bag in her hand. She sat it in front of him.

He looked up. "I don't need..." Before he could finish the statement, his head was in the trashcan emptying the contents of his stomach. He looked up to find her standing there with a glass in her hand.

"Rinse."

He did.

That routine happened three more times until he fell asleep. When he woke during the wee hours of the next morning, there was a blanket over him. He was stripped down to his pants, the trashcan was gone, the room was clean and he felt lousy. He looked around, somewhat disoriented, until he saw Chrystina. She was curled up in an overstuffed chair and ottoman with a blanket wrapped around her.

Concern filled her eyes as she sat up. "Hi."

"Morning." He looked around. It was still dark outside.

"There is a clean towel, wash cloth and toothbrush in the hall bath. I'll fix you some coffee." She threw the blanket aside then walked into the kitchen.

Feeling like crap, he stood under the shower for more than twenty minutes. When he stepped out there was grey sweat pants, and a black tee shirt.

"She thinks of everything," he said, then wondered if she had a magic potion to stop the headache from vibrating when he brushed his teeth. He dressed then walked out to the living room to find her at the table in the dining area pouring a cup of coffee. She was dressed in a long black night shirt that came to her knees, her hair was in one long braid that fell across her shoulder, and on her feet was a pair of bunny slippers with the ears flopped down on the side. The sight of her made him smile.

"Here, sit and drink this first." She pointed to a glass of cloudy water.

He sat to find eggs, toast and coffee on the table next to the cloudy water.

"This is?" He raised an eyebrow.

"Lemon water with honey to help with your hangover."

He sighed. "Yeah, I need that." He downed the glass in its entirety.

"Alcohol dehydrates you. The lemon water will help with that. The toast and eggs will absorb the alcohol out of your system. Together the two will flush you out. Now eat." She sat in the chair to his left.

"Aren't you going to eat?" he asked as he bit into the toast.

"It's a little early for me." She smiled as she put her elbow on the table using her arm to brace her head.

He nodded. "Your hair is down."

"Hmm?"

"Your hair," he repeated. "You always wear it up at work. It's down."

She picked up the end of the braid. "It's pinned up all day so at night I brush it out to let it breathe then I braid it."

He nodded. "You look different."

"It's three in the morning and you're drunk. Everything looks different."

"True." He sipped on the coffee. "I busted in on you, I'm sorry about that. I just needed to get away from it all."

She put her hand on his. It closed around hers as if he was grabbing onto a lifeline.

"They say the pain will ease. But it will never go away. It will be replaced by warm memories of your father. That is what is going to sustain you. Myles, you have a rich history dating back to 1650 that your great-grandfather, grandfather, father and faith have instilled in you. It is now up to you to carry that history forward. That is what your father has given you. For now you grieve, for it's the only way you can heal. What you cannot ever do is lose control. Too many lives are depending on you to make it through this difficult time. Until you are strong and can deal on your own, you have my shoulder to lean on."

His hand tightened on hers. He leaned forward placing his head on her hand. The tears dropped. No sound was made, only tears dropping onto her hand.

She kneeled beside him, placing his hand on her shoulder as he slid to the floor. His arms wrapped over her shoulders, around her neck pulling her closer as the heart wrenching sobs left his body. Her arms circled his waist, holding him tight, doing all she could to take the grief from him. Her hands rubbed his back, consoling him with her touch.

"Let it out, Myles." Her soothing words continued to flow. "This sharp pain will pass but for now, you feel it, embrace it, then let go, baby, just let it go." She kissed his neck. "It will be all right, Myles. It will." Her tears fell to his cheek.

That was when he realized he had brought his pain to her. "I'm sorry, Chrystina." He kissed her neck. "I never meant to bring my problems to you. I'm sorry, baby. Please don't cry." He kissed her cheek, then held her at arms' length, wiping her tears away with his thumb. She cupped his face in her hands, then wiped his tears away with her thumbs. The gentle caress sent shivers through his body. Their eyes met and before he knew it he was kissing her and she was kissing him.

The sweetness of her tongue was smothering the hurt. The deeper he explored, the less intense the pain was. Suddenly there was a driving need for her touch, her taste building up in him. They moved from their knees to the floor, his hands roaming her body. His tongue ravishing her mouth; her sweetness encompassing his hurt. It was as if he never needed anything more in his life than her...just her around him. Falling between her thighs sent a surge of heat to his groin. He wanted her, had to have her. She was his lifeline.

"Chrystina," he called out as his hands moved to her thighs, feeling the smooth thickness in the palms of his hands. "Tell me to stop, Chrystina."

"Don't stop, Myles," he thought he heard her say.

His fingers felt the moistness between them as he pushed the thin material aside. He freed himself from the sweat pants and entered her.

He gasped. She gasped. They were one. Her inner lips clung to him. Pulling the hurt, replacing it with pure joy, the likes of which he had never experienced.

"Chrys," he moaned out.

"You're safe, Myles." She pushed up to him.

"Chrys." He pulled out then entered her again. This sensation was more intense than the first. Every time he went deeper the less pain he felt. His body went deeper in search of the joy, the pleasure, the explosion. It filled the air. He lay on top of her, his head in the crook of her neck, her rapidly beating heart radiating through her breasts and her arms still caressing his back.

He rolled to the side, withdrawing from her. They both lay there on their backs trying to control their breathing. Neither saying a word.

He needed to say something, do something. The words would not come. He slid his hand over, taking hers.

"Chrystina..." He couldn't think of one word to say to explain or excuse his actions. What he did was wrong. He used her to relieve his anger, his pain. Lying on the floor was not going to solve the problem. He stood, pulling her up with him.

He brushed the strands of hair that had come loose away from her face then immediately felt ashamed. He wanted to kiss her again. He never thought of himself as a selfish person, but there it was.

He was still holding her hand when she said, "Umm..." She swallowed. "I get tested regularly for certain things. As of three months ago I was clean."

She looked as if she was going through a checklist in her mind. "Chrystina...."

"This is important." She squeezed his hand. "I'm on birth control. You can thank my sister and her children for that. This happened in my home. Only you and I know. Therefore you don't have to be concerned with HR, harassment, you know all that stuff." She waved a hand through the air. "We're okay," she said as she looked into his eyes. "We're okay."

But he wasn't okay. Something changed within him. He just couldn't put his finger on what.

Hours later he buried his father.

Myles pushed his chair back from his desk forcing the memory away. He walked across the plush carpet of his office to the bar. Taking down a glass from the rack, he dropped in two cubes of ice from the mini bar, then poured cognac over them. That night changed his life. His father was no longer with him, that was true. However, a rich heritage and the responsibility to carry the bank forward, in addition to being strong for his family were instilled in him. They depended on him now. The question in his mind was whom did he turn to now?

"Mr. Dunning." Chrystina's voice came through the intercom. "Michael is here."

"Thank you, Chrystina."

Taking a swallow, he sat on one of the bar stools and allowed the smooth liquid to coat his throat.

Looking down into the glass, he sighed. "Dad, how am I supposed to fill your shoes? You wore a size fourteen, I'm barely a twelve." He bowed his head to say a silent prayer.

## Chapter Four

**"Y**ou are going to need a little bit more than prayer here, big brother. It's all on your shoulders now." Michael smiled as he stood in the doorway.

Myles looked up to what he considered a stupid grin on his brother's face. He smiled as he stood to walk back over to his desk, placing the glass there.

"This is the last thing I wanted, you know that," Myles said as he pointed to Mike. "Grace could have easily taken the CEO position."

"Mitch would have taken Grace through too much crap and she would have eventually killed him. Her temperament is not the best when it comes to him. As for the alternative, how would the employees fare with Mitch at the helm? What's more important is how would Dad feel knowing you let Mitch do what he has been trying to do behind his back for years?"

Sitting back in the chair, Myles sighed. "I know. Now, he'll try to do it behind my back."

"No questions about it, Mitch is going to try you at every turn, Myles, that's for certain. Knock him out with a firm punch. Let him know from jump you are not taking that crap off of him."

"He is a valued employee, Mike. Let's keep that in mind."

"I beg to differ with you on that. As I see it, I saved you a lot of embarrassment." He shook his head as he walked to the bar and poured himself a drink. "That mother of ours was ready to do whatever was needed to keep DBT in the family."

"It was in her eyes for everyone to see," Myles agreed, "including Mitch."

Michael took a seat in front of Myles' desk. "What are your plans for Mitch?"

"What do you mean?"

"You are going to get rid of him, aren't you?"

Myles shrugged. "Not if he doesn't give me reason."

Michael sat up. "Are you serious? You know how many times he attempted to do little deals behind Dad's back?"

"No, Mike, tell me about them," Myles replied sarcastically.

"Myles, I am not trying to tell you how to handle your job, but even Captain Kirk never let Kahn onto the Enterprise."

Myles laughed at his brother's obsession with all things Star Trek. "Protect the Enterprise at all cost."

"Damn straight."

"Hey," Grace interrupted, as she knocked on the open door. "Where is Mr. Spock when you need him?" she joked then looked at Myles. "So, do I have to call you Mr. Big Brother CEO now?"

Myles smiled at his sister with the split personalities. There was the very conservative, stubborn professional Grace that she portrayed in the office and the wild, uninhibited Heather outside. "No, you can just call me Mister."

"Ah, like in The Heat of the Night?" she said as she took the other seat in front of Myles' desk. "You know the famous line, 'They call me Mister Tibbs.'"

"I'll just call you grouchy," Gary stated, as he walked into the office behind Grace, then slumped on the end of Myles' desk. "I can't believe you were that mean in the meeting."

"This was your first board meeting. Wait until you really see him in action," Grace said, as she walked over to the bar. She pulled out two bottles of water, tossing one to Gary just as he hopped into her seat.

Gary grinned at her as Mike spoke.

"Yes, he and Dad were a tag team match of decorum in the board room. Where one left off preaching, the other one picked up. At the end of the day it felt as if you were leaving the principal's office."

"You should know," Myles laughed. "As much as Dad had to pick you up from there."

"That was his own fault for insisting we go to public schools." Gary laughed. "We never would have experienced half the stuff we did if we had gone to private school."

"True, nor would we have had such a plethora of women." Michael reached out as Gary gave him a fist bump.

"That's why you were always in the principal's office, Mike," Grace laughed from the edge of Myles' desk.

"One fight after another over someone's girlfriend," Myles added.

"If he only knew how much I learned from the girls in the public school system, he might have sent all of us to boarding school."

"Ah yes, my first was Mrs. Granger." Gary closed his eyes and sighed as if remembering.

"Mrs. Granger?" Myles raised an eyebrow. "Wasn't she your history teacher?"

"Memorable lessons she taught, whew...." He nodded. "That's why I'm a history buff to this day."

"Are you serious?" Grace glared at her youngest brother.

"I loved Mrs. Granger," Mike added. "She was the best teacher I ever had."

Gary laughed as he opened his eyes. "And she liked you too. Told me so several times."

"I don't believe you... either of you." Grace frowned.

"Umm, believe them." Myles nodded.

Gary laughed as he looked at Grace's expression. "Well, Mother always stated she did not want pampered millionaires for children. She wanted her children to have normal childhoods."

"There is nothing normal about having sex with your teachers." Grace gasped.

"Hmm....." Myles chuckled. "It was in our world. Look we all know Dad's purpose in life was to make Winnieford happy. She wanted us in public schools so we would not turn out like Uncle Walker."

"As Dad always said, 'happy Winnie, happy life'."

Silence fell on the room as Myles took a moment to remember their larger-than-life father.

Gary held up his bottle. "Here's to Dad and his relentless lectures on the importance of having a happy family."

Myles smiled, remembering the many talks about supporting each other, and finding true love.

"To Dad," they said in unison then took a drink in their father's honor.

"Dad had two passions in life." Myles sat his glass down. "Winnieford and Dunning Bank & Trust. It's up to us to continue his legacy. Michael, close the door," Myles said in a somber tone.

Michael complied as they all took a seat to listen to their big brother who was now the head of the family.

"We have some issues that have to be addressed. First will be the reading of the will."

"Mother was right to delay the reading until after the vote on Dunning was settled," Grace sated. "There is going to be push back, Myles, especially from Uncle Walker. That letter the attorney gave to Mother granting her control of the bank is going to send him into a tailspin."

Nodding, Myles sat forward in the chair. "My only concern with Uncle Walker is Mother. Once the will is read in its entirety I am certain he will attempt to contest it. Proclaim Mother is not the legal heir."

"On what grounds?" Mike sat up.

"It's no secret how he feels about Mother," Grace said. "He has always believed Dad married down. That she only married him for his money."

"We know that couldn't be further from the truth." Gary smirked. "Anyone with a grain of sense could see those two were written in the book."

"Operative word, sense." Mike shook his head. "Uncle Walker doesn't have any. He deals in greed only." He turned to Myles. "Would he have any ground for contesting Dad's will?"

"No," Grace replied. "But he will still try. I say we leave Uncle Walker to his own demise."

"Yes, he is pretty good at destroying himself." Mike shrugged.

"How could he be so different from Dad and Aunt Vivian?" Gary sighed. "Are we sure he is a Dunning? I mean do we have proof?"

"That is not our cross to bear," Myles stated. "He carries the last name of Dunning, therefore he is family. What he is not going to do is upset Winnieford. She is going through enough as it is with Dad's death and AnnieMarie feeling guilty."

"Have you talked to her, Grace?" Mike asked.

"I have tried." She shook her head. "No progress. That guilt is eating her up."

"Well." Myles sat forward. "It is our duty to help both of them through this. For now, Grace, keep tabs on the reading date for the will. I want us to all be home for that. Above all, make sure Winnieford is protected. Now." He cleared his throat. "Let's talk about Dunning."

"The serious voice just came out," Grace announced. "What's up?"

"There are some issues that could be potentially damaging to the bank. It seems we are being hit from different directions. Until I know who is fully committed to our success we are keeping this within the family."

"What about AnnieMarie?" Gary asked.

"As soon as she is ready to come back we will fill her in." Myles stared at him. "That goes for Mother as well. I do not want her concerned about Dunning. Everyone get my drift?"

The siblings nodded.

"Good." He turned to Grace, who was the attorney in the family and human resource department of the bank. "Grace, there are reports of issues concerning illegal immigrants in Texas, California, Illinois, Mississippi and Arizona. From what Dad was saying some of their situations are quite complicated."

"Has Homeland Security been notified of any violations?"

"Not that I am aware of," Myles replied. "But I want to know what the situations are before they become involved. The last thing we need is a federal investigation into our employment practices." He gave her a folder from his desk. "Here are the names of the 20 or so employees who are in question. See what you can do to get this cleared up before we are hit with subpoenas."

"Did someone report these employees? How did their names come to light?"

"That I do not know and I don't believe Dad knew either. The names were given to him by one of our competitors. I had Chrystina to do a check and there are un-answered questions regarding their citizenship. So let's start with them."

"Do you think there may be plans to get bad press for us?" Gary asked.

"Just the mention of allegations of an investigation by Homeland Security could cause problems," Mike suggested. "Cleaning up the bad press would put AnnieMarie's PR skills to the real test."

Grace took the folder and began scanning through it. "I think we should expand the inquiry to all employees. We have banks in a number of Border States. I'll make certain we are clear on all fronts."

"Sounds good." Myles turned to Gary. "Do you believe our competitors will go that far to discredit us?"

"That and deeper," Gary stated. "The entity with their finger on the world financial purse strings controls the power in this country. Right now China holds a number of loans on US government interests. Phase International or America's bank has connections there and in London. Any bank or entity coming close to world ranking would be considered a threat."

"Are we in that position?" Grace asked, unbelieving.

"No," Gary admitted. "However, the acquisition of Hershel Automotive will put us in a solid third-place ranking. Being in that number three slot makes Dunning a target of PI and America's Bank. You better know they will throw everything in the mix to protect the control of the world market."

Myles nodded as Gary spoke. Gary was new to the executive level. A recent graduate with an MBA in International Finance, Gary worked through the ranks, as they all did, until he obtained his degree. When the position came open he had to apply just like everyone else did. An outside agency handled the hiring to ensure the best person for the position was hired. Gary prevailed and at the young age of 25, to Mitch's dismay, he was named Chief Financial Officer.

"Gary is right," Myles surmised. "It is not a position we sought after, yet here it is. The ranking comes with the assets and customers we acquire. Herschel Automotive is a multi-billion dollar asset transferring from Phase International if we succeed. They cannot be happy about that."

"So you think they may be coming after us?" Mike asked.

"Oh yes." Gary grinned. "With guns loaded and ready to fire."

"I know one of the executives at Phase." Grace shook her head. "I don't believe he will allow PI to come after us in this way. Fair competition yes, but nothing under handed like this."

"There is no telling what people will do when it comes to their economic stability," Mike replied.

The siblings looked to Myles.

"We handle one concern at a time." Myles sat back. "Let's keep our eyes and minds open to all possibilities."

"What impact do you think the board's actions will have on this?" Grace asked.

"Concern at this point," Gary replied. "Myles is an unknown factor. He has yet to prove himself. They would have breathed a little easier if Mitch had been named."

Mike sat back in his chair. "Keep your enemies close," he said then sent a poignant glare at Myles.

Myles nodded. "That's why Mitch stays, for now. Losing him to one of our competitors could hurt us. Until I know the depth of his control I want to keep him right where he is."

"Good move." Mike smirked. "Now I understand."

Myles turned. "Gary, I'm afraid your situation is going to be a little more difficult. There has been some unexplainable activity on a number of the dead accounts. An intern in one of our Virginia branch offices noticed some transactions taking place on several accounts she reviews. The transactions did not generate from her office. She believes someone from headquarters has been tampering with the accounts. Inaccuracies were found totaling a little over a half million dollars on her accounts alone." He handed a file to Gary.

Looking at the file, Gary frowned. "We have branches all over the country, has any other branch reported strange activities?"

The question pleased Myles. His baby brother might be young but his mind was sharp. He only wished Gary was as wise with women as he was with numbers.

"I don't know. You will have to investigate all the accounts to identify any additional discrepancies. If possible determine where the money is going."

"With 398 branches in this country alone, I would hate to think of the amount of money we're losing."

"Whew, that could add up." Mike whistled. "You want me with Gary?"

"No. You have a more pressing situation." He cleared his throat. "Grace and Gary, the next situation is sticky. I need to talk to Mike alone."

Gary and Grace looked up from their files. "Sounds serious," Grace stated.

"It is and when the time is right, I will let both of you in on it. For now I need plausible deniability on your part," Myles instructed.

"That's good enough for me," Gary said as he stood.

Smiling, Grace walked over then kissed her big brother on the cheek. "This is not an easy gig...Dad knew that. He would not expect you to conquer all in one day."

"I know," Myles replied as he hugged her.

Gary saluted his brother. "You are the man, Mr. Dunning," then followed Grace out the door.

Myles waited until the door closed then turned to Michael. "You are going to have to investigate Cainan Scott."

Michael frowned. "The guy in investments?"

"Yes." Myles hesitated. "When Dad had his heart attack he and AnnieMarie were arguing because he did not want her involved with Scott. Dad tried to tell me why, but he died before he could say. I want to know what was so important about Scott that Dad used his dying breath trying to tell me."

"Is that why AnnieMarie is so withdrawn? I tried several times to get her to talk to me, but she just sits in her room and cries."

Myles shook his head. "I don't know if the tears are from heartbreak over Scott or guilt over Dad. I have tried to tell her the heart attack was not her fault but she's not listening to me either."

"Do you have any idea what I'm looking for on Scott?"

"No. This is about family. I don't think it has anything to do with Dunning. I know Dad has put you on special projects before. If he believed in your ability to get to the bottom of things I'm going to follow suit. Before I make any judgment on this man or allow him into AnnieMarie's life I need to know what Dad's concerns were."

"I appreciate the vote of confidence. Scott is handling investments, isn't he? Is anyone checking behind him?"

"Not at the moment. I think I will put Chrystina on it."

"Yes, she could work after hours and on the weekends when he is not around. It's not like she has anything else to do."

"I don't know if that's true or not. I'm sure she has a life outside this office."

"She is a loner if I've ever seen one." Mike chuckled.

"Why would you say that?"

"Man, look at her. She's got to be a good fifty pounds overweight. And what's with the bun on her head?"

Myles wasn't sure why but he felt humiliated by his brother's words on Chrystina's behalf. "What does her weight have to do with her social life?"

"She's a little on the heavy side. Most men like a trophy on their arms. You know what I'm saying?"

"No, I don't. Chrystina and I go out to lunch all the time."

"Lunch," Mike replied. "That's business. I'm talking about a date. And since you brought it up, you'd be wise to rethink being seen out with her. You are now the CEO and you have a reputation to uphold. Are you going to make Nancy your new assistant?"

"Nancy? Why in the hell would I do that?"

"You're going be moving into the front office. Chrystina is not going to fit in there."

Myles felt himself about to lose his temper. "And you think Nancy would?"

"Well, she looks a lot better than Chrystina."

"What are you talking about?"

"Don't get me wrong, Chrystina is a beautiful woman. There is just a lot of her."

Myles shook his head, not believing he was having this conversation with his brother. "Let me get this straight. You think that I should go with size versus competence?"

"When executives meet with you in the office at the end of the hallway, Chrystina should not be the first person they see. As incredibly chauvinistic as that may sound, you know I am right."

"What I know is you better change this subject before I whip some sense into you."

Michael shook his head. "I'm telling you, my words are going to be kind compared to some she will hear from those women down the hall."

"This is the name and address of the person Dad had in Scott's employment folder." Myles ignored his brother's last statement by handing him a card. "Start there."

Michael looked at the card. "Landover, MD?" He looked up at Myles as he raised an eyebrow. "I'll see what I can find out."

"Mike, no one is to know about this. If I'm wrong, I don't want any questions from the board surrounding Cainan Scott."

"I have you covered on this one." He started towards the door. "Myles, don't take any crap off Mitch. Dad would have never put Dunning in Mitch's hands. Nor would he ever trust Uncle Walker. Watch your back with those two."

Myles nodded as Michael walked out the door.

# Chapter Five

"Chrystina, will you step in here for a moment?"
"Yes, Mr. Dunning," Chrystina replied to the intercom, stood then tugged at the bottom of her skirt. She knew it was too tight, and she should be in a size sixteen, but all of those clothes looked like they should be on an old woman. At twenty-eight she did not want to wear clothes that made her look fifty. Shopping at high-end retailers was out of the question. While she made a decent salary, she had rent on her apartment, a car note and over $100,000 in student loans to pay. Spending money on clothes was a distant fourth place on her budget list. Therefore, for now, it was the best she could get on sale or at a second hand store. With that said, she still looked good for a girl dressing on a tight budget. Stopping at the door, she consciously spread her legs, then walked in.

"Yes, Mr. Dunning."

Myles was sitting behind his desk reviewing a file. "Did you speak with Mr. Mitchell?"

Chrystina was hoping she had a little more time to work on Mr. Mitchell.

"Yes, sir, I did. His earliest free moment is on Wednesday afternoon."

The expression on Myles' face was comical. Chrystina couldn't help but laugh. "I urge you to begin working on controlling your facial expressions before you move down the hall."

Myles laughed. "Was it that bad?"

"Yes, sir, it was. But I understand because I had the same expression when his secretary told me."

"Are we playing cat and mouse here?"

Chrystina nodded. "I believe he is. He expects you to walk down the hall to see him."

"I could do that." Myles stood.

"Umm...excuse me. No, you cannot," Chrystina declared with a sister-girl neck roll. "You are going to sit right back in your seat. Next you are going to instruct me to contact Mr. Mitchell and tell him that he is to be in your office for a meeting at two o'clock this afternoon. You are also going to instruct me to tell him to rearrange his calendar to accommodate your request."

Myles was still half standing when Chrystina continued.

"Shall I make that call for your now, sir?"

Myles stared at her for a moment, then nodded. "Yes, I think you should."

"Very well, sir." Chrystina turned and took two steps. As soon as she heard her thighs rubbing together she stopped.

"Is there something else I forgot to instruct you to tell Mr. Mitchell?"

She laughed over her shoulder. "Not at the moment." Taking wide steps she walked out the room.

#

Myles sat back and laughed at Chrystina's antics. There was no way he would give up Chrystina for

Nancy or anyone else. He did not see anything wrong with the way she looked. Yes, she could spend a little more money on quality clothes that fit better. From his point of view she came to work each morning professionally dressed. As to her size, she was a thick sister with nice, smooth, thick thighs. He closed his eyes. That wasn't what he was supposed to be thinking. That was one night, a month ago. He refused to look at it as a mistake. It was simply something that happened that was not planned. As for her looks, he never paid much attention because her smile, warm heart and mind, captivated him. The quality of work she produced for the organization impressed him early on and continued to this day. Bottom line, Chrystina was the best he ever had...at work, that is; the best assistant he ever had. Michael's words played in his mind again. What if others thought the way Mike did? People could be cruel...especially women. All he had to do was remember the contention between him and Savannah Whitfield over Chrystina.

Savannah was beautiful, elegant, petite and a pain in the butt as far as Myles was concerned. A while back, his mother felt it was time for him to settle down. "Your father and I plan to retire to play with grandchildren. We can't do that if you are still playing the field." He put in a good effort to make things work with Savannah. And for a while he thought about marrying her. The two had been dating for over a year when Savannah decided Chrystina was not the right assistant for Myles. Something about the chemistry between him and his assistant was unsettling and improper in her opinion. An assistant should not have access to his condo, or personal bank accounts. That should be reserved for his significant other. Myles disagreed with her point of view. When that did not sway him, there were several accusations here and there about her calls not being put through, or her messages disappearing. The topper was the suggestion that Chrystina had a crush on him. Savannah felt it could lead to sexual harassment accusations. That caught his attention. He immediately replaced Chrystina with someone Savannah recommended. That was a mistake. The friend's sole purpose was to keep Savannah posted on him. Two weeks later, Chrystina was brought back with a raise and a personal apology from him. The thought of replacing her never entered his mind again.

It was clear he needed to make plans on how this transition would go. The smoother, the better for all, including Chrystina. He had already proven to be selfish by using her to ease his pain the morning of his father's funeral. That was something he never wanted to do to her again. Not the sex part. That he found himself thinking about too often. He closed his eyes trying to shake the memory. No, he would not use her in that way again. Selfish or not, he wanted her near him. He thought for a moment to call his mother, to discuss the dilemma with her. However, he was certain she wanted him to take the reins when it came to personal issues. She would listen, of course, but would feel giving an opinion would be interfering. That left only one other person. His mind set, he stood and walked out of the office.

"Chrystina, I'll be out of the office for a while."

She looked up from her desk and frowned. "You are not going down that hallway to talk to Mr. Mitchell."

Myles grinned. "I am going down the hallway to my father's office. Is that all right with you?"

He received a side-glance. "Do not go to that man's office. He is to come to you. Do I make myself clear?"

"Loud and clear, little general."

Chrystina raised an eyebrow at him. "Little general? Where did that come from?"

"Oh, I don't know. Could be the way you take control and give orders." He winked as he turned to walk into the hallway.

"Are you going to be okay down there?"

The concern in her voice touched him. "I'm good."

The Risk Management suites consisted of Myles' office, with Chrystina's office directly outside his door. Across the hall were the secretaries and administrative assistants who reported directly to Myles. While Chrystina's area was the same size, the ten assistants had cubical style workstations. The hallway was lined with rich burgundy and gold design carpeting that lead to the main hallway.

Myles followed that hallway waving at the employees across the hall, then took a left once he reached the marble flooring that flowed throughout the building. The circular foyer had a balcony with a view eight floors down to the main lobby. Myles nodded and smiled at employees as he followed the circle leading to his father's office. He passed by the Financial suites, where Gary worked, Human Resources, where Grace's offices were located, around the corner to the Technology Center where Michael's office was located, Global Investments, where Cainan Scott, and Elaine Jacobson worked. If he continued around he would have reached the Public Relations suites, where AnnieMarie worked and Small Business Management, where Preston Long worked. Instead, he turned left stepping into what everyone referred to as The Vault.

The Vault was named so because it was the original vault of the building before it was redesigned. The gold trim still gleamed in the sunlight. This was where the 'beautiful people' of the CEO's office were housed. The vaulted door at the far end of the area was his father's office...well his office now. Before reaching there, you had six offices on your left and right, a receptionist at the very entrance and Mrs. Vazquez sitting directly in front of the vault. No one, absolutely no one, entered the vault without Mrs. Vazquez's approval. Period. The offices consisted of four secretaries, each speaking several languages and looking as if they stepped of off a runway each morning.

Annatasha Bessant was said to have been Ms. Universe at one time. Myles had no idea if it was true or not. What he did know was any man would take the opportunity to come to the vault just to get a glance at her. If looking at her did nothing for you, the moment she spoke, you were a goner. The sensual, accented voice made your insides melt without her putting any effort into it.

"Congratulations, Mr. Dunning. Are you here to see Mrs. Vazquez?" The dark hair mother of three smiled, making the gold trim sparkle that much brighter.

"Thank you, Annatasha. Yes, I would like a moment of Mrs. Vazquez's time, if she is free."

Annatasha's laughter rang out. "Of course she is free for you, sir. I will notify her that you are here."

"Annatasha, it's still Myles."

Picking up the phone, Annatasha glanced at him. "No, get used to it, sir. You are Mr. Dunning now." She held up a finger as she spoke into the receiver of the phone. "Mr. Dunning is here." She hung up the phone.

Myles noticed employees walking out of their offices.

"Congratulations, Mr. Dunning." Sean Papia, a young man with roots connected to India extended his hand as he walked out adjusting his suit jacket.

"Thank you," Myles said as he shook the young man's hand.

Next came Paulette Brittan, a blonde hair, blue eyed Swedish beauty who considered herself the fashion barometer for the area.

"Congratulations, Myles. Welcome to the Vault."

"Thank you, Ms. Brittin."

"She may have missed the point. That is a directive for you to address him properly, Paulette." Sonya Scaife smiled as she extended her hand. "Hello, Mr. Dunning. Congratulations, sir."

"Myles. My apology. I have to call you Mr. Dunning now." Lynn Sterling laughed, giving Myles a point and shoulder bump. "I can't tell you how relieved I am that you received the nod. Seriously, man, I know you will handle this better than you do the basketball court."

"Thank you. Save those wolf tickets for the court," Myles laughed.

"We were a little concerned," Sean acknowledged. "With you at the helm, Dunning will continue to rise."

"Mr. Mitchell indicated there is a possibility you will bring in your own staff. Is that correct?" Paulette asked.

"Things will remain as they are, for now," Myles replied.

"That's a relief," she laughed. "We here in the vault are a very efficient group. Adding someone new to the mix may have an adverse impact on our goals. We wouldn't want that, now would we?"

"Please know she is not insinuating you would have an adverse impact to the group, Mr. Dunning," Annatasha stated as she glared at Paulette.

"Of course not." Paulette supplied an adequately appalled look as a delicate hand flew to her chest. "We are looking forward to your leadership, Myles. Besides we all know Mr. Mitchell will be there guiding you."

"You are to address him as Mr. Dunning." The group turned as Mrs. Vazquez approached. "It will be Mr. Dunning guiding us. Not Mr. Mitchell. Have another slip of the tongue and it will be your last day here. Do I make myself clear?"

The reprimand was conducted in a calm, direct manner. The woman never raised so much as an eyebrow as she spoke; yet Myles felt as if Paulette was just slapped with Thor's hammer.

"I meant no disrespect," Paulette countered.

"None taken," Myles replied as he noticed the woman still did not address him as sir or Mr. Dunning. She was clearly a Mitch person. "Mrs. Vazquez, may I have a moment of your time?"

"Of course, sir. Right this way." She held out a hand in the direction of her office as she glanced over her shoulder one last time at Paulette.

"Mr. Mitchell and Paulette are...close. Be aware of their displeasure on the vote."

"And the others?" Myles questioned.

"They are all very good at what they do. You will find the majority are very pleased with the outcome." She nodded to the closed door that led to William's office. "The alternative wasn't something any of us were looking forward to. Did you want to peek in on Mr. Mitchell?"

"No."

"Very well." With a nod, Mrs. Vazquez opened the heavy gold trimmed door to what was now his office.

Myles hesitated.

"Why don't we talk here, at your desk. This is your office now. Dunning Bank & Trust needs its leader to lead. Each employee in this company is watching every step you take. Any sign of hesitation on your part will be looked upon as a weakness. Now, come inside and take your place."

Myles inhaled then stepped into the office he had not been in since his father's death. The circular window with sliding doors that led out to the balcony allowed the sunlight to flow inside. The massive cherry wood desk was to the right. Matching bookshelves lined the wall behind the desk. A door that led to the spa like facilities was on the left of the shelves. The big chair his father sat in every day, working at times until the wee hours of the morning, was pushed in. The rich burgundy leather sofa and two chairs were on the wall by the entrance. To his left was a wet bar, conference table that seated ten, four monitors mounted on the wall covering the different markets around the world and a door which he knew led to Mitch's office.

The beautiful wood furniture glistened from the sunlight, bringing cheeriness to the room. For all the hard work that was done in this office, the sunlight always made it look like a place of joy. 'You have to love the place you work. There are times it is the only way to make it through the craziness of office politics,' his father would say.

"It brings a smile to your face when you walk in, doesn't it?"

Myles realized he had not said a word since the door closed behind them. Mrs. Vazquez was kind enough to give him the moment he needed to compose himself.

"It does," Myles acknowledged with a nod of his head. "I thought it would be depressing to walk in without him sitting behind that desk."

"I like to think his spirit is still in this room. And there was nothing depressing about his spirit." She walked to the desk and stood next to the chair. "There are a number of documents here that need your signature." She picked one up, looked at him then waited.

Myles walked around the opposite side of the desk, took a deep breath then sat in his father's chair.

Placing the document in front of him, Mrs. Vazquez continued. "This document gives authorization to change the charter to add your name as the CEO. This takes priority." She pointed to another document. "This document gives Chrystina a higher security access."

Myles glanced at her. "How do you feel about Chrystina coming with me?"

"I was your father's executive assistant. You need to have your own. I am not privy to your decision making process, however you would be a fool not to bring her with you."

Myles smiled at the direct speaking woman whom he has always admired. "Will you remain as my personal secretary?"

"Not interested in brining Nancy along? Hmm...smart move." She laughed. "I'll hang around for another year or two. But you need to have someone prepared to take my place."

"You're planning on leaving?"

"I worked for your father since before you were born. Yes, I am ready to retire, travel and enjoy my grand babies."

"How many do you have?"

"Twelve."

Shocked, he glanced up at her. "Twelve."

Mrs. Vazquez nodded proudly. "Yes. You should settle down and give your mother one or two soon.

Believe me it will fill her life like you would never imagine."

"Can I just give her a puppy?"

Mrs. Vazquez poked his shoulder as she laughed. "Sign this document, please."

Myles did as he was instructed.

"Thank you." She took the document then walked to the front of the desk and took a seat. "The rest you can read through, then sign. I need them by the end of day. Now, what do you need to talk about?"

Myles sat back. "My first concern is Chrystina. How do you feel she will be accepted by the occupants of this wing?"

"It's a non-factor. Chrystina is your assistant."

Myles sat forward and nodded. "I know, however, it's been brought to my attention that she does not fit the pattern of employees in this area."

"Oh." Mrs. Vazquez hesitated. "I see."

"I don't want to put her in a position where her feelings would be hurt. Employees in this area are known to the outside world as the beautiful people. Some feel Chrystina will not be welcomed because of her appearance."

"That firecracker who works for you? Ha Ha. You should be more concerned about their feelings. I am certain Chrystina can hold her own."

"You may have a point there." He sat back visibly more relaxed. "For office space, I will need her nearby."

"She will move into my space."

"No." Myles shook his head. "I want you to remain where you are. Chrystina is to have the adjoining office. Move Mitch to the front office. It's larger so there should be no complaints from him."

"Of course there will be." She waived off the statement. "I'll have him moved anyway."

"None of this needs to take place until I move into this office. For now things can stay as they are."

#

The office was quiet for a long moment until Mrs. Vazquez spoke.

"Ask your questions, Myles. Nothing we discuss will leave this office."

Myles held her eyes for a moment then asked, "I've come to learn the loud mouth is usually not the person you need to watch. Who was my father's major concern? Who could hurt Dunning the most?"

"Internally he had his eye on one or two employees he knew had connections with some of our competitors. However, your father was a firm believer that what was due for Dunning would happen. No one will be in a position to stop us from moving forward."

"Moving forward is relative. For him it was strengthen our resolve to help improve lives, sustain families and give everyone a chance at economic security."

"That's right." Mrs. Vazquez smiled. "Keep talking like that and I may stay around longer." She then sat forward and her smile disappeared. "Hep's major concern was Walker Jr.'s antics and of course the way he treats your mother."

"You believe Uncle Walker can sway my mother?"

"Yes. He has been the one member of the family who has always been able to get under Winnie's skin. You see, her family was middle-class. Walker always thought she was beneath Hep. Truth be told Hep would have left this gig long ago if it wasn't for Winnie."

"Why?"

"Your uncle Walker was concerned with you."

"Me?"

"Yes. When you were born your grandfather made a toast to Hepburn. He said 'to the future of Dunning.' Walker, of course, took exception. He stated the future of Dunning flowed through his family for he was the oldest child. Then he said something Hep could never forgive. He said his family would be pureblood, not tainted by hood rats. Which was how he referred to your mother the first time Hep brought her home to meet the family. Your father was ready to leave the business right then and there. It was your mother who stepped in and convinced Hep to stay. Now it seems his prediction has come true."

"The hood rats are taking over?"

"With you as their leader." Mrs. Vazquez smiled. "However, Walker's vision isn't the one I was referring to. It was your grandfather's wisdom and foresight when he said the future of Dunning lies within you."

Myles nodded at the comment. "I have one more question for you. What can you tell me about Cainan Scott?"

There was a noticeable pause in Mrs. Vasquez's armor.

"He is a nice young man, very intelligent, and analytical. In the last two years, Hep did not make investments without consulting with him." She answered this while averting her eyes, then looked at him. "Why do you ask?"

She was holding something back. Myles knew that the moment her eyes veered from his. Mrs. Vazquez did not lie, however, she was not telling him all she knew.

"Dad mentioned his name on his dying bed. I need to know the significance of that."

"I'm afraid there isn't much I can tell you on that." She stood. "However, this is now your office, you are free to explore every corner." She put emphasis on the word every. Myles made a mental note of that. "When you are ready, we will approach the subject again. In the meantime, I will coordinate office moves." She walked towards the door. "Is there anything else I can help you with?"

"No," Myles replied. "I will review these documents and sign them before I leave."

"You should spend a little time here, Myles. After all, this is now your new home."

## Chapter Six

Entering the house was getting a little easier for Winnieford; however, it would never be the same. The house, the grounds, the entire estate was all about Hep and Winnie together. It was never supposed to be Winnie alone. Standing in the doorway of the side entrance into the home, Winnie hesitated. Hep was usually there opening the door for her, holding her waist then guiding her inside. That was never to be again.

"Will you need the car anymore today, Mrs. Dunning?"

She turned with the welcoming smile she had perfected over the years. "No, Jerome. I'm pretty sure I'm in for the day."

Jerome Morgan returned the smile. "You know, Mr. Dunning would say, it's a beautiful day and it should not be wasted inside. The breeze is nice. I think a walk around The Park will do you some good. I will be happy to take you if you don't want to walk. You could go and just sit for a while."

The Park. That was the Dunning family's burial grounds. She and Hep would visit his grandparents and parents from time to time. It was also where they both planned to be buried, just never this soon. The area was never referred to as a cemetery. That just did not fit the Dunnings' personality. With the family crest statue in the center the area resembled more of a family gathering spot than anything else. Each of the original four Dunning brothers and their families had been moved to the grounds when Hep's grandfather first purchased the land years ago. Since then, Hep and his father had the ground set up like a walk in the park from one generation to another. A stone stood at each section of the resting place, telling the history of the family members buried there. Hep was the only person buried in the new section, Winnie thought as she stared at Jerome.

"He may be lonely," she said as tears burned at her eyes. "I may do that later, Jerome." She smiled then opened the door and walked into the kitchen.

The Dunning home was a mini palace built on a twenty-acre estate. Pulling up in the circular driveway the stained glass above the entrance displayed the family crest glistening against the sun. The front entrance, with its grand double doorway of clear glass, allowed visitors an unrestricted view of the gardens via the floor to ceiling windows at the end of the foyer.

Lined with accented Greek columns at the entry of each room to the left and right, the walkway of the foyer led into the round sitting area that was furnished in ancient Greek with rich tasteful gold and red trim. Between the third and fourth columns on both sides were grand winding staircases that led to the second landing of the home, meeting in the center upstairs foyer. Many who attended functions at the home often wondered if the occupants ever lost their way. Then after being there for thirty minutes or more, most of them will tell you the mini palace was indeed a home. The flow of the house was easy and the welcoming feeling quickly overtook the intimidation felt upon entering. When asked about the Dunning house, many visitors would tell you it felt just like being at home.

The kitchen was the heart of their home. The table in the corner surrounded by bay windows overlooked the veranda. It seated eight and was used regularly. However, the breakfast bar that seated ten was the focal point. It seemed like a mini hub for the family of seven - well, now six. The double level bar with Italian marble countertop sat in the center of the large kitchen. An eight-eye stove, double oven and various other appliances of convenience known to man, was where the family gathered. For they knew within a matter of minutes of them taking a seat, a cup of coffee, tea or maybe something stronger would be sitting in front of them. On the far side of the bright sunny room was one of the four staircases in the house. This one was used more frequently than all the others. The entry from the private driveway was where the family entered, as Winnie was doing at that moment.

"Mrs. Dunning, how did it go?" Daisy, the housekeeper, cook, and all around friend, asked as Winnie walked through the door. "Did Myles get the vote?"

"Yes, he did." Winnie smiled, then exhaled as she removed her hat and gloves. "For a minute there I was sure he was going to turn down the nominations. But thank goodness for Michael and Grace. Neither gave him a chance."

Daisy took Winnie's hat and gloves from her. "But you did...didn't you? You were willing to let that boy turn away from all his father and grandfather built just so he could live his life doing what? Nothing is more important than keeping that bank going."

Winnie had taken a seat at the table in the kitchen as Daisy strolled from the room to put her things away. She knew when Daisy was on her righteous roll there was no stopping her until she had said her piece. Never taking a breath from her sermon, Daisy reentered the kitchen.

"He has the rest of his life to build that school he been talking about. Hell, he could hire somebody to build it for him." She walked over to the cupboard, took down a teacup and saucer, then placed it in front of Winnie on the table, with a rattle. "That girl who works for him...."

"Chrystina?" Winnie offered.

"Yes." Daisy nodded as she put the sugar and teabag in the cup. "That Chrystina girl is bright. Hell, she could set it up to his specifications and have that school running in no time." Pouring the hot water from the teapot with one hand and the other placed on her hip, she continued. "You were just going to let Myles walk away from all Mr. Hep worked so hard for."

Winnie looked up, raising an eyebrow. "Are you finished?"

"I don't know if I'm finished or not. It depends on your answer."

"Why did we hire you?" Winnie teased.

"Because y'all need someone around here to keep the foolishness in order, that's why. Now answer my question."

Winnie took a sip of her tea, then closed her eyes as the warmth began to ease the tension from her body. Opening her eyes she looked at Daisy, who stood with hands on hips waiting with an 'I know what you did' look on her face.

Winnie sighed. "Yes, I was going to give Myles the opportunity to walk away." She looked straight into Daisy's eyes. "Hep would never force any of his children to do something they did not want to do. And neither would I."

"Humph," Daisy stammered out as she walked back over to the stove. "You and Mr. Hep and those high ideas of children knowing what is best." She placed the teapot on the eye of the stove with a thump. "When I was growing up as a child I did what I was told and liked it."

"A hundred years ago," Winnie mumbled as she drank her tea.

"What you say?"

"I said the tea was cold." Winnie looked innocently at the woman.

"Don't you sass me, Winnieford Dunning. I knew you before you were born."

Why did people say things like that, Winnie wondered. "How could you have known me before I was born, Daisy? I'm older than you are."

"My spirit knew you. That's how."

Winnie stood and muttered, "I wish my spirit had warned me before we hired you."

"And it would have told you what you already knew. I was the best thing to happen to this family."

Winnie walked over and kissed the woman on her cheek. "That's the first thing I can agree with you on since I walked in the house." She patted Daisy on the shoulder as she sat the teacup in the sink. "Has AnnieMarie been down this morning?"

Daisy sighed. "No. That child is so torn up inside. I just don't know what to do to help her."

The telephone rung just as Winnie replied, "Time, Daisy, time and understanding will heal her."

"Dunning residence," Daisy said into the telephone as she nodded her agreement. Winnie was walking out of the room when she heard Daisy say, "Mrs. Dunning is unavailable, Mr. Dunning. But I will give the message along with the others you left earlier."

Winnie turned back with a questioning look and waited for Daisy to finish with the call.

"Which Mr. Dunning was that?"

Daisy hung up the telephone. "Never you mind. You don't need to be bothered by them right now." Not looking in Winnie's direction, Daisy went on preparing a snack. "You want some of this soup I'm putting together for Annie?"

"No. I want an answer to my question."

Pulling ingredients from the refrigerator, Daisy huffed. "Well if you must know, that was Walker Jr. calling. He wanted to know if you talked to the attorneys yet about Mr. Hep's will."

Somewhat surprised, Winnie asked, "Walker asked you about that?"

"No." Daisy shook her head. "I overheard him talking to you as if you were a child about Mr. Hep's will. It ain't none of his business what your husband put in his will. Hell, Mr. Hep ain't even cold in the ground and the vultures are after the bank," she huffed. "He wants no part of the hard work it takes to keep that bank running. Hell, soon he gonna be wanting this house and you too."

Daisy was off on one of her tantrums again, but this time Winnie did not have the patience to wait until she finished. "What..." she cut in, "did he say...exactly. Not your interpretation."

Daisy gave her one of those 'watch your tone' looks, then answered.

"Mr. Walker Dunning Jr. wants you to call him the minute you get in to discuss the terms of Hep's will. He specifically asked if there was anything in the will reinstating the shares of the bank back to him."

Winnie was stunned at the question. "Was there supposed to be?"

"How would I know, I'm just the cook around here."

Winnie stomped her foot. "Don't play that game with me, Daisy. You know more about what's going on with the family than any of us do. So spill it. Why does Walker think Hep would have gone against his father's wishes to give shares of the bank back to him?"

"Because a few years ago Mr. Hep said he would think about it if Walker made an effort to stop gambling."

"Oh," Winnie sighed. "Well, Hep never mentioned that to me."

"That's because as soon as Walker Jr. left that day, Mr. Hep said he would give the shares back to Walker as soon as Lucifer stopped beating his wife. Then he told Myles the only way Walker would get his hands on any shares of stock to the bank was over his dead body and even then he would haunt his ass until he dropped dead with him."

Winnie laughed lightly at first, then it turned into a full-fledged roar, with tears and all coming from her eyes. Reaching down she took off her shoes and pointed one at Daisy. "Now that sounds like Hep." She could hear Daisy laughing as she climbed the back stairs.

# *Chapter Seven*

Daisy watched as Winnie walked up the stairs. She sobered and shook her head at the thought of what this family was about to go through. Mr. Hep was the true leader of the family and he had died too soon, way too soon. Daisy checked the stairs to make sure Winnie was out of hearing distance and then she picked up the telephone and dialed.

"Dunning Bank & Trust executive offices, Mrs. Vazquez speaking."

"Marie, this is Daisy. Has Walker Jr. tried to contact Myles today?"

"Not that I'm aware of. Why? Is he bothering Winnie?"

"He has called several times trying to reach her. This whole will reading needs to be done so things can settle down."

"I agree, Daisy, however, neither you nor I have any control over the timing." There was a slight hesitation, then Marie continued. "Myles just left here," she said in a low voice. "He asked about Cainan Scott."

"Did you tell him anything?" Daisy gasped. "What did he want to know?"

"No, I did not. Legally we can't. I hate withholding information from Myles."

"It seems to me, with Mr. Hep gone, they gonna have to talk to Myles eventually. For now, it ain't no need causing more problems for him or us. All we can do now is pray Mr. Hep put something in his will to let Winnie know."

"If this goes public it could be a PR nightmare. I think we should turn it over to Myles."

"At some point, I think you are right. But ain't no need putting anything else on that boy right now. He has that bank to deal with. You just make sure the investigation file is somewhere he will eventually see it. If he finds out on his own that will take us off the hook."

"Already done. In the meantime, I'll keep Walker Jr. away from Myles, you keep him away from Winnie." Mrs. Vazquez cleared her throat. "Daisy, tell me something. Is there anything personal going on between Myles and Chrystina?"

"You mean like man woman stuff?"

"Yes."

"No, not yet. She's a nice girl. Got her own for all I know. She ain't looking for no one to take care of her like that Savannah Whitfield. Why you asking?"

"I don't know. Something in the way he talks about her. I could be wrong. Seeing something that's not there."

Daisy shrugged her shoulders. "Keep an eye on it. Lord knows that boy is going to need someone to have his back. In fact I need to put him on notice about Walker Jr. and his mother."

"All right, Daisy, you take care."

Daisy held the disconnection button down for a few seconds then dialed another number.

"Mr. Dunning, please. Daisy Smithers calling." Daisy waited until the call was picked up on the other end. "Myles, I thought you might like to know the vultures are beginning to circle around your mother. And if you are the man I know your father raised you to be you will put a stop to it right now."

Myles held the telephone for a minute because it sounded like the no-nonsense woman who helped to raise him was in tears.

"Daisy, what's going on?"

"That no-good uncle of yours has been calling here looking for your mother all morning. Now I have put him off as long as I can. But he is going to get to her sooner or later. Now she got too much to deal with to have to put up with that nonsense."

Myles just groaned.

"And you know what he's after, the same thing that Mr. Mitchell is after. Your mother is a sweetheart with a heart of gold and you know what vultures do with sweethearts like her. Now, what are you going to do about it?"

"What did Walker Jr. want?" Myles asked.

"He wants her to give him back those shares to the bank your grandfather took away. He thinks your daddy put something in his will. If he didn't you know he is going to try to sweet-talk your mother into doing it. And are you watching your back at that bank?"

Myles never had a chance to answer.

"You know that William Mitchell is as much of a snake as your Uncle Walker. He's going to try to take that bank over. And you can't let that happen. Your father and grandfather would turn over in their graves if you let that man get his hands on that bank. Now, what you gonna do about that?"

Myles had to chuckle. "It is my first day as CEO, Daisy. There is a lot on my plate. Can I get a little time to take care of all of this?"

"Ain't nobody give President Obama no time. That cartoon character-looking man demanding his birth certificate and such. Can you imagine that? That clown needs to be paying attention to his own finances. Maybe then he won't be filing for bankruptcy so many times. You're battling just like President Obama did. The old trying to turn things back to the way it was. Don't nobody want to go back there. I was raised during that time, I know what I'm talking about. We need to go forward and just like him it's your job to take that bank forward."

"Daisy...Daisy," he called twice to get her attention as she rambled on.

"Are you interrupting me, boy?"

"Yes, ma'am, I am. I want you to listen to me. Walker Jr. is not to talk to Mother until I give you the okay."

"All right, son. I can do that."

"Also, Daisy, there is something I have to tell you."

"What?"

"My father trusted you with his children. Now I'm going to trust you with my mother. She is vulnerable right now. Neither of us is going to let anyone take advantage of her. You know I have to be here at the bank. So I am depending on you to handle things at the house. Set up the master guest suite on the first floor for me. I'll be staying there until things settle down." Daisy choked up.

"You're a good son, Myles Dunning." Daisy sighed.

Daisy heard the intercom in his office buzz. "Mr. Mitchell is here to see you, Mr. Dunning."

"We'll talk more when I get home, Daisy."

Daisy disconnected the call, hesitated then walked behind the kitchen staircase to Hep's home office. She closed the door behind her then walked over to the bookcase on the left of the room. Pulling out the red dictionary, the shelves separated revealing a safe in the center of the wall. Placing her thumb on the screen, the green light flashed. The door popped open. Inside she pushed the small recorder and disc to the side Hep put in her care and reached for the documents needed to stop Walker Jr. if he created any issues that will harm Winnie.

She pulled the document out along with the business card that was attached to it. The FBI agent on the card was Byron Roark, Washington DC office. She opened the document and read. It was an arrest warrant taken out by Hepburn on behalf of Dunning Bank & Trust against Walker Dunning Jr. for embezzlement. If Walker was to try to do anything to Winnie, Daisy had been instructed to call the number on the card and turn the document over to the agent. If that were to happen Walker Jr. would be prosecuted to the fullest extent of the law.

Daisy exhaled, relieved to know the document was still in place. She folded the document and placed it back inside the safe.

"Don't you worry, Mr. Hep. I'm going to make sure your Winnie is okay. If he comes anywhere near her again with this crazy talk about your will, I'll have his no good behind arrested and put away for life. I'm gonna make sure of it." She put the dictionary back in its place and watched as the shelves connected again.

She opened the door to find Jerome standing outside the office. Startled, she gasped. "You scared the crap out of me."

"What going on with Mrs. Dunning?"

"That Walker Jr. called again." Daisy shook her head as she rolled her eyes.

"Questions on the will again?"

"You know it," Daisy replied as she walked back to the kitchen with Jerome. "That man is the worst."

"There is always one dark horse in the corral," Jerome acknowledged. "Walker Jr. is it for this family."

"I'm surprised he hasn't gotten himself killed or something."

Jerome shook his head as he took a seat at the breakfast bar. "Nothing happens to men like Walker Jr. It's the people around him who usually end up paying the price for his wrong doings. That's why I'm here."

"Are you going to stay now that Mr. Hep is gone?"

"That is going to depend on Myles. Where is Mrs. Dunning?"

"Upstairs." Daisy smiled. "She's going to be all right. Just going to take a little time."

"Oh yeah, she's made of good stock. She's going to make it through this," Jerome agreed. "How is AnnieMarie?"

"The same," Daisy replied. "Marie mentioned Myles is asking about the Scott boy."

Jerome hesitated. The reason he was there was because of Cainan Scott. The information was told to a few select people Mr. Hepburn trusted in the strictest of confidence. He was given a recording of the meeting between Hepburn and Scott's people. He put it in a safe place with no intention of turning it over to anyone unless it became a life or death matter.

"Why is he asking about Scott?"

"AnnieMarie is blaming herself for Mr. Hep's heart attack. They were arguing about Cainan Scott when it happened. He didn't want AnnieMarie seeing him.

Did you listen to the recording? Is there anything in there that could help her?"

"No, I didn't listen to it. I only secured it."

"I hate seeing her walking around with a broken heart about her daddy and that boy."

"She will figure things out on her own." Jerome rose to leave. "Has Mrs. Dunning been eating right?"

"Not really. She's been faking it so Mr. Myles and the children feel better about going into the office. I talked to him about it. He's going to be staying here for a while. His assistant Chrystina is going to send some of his things over."

"His assistant," Jerome laughed.

Daisy joined in. "Yes, that is what he is still calling her."

"When is that boy going to figure out he is in love with that woman?"

"Probably not until it's too late and somebody else done scooped her up."

"That girl isn't going anywhere." Jerome shook his head. "She is just as bad for him as he is for her. Love is just wasted on young people these days."

"Amen to that," Daisy laughed. "Those two are just wasting time that is not promised to anybody."

"You know he went to her house the night of the wake."

"Stop it I say." Daisy turned to him, surprised.

"Sure did." Jerome nodded. "I took him there myself and picked him up the next morning. He was in bad shape when I dropped him off. But walked out a man when I picked him up the next morning."

"Do you think....?"

"I don't think so. He was in pretty bad shape. Wouldn't have been able to get it up if he tried."

"Poor baby." Daisy frowned. "Well, they'll have time to get it all together before it's over with. As least that is what Mr. Hep said."

Jerome nodded. "I think they could stand a little push. Like you said, tomorrow isn't promised to anybody."

## Chapter Eight

Myles' voice came through the intercom. "Tell Mr. Mitchell I'll see him as soon as I finish with this conference call."

Chrystina smiled inside. He was making Mitch wait on him. Good for him. She knew Myles was talking to Ms. Daisy on the phone, but had hung up a few minutes ago.

"Mr. Dunning will be with you in a few minutes. Would you like to have a seat while I get you a cup of coffee?"

"I'll stand and I don't want any coffee," William snapped. "What is so important to make me cancel my afternoon appointments?"

"I have no idea, Mr. Mitchell. But I don't believe Mr. Dunning will be too much longer."

"Don't give me that brush-off. We all know you are his right arm, for the moment that is. So what does he want?"

Chrystina did not like the implication, but was used to shielding her thoughts. After all, technically, Mr. Mitchell was her boss so she sweetened her reply.

"I was only asked to make the appointment, sir. I really do not know what the meeting will be about. Perhaps it's concerning whether or not you are going to continue in the role as Vice-President of the bank."

Mitchell was stunned by her response. "Of course I am," he said with an air of superiority as he adjusted his blazer. "He cannot run this bank without me. Huh, if anyone should be concerned about their tenure here it should be you." He looked Chrystina up and down. "There is no way Myles is going to take you down the hall to the corner office." He smirked.

The office door opened and William's whole demeanor changed. "Myles." He turned with his hand extended with an air of sincerity all knew was manufactured. "I understand you wanted to talk. I'm here for you, son. What do you need?"

Chrystina looked over William's back at Myles then rolled her eyes. She could tell Myles held his laughter as he shook William's hand, then patted him on the shoulder.

"Let's go into the office and talk."

Myles shot Chrystina a look. She raised her eyebrow as she watched them close the door.

"He is right you know," Nancy said from the hallway as she leaned against the opening to Chrystina's office.

Chrystina looked over at the slim blonde with the fake eyelashes, nails, and booty pads.

"Right about what?" she asked as she fumbled with papers on her desk.

"There is no way Myles is going to take you down the hall to his new office." She took a step inside and shrugged her shoulder. "Oh, I don't think for a minute he is going to let you go. However, I just don't see you fitting in down the hall."

"And why not?" Chrystina looked at the woman with a curious brow raised.

Nancy laughed. "Come on, Chrystina. You know why."

"No, I don't. Enlighten me."

"Now, Chrystina, Mr. Hep selected every person in the front office for two reasons. They look good and they know how to socialize with the elites." She shook her head. "No disrespect intended, but you don't fit either category. I, on the other hand, grew up with the socialites. I know how to mingle." She flipped her long blonde hair across her shoulders. "And the looks, well, we both know I have you heads over heels on that front."

"Some people in this building are chosen for their skills and knowledge. Not on what you can do with your mouth." Chrystina tilted her head, then turned back to her computer.

"You are right." She removed her lean body from the doorframe and smirked. "But none of them is in that office down the hallway." She ran her hands down her hip-hugging short skirt, then looked over her shoulder. "This mouth will get me where you want to be." Nancy took a step to walk away and stopped. Turning back to Chrystina, she placed a finger on her cheek. "You know, I think I will go down to the mailroom to get a few empty boxes. I'm pretty sure I will be moving soon." She walked out of the office smiling.

"You are right. You will be moving straight out the front door," Chrystina mumbled to herself. But inside she knew the wench was right. Everyone in the front office looked and acted the part. None of the females were bigger than a size six and the men...well most of them looked like GQ magazine cover models. Every one of them had come to her for help when they could not find the answer or figure out exactly what Mr. Hep needed. But, they weren't friends that would look out for her. They were co-workers who used her when it benefited them. She knew even if Myles wanted to take her along, she would not fit in with the group. That meant she would probably no longer work directly for Myles. A new boss would not be too much of an issue for her, because she knew her stuff. The thought of being without Myles would shatter her world.

For the last ten years he'd been more than her boss. Myles was her mentor, her confidant, her friend, her wildest fantasy. Myles Dunning was her everything. Opening her eyes in the morning there was a picture of him on her nightstand. The last voice she heard at night was Myles, on her recorder. A message he sent telling her to get well soon two years ago when she was sick. All day, every day, Myles was around, needing her, more now than he ever did before. That need materialized right before her eyes the night before his father's funeral. One minute she was consoling him, then the next minute...well, all she could say was her fantasy world became a reality.

The way he drove himself into her still made her inner lips moist, her thighs shake and her knees weak. To this day she had not told anyone what happened between them. That was a memory she was keeping tucked away, in her heart. The feel of him inside of her, even though she knew deep down it was just a weak moment for him, filled her in a way no man ever did before and she had no doubt if anyone will in the future. Her inner lips were throbbing at the memory.

Oh God, was she obsessed, like her sister Gina said? No, she was in love with the man. She admired his drive to make the world better. She loved the way he was every glass half-full rather than half-empty.

She idolized the way he took care, even when he did not want to. But most of all and this was the most important to her. She loved the way his thighs looked in a pair of jeans. It did not happen often, but when it did, that butt of his and those thick thighs just did something to her on the inside. That was her only regret of their one night together. She did not get to put her hands on that butt, to feel the firmness in her hands. She will probably never get the opportunity again.

Chrystina closed her eyes, willing herself to stop thinking about that night. "All hell is about to break out around here and I need to focus." The telephone sounded just as she turned to her computer to pull up the files on William Mitchell she was sure Myles needed.

Racing over, without checking the number on the caller ID, she answered, "Dunning Bank & Trust, Risk Management office, Chrystina Price speaking."

"Hello, Chrystina. This is Ms. Whitfield."

The voice grated on her nerves, like always, as Chrystina stopped and stared at the telephone. The woman treated her as if she was an insignificant entity in this world, then had the nerve to damn near cause her to lose her job. Well, two can play that game.

"I'm sorry. I did not get your name."

"It's Savannah Whitfield, Chrystina."

Chrystina could hear the woman holding in her temper as she spoke. She must have heard the news about Myles.

"Oh, Ms. Whitfield," she put emphasis on the Ms. "I do apologize. I did not catch your voice. How may I help you?"

"It has been a while. Would you be a dear and tell Myles I'm calling?"

People treat you bad, forget about it, then always come back to ask you to do something for them. What did she think, I'm just going to jump through hoops to help her. I don't think so, Chrystina thought to herself. Savannah Whitfield had no shame in her game. She wanted to be a Dunning. When her relationship with Myles ended she tried to snag Michael. That didn't work, so I guess it's back to Myles again.

"Mr. Dunning is in a meeting. Would you like to leave a message?"

"No, I do not want to leave a message." The testy words filtered through the telephone line like spikes. "I would like to speak with him now."

Chrystina smiled. Now that was the Savannah she knew and hated. She just held the phone and waited. The she heard the sigh.

"Chrystina, for a girl from the streets you do your job very well. It is a shame it's all about to come to an end for you." She smirked. "Be a dear and tell Myles to return my call. And Chrystina, if you don't give him my message, I will make sure he knows." She paused. "You do remember what happened the last time you did not give him my message. Let's not have a repeat. You don't want to end up back in the gutter."

There was no way she was going to let this woman think for a moment she had touched a nerve...she had, but she didn't need to know it.

"I will be sure to give Mr. Dunning your message. Have a nice day, Ms. Whitfield," Chrystina replied in the most professional voice she could manage. As she disconnected the call she could only sigh. Everyone seemed to have an opinion about her future at Dunning. First Mr. Mitchell, then Nancy, now Savannah, all within an hour. They were all so sure she was going to be replaced, and why...because she was a little overweight. None of that had anything to do with her ability to get the job done. That's why Myles kept her around.

She pushed her chair back and walked over to the mirror that was on the far wall in the corner of her office. She took a good look at herself. It was as her grandmother said; she had the cutest face this side of the Dixon. Of course that was her grandmother's opinion. But when she looked into the mirror the more she had to agree, to an extent. Reflected back in the mirror was a very pretty woman with beautiful natural shoulder length hair that she kept up in a roll most of the time. She had long lashes that most women would kill for, a cute perky nose, smooth copper-tone skin and lips that she deemed to be quite kissable. But, and it was a big but, no pun intended, as she traveled lower, it was clear where her problems lie. There she stood with a beautiful face but a body that was curvier than she would like for it to be. Slightly overweight...oh okay, more than slightly. She ran her hands down her body and wondered what it would be like to be a size 10 or hell, a 12 for that matter. Losing a good 20 pounds or so will do the trick. Would men take a second look at her then...would Myles? What did he think about that night, she soundlessly wondered. Things happened so fast, so intense he didn't see the fat. Thank God for blind passion.

She quickly turned away from the mirror. Who has the time to lose weight? She sat back down at her desk. It was what it was and if she was not moved to the office down the hall so be it.

"Stop allowing people to mess with your mind. Do what you have always done...work hard." With that said, she turned to her computer and pulled up the file she should have started working on twenty minutes ago.

#

As William took a seat in front of Myles' desk he wondered how the man was going to come at him. When he received the call from Chrystina demanding a meeting today his first thought was the nerve of him to demand anything of him. But then he thought about the way he handled Hep. The man never knew how deeply he hated him.

"The initial meeting with the group from Hershel Automotive was this afternoon. You know they plan to have us as their main banker here in the states. Otherwise, you know I would never have disregarded your request to meet today."

Myles took a seat behind his desk then sat back. "I was under the impression that meeting was set for tomorrow."

"Yes, yes the main meeting is scheduled for tomorrow. Today was a get to know your client. You know...work them outside the office in a social setting," William explained, as he fidgeted in his seat.

Myles frowned as he reached over to take a look at his calendar. "I don't recall having anything on my schedule. Who was attending with you?"

No this boy did not just question me. "No one. Your father trusted me to handle events like this."

Myles stopped clicking through the pages in his calendar, then sat back. He shrugged his shoulder. "Well, Dad had his way of handling things and I have mine. I tend to have a more hands on approach. Check with Chrystina before you reschedule the meeting. I think I will join you." He sat forward and clasped his hands together on the desk. "Mitch, I felt it was imperative for us to meet today to ensure we present a united front to the employees when the announcement is made."

"We are united, Myles," William replied, as he thought of ways to keep Myles from moving down the hallway. Earlier in the day when Paulette informed him Myles was in the area his initial thought was Myles had given into the standoff. However, after more than an hour had passed and Myles had not knocked on his door, William realized moving into Hep's office was going to take a little more finesse.

Myles put up his hand. "I know, Mitch," he said, as he nodded his head. "However, there may be some undercurrents that could undermine the plans I have for the bank."

"Plans...what plans could you have, Myles? You were only voted CEO a few hours ago."

Myles smirked. "As you know, Mitch, Dunnings never sit on their hands and wait for things to happen. My father shared his vision for Dunning with all his children. My plan is to take that vision and add a few of my own to move us forward. I would like for you to be a part of that journey." He adjusted his position. "In your position I can understand some resentment on the way the vote turned out. If you are willing to stay on board, your knowledge and experience is welcomed."

"Well, yes, the vote was a disappointment. Hep would have valued my dedication a little more than his family has," Mitch huffed. "But that's neither here nor there. We are where we are. It's good that you understand your limitations. You are not prepared to take on the responsibility of a bank this size. You can always take a branch manager's position and work your way up. Now, if you would just give me the reins, I will know who to put in place to get Dunning established in the banking industry where it should have been years ago. First on the agenda is ensuring a strong presence in the front office. Now, it would be a sacrifice, but I am willing to move my office next door. That way the employees and customers alike will know who is in charge. Unfortunately, we will have to let a few people go, starting with that Scott kid. I never knew what Hep saw in him. Don't get me wrong, he has shown an above average profit for our clients since he has been here, but, there is something about him I don't like."

Myles sat back in his chair and continued to listen as the man spoke freely. He wondered if the man knew how many ways he had insulted him and his father in the few minutes he had been in the office.

His father once said if you let a person talk long enough you will eventually hear what is truly inside their heart. Mitch was certainly proving the point.

"Then too, there is AnnieMarie. The public relations on Dunning has suffered since Hep's death. I know she is your sister, but at times like this we cannot let family ties hold us back. If she is not capable of doing the job, we are just going to have to let her go. And that Chrystina. She has too much power for an assistant. Hell, before some members of my staff do what I tell them, they check in with her. I don't know what you or Hep saw in her, but she runs this place like it's her own. There is no way I can put things in place with her around contradicting my orders. She simply has to go."

Before he could control it, Myles' fist came down on the desk with a bang. William jumped a foot in the air landing behind the chair. He glared at Myles.

Trying with all his will to pull in his temper and not laugh at Mitch, Myles closed his eyes then began counting to ten. He opened them to see Mitch staring at him, not certain what in the hell had just happened.

Myles exhaled, then stood, turning his back on Mitch as he looked out of the window silently asking God to guide him in this moment. Myles dropped his head to his chest then turned back to the man he was trying to tolerate.

"Mitch." He hesitated. "I believe you misunderstood my meaning." He saw the man flinch, so he tried to readjust his harsh tone. Myles pointed to the chair. "Please sit down and forgive my outburst."

Mitch hesitantly retook his seat and stared suspiciously up at Myles who remained standing behind his desk. The look on the man's face almost made Myles laugh. In fact he would have if the situation weren't so serious.

"Contrary to what you think, my father has been preparing me for this position since I was born. I am more than ready to take over as CEO of Dunning and have every intention of doing just that. None of what you said is taken lightly." He sat back behind his desk. "Let's address your issues one at a time. Cainan Scott has been a model employee since his arrival. You stated he has made significant investments for our customers. Now, unless you know something I do not, I have no reason to let the man go. As to AnnieMarie, she is overqualified for the position she is in. If she was not doing the job and doing it well...family or not...I would relieve her. However, the truth of the matter is we have had world-class public relations under her rule, and as you indicated, she is family. Now to Chrystina, I want you to listen carefully and take this in the light it is meant. Chrystina will always have a position here as long as she wants one. You, on the other hand, have a choice. You are welcome to stay on in your position, for you, just like the others you named are valued members of this organization. If, however, you feel you are not able to work under an unprepared man as you indicated I am, you are welcome to leave." Myles sat back and watched as the man squirmed.

## Chapter Nine

Mitch walked into Elaine Jacobson's office and slammed the door behind him. Looking up at the sudden sound, Elaine pushed back from her desk, crossed her legs and waited. The fool was at it again, she thought as she watched him angrily pace in front of her desk. It was actually funny, for he reminded her of a real life Elmer Fudd after missing another opportunity to catch the silly rabbit. Like Elmer Fudd, Mitch just did not know when to quit. How long was it going to take him to realize he was not a Dunning? He will never have control of this bank. It became clear to her years ago. His sudden stop took her from her thoughts. She turned her focus on him.

"The audacity of that son of a b....!"

Doing all she could to stop the image of Elmer Fudd marching with the rifle on his shoulder and smoke coming out of his ears, Elaine took a sip of her coffee, then asked, "Which son of a blank would that be?"

"Myles," Mitch shouted, and began the angry march again as he relayed to her the details of the meeting he'd just left with Myles. As always, Mitch had shown his cards too soon. The old fool, Elaine thought, as he continued to pace angrily across her floor. The office wasn't large, therefore, it did not take many steps or, in this case stomps, from one end to the other. His stomping became a rhythm in her mind...11,12,13,14, turn. 1,2,3,4,5,6,7,8,9,10,11,12,13,14, turn. After the fourth time around she had had enough.

"William, stop!" Her voice was a little higher than she meant it to be, but if he did not stop his Elmer Fudd impersonation she was going to scream. She sighed. "First you need to calm down." She motioned towards the chair in front of her desk. "Have a seat. Let's try to sort through the conversation rationally."

"Rationally...hell, the man all but offered me walking papers," he yelled.

"But he did not give you walking papers, William." She stood, walked around the desk, then hugged him. "Come on." She rubbed his shoulder. "Have a seat. Let's talk it through."

Mitch calmed down a bit, then did as she asked and sat in the chair. Instead of returning to her seat, Elaine leaned back against the edge of her desk, then crossed her legs. She knew Mitch's attention would go to her nice firm thighs as the form-fitting burgundy dress rose.

"Now, based on what you said, the option of you staying and remaining in your position is totally up to you. So how did you leave things?"

Mitch's eyes focused on her thighs, so it took him a moment to reply. Elaine held her patience and called out.

"William?"

His head jerked up. "What?" he asked, now looking into her light brown eyes.

"With Myles...how did you leave things?"

"I told him I would remain his second in command, of course."

Of course you did, Elaine thought. God forbid you grow any balls. It seemed the men involved with this organization have an issue with that when it comes to going up against the Dunnings.

"Well, it's difficult to give up a six-figure salary plus bonuses," she rationalized as she stood and walked back around the desk to retake her seat.

She knew he was watching her behind as she walked. He couldn't help himself, she summarized. Elaine knew William always wondered if she had ever slept with Hep. The rumors were out but never any proof. He tried to catch them, to get anything on Hep. But it never materialized. The first years of her employment she wanted the man. William even encouraged her. She wasn't stupid. Elaine knew when she was being used. William was trying to put a wedge between Hep and Winnie. It did not work.

"If the Hershel Automotive group accepts our offer your salary will double. So will Myles'. If you really think about it his bonus will be more than your salary."

That snapped Mitch's attention back to where it should be. His brows drew closer together. "As president he will get the $250,000 signing bonus."

Elaine nodded. "Not to mention the notoriety." She let that one hang in the air for a minute. "Then if we get the Boeing Industries Technology account, and it looks as though we will, that will be another 250K bonus for him. Looks like Myles is coming out on top all the way around. And the Dunnings get richer."

"Yes...that will be an additional half-million on top of his regular salary."

"If the board had voted later in the week that bonus would have been yours."

Mitch stared past Elaine's shoulder out the window behind her. His eyes returned to her. "Who has the lead on the BIT account?" BIT was their acronym for Boeing Industries Technology.

"Preston, I believe. You know he is looking to be promoted. If he pulls BIT off, well, he may be moved from Small Business acquisitions, to my position."

Mitch nodded, acknowledging her statement. Then she folded her arms across her chest, pushing her breasts up, revealing a little more cleavage at the v of the dress she was wearing. Mitch all but licked his lips.

"You know, I think you should be the lead on BIT."

Elaine unfolded her arms, sat forward and smirked. "No, I'm sure Myles will not agree. He has his people and I'm pretty sure I'm not one of them. But thanks for the vote of confidence." She flashed that hundred-watt smile of hers on him.

"Let me talk to Myles."

"About what?"

"Giving you the lead on BIT. I think you can close that deal."

"Listen, I appreciate the thought. But you just had a run-in with Myles. It's not a time for you to be asking for favors. Take cover for a minute. Just make sure you are okay. I kind of like having you around."

Mitch smiled as he stood and adjusted his suit jacket, while sucking in his stomach. "Don't underestimate what I can accomplish. I still have a little pull around here."

"I never underestimate you, William." She held her smile.

"We'll talk later," Mitch replied, as he opened the door.

Her expression turned to one of concern. "You feel better now?"

"I always do after one of our sessions." He smiled and walked out the door.

Elaine pulled out her cell phone. She pushed one button and waited. When the call was answered on the other end she smiled. "He is poised and ready to pop."

A deep snicker flowed through the phone. "The thighs reeled him in?"

"Works every time." She grinned as she crossed her legs and sat back in her chair.

"Any word from PI?"

"It's still early yct. Give them time. Whatever they do it has to appear to be random. If it appears they are attacking Dunning it would be a PR nightmare for them."

"You are certain they are going to react?"

"I'm betting my future on it. Have you taken steps on the home front?"

"I'm on my way there now."

"Keep your temper in check."

"Winnie is no match for me. I'll get what we need." The call ended.

"Men are suckers," Elaine said as she turned back to her computer. The file on BIT, waiting for her to return, lit up. "You are going to be my ticket to bring down the mighty Dunnings, once and for all." She laughed, and began reviewing the account.

# Chapter Ten

It was well after eight at night when Chrystina knocked lightly on Myles' office door before walking in.

"Are we done for the night?"

Looking up from the file on his desk, Myles allowed Chrystina's smile to ease some of the tension of the day. He sat back and sighed. "It has been a hell of a day."

"Tell me about it," Chrystina replied with a weary sigh as she dropped into her usual seat. "Twelve meetings, four hundred and seventy-two calls and I don't even want to discuss the emails."

The beat look became her, Myles thought, as he watched strands of her hair fall from the customary French roll. He thought back to the night at her place then quickly wiped it from his mind.

"Have we responded to all of them?"

"No, but we put a big dent into them. The calls, yes." She hesitated. "All except one. Well, make that five," she corrected as she placed the pink slips of messages on his desk.

Myles smirked as he read them. "All from Savannah." He placed them to the side. "That doesn't surprise me."

"Me either, but please return her calls. I can deal with being replaced due to your promotion. However, I cannot handle losing my job again because of Savannah Whitfield and her holier-than-thou attitude."

Myles laughed. "She can be a bit dramatic. Losing your job because of her antics should not be a concern."

"I'm happy to hear that." She inhaled, then gave him the other piece of paper. "The top person on that list is actually with another agency. But I'm pretty sure she could be persuaded to make a move here."

Myles glanced at the list. There were names of Executive Assistants on it. "Why are you giving me this?"

Chrystina stopped talking and looked up at him.

"I'm sorry, did you want me to handle the hiring?"

"No. I want you to answer my question," he snapped. Sitting back and shaking his head, he exhaled. "You know, I expected this from others, but not you, Chrystina. All day, I've dealt with employees, one after another with concerns about their jobs and how my becoming president of the bank will impact them. Everybody is positioning themselves as if this was a game of chess. Preston, Mitch and a few others, I expect it from. But not you. I am baffled as to why you want to leave now, just when I need you the most."

Chrystina shot up from the chair with hands on hips and fired back at him. "Now wait a minute. I don't want to leave. But it seems to be the general consensus around here that you have to replace me. I was simply trying to streamline the process for you because I knew you would not have the time to deal with hiring an assistant."

Myles stood with his hands on his desk and leaned towards her. "Did I ask you to find a replacement for you?"

Chrystina replied, "You don't ask me to do a lot of things, but..."

"But what, Chrystina? But what?"

"Well, everyone believes I will not fit in down the hallway." Her tone a little less combative this time.

"When did the sassy Chrystina begin allowing others to define her? Do you have a problem fitting in down the hallway?" His tone more questioning, than angry now.

"Myles." Chrystina held her arms out and smirked. "Look at me."

"I'm looking at you, Chrystina. You want to give me an idea of what I'm looking for?"

Chrystina huffed, "Myles." She gestured with her hands. "All of this. Look at it in all its glory."

Myles stood back and folded his arms across his chest. "You care to be a little more specific?"

"Arrrrgh...my weight, Myles. Everyone down that hallway is a size six or lower."

Myles shook his head and sat back down. "Chrystina, I don't have time for petty stuff."

"Petty?"

"Yes, petty. If you don't like your size, do something about it. But don't ever presume I'm so shallow as to hire and fire based on someone's looks. This is not a beauty pageant. You don't get points because you can walk upright in a pair of heels." He picked up the piece of paper she had given him. "Is everyone on this list a size six?"

"Yes, except for the male. He's about your size."
The bluster all gone, she sat back down. "I was kind of
looking forward to interviewing him."

Myles' lips curved a little at the end. "You would
be," he murmured.

"What was that?" Chrystina asked with a raised
eyebrow.

"I said you still can see him." He handed the paper
back to her. "Hold interviews for an assistant for
whomever will take over my position. When I move
down the hallway, you are going with me. So I suggest
you start walking thirty minutes a day, drink plenty of
water and eat healthier. If you ask me a size six will
not do you justice. Size ten or twelve will do just fine.
A man needs a little something to hold onto."

"Myles," she laughed.

"I'm just saying. I know what I like." He shrugged.
"This brother likes flesh, opposed to bones."

"Ha, you seemed to like that boney Savannah
Whitfield just fine."

"Where is she now?"

"Hmm? On a pink slip."

He smiled at her. "Go home. It's been a long day.
I'm sure tomorrow will be longer."

She stood to walk out, then remembered the sound
her thighs would make. She took wider steps. "Are you
calling it a night too?"

He looked around. "Yes. I don't think there is too
much more damage I can do tonight. Besides I need to
check in on AnnieMarie."

"Please tell her hello for me. I really miss her
around here."

"I will do that."

"Okay, I'll see you tomorrow," Chrystina said as
she walked away.

"Do me a favor," Myles started.

She stopped at the door and turned back to him. "Sure, anything."

"Stop with the penguin walk. You got thick thighs...live with it."

She gasped. "You knew what I was doing?"

"Swish-swish-swish," he laughed.

She laughed with him then waived him off. "Myles Dunning, you are certifiable."

"Look, all jokes aside. If you need a walking partner, I'm here."

"I can't keep up with you. You work out every day."

"So join me. You know the schedule. Meet me upstairs in the morning."

"Are you serious? You would help me?"

"Together we can conquer anything, even the battle of thick thighs."

"No one has ever volunteered to help me lose weight before. Others have all had opinions on how I should do it, but no one ever said I will do it with you." She nodded. "I may take you up on that."

"Please do. See you tomorrow."

"Good night, Myles."

"Good night, Chrystina."

# Chapter Eleven

As she clicked the lock on her car all that was on Chrystina's mind was a nice long bath in her soaking tub, smooth music and a tall glass of wine. Opening the front door to her apartment she knew it was not to be.

"Turn off the damn water, Money. I'm trying to listen to my show."

"You told me to give Crystallite a bath. That's what I'm doing."

"Don't you talk back to me. Turn the damn water off."

A stunned Chrystina stood in the open doorway gaping at her living room.

"What in the hell is going on here?"

Her sister, Gina-the gorgeous one, turned towards the door. "Oh, hey. You're home."

Chrystina's purse fell off her shoulder. She caught it just before it hit the floor. "Operative word, home. Why are you in my home?" The door slammed behind her as she picked up a trash bag filled with clothes.

"Oh that. My water got cut off and I needed to wash some clothes and give the kids a bath."

"In my apartment? How did you get in?"

"Mom dropped us off then went to the store. She tried to call you. Didn't you get her message," Gina said as she turned up the volume on the television.

Frustrated with the answers she was getting, Chrystina stomped over to where her sister sat, grabbed the remote control then turned the television off.

Gina's head snapped back. "What the hell is your problem? I was looking at that."

"YOU...you are my problem at the moment." Chrystina put the remote on the coffee table only to find it covered with empty plates. "Get this food off of my coffee table. Your trash bag full of clothes from in front of my door and your feet off my white sofa." She turned and dropped her keys onto the breakfast bar. When she looked back Gina hadn't made a move. "Are you deaf?"

"You cut off my show."

"Your ass is going to be next if you don't get off my sofa...now!"

"Damn, you think more of your sofa than you do of your own sister," Gina huffed as she stood and grabbed the chips and empty plates off the glass table.

Chrystina decided to ignore that statement when she saw the red stain on her kitchen floor. "What is this?"

"Oh, Lilwayne had a drink in his hand when he was running through the house."

"He wasted it and you didn't think to clean up a red stain?"

"I was going to get to it. I just haven't had a chance yet."

"You were sitting on your ass watching television when I walked in."

"That was my show. I was going to clean it up after my show."

"And my kitchen?" Chrystina asked as she walked in to see pots and pans where someone cooked spaghettios and hot dogs. She could tell because the tomato sauce from the spaghettios had dripped from the pot to the stove. The can was sitting on the cabinet, next to the open hot dog roll bag. "When were you going to clean this up?"

"Damn, Chrystina, why don't you chill out." Gina started picking up the mess. "The house was peaceful before you walked in the door."

"This is my apartment. You want peace take your children and go home."

Gina looked at her and rolled her eyes. "I told you the kids needed a bath and I had to wash clothes. We are family, Chrys. We are supposed to help each other."

"Help each other? How are you helping me right now? I've been at work for the last twelve hours. Where have you been?"

"Mommy, what do you want me to put on Crystallite?"

The two sisters turned to see the oldest girl, Money holding her baby sister's hand in the hallway, dripping wet with a towel wrapped around her.

"Take your ass back into the bathroom until I come in there," Gina yelled.

Chrystina walked over, picked up the baby girl, then leaned down and kissed Money on the forehead. "Come on, lightening bug, let's get you dried off. Money, go into the bag by the door and get some clothes for her." She looked over her shoulder and frowned at her sister. "Clean my kitchen."

"You talk to them all sweet and treat me like dirt. I'm your sister or did working around those uppity people at the bank make you forget that?" Gina started grabbing things off the counter.

Chrystina dried the baby off, dressed her, then combed her hair. She held the four-year-old at arms' length. "Look at that pretty girl."

Money stood in the bathroom next to her aunt. "Now, I have to give Lilwayne his bath."

"Where is he?" Chrystina asked.

"Taking a nap on your bed."

"What?" She shoved the baby aside then walked down the hallway to her room. Turning on the light she saw the two-year-old baby lying on his stomach asleep. The sight would have been precious if he wasn't lying on her white comforter with dirt and red juice on the front of his shirt. Closing her eyes she walked over, picked up the child and saw the red stain she knew would be there.

"Come on, baby, we have to give you a bath." She carried the sleeping child to his big sister. "Money, run the bath water for him," she said as she removed the soiled clothes. The baby opened his eyes and smiled up at her. Chrystina smiled back and kissed his cheek. "Hi, Lilwayne. Are you ready for your bath?"

He shook his head.

Money laughed. "He doesn't like taking a bath."

"He doesn't? Let's see what we can do about that." She reached into her vanity, poured bubble bath into the tub then turned the water up full speed. "Let him play in there for a while. You stay here with him."

"Can I play with him too?" Crystallite asked.

"No, you already had your bath."

"It didn't look like that," the child cried out.

"You can do it the next time." Chrystina took her hand and carried the child into the living room only to find Gina had turned the television back on with the volume down low. She took the remote, then turned the channel.

"Hey, I'm looking at that."

Chrystina sat the little girl on the floor. "You look at tv while your mom cleans up my house."

"You are a bitch. You think because you work at the bank that you are better than me. You need to remember you came from the same roach invested hood that I came from. You ain't no better than me and everybody else we grew up with. Just cause you got a college degree and a funky ass job don't mean shit to me. You are still and always will be big ass Chrys from around the way. So what you live in a fancy apartment, with good furniture and a car to take you where you want to go, you still ain't shit and you ain't never going to be shit. And I'm going to be in your face every day to remind your uppity ass where you came from." She took the dishcloth and threw it in Chrystina's face.

"What in the hell is going on here?"

They both turned to see the stern Beverly Price standing in the doorway with the key in her hand.

"Mommy." Gina ran to the door, looking the spitting image of her mother. "Chrys came in the house yelling and throwing her weight around because I fed the kids in her all white kitchen, then washed them in her bathroom. I told her about the water being turned off, but she didn't care. All she's been doing since she walked in the house was bitch about her sofa and her table and her kitchen. She is selfish, just selfish. She don't care about nothing or anybody but herself."

Beverly saw the expression on her oldest daughter's face and knew she was pissed. She knew a con when she heard one.

"Gina, I washed and folded these clothes before I left. Why are they still in front of the door?"

"Chrys just sent Money in there for something," Gina said as she bent down to pick the bag up.

"I sent Money in there to get clothes for Crystallite because your lazy behind was sitting on my sofa, stuffing your face looking at television while your daughter was giving your baby a bath." Chrystina spoke calmly and directly to her baby sister. "Yes, I yelled at you and will do it again if I walk in my house, that I left clean, to find you here and it dirty from your actions." She walked slowly to where her sister stood next to her mother. "And let's be very clear on something. I don't need you or anyone else to remind me where I came from. I know from where I came. I made the choice to go to college to get a different life. I don't think I'm better than you or anybody else. But I will be damned- excuse me, Mother- if I am going to be chastised because you chose something different and your life is not as you want it to be. I didn't tell you to spread your legs and have three babies by different daddies. That was your choice."

"Chrystina, that's enough."

"You see what I mean, Mommy, she is always downing me because I have children."

"No, I don't down you because you have three beautiful children. I down you because you force your daughter to take care of them when you should be taking care of her. Let me tell you one more thing. I will not be your punching bag whenever one of your baby daddies is not doing their part to take care of you. You are right about one thing; we came from the same mother. She gave both of us the same chances. You chose one direction, I chose another. Do not blame me for your short falls. Go out and get a job so you can have your own apartment, with running water and stop trying to live off of me and your babies' daddies."

Gina started crying. "See, Mommy, see how she is always talking down to me."

"Chrystina, stop it right there," Beverly yelled. Gina started to speak but one look from Beverly and she stopped. "Not another word." She turned to Gina. "I left you here to give the kids a bath and have them dressed by the time I got back."

"I know but they were hungry. I had to feed them."

"Then you should have cleaned up behind yourself," Beverly reprimanded, then turned to her oldest daughter. "Chrys, everyone needs a little help every now and then. You could be a little more understanding. Your sister can't do much about her situation."

"Yes, Mother, she can."

"Well, she can't do it tonight." Beverly turned to Gina. "Finish cleaning the kitchen, while I check on the children."

Gina huffed off to do as her mother instructed.

"You" -Beverly pointed to Chrystina- "come with me."

Chrystina followed her mother into the bedroom.

"What happened to your comforter?" Beverly gasped.

"Your daughter put her son on it with red drink on his shirt."

"Oh, Chrys, I'm sorry. This is my fault. I'll have it cleaned."

"What are they doing here, Mother?"

Beverly sighed. "She called me at work and said her water had been turned off two days ago. They needed to take a bath and wash a few clothes. You live closer to work, so I dropped them off here and went back to work. I didn't mean for all of this to hop off."

"Mother." Chrystina sat on the bed next to her. "Gina lives in subsidized housing. She pays literally no rent. She gets a check for each child and child support for Money. Why can't she pay her water bill?"

"She has other expenses, Chrys."

"Yes, I noticed her nails are done, the hair not a strand out of place and the designer clothes she's wearing. I work every day and can't afford that. Yes, she has expenses and none of them have to do with her children."

"She has her priorities a little mixed up."

"Duh, you think?"

Beverly smiled. "Look I'll get the kids dressed and out of your way."

"Thanks, Mom. I'll try to help her in the kitchen."

Still frustrated, but more focused on getting her sister and her children on their way, Chrystina walked into the kitchen, picked up the hand towel and began drying the dishes as Gina washed them. They worked in silence until Gina spoke.

"We did you a favor and ate those hot dogs you had in the refrigerator."

"How is that doing me a favor?"

"You keep saying you want to lose weight. Well, if we ate all your food, that's helping you lose weight." She shrugged her shoulder. "If we came by once a week and cleaned your fridge out you might make it down to my size and look as good as I do."

Chrystina closed her eyes and shook her head. "In your own way I am sure you think you are helping me." She looked over at her sister. "It would help a lot more if you used your food stamps to buy food for you and your children instead of selling them to get your hair done."

"So what am I supposed to do about my hair?"

"Get a job, Gina. You know that thing you do Monday thru Fridays from 9-5. Hell you like children. The school system could always use help."

"If I get a job, when am I supposed to be with my man?"

"You got three children, you don't need another man. Besides, a man should be at a 9-5 too."

"If he is at a job how is he supposed to take care of my needs? You know I get those urges during the day and I got to have what I got to have."

Chrystina stopped wiping the dishes and glared at her sister. "Are you serious right now?"

Gina's lips curved up as she burst out laughing. "You should see the look on your face. You know I'm just joking."

Chrystina shook her head and laughed. "Sometimes, I swear I can't tell when you are joking or being serious."

"I know." Gina sighed. "I don't have your brains, Chrys. I mean, I could get a job, but to be honest, why should I? I have a roof over my head and food for me and my children."

Folding the dish towel, Chrystina turned to her sister and leaned back against the countertop. "Sometimes it's about being in control of your own destiny. Not having to depend on the city to feed your children. Or a man for your needs."

Gina sighed and mirrored her sister's stance. "You could put a little more effort in finding a man to meet your needs. It would be easy if you lose a little weight and loosen up that damn French roll on your head. You know that went out of style when we were in high school, right?"

Chrystina touched her hair. "Hey, it's simple, no mess. I don't have time to be doing hair and makeup every day. Girl, my job keeps me running."

"Nothing is more important than spending a little time on you." Gina sighed. "You know I've spent the last ten years watching you go to that bank, working from sun up to sundown. When do you get to enjoy life from all that hard work?"

"All right, we're ready," Beverly said from the door. "I see you two got the kitchen clean."

Gina reached out and took Lilwayne from her mother's shoulder. "Yeah, but I did most of the work."

"You're the one who messed it up in the first place," Chrystina said as they walked towards the door.

"Don't you two start again," Beverly said as she took Crystallite's hand.

"Bye, Aunt Chrys." Money tiptoed up and kissed her cheek.

"See you next time, Money." Chrystina smiled while standing at the door.

"Umm...Chrys, do you think you can help me with the water bill?"

Chrystina exhaled and looked at her mother then back to her sister and asked, "How much is it?"

"Just one hundred and seventy-five dollars."

"You have a water bill for a hundred and seventy-five dollars? When was the last time you paid it?"

"I don't know, months ago I guess."

Beverly sighed. "We'll split it."

"Aren't you supposed to go on your cruise in two weeks?" Chrystina asked. "You are going to need spending money. Send me the account number and I'll pay the bill tomorrow. For now just get out of my house so I can get some rest."

"You're a good sister, Chrystina." Beverly smiled.

"That's taking it a bit far," Gina groaned.

"What you say?" Chrystina asked.

"Nothing, I didn't say nothing. I'll call tomorrow with the account number." Gina smiled.

"That's what I thought you said."

They all said their good byes and Chrystina closed the door. She walked into her bathroom and knew the soaking tub was out of the question unless she cleaned it first. She opted for a shower instead.

Shower done, she walked into the bedroom and sighed. She had to change the bed before she could get in it. "What a freaking day."

It was well after eleven when she finally crawled under her clean sheets. No television tonight, she was just too tired. Instead she reached over and hit the play button on the message from Myles.

'Hello, Chrystina. I want you to take a few days. Drink plenty of fluids, get between the sheets, and rest. I'll handle things at the office. You take care of you. See you on Monday. Not a day sooner.'

The message did what it has done for her every night since he sent the message two years ago, put a smile on her face. Now, when she closed her eyes she had more to add to it. The memory of the morning they made love. Oh, she was delusional. She understood for Myles it was just sex. She was the person who happened to be there in his time of need.

One minute she was on her knees holding him, comforting him, then the next minute she was kissing him and he was kissing her back. His tongue stroking hers, causing a heat so intense, no fan could have cooled it. Her body shivered with every stroke of his tongue. The deeper his tongue plunged, the more sensations flooded her body. Their breathing quickened, her muscles tensing, longing for him to touch the area that has gone so long, waiting to be awakened. His hands began to roam to her thighs, then they were caressing them causing sensations to surge through her body. Then his finger touched her wetness. A gasp escaped her throat. Lord she hadn't been wet in so long, she didn't even know how her body knew to generate the moisture. But it did, for Myles. Things were happening so fast. She remembered him calling her name, asking permission to continue or asking her to stop him; she didn't know which, but there was no way she could stop. She didn't remember if she answered him or not, for in the next moment her legs parted and a piece of heaven entered her, demanding her attention. The thickness filled her, the warmth caressed her and the power, oh the power each time he thrust into her, ignited a sensation that crawled through her, building more and more until it exploded. Leaving her heart pumping vigorously, her mind spinning and her body humming.

"Hmm," she sighed as she slipped deeper under the covers to let the memory caress her to sleep.

## Chapter Twelve

T he light tapping on the door startled Myles as he
sat straight up in bed and looked around. It took a
moment for him to recognize the guest suite in his
parents' home. Then he remembered. It wasn't a
dream. He was voted in as CEO and President of
Dunning Bank & Trust. He fell back against the
pillows and threw his arms over his eyes.

"Myles, are you in there?"

The soft sound of AnnieMarie's voice caught his
attention. He replied as he sat up, "Yes, come in."

The door opened and the face of his beautiful baby
sister appeared.

"Myles!" She immediately covered her eyes and
turned her back as she yelled.

Looking down, he threw the cover over the lower
part of his naked body. He adjusted the pillows
behind him then sat up in bed.

"Okay," he said. As he wiped his face, he saw
AnnieMarie peeking through her fingers. "Oh cut the
act. It's not like you have never seen a naked man
before."

AnnieMarie smiled, then jumped on the bed with her brother. "That's why I love you, Myles. You are the only one around here that doesn't treat me like a baby."

He tapped the bridge of her nose with his finger. "That's because you are not a baby. You are a grown woman and it's time for you to come back to work."

"Myles," she exhaled and looked away.

"Do you want me to fire him?"

"Cainan?" Her head snapped around to look at him. "No, he didn't do anything wrong." She looked away from him.

He reached out using his finger to turn her face back to him.

"Listen to me, AnnieMarie. I know you are intelligent enough to know you did not cause Dad's heart attack. The only reason you are avoiding work is because of Scott. At this time I have no reason to let him go. However, if it will make you more comfortable I will move him to another location."

AnnieMarie stood and walked over to the window that overlooked the gardens. She looked so much like his mother at times it was hard to tell them apart from the back. The only difference was AnnieMarie wore her hair in a ponytail these days while his mother wore hers down.

"Myles," she began, without turning back to him, "do you know why Daddy wanted me to stop seeing Cainan?" She turned to him with a hopeful look. "I mean, was something happening at the bank?"

"Nothing we've been able to find."

She seemed to physically relax. "I never thought so. Cainan is so anal when it comes to some things."

The last thing Myles wanted to do was question AnnieMarie. But there were certain things he needed to know.

"Turn your head."

When she did he threw the covers back and put on his robe. Thank goodness for Chrystina. She had all his favorite things sent to his mother's house.

"Do all men sleep in the nude?"

"I don't know. I never slept with one," Myles replied as he took her hand.

She laughed at him. "Thank goodness. Think of all the women's hearts you would break."

They sat at the table next to the window. "Tell me about Cainan."

AnnieMarie shrugged her shoulder. "What do you want to know?"

He squeezed her hand to get her to look up at him. "Anything you want to tell me...no pressure. I just want to know more about the man you seem to have a thing for." He waited as he saw the tears come to surface.

AnnieMarie looked up just as a tear ran down her face. "I love him, Myles." She pulled her hand away and sat back in the chair. "I know the family hates me for it." She wiped the tears from her face. "Mother can't even look at me she is so hurt by what I did. Grace and Gary keep their distance. And Mike, well, he's just straight up with his disgust."

"Look at me, AnnieMarie." When she did not look, he raised his voice. "Look at me now!"

She turned to him with tears streaming down her face. "No one...no one in this family hates you or holds you responsible for Dad's death. I want that out of your mind."

"Feelings don't just disappear at your command, Myles."

"They don't? I thought they did. Hell, it worked when Dad gave the command." He pointed his finger imitating his dad. "Myles, stop lusting after that girl."

AnnieMarie laughed. "You sound just like him."

"Good." He smiled. "Is the command working?"

"No, but it was a good try," she said holding a solemn smile.

"AnnieMarie, Mother is reflecting what she sees in your eyes every time she looks at you. She sees the hurt and guilt you are carrying around about Dad. Mother is so worried about you she cannot function. Think about it. She has lost her husband and her fear is she may be losing her daughter as well. As far as Grace is concerned, she doesn't come near for fear you are going to break down. Seeing her free-spirited baby sister so distraught up close upsets her. And Gary, well, he's so into women he doesn't have time for anything else. Not your sadness or dealing with his own loss. As for Michael frowning every time he sees you, well that's because he wants to beat the pulp out of Scott for taking the spark from your eyes."

"Cainan did not take that away. He is more miserable than I am. He doesn't understand why I'm refusing to see or talk to him. You tell Mike to stay away from Cainan," she cried out as she jumped from the chair. "I would never forgive him if he puts one finger on Cainan. Do you understand me?"

Happy to see the flare of anger in her, Myles stood and held up his hand. "Hold on there, Hidden Dragon gone wild. Michael is not going to harm Cainan. But you did leave the man with no backing."

AnnieMarie stood there with her hands on her hips just staring up at Myles with a confused look on her face. Then she broke out into laughter.

"Myles," she continued to laugh. "Who in the hell is hidden dragon?"

With a low rumble in his chest, Myles replied, "I have no idea. It's something I've heard Chrystina say."

"By all means take that woman to the big office with you. She keeps you young. You are always so serious. It's kind of nice to see the silly side of you."

"It would be nice to see the business side of you back in the office," Myles countered. "Do you have any idea how much flack I'm getting from Mitch because you are not there? Not to mention we have a PR nightmare going on with the vote. Somewhere along the line we have moved to the number three ranking in the world banking industry. The vote and the ranking have phones ringing off the hook. It's my understanding a number of reporters are asking for comments and interviews. Bottom line, I need you in the office."

"I realize my absence is putting you in a bad position. I apologize for that. But know my people are keeping me abreast of the interview requests and the calls. Give me the day to build up my courage to face Cainan and I will report to work tomorrow."

Myles gave her a bear hug. "I'll take it. Chrystina misses you. I think the folks in the office are giving her a hard time about moving to the vault area. It is going to get worse when I have offices moved around. An ally in the office would be nice for her."

AnnieMarie exhaled, then pulled out of his embrace. "Nancy is the culprit, isn't she? Now that you've been named CEO she thinks you will select her."

"Nancy has no reason to think that." Myles shook his head. "Nancy is the worst assistant in the office. Why would I take her anywhere?"

"One, because she looks good and people like Nancy think that's all it takes. Second, she has no idea what you think of her."

"What is this obsession with looks? Chrystina looks good to me. As for Nancy, I've expressed my dissatisfaction with her work on a number of occasions."

"To Chrystina you have, but not directly to Nancy. Chrystina always softens your comments to others. That's why no one in the office knows you are a tyrant."

"I'm not a tyrant."

"At work you are. That's another reason you have to keep Chrystina with you. She is the barrier between you and us. She saves us from you. As for the way Chrystina looks, her weight is going to cause her problems with some of the more superficial people in that office. They are smart, but arrogant about working in the vault. In fact, now that you are the president you should look into renaming that area. Maybe the elitist attitude will dissipate."

"So you think they will shun her?"

"Who?"

"Chrystina."

AnnieMarie glared at her brother. "Did you hear what I suggested about the vault?"

"Yes, changing the name. I think Executive Office would be fine. Now, with Chrystina, how do I prevent them from shunning her?"

A small smile creased AnnieMarie's face. She tilted her head. "It's nice that you want to, however, this is one time you will have to let Chrystina fend for herself. Believe me, she will handle it."

"You're sure?"

"Yes, I am."

"I don't know, AnnieMarie, with everyone gone, I feel vulnerable and I'm sure Chrystina does as well. It would be nice to have someone around that we knew was on our side." He took a step towards the window, then stood and looked out. Contemplating his next words, he spoke as if to himself. "Dad left me with the

responsibility of taking care of this family and
carrying the legacy of Dunning forward. It all falls on
my shoulders. I'm not sure I'm the man to handle
both."

"Of course you are." AnnieMarie touched her
brother's big shoulders. "You can handle it, Myles.
Don't you think Dad knew that? He's been grooming
you since I can remember. How many times did he
send us to you whenever we had an issue? Mother
knows it too. All she needs is a little backup when it
comes to Uncle Walker. As for the office, well, your
biggest headache there is Elaine. Keep an eye on her
and you will be fine."

"Elaine? Elaine Jacobson?"

"Yes, I know everyone thinks Mitch is the
competition, but he's not. Every time he tries
something he gets caught. His execution is off. Now,
Elaine - that chick is slick. They say any time a woman
scorned is in the midst, it's a danger zone."

"What are you talking about? I've never been
involved with Elaine."

"I hope not. She is old enough to be your mother."
AnnieMarie laughed. "But I wasn't talking about you.
I was talking about Dad."

"What?" Myles could not hide his shocked
expression. "What are you talking about?"

"You really need to get out of your office more,"
she huffed. "The rumor had it that Elaine was crazy
about Dad back in the day. He never encouraged it, so
I was told, but they did work very closely together.
Mother even thought Elaine had broken through. But
once Daddy discovered her feelings about him, he had
her position changed and her office moved from the
front office next to his. Mitch was on the right and
Elaine was on his left. The three of them ran things at
Dunning. I don't know the entire story, but from what

my people told me, something went down years ago and Dad moved her out. The office became Mother's place whenever she came into the office." She frowned. "Chrystina never mentioned any of this to you?"

"No. This is the first I've heard of anything involving Dad and Elaine. How did Mother react?"

"From what I was told, there was a major pow-wow in Dad's office one day between Dad, Mother, and Elaine. Elaine emerged, packed a few things and disappeared for about a month. While she was gone, her office was moved to where she is now. Her position was changed, but she wasn't demoted, or removed from the board. However, she did not spend time alone with Dad anymore."

"Is Elaine married?"

"No, she never married as far as I know."

"How did Mother handle Elaine?"

"From what I'm told she handled it like she did everything else, cool and collected. She trusted Dad to handle whatever it was. It seemed he did. But I still don't trust Elaine Jacobson and you shouldn't either."

"How do you know about all of this and I don't?"

"First of all, I venture out of my office on occasion. Second, I'm the public relations manager. It is my job to know everything about everyone connected to Dunning. The last thing I ever want to happen on my watch is a scandal involving personnel."

"I'm planning on moving Mitch to that office you said was once Elaine's and Chrystina into his office."

AnnieMarie raised an eyebrow. "That is going to cause a stir. Have you told him yet?"

"No, I've instructed Mrs. Vazquez to hold off until things settle down. But Chrystina is going to be next to me. I don't trust Mitch to have access to my office."

Nodding, AnnieMarie agreed. "I think that's a good move. You do realize that is positioning Chrystina as your second in command."

"No." Myles shook his head. "I just need her there."

"So you are moving into Dad's office. Good. Dunning employees need to know they have a leader. The financial world needs to know as well." She took her brother's hand. "I know it's going to be difficult for you to occupy that space, just as it will be rough for Mother to visit. But with the right mindset I know you will take Dunning to the next level. So say it with me. I can do it."

Myles smiled. "I can do that. Just as I know you can come into the office, look people in the face and move past this moment in your life. As for Cainan Scott, I don't know how you are going to handle that situation. I can't give you my blessings until I know what Dad's concerns were. But you are an adult. I can't forbid you from seeing him. However, I hope you will honor my wishes until we know more."

AnnieMarie sighed. "If Mother was able to handle the situation with Elaine I should be able to handle Cainan."

"Office romances." Myles looked out as if thinking. "They are bound to happen because we spend so much time with each other."

AnnieMarie stared at him. "Are you referring to me or someone else?"

"No, just thinking overall," he explained.

## Chapter Thirteen

Elaine turned in her office chair looking out the window while she waited for the call she had just placed to be answered. It was noon in London. Jonathan should be available.

While she waited she watched Cainan Scott pull into the parking lot. He did not get out of the car immediately. He was sitting inside talking on his cell phone. The call seemed to irritate him.

She, like other members of the board, wondered how someone so young gained Hep's trust so fast. She shook her head correcting her thoughts. It wasn't just Hepburn's trust; the man admired Cainan Scott to the point where he put him on the board without the usual vetting done by the members. One day he showed up to work, the next day he was sitting as a full voting member of the board. In the Dunning atmosphere, that was unheard of.

"Hello." The masculine accented voice pulled her from her thoughts.

"Jonathan." She turned from the window. "I expected a call yesterday. What was the PI brass' take on the news of Myles Dunning's appointment?

"I see you are straight to the point today," Jonathan replied. "Mild curiosity at this point."

Elaine sat forward. "Any plans for counter actions?"

"Dunning isn't a concern for us at this time. I must say I question your motives. You are working for a progressive mobile company. Why are you taking a chance on losing what must be a trusted position by attempting a sabotage? What happens when this becomes public knowledge?"

"I don't plan on it being publicized. Do you?"

"You offered to bring a major contract to us in exchange for employment considerations. I would think Dunning would notice if you and BIT signed with us."

"We have plans to cover us."

"We? It's been my experience, when more than one party is involved in a scheme there tends to be individual agendas. I would implore you to examine the 'we' factor."

"I've covered all my bases. My only concern is where does PI stand? If I deliver BIT, signed and sealed, will I have a position with PI?"

"We are noncommittal at this time. However, we will continue to monitor your actions." The call was disconnected.

Elaine hung up the phone then turned back to the window. "I never put all my eggs into one basket, Jonathan...never."

#

Jonathan stood at the window in this office. He had made a decision. The offer from Elaine Jacobson to deliver BIT would guarantee Phase the number one ranking for years to come. If he was the one who brought the multi-billion dollar company on board his position with Phase would be etched in stone. All that at the cost of selling out Dunning. That price was too high. The entity known as Dunning was too important to not only the African American community, but to the world. Its value debunked the myth that the good guys always finish last. He could not in all good conscious interfere with its progress. Turning down Elaine's proposal would leave Dunning in a vulnerable position. He was certain she would shop the offer around. Another financial entity would take it. He had to take steps to prevent her from succeeding.

It was evident to him Elaine Jacobson was working with someone to disrupt Dunning's operations. If she contacted him regarding the BIT account she had certainly reached out to others. His first choice would be America's Bank. He knew the acquisition manager over there would be hesitant to get his hands dirty with the banking commission, the same as he was. That left who will benefit the most from acquiring BIT.

Jonathan touched the Bluetooth in his ear. "Sydney, would you step inside please?"

A very attractive slim brunette stepped inside with a tablet in her hand. "Whatever you decide to do, I'm going with you," she said, sitting in the chair in front of his desk.

Jonathan smiled as he took a seat at his desk. "What makes you think I'm going to do anything?"

"You're a good mate. There is no way you're going to allow a takeover of Dunning by us or anyone else."

"You know me too well."

"How do you wish to proceed?"

Jonathan sat forward. "Whoever is behind this is not out to just acquire BIT. My gut tells me they want

Dunning cut to bloody hell. It's not Phase or America's Bank. It will be one of the others who will take Dunning's place in the rankings. Let's look at the financials of the top 10."

Sydney was keying into her personal phone. "I'll pull those reports. How do you want to handle Mr. Dewberry?"

Sitting back, the regret was clear on his face. "I don't want to lie to him."

"You certainly can't tell him what you are planning to do. He will never understand your emotional tie to Dunning's history."

"The man has done so much for me. Hell, he orchestrated my career to this point."

Sydney sat forward. "The company has rewarded you for a job well done. You should be running this organization. If it hadn't been for the color of your skin you would be running it. I know we like to think here in the UK race is not an issue, but in the business world that would be naive of us. Jonathan, you have gone as far as you can with Phase. It is time for you to start your own investment firm, financial advisor firm or your own bank if that's what you want. Whatever direction your heart takes you, it's time for you to make that move." She sat back. "I commend your loyalty to Phase and all that you have accomplished here, but it is time."

Jonathan sighed. "For now, let's get the information on the top ten. Then find me a place stateside."

Sydney smiled as she stood. "Any particular sate?"

"Virginia."

"Virginia?" Sydney slowed her stride and frowned. "Is that a real place?"

"Yes," Jonathan laughed. "It is one of the original thirteen colonies."

"Oh. Then they are sure to have pubs there."

The words from Sydney lingered in the room long after she left. He had hit the ceiling at Phase. While he felt a certain loyalty with Phase he did not feel content, the kind that fills you with the satisfaction of getting up every morning and working towards something meaningful. Something you can look back on and see where you made a mark in the world. The drive and desire to do more is harder to fulfill once you've reached the top. The fear of losing it all is also greater. Then why in the bloody hell was he considering leaving Phase?

He pushed away from the desk. His spirit was telling him to make a move, but was it the right move? The telly rung. The smile on his face was instant.

"Hello, Mum. You sensed I needed to hear ya voice?"

"I did, son. How are you?"

"Torn," he sighed.

"You are restless. I can hear it in your voice. Why don't you take some time off? I would love to see your Aunt English and S'mone."

Jonathan froze. "In New York?"

"Yes, son. Are you okay?"

"Yes, yes of course. I think we should."

"Should what?"

"Visit Aunt English and S'mone. How about we leave next week? You can have a long visit while I work through some issues. I say, a month or longer should do the trick."

"You are going to take a month off from work?"

"Maybe longer. We'll see."

"Are you all right, son? It seems you've lost your knocker."

Jonathan laughed. "No, Mum, I'm fine. Really. I think this may be the very change that I need."

After disconnecting the call with his mum Jonathan dialed another number. It wasn't programed in his phone where he could just push a button. No, he knew the number by heart.

"Hello."

"Your voice is music to my ears, love." There was laughter on the other end of the line.

"I know that seductive accent anywhere. Jonathan Michael. Tell me who I owe for this call and I will pay them double the fee."

"Then write yourself a check, Love. You are on my mind. I wanted to give you a little time before I bell you up. How is life treating you?"

"Day by day."

"I was on a bit of business when I heard of your father's death. My heart was with you."

"I know. The flowers were lovely. Thank you."

"Anything for you, Love. How is your mum?"

"Amazing. I have no idea how she does it, but she keeps us together."

"I imagine her nights must be bloody hell."

"I try not to think about it."

"How are your nights?"

"You know me. I find a way through."

"I wish I could help with that. Listen, Love, I will be in New York in a fortnight. Will you grace me with a bit of your time?"

"When you ask in that voice, how can I resist?"

The smile in her voice warmed his heart. "You can't, Love, that's why I gave you a bell."

"I would love to see you," Grace replied. "Are you coming for business or pleasure?"

"Now that I've had a word with you, it's strictly pleasure, Love."

"Let me know when you land and I'll fly out."

"Bees' knees. I'll give you a bell from the hotel."

Grace's laughter rang out. "Jonathan, when you arrive, please don't say bees' knees. Just say awesome."

"I will try to remember, Love. See you soon."

"I'm counting the nights."

Jonathan smiled as he disconnected the call. His life was about to change in multiple ways. It was time to prepare for it. Sitting at his desk, he pushed a button on the telly.

"Sydney, get me everything about Dunning you can put your hands on and set up an appointment with Richard as soon as possible."

"Yes, sir. Shall I pack my bags?"

"Are you willing to leave London without a job or a clear future?"

"You need a PA to help you figure things out, mate. You can't do it without me."

"All I can promise is when I land on my feet so will you."

"Brilliant. Count me in."

#

Cainan was serious as he sat in his car listening. "Why can't we just tell her or her brother the truth? I'm out here with no backup now that Mr. Dunning is gone."

"People are out to kill you. What part of that do you not understand? Until you testify, no one and I mean no one, can know who you are or where you live. Your life depends on that."

"Has it occurred to you that they may have found me? Is it possible that Mr. Dunning's death wasn't a heart attack? It's occurred to me."

"We're checking into that. But there is no reason to believe there was foul play here." There was a hesitation on the other end of the line. "Look, I know you feel something for this young woman. I get it.

However, bringing someone else into the mix jeopardizes you and them. Keep that in mind. We'll talk again soon." The call disconnected.

Cainan laid his head back. He was twenty-nine years old and felt the weight of a sixty-year-old on his shoulder. For the last two years it's been one delay after another with this case. Nothing could have prepared him for the loneliness he felt away from his family. His parents thought he was dead. As cruel as it seemed, it was for the best. His fake death was the only thing keeping them alive. So for now he would have to deal with the deception.

"Deception," Cainan sighed as he stepped out of his car. Everything about him was a deception, from the lifts in his shoes, to the color contacts in his eyes. The braids and beard from his undercover days were all gone. Now he was sporting a clean-cut nerdy look with glasses. One would think it would cost him women, but it didn't. It seemed nerdy guys were in. But there was only one who touched the very core of him, AnnieMarie.

He smiled as he walked across the parking lot, just thinking of her. Even her name sounded magical to him. The way she walked, talked, and the laughter, it was all genuine and he loved her. Loved her more than life itself. But for some reason, since her father's death, she would not take his calls, or visits. No reply to text messages – nothing, and he had no idea why. He knew she was well. Saw her at the funeral, where he kept his distance trying not to create a scene. He asked her family members and Chrystina about her daily. The response was always the same. 'She's not taking her father's death well. Give her a little time.' It'd been well over a month now and still, nothing.

There was so much he needed to tell her. Like, how the three months preceding her father's death had brought him out of despair. How her outrageous positive outlook on life had made him see the good in people again. How after so much senseless death she breathed life into him again. How the last month of not seeing her, touching her, kissing her has been like dying all over again. Something had to give soon or his natural instinct to take charge of his own destiny was going to take over.

"Cainan, Cainan."

Turning he saw Preston Long running up to join him.

"Good morning, Preston," Cainan said as he held the employee elevator door open. "You're in early."

"Elaine wants to give me some pointers on the BIT account I'm working on."

"At seven in the morning?"

"Hey, I'll take advice anywhere I can get it. I need to land this account. These are strange times, my friend. I'm getting weird vibes from Mitch since the vote did not go in his favor. It's like he's up to something."

"Is there ever a time that he isn't? Cainan asked sarcastically.

"You have a point. Tables have turned. He has no chance of taking Dunning over at this point. Myles is not a sit back and take the punches kind of guy like Mr. Dunning. That brother is going to come out punching."

"He seems to be a pretty fair person. If Mr. Mitchell understands his place, he'll be okay."

"I don't see it. If I were Myles, I would move his ass out of the vault, if not the building."

The elevator opened to the first floor where they had to get out at the lobby then switch to the main elevators.

"Aren't you one of Mr. Mitchell's biggest supporters? You did nominate him for president."

"Office politics. He offered me a promotion."

They boarded the next elevator. "You knew he would make negative changes to Dunning if he had been voted in. Why would you want that?"

Preston waived Cainan off. "There was no way the family was going to let that happen."

"The vote came down to me. How do you know I wasn't offered a promotion by Mr. Mitchell?"

"You're sleeping with a Dunning. I knew where your vote was going."

Cainan turned on the man. "I'm not sleeping with a Dunning. I'm in love with AnnieMarie. There is a difference. Watch how you talk about her." He pushed the cafeteria button. "I'll get off here," he said as the door opened.

Preston reached out and stopped the door from closing. "My apology, man. I didn't mean anything by it."

Cainan exhaled. "No problem. Look, watch your back with Elaine. She may be picking you for info rather than sharing."

"Why would she do that? She is already an executive account manager."

"BIT is a big account. It can make or break a career. Just watch your back." Cainan turned and walked into the cafe. "Large coffee, black, please," he said to the cashier, then took a seat at a table next to the window. What now, he wondered. Mr. Dunning was his protector. The only person at Dunning who knew his background. There was going to be a power struggle within the company. He had no doubt Myles will come out the victor. His concern was simple. Once the dust settles how much of his story will be revealed in the process? Duck and cover, his father would say. Duck and cover.

## Chapter Fourteen

Exercise was never on Chrystina's to-do list. However, after the many comments about her job and the relationship to her weight, she decided to take Myles' advice. A little walk a day couldn't hurt. If he was still in the gym when she arrived, she might...might, join him for a workout...Might.

Standing before the scale, she took a deep breath, closed her eyes and stepped on. When both feet were planted on the device that took some kind of electronic pleasure every time she used it, she opened her eyes. Looking to the sky she said a short prayer.

"You are a compassionate God. Be kind this morning. Know that this is one of your children asking for your help and guidance."

The device beeped before she finished her prayer. She looked down. The damn thing read, 'step off'. She complied, thinking at least it did not play the music indicating she was over the desired weight she programed in. She took a breath, finished her prayer then put one foot on, closed her eyes, inhaled, then put the other foot on the device.

"Arrrgh!" She looked down the minute the tune began playing New Attitude by Patti Labelle. She stepped off and began shouting, "I asked you to be kind. That wasn't kind. That was downright mean."

"The scale is designed to tell you the truth, whether you want to hear it or not."

Chrystina turned to see her mother standing in the doorway. "What are you doing here?"

"I wanted to apologize for last night and to take your comforter to the cleaners. You didn't answer the door so I let myself in. I guess you were too busy praying the scale would lie to you," Beverly teased then walked back into the adjoining bedroom. Beverly fell into the overstuffed chair near the fireplace laughing as Chrystina sat on the bed.

"Very funny, Mother." Chrystina smirked. "Why can't I be slim like you and Gina?"

"That's all on you, little girl. When you left for college, you and Gina were the same size. Somewhere along the line, you chose not to be active."

"Mom, I was studying."

"And working your mouth along the way it seems." Beverly sat up. "I'm sorry, Chrystina. Gina is a work in progress and has a lot of nerve to talk, but some of what she said to you is right. You really should spend a little more time on yourself and stop spending so much time at the bank."

"It's my job, Mom. I have bills to pay and I don't want to have children to depend on getting a check every month. I just want something a little better out of life. And I don't mind working for it."

"I can understand that. But don't you think there is a balance that can be reached? You work hard during the day, but at night or on the weekends, take a little time for yourself." She reached out and patted her daughter's knee. "So, tell me, what has you on the scale this time?"

Chrystina sighed, then rolled her eyes upward. "Whew, crazy day at the bank yesterday. Myles was voted in as CEO and President."

"Good for him. That's the natural progression of things," Beverly stated. "What does that have to do with you and the scale?"

Chrystina fell back on the bed with her hair loose and legs kicking. "Everyone at the office thinks Myles will take someone else as his assistant because of my weight."

"What does your weight have to do with the job?"

Chrystina sat up. "Mom, have you ever been to the presidential offices?"

"No."

"Well, everyone in the suite of offices is referred to as 'the beautiful people.'" Chrystina moved to her closet as she spoke. "No one believes I can fit in down the hall with the beautiful people. So the majority think Myles will replace me."

Beverly jumped to her feet. "Did he say that?"

Chrystina walked out of the closet with a Jones of New York black pants set and black heels. "No."

"So what did he say?" Beverly asked ready to attack.

"Down, Momma Duke," Chrystina laughed as she walked by her mother. "Myles said I go where he goes."

"Oh." Beverly sat back into the chair. "I always knew Myles was a smart man." Beverly grinned at the smirk on her daughter's face. "So back to my original question. Why are you laying God and the scale out?"

Chrystina began dressing. "Myles said if I felt uncomfortable with the way I look I should do something about it. But I'm going down the hall with him, comfortable or not."

"The visit to the scale is your decision. Myles didn't indicate you had to do this?"

"No, he didn't. But now I wish I hadn't stepped on that evil device. It only made me feel worse than I did before."

Beverly stood and pointed to the bed. "Sit down."

"I have to get ready for work, Mom."

"Sit your ass on that bed and listen to your mother."

Knowing the tone, Chrystina did as her mother asked.

Beverly checked her watch, then looked at her daughter. "I had to see how much time I had before I'm late for work so I know how deep I can go right now." She exhaled. "You are a beautiful girl just the way you are. If people don't take the time to get to know you because of your physical appearance, they are not worth the air you breathe." She sighed. "However, you do need to think about your health. Dropping a good thirty or forty pounds would make a world of difference in your appearance and in your health." She saw the frown on Chrystina's face and laughed. "Don't think about the end goal. Think about ten pounds. Let the rest fall where it may."

"Ten?"

"Yes...ten." Beverly put her hands on her hips. "I promise you, after that first ten is off you will want to do the rest. Now, if you are serious I will help. For the next three months ride to work with me. You can walk from my office to your job in no time. Start drinking at least eight glasses of water a day, more if you can. I will cook all your meals including lunch and snacks. Let's see how that impacts your look."

Chrystina gave her a suspicious look. "I work late sometimes. How am I supposed to get home if I don't drive?"

Beverly frowned as she thought. "Well, for the next three months, if you have to work late, call me. I'll come and pick you up."

Chrystina gave her a doubtful look. "Mommy, you don't like to cook."

"You're right, I don't; but I dislike my daughter doubting herself more. So if you are willing to take the first steps, I'm willing to help."

"Myles said he would help too."

"He did? How is he going to help you lose weight? When will he have the time?"

"He works out in the gym every morning before starting work. He said I could join him and he will exercise with me each morning."

"Hmm." Beverly nodded. "Well, that's nice of him. But neither him nor I can help unless you are ready to make this commitment to yourself."

"Three months, huh?"

"Three months, or hell, you might reach your goal before then and may not need me or Myles to keep you motivated. So what's it going to be, girl?"

"I'll think on it."

"While you are thinking I'm going full throttle."

"Whatever it's going to be will have to wait. I have to get to work," Chrystina stated as she stood and continued dressing.

Beverly grabbed Chrystina's black heels and walked back into the huge closet.

"Mom, what are you doing with my shoes?" After a minute or two of no response, Chrystina called out to her again. "Mom, what are you doing?"

After a few more minutes of mother butt-thumps against the wall, Beverly reappeared in the closet doorway. "Girl, you don't have any sneakers?"

"No," Chrystina replied.

Beverly walked over to the chair she previously occupied with a pair of flat shoes she'd found in the closet. She sat down and began to remove her sneakers that she wore religiously in her job as a librarian.

"Mom, what are you doing?"

"Giving you the shoes off my feet. What does it look like?"

"I can see that. But why?"

Beverly stood and handed the sneakers to Chrystina. "There is no time like the present to begin your new lifestyle." She raised an eyebrow when Chrystina hesitated to take the sneakers.

"Mom," she laughed. "I can't wear these. I don't have any socks."

Beverly sat back down in the chair with a huff. She pulled off her socks and threw them at Chrystina.

"You are not serious." She stared at the mother laughing.

"Serious as a heart attack." Beverly slipped on the flats, then twisted her feet one way, then the other and smiled. "Put those on over your stocking feet, then put on those sneakers." She went back into the closet, returning with a cloth bag. She placed the black heels inside the bag as she walked by her daughter. "When I'm finished with you, your sister is not going to be able to stand you."

"She can't stand me now."

"Hmm hmm, I know. What do you think will happen when you are the same size she is?"

Chrystina grinned. "I can't get that small, can I?"

Beverly nodded. "You can get to whatever size is comfortable for you. While you put on those sneakers, I'll check out the kitchen to see what I can throw together for your lunch. Girl, this is going to be fun." Beverly laughed as she walked out of the door.

"Gina is going to be mad at you."

"You let me worry about Gina. I got some plans for her too."

Chrystina sat on the side of the bed staring at the sneakers.

"Put them on!"

"Okay...okay," Chrystina huffed then began laughing. "If Mom and Myles are willing to help, the least I can do is make them proud."

Chrystina put the sneakers on then stood. If felt weird to have her feet so close to the floor, but hey, it's time to look at the bigger, or in this case, smaller picture. She looked in the mirror. "Forty pounds, hmm. Why not make it an even fifty. Fifty pounds...I guess that's possible. Wrong sentiment," she said as she grabbed her purse and bag. "Hell, I can do that with my eyes closed." She snapped her fingers as she walked towards the kitchen. "Look out world, here comes the new Chrystina. Get Vera Wang on the line, Mommy, I'm going to need a new wardrobe."

## Chapter Fifteen

At her mother's insistence, Chrystina found herself walking from Ninth and Broad Streets, where Beverly worked at the State Library of Virginia, to Third and Marshall where Dunning's headquarters was located. A total of six blocks, five up and one across. What the heck, she thought. It was a beautiful morning, the sun was shining. The streets were moderately busy with people on their way to work, just like her. This would be a breeze, no effort.

With purse, bag with shoes and lunch in tow, Chrystina was cursing by the time she reached Fifth and Broad.

"City blocks, my butt," she huffed at her mother's description for the walk. "Five city blocks, she said. Somebody needs to teach that woman how to count," she fussed as she stopped to pull the bag up on her shoulder. "Fifteen minutes and you will be sitting at your desk," Chrystina mocked her mother's words as she peeked at her watch. "Seven fifteen and I am not at my desk yet." She huffed, but felt like yelling. She didn't think the people walking down the street would appreciate a full-grown woman yelling in the middle of the sidewalk. So she continued.

Two more blocks and she was now at Third and Broad Street. "Okay," she huffed and decided to walk down Third to Marshall, then take that straight into the employees' entrance. As she turned the corner she smiled. The building was in sight. "Two more blocks." Seeing the destination in sight Chrystina adjusted her items and continued to conquer this first step into her new lifestyle.

Okay, not so bad. She will use the remainder of the walk to set up her day. Complete the documents from Mrs. Vazquez to change over names on the corporate documents. Start the new organizational chart. Organize the move of Myles' office to the vault area. Send a request to human resources for a new risk management director and assistant.

It was the last thought that was interrupted by the time she reached Second and Marshall. A heavenly scent invaded her nostrils as she waited for traffic to stop so she could cross the street. Looking around, she spotted a bistro directly across from where she stood. She could smell the fresh pastries and coffee.

"Now, that is downright mean. Why would you do this to me on the first day, Lord? The first day. You are testing my will on the very first day."

"Excuse me?" The woman standing next to her on the corner looked at her with a raised eyebrow.

"Oh, nothing. I was just thanking the Lord for such a beautiful morning," she replied then crossed the street. When she reached the door of the bistro, she stood there and inhaled. "Ahhh, muffins, blueberry. Aw man." The urge to go inside was overpowering her will.

"Don't do it, Chrystina. Just say no...just say no. Keep walking."

The door opened. A tall dark-skinned brother dressed in a suit walked out. He held the door for her.

Chrystina started to walk in, then froze.

"Are you going in?" the man asked.

"No...no, thank you."

Chrystina quickly stepped to the side. The man closed the door then walked away. Chrystina looked back in through the window just to be sure she was not imagining things. No, she was right. William Mitchell, Paulette Brittin, Nancy Charles and was that...? She peeked in again. "Yes, that is Walker Dunning." They were seated towards the back of the bistro with documents on the table in front of them. "Why would those four be together?"

The hairs on her neck stood up. Something wasn't right. She hurried by the window to make sure she wasn't seen. Not certain why it was important, but she knew it was.

"Okay, Lord, I forgive you. You brought me this way for a reason. At first I thought you were messing with me, but no. You wanted me to see those four together...Why?" She looked up to the sky as she quickly walked the last block to the office. "No answer? Okay, you want me to figure this out myself."

She took the parking lot elevator to the lobby, then switched to the employee elevator, speaking to people along the way but not stopping for conversation. She needed to get to her desk. Chrystina dropped her bag and purse to the floor as she turned on her computer. The first thing she did was check the online calendars for Mitch, Paulette, and Nancy. The only one scheduled for a meeting was Mitch at 9 AM with Herschel automotive representatives.

"Hmm." She did not recall the meeting with Hershel on Myles' calendar. She double-checked it to find Myles' calendar was clear until 11am. "Why is Mitch meeting with the Herschel representatives without Myles?"

Looking at the attachment to the appointment she noticed the memo was password protected. Not wanting to get up Chrystina right-clicked to check the properties on the memo. It listed the author of the memo as Nancy Charles.

"Oh hell no." Now Chrystina knew something was amiss for sure.

"Let's see," Chrystina thought, "the current boyfriend is...Craig, that's right Craig."

She knew Nancy's passwords were always the current boyfriend and a number. She tried Craig one, Craig two and hit pay dirt when she put in Craig three.

"Made it to three weeks, good for you, Nancy. Now what in the hell are you up to?" She printed the document and closed the file.

The memo was addressed to William Mitchell. It was a list of talking points to discredit Myles with the Hershel representatives. By the time she finished the memo she was beyond pissed. But looking at the clock she knew she had to put her level of pisstivity in the pocket for now.

"Okay, Chrystina, you can do this. Herschel reps will be offended if Myles does not greet them at the 9 a.m. meeting." She checked her watch. "There is time." She shot Myles a quick text message. 'Talking points bullets.' She turned on her computer and did a document matching bullet point for bullet point. She then added some information she knew would impress the Hershel representatives. She sent that document via email to Myles.

"Now," she exhaled. "To take over at the meeting. We need a quick presentation." She now had a game plan on how to handle the meeting without damaging the reputation of the bank. Afterwards she would think of a way to handle little Miss Nancy. With the solution in hand she picked up her cell phone and called Myles.

#

In the time frame it would take Myles to get into the office Chrystina had to secure the conference room on the fifth floor to keep anyone on the higher levels from knowing what she was up to. Then she called her favorite diner Stokes, which was right around the corner. She asked him for all the croissants, fruit, and coffee they had prepared for breakfast. Next she pulled three of her most trusted coworkers together to set up a conference room. Then she bribed the receptionist to send her a message the moment Mitch walked in the door. Now, she had one last piece to get done and they would be ready.

Chrystina knocked on the office door and thought it was times like this she really missed AnnieMarie. The woman really had a way with people, especially this man.

"Excuse me, Cainan. I know you are busy, but there is a situation Mr. Dunning needs your assistance with. Do you think you can spare us a few minutes, or hours?"

Cainan glanced up with pleading eyes. Chrystina smiled. "When you give a definite time frame range from a few minutes to a couple of hours, how can I say no?" Cainan laughed as he sat his coffee cup down. "How can I help you?"

"I need you to come with me to the fifth floor conference room. Bring your laptop and anything you will need to put together a presentation." She spoke as she walked. Looking back over her shoulder she saw Cainan was still seated. "I need you to move now."

"Oh sorry." Cainan stood as he gathered his things. "I was waiting for more direction on what you needed in the presentation."

"We don't have time for a sit down chat on what's about to happen. We'll have to wing it as we go."

"I'm winging it with you."

"You are so nerdy, but you are cute," Chrystina laughed. "Grab your suit jacket. You need to be suited up for this."

Cainan grabbed his jacket from the back of the chair. "Thank you, I think. You said this is for Mr. Dunning, why aren't we using his conference room?"

"We have traitors amongst us."

"Already?"

"Some of them were already in place. They have chosen this moment to try us." Chrystina tilted her head and shrugged her shoulders as the elevator doors opened. "What they don't know is I don't play games."

"Is Mr. Mitchell involved in this?"

"I'm afraid so." Chrystina smirked as she pushed the button to the fifth floor. "Why do you ask?"

"Preston mentioned something about him earlier this morning. He thought the man was up to something, he just didn't know what."

"Well, for his sake, I pray Preston is not involved in this matter. Mr. Dunning is a nice guy, but when you bring customers into some mess he's not going to take any prisoners. Heads will roll."

"Is this about Hershel Automotive?"

"Yes." Chrystina glanced at him as the elevator doors opened. "How did you know?"

"One of Mr. Mitchell's assistants, Paulette asked me to put together some numbers for Hershel yesterday."

"Did you give it to her?"

He nodded. "Before close of business yesterday."

Chrystina stopped walking. "Tell me you still have it on your computer."

"The entire presentation." Cainan smiled. "How you like me now?"

"Like you? I love you in this moment." Chrystina beamed

Ten minutes later Chrystina and Cainan set up the projector and connected the sound system. He was sitting at the table running through the presentation when Chrystina felt her cell phone buzz. She checked the message; it was the receptionist advising her Mitch had just walked into the building. He had entered the executive elevator.

"Of course. He would not be caught dead riding with the employees."

"Did you say something?" Cainan asked as he looked up from the computer monitor he was working on.

"No, sorry." Chrystina smiled. "Things are falling into place. I'll be able to breathe a sigh of relief in about two shakes of a tail feather."

Cainan looked at her. "If I'm nerdy, you are corny."

She nodded and stepped away. "That I am." She laughed then sent a text message to Cory in the maintenance department. 'Please shut down the Executive Elevator as previously discussed.' A minute later she received a text back with a single word, 'Done'.

She smiled, then looked at Cainan. "Are we ready?"

"We will be in two minutes," he replied as he continued to work.

"I don't have to tell you how important this presentation is to Mr. Dunning."

"I have a feeling there is more to this than you are saying." Cainan stopped keying and looked up at her. "If this is for Mr. Dunning, I don't need to know why."

Chrystina smiled as she walked out of the room. "That's why I'm calling AnnieMarie to tell her if she does not come back to work soon, I'm taking you." She turned to walk out the door, talking over her shoulder. "I will send you a text in ten minutes to let you know where to meet Mr. Dunning."

"Hey, since I know this stuff do you want me to present? That will save Mr. Dunning some time."

"Bless you. I am certain Mr. Dunning will not have an opportunity to review those numbers ahead of time. He will welcome your input."

"You got it. One more thing," he said as she walked away.

"Cainan, I really have to go."

"I understand and in the scheme of things happening today, this is relatively small. But, do you know you have on sneakers and not heels?"

Chrystina looked down at her feet. "Damn it." She ran out the door closing it behind her.

"Everything set, ladies?" she asked Holly Helberg, a sweet brunette from accounting and Serena Lamb, a dark hair feisty woman from human resources, as she met them in the hallway.

"Ready." They both stood with presentation packages in their hands.

"Good. Holly, run to my office. There is a bag on the floor. Grab my shoes and meet me by the elevator."

"Will do." Holly ran off. "Remember, don't talk to anyone."

"Got it."

Chrystina turned to Serena and sighed. "We've done all we can do. Now let's show them how Dunning represents."

# Chapter Sixteen

Daisy was sitting in the kitchen having breakfast when Myles and AnnieMarie walked in. The surprised look on her face told all.

"Annie, baby." She held her arms out and embraced the young woman with all the love a second mother could give. "It's so good to see you out of that bedroom." She took her by the hand. "Now come right over here and sit down. You too, Myles." She smiled brightly. "It is nice to have both of you at the breakfast table again. How about some nice big waffles with fresh strawberries and whipped cream?"

"I'll take two, Daisy, but AnnieMarie needs five," Myles joked. "Look how skinny she is."

"Stop teasing your sister. She looks wonderful, with the exception of the dark circles under her eyes." Daisy walked over to the double wood-grain refrigerator and pulled out the waffle mix. "Your father would have a fit if he could see those circles. I think you need to take a walk down to the park and have a nice heart-to-heart with your daddy."

"I think that's a wonderful idea," Winnie said as she walked into the kitchen. She never stopped, but went right to her daughter, pulled her out of the chair she had taken and hugged her with the love only a mother could give. She pulled out of the embrace and checked her daughter over as if it had been years since she had seen her. Palming AnnieMarie's face in her hands, she looked directly into her daughter's eyes.

"I love you so much, my baby. When you hurt, I hurt. It's just that simple." She hugged her again.

Daisy smiled as Myles winked at AnnieMarie.

"Stop treating her like she is a baby. AnnieMarie is a grown woman and both of you need to realize that." Daisy placed a cup of coffee in front of Myles, then popped him on the back of his head with the palm of her hand. "Ouch."

"Mind your mouth," she said, then walked back to the stovetop where the waffles were cooking.

Winnie looked down at her daughter's face again. "You will always be my baby. I don't care how big or beautiful you get." She took the chair next to AnnieMarie. "Now tell me, are you going into the office today or can you spare your mother another day here at home?"

"She needs to come into the office," Myles said as he took a sip of his coffee. "With Michael, Gary and Grace gone, I can really use the support."

"Your Uncle Walker is coming by today. You know AnnieMarie is the only one he tends to watch his mouth around."

"He's coming today, why?" Myles asked as he glanced at Daisy, who shrugged.

Winnie exhaled. "I couldn't keep putting him off. I made an appointment with him at ten this morning. Lord knows I don't want to deal with him today, but I have no choice."

"Hmm, I'm sure I have back-to-back meetings today." His phone buzzed. Daisy stopped cooking and glared at him. Myles pulled out his phone. He looked up to see Daisy frowning. "It's an urgent message from Chrystina."

"Umm, Myles. Telephones are prohibited at the kitchen table." AnnieMarie frowned. "You know that."

Myles stood, remembering his father's command. "I'll take this outside."

Daisy nodded her approval.

"He looks so much like your father when he was that age. Lord I miss him." Winnie turned to her daughter. "I miss you too, AnnieMarie. I miss your laughter and the instant joy you bring into this house." She took her daughter's hand. "Would you go to the park with me today to visit with your father? I know he would love to feel your presence and I could surely use the support."

Daisy continued cooking as she watched and listened. She held her breath for AnnieMarie's response.

"Of course, I'll join you. But I have no idea how much support I will be."

Winnie beamed. "Just having you near is all the support I need."

Daisy released a sigh of relief, placed waffles on a plate and put them in front of AnnieMarie.

"Daisy, I can't eat all of this," she cried out.

"Of course you can. Myles is right. You are too skinny. Eat up." Daisy walked away smiling. "It's good to have you at the table, Annie."

She removed four of the waffles from her plate and put them on the plate at Myles' seat. "Let Myles be the one to get fat."

Daisy laughed, then turned back towards Winnieford who was watching Myles talking on the phone.

"Something is happening. We need to make sure he goes into the office. He's not going to leave if he thinks we need him here." She glanced at Daisy and AnnieMarie. "Follow my lead."

AnnieMarie nodded.

Winnie reached over, took Myles' plate and began eating. She had just put the first fork filled with waffles and strawberries in her mouth when Myles retuned to the table. He looked suspiciously at his mother, then glanced at Daisy. Daisy did all she could to keep a straight face.

"Oh, sorry. Can I have this?" Winnie innocently asked, with her mouth full.

"Looks like you already have them to me." Everyone laughed. "A brother can't get a break around here."

Daisy continued to watch the family she loved. It was good to see a partial smile on AnnieMarie's face, to hear laughter in the house again, to see the frown soften on Myles' face. Now, if he could just get things under control at the office, Mr. Hep could rest in peace.

"Enjoy them. It seems my enemies are not wasting any time to try to take me down." Myles finished his coffee. "Chrystina needs me in the office as soon as possible. Are you two going to be okay with Walker?"

Winnie waved Myles off. "Of course. You go to the office and establish your position. AnnieMarie and I will handle Walker."

"Don't choke trying." Myles smiled as he bent down and kissed his sister. "I need you back in the office as soon as possible. But not before you are ready."

"Thank you for understanding, Myles."

He nodded. "And Mother." Winnie looked up with whipped cream on her lips. Myles laughed, then gave her a napkin. "Try not to give the farm away to Walker. Let Grace handle any legalities of the will."

Winnie, whose eyes were shining with laughter, took the napkin and wiped her mouth. "I will try. Now go save Dunning from Mitchell."

"How do you know it's Mitchell?"

"He's been trying that petty crap behind Hep's back for years. You being in charge is not going to change that. Just make sure your customers get to know you. You will be okay."

"Thanks, Mother." He kissed her cheek then left out the door.

AnnieMarie turned to her mother. "You can stop now. He's gone."

Winnie dropped the fork. "Thank goodness. I thought I would pop if I had to eat another bite."

Daisy dropped the dishcloth and fell out laughing at the sight of Winnie with pancakes dropping out of her mouth. AnnieMarie joined in.

"You know you don't have to put a front on for Myles."

"Oh, baby, I do. Myles worries about all of us these days. In his mind we are now his responsibility. He is just as overprotective as his father. If he thought for one minute I was concerned about Walker's visit or you were still locked up in that room, he would delay going into the office. We both know that is where he needs to be." She reached over and took AnnieMarie's hand. "Thank you for your help this morning. I don't know what you said to him, but he seems at ease leaving us today. I can't imagine who called and made him feel he had to be here in the first place," she said, as she looked directly at Daisy.

"Oh, I'm sure it was an angel looking out for us." AnnieMarie winked at Daisy.

Daisy looked from one to the other. "Damn right. It's my job."

## Chapter Seventeen

Walking into the building was different today for Myles. This was now his building. Every floor, every employee, every account, every problem, it was all on his shoulders. It was difficult at this point to determine if that was a curse or a blessing.

"Good morning, Mr. Dunning." A young lady smiled brightly.

"Congratulations, Mr. Dunning."

"Good morning and thank you," Myles replied, as he continued on to the elevator.

"Congratulations, Mr. Dunning," a young man said, as he entered the elevator.

"Thank you." Myles nodded his head just as a hand slid between the closing doors.

"Good morning, Myles," came the cherry sweet voice of Savannah Whitfield. This was the last thing he needed this morning.

"Savannah. This is a surprise."

"I thought it would be." She stood right in front of him. "Normally I would say congratulations, but under the circumstances I will say the best man was voted into the position. It will be difficult, but I believe you will prove every praise your father ever gave you to be true."

The statement caught him off guard. It was the most thoughtful thing anyone could say to him at this time. He wondered if she sat up all night thinking of the perfect thing to say to him this morning. "Thank you, Savannah."

"Your father believed you were ready for this a few years ago and I agreed with him. You are going to do great things here, Myles."

The elevator stopped on the third floor. "It was good seeing you. Have a wonderful day." Savannah stepped off the elevator with a parting smile.

The fact that she did not try to get him to spend time with her was a surprise. Myles was sure when she first stepped into the elevator, she was there to see him. As it turned out he was wrong. She got off on the floor her friend worked on. Shrugging his shoulder, he dismissed thoughts of Savannah as another employee started to enter.

Cainan stepped from behind Myles and hit the close button. "We need the elevator."

The employee stepped back as Myles turned to stare at Cainan. He had no idea anyone else was in the elevator.

"A simple congratulation just doesn't work for someone trying to make an impression." Cainan nodded. "I did not have a chance to say it yesterday during the meeting." He extended his hand. "Congratulations."

Myles hesitated, then took the young man's hand. "Thank you, Cainan. I appreciate that." He tapped the man on the shoulder as he shook his hand. The man visibly relaxed. Cainan Scott was a nice young man in Myles' opinion. Standing a solid six-two, he was a bit shorter than Myles, but had a menacing appearance. For some reason Myles always thought it would be better to have this man on your side, he could be a ferocious opponent. Unfortunately, they found themselves on opposite sides at the moment. There was some reason his father did not want Cainan involved with AnnieMarie. It was now his job to discover why.

"Ms. Price is waiting for you with some information for this morning's meeting."

"Thank you." Myles nodded. He stared at Cainan remembering what AnnieMarie said about him. "How are you holding up?"

Cainan, dressed in a suit and tie, shrugged. "Could be better."

Myles had to smile. "My sister giving you hell?"

He stood from his leaning position. "Has she said something to you?" he asked curiously, a tad anxious.

"Only that she would take anyone's balls off who puts a finger on you."

The menacing man grinned and nodded his head, relaxing a little more. "She would, too." The elevator stopped on the eighth floor and both men stepped out.

Chrystina was there waiting for Myles. "Was anyone on the elevator?" she asked Cainan.

"Savannah Whitfield."

Chrystina stopped. "What is she doing here?" She turned to Myles.

"She just happened to get on the elevator."

"No, everything with that woman is calculated." She then turned to Cainan. "Thank you, Cainan. I'll see you in a few minutes." She then began walking down the hall with Myles. "We have a situation that needs your immediate attention."

Myles stopped and turned to Cainan, who was walking in the opposite direction. "Cainan, do you have any free time to meet with me today?"

"You're the president of the bank. My time is yours."

"I have something I need to handle this morning." Myles nodded. "Join me for lunch."

"I'll see you sooner than you think, sir." Cainan nodded then walk ... way.

Myles stared at ainan walking away then turned back. Chrystina and Myles began walking towards their suite of offices.

"Now, that's the way you are supposed to reply when the boss requests a meeting with you." She handed him a document. "This is the document I mentioned this morning." She then gave him a folder as she followed through his office door, closing it behind her. "This is what you need to know about the Hershel representatives." Myles walked behind his desk, placing his briefcase on the floor as they entered his office.

Chrystina continued, "I've made some notes for you on the side. The main thing to remember is while Marty Wassermann is the outspoken one, it is Herbert Chadwick that will make the final decision. He does not, I do mean does not, like to be called Herbert. He goes by Herb. Also, he was recently divorced. That's why I think Nancy was brought in on this little coup d'etat attempt. However, it is known that Mr. Herb likes his coffee dark. I'm not certain whose brain-child this was, but it was Nancy that put together the memo." She paused, took a breath and checked her watch. "You have about fifteen minutes to familiarize yourself with Herb Chadwick. You will open the meeting, then Cainan will handle the presentation."

"Cainan?"

"Yes, they went to him for the numbers yesterday. Keeping you out of the loop on this meeting was planned. Not well, but it was intentional. However, that's something we will deal with later. In the meantime, I need to put a few more touches in place to ensure this goes smoothly." She walked quickly towards the door. "Fifteen minutes, Myles. I'm holding all your calls."

Myles watched as she walked out of the door. God, she was a powerhouse. What would he do without her, Myles thought, as he settled into reading the document Chrystina had written. 'Read this first,' was written in red. It was the document outlining his weaknesses, according to Nancy. It was full, most of them he considered strengths. But there was one that hit close to home. Chrystina Price was listed as his greatest strength, and his weakness. The notes read, 'While Myles Dunning is an astute businessman; it is Price who runs the day in, day out operations of his department. Could Myles find an assistant to handle operations, yes. But it would take years to get them to the proficiency of Price.'

The next item also struck a chord. Listed as a weakness was family. 'Dunning is a family owned establishment. With the death of Hepburn it was evident that vital functions ceased. Case in point, the human resource director left several key positions unfilled. Several remain unfilled to this day.'

Setting that document aside, Myles moved on to the next. While the first document was meant to hurt the company, he believed it could be useful and would revisit it once this coup was stopped. He pulled out the document on the Hershel Automotive group.

The Hershel account was a multi-billion-dollar account with its headquarters in Japan. The executives want to move the operations back to the

United States. This was the kind of account Myles wanted, a company who's looking to bring jobs back to this country. The only issue for him lies in the fact that Hershel was a Phase International account. He was certain this move would start a bidding war with Phase.

His cell phone buzzed. Knowing he had to get through the documents he glanced at the number. He had to take it. The call was from Michael.

"Mike, can it wait? We have an issue here."

"We have a bigger issue than you think. I'm getting blocked on every turn trying to get into this building. The address on the card you gave is the Department of Justice. Know what's inside? I'll tell you, the US Marshall's Service. Know what they do? Head up the witness protection program."

Myles sat up. "Are you telling me Cainan Scott is in the witness protection program?"

"That's just it, I can't tell you because no one is talking. In fact I can't get in to talk to anyone."

His phone buzzed again. This time it was a message from Chrystina. It was time to go.

"Mike, I have to run. Find out what you can and get back to me."

# Chapter Eighteen

"Mr. Wassermann, good morning. "Myles extended his hand. "Mr. Chadwick, thank you for joining us this morning. I am Myles Dunning. This is my executive assistant, Chrystina Price. Mr. Mitchell will join us upstairs."

"My brother, Herb Chadwick and my assistant, Carrie Oliver. My deepest sympathy on the loss of your father." Marty Wassermann patted Myles on the shoulder.

"Thank you, sir. It was a significant loss to our family."

"I so admired your father," Herb Chadwick said as he shook Myles' hand. "I must say his loss has left a few concerns with the deal unfinished."

"I can understand that. It's the reason I felt it was important that we speak face to face."

Marty nodded his head. "That is exactly what I stressed to William. He informed me the family was too devastated to meet with the public at this time."

"My father was dedicated to providing world class customer service. I will never defame his memory by providing anything less." Myles could see Herb Chadwick's expression soften.

"Business has become too automated. I prefer the personal touch. Shall we take this upstairs? We are eager to share Dunning's plans for you."

"I'd like that," Marty responded as they all entered the elevator.

"Mr. Chadwick, I understand you are a jazz enthusiast. Do you happen to enjoy a little Miles Davis?"

"I am and I do." Herb nodded.

"My parents have told me I was conceived while listening to Kind of Blue by Miles Davis, hence the name."

"Released in 1959. The man was a musical genius."

Pleased he could spark Herb's interest, Myles continued. "Indeed. They have the original. It's a treasure I happen to possess."

"We should take a listen to that, perhaps with a cigar and a good cognac," Herb offered.

"It would be my pleasure," Myles agreed.

"I believe it was a good cognac that had you married for the third time," Marty joked with Herb.

Herb nodded with a smirk as the elevator arrived on the fifth floor. "It's the reason I no longer drink or travel with an assistant."

"Your assistant?" Chrystina questioned.

Marty laughed. "Yes, they traveled to Vegas and returned married. We refer to her as the unfortunate mistake."

"Yes, it cost me a fortune. As it turned out during my divorce proceedings she knew more about my finances than I did."

Chrystina smiled. "My apologies, sir. I didn't mean to pry."

"No problem, darling. As long as you never speak her name in my presence we'll do just fine."

"Should be easy, since I do not know the unfortunate," Chrystina said as she ushered the party into the conference room.

"Been married thirty-two years," Marty boasted as he took a seat at the table. "One look across the room and I knew my Lizzy was the one."

"Are you married, Myles?" Carrie asked.

Chrystina gave the petite blonde a quick glance then moved away from the table.

"Carrie never misses an opportunity to seek out the bachelors in a room. Forgive her," Marty joked.

"No. I haven't been so honored," Myles replied taking a step to block the look on Chrystina's face from the guests.

"Take your time locating the one," Marty offered.

"Whatever you do stay away from Vegas," Herb suggested as he took a seat.

Myles laughed as he stood at the head of the table, privately amazed at the setup. He knew the employees put this together in a very short period of time.

"I take the wisdom from each of you to heart." He smiled. "Allow me to introduce Cainan Scott who will be assisting us with your presentation."

Cainan stood and extended his hand. "Mr. Wassermann, Mr. Chadwick, thank you for the opportunity."

"I took the liberty of pouring each of you a cup of coffee." Chrystina moved towards them placing the cups of coffee in front of each of the men. "Mr. Wassermann, I believe you take cream and sugar. Mr. Chadwick, I understand you enjoy yours strong and black."

"That I do." He tilted his head to the side.

Myles hoped he was wrong, but was Herb watching Chrystina walk around the table? He shook the thought off not certain how he felt about it.

"I'm afraid I am not clear on your preference, Ms. Oliver, cream or black?" Cainan asked.

"I'm easy," Carrie replied.

"I can see that," Chrystina mumbled.

Myles cleared his throat. "Serena, will you take care of Carrie's order. Chrystina, I would like you at the table. Shall we begin?"

"Yes." Cainan nodded. "Gentlemen, if you would open the presentation package in front of you. You will be able to follow what is on the screen."

Cainan began the presentation as Holly and Serena moved around the room almost invisibly filling pastry plates, coffee cups, and documents as needed. About fifteen minutes into the presentation, William, Paulette and Nancy walked through the open door.

"Forgive the delay, Marty, I was stuck in an elevator that is in need of desperate repair. Myles is new to all of this. He will soon learn the building needs care the same as people." William laughed as he ignored Myles and went straight to Marty and extended his hand. In an anger laced voice he continued. "Imagine my surprise to learn the meeting had been moved from the main conference room."

"Imagine that." Myles smiled, then continued, "It is important to stay on top of all the moving pieces of the business world, Mitch."

"Yes, well." Mitch nodded. "Herbert, it's good to meet you in person. Marty tells me you're the brains behind Hershel's success."

Unlike Marty, Herb did not extend his hand. "Yes." He glanced at Myles. "I see more of your employees decided to join us."

"Yes, they have." Myles stood. "Nancy and Paulette, thank you for coming. I believe we can take it from here." He then turned to William. "Mitch, if you would take a seat." Myles nodded to Chrystina as he re-took his seat then looked to Cainan. "Continue with the presentation."

#

Chrystina eased from the table. Taking Paulette and Nancy out the conference room she closed the door, then walked them towards the elevator before speaking.

"It seems you two have found yourselves in a bit of a situation. While Mr. Dunning may very well excuse your part in this poorly orchestrated coup, I will not. At this time I strongly suggest you each take some time to reflect on the events of this morning. Your actions starting this very moment will determine if you remain in your positions here at Dunning. Is my meaning clear?"

Paulette started to speak just as Mrs. Vazquez stepped off of the elevator. "This way, ladies," she spoke as she held the door open.

The look Chrystina received from Paulette was defiant and definitely would have killed if she cared, but she didn't. As for Nancy, she looked terrified.

"I believe Mr. Mitchell would prefer I remain in this meeting." Paulette glared at Chrystina.

"If I were you I would be more concerned with remaining in the job after this meeting is over," Chrystina replied then walked back into the conference room.

#

By the time Chrystina returned to the meeting William had taken her seat next to Myles. She removed her documents from in front of him down to the seat across from Herb. She then moved the documents meant for William and put them in front of him. "We are on page twenty-three if you'd like to follow along," she whispered. She sat, shared a smile with Herb, then put her attention on the presentation.

She settled, then watched William seething as Cainan meticulously covered each aspect of corporate level services and benefits Dunning would provide to Hershel. The presentation was good...very good. It was clear Chadwick was impressed with the human factor in the presented.

It was in that moment William cleared his throat. Chrystina turned towards him.

"Where are the profit margins from investments?" William asked.

Chrystina glanced at Cainan. She knew William asked the question to break the momentum Cainan had gained.

"It was covered on page ten of the presentation," Herb replied without looking at William. "Please continue." He nodded to Cainan.

Chrystina coughed to cover her laugh. To her dismay he tried again a few minutes later.

"What is the earning timespan for the numbers you have here?" William spoke again before Cainan was able to respond.

"There is a twenty year projection of investment earning which includes possible downturns in the market," Cainan responded. "Those figures are on page twelve of the document."

"Let's take a break here," Myles suggested as he pushed his chair back from the conference table. "It will give Mitch an opportunity to catch up by reviewing the documents."

"Yes, yes, let's do that." William stood. "Marty, a moment of your time."

Chrystina glanced at Myles, shook her head and walked in the opposite direction.

#

Myles walked over to the refreshment table and poured another cup of coffee. His patience was wearing thin. He needed a moment to get it under control.

"For every action there is a reaction." Herb joined him at the table holding his cup out. Myles filled it as Herb continued to talk. "You were voted in, technically voting him out. His reaction by attempting to take control can be self-defeating as demonstrated here this morning. Use your circle to earn control. Longevity is what you are seeking, not instant gratification." He took a sip of his coffee. "I can see in your eyes, you are pissed at what Mitchell attempted here. It was to be expected. Use that anger, but never let it control your reaction."

Myles nodded as he took a drink of his coffee. "You seem to have a decent insight on the situation. Do you think I should let him remain in his position?"

"Hell no. Move him out of your front office. Not because he attempted to take you down. Take him down because he was so bad at it." He laughed. "This is a new position of power. You have established yourself as Dunning's leader. Today, you accomplished that. Surround yourself with people you can trust next to you. From what I see, you have a strong inner circle. They put together a strong presentation in a short period of time."

Myles' attempt to control his expression must have failed.

Herb laughed at Myles' surprised reaction. "Oh, we saw this coming the moment Mitchell contacted us about changing the time of the meeting. It is his intention to show your customers you are weak, not ready for the leadership role. He took the vote personally. This is why you are getting our account, Myles. You put the bank before personal preference. The way this situation was handled this morning stripped him of his power with his allies as well as with us. I must commend you. You left his pride intact. Not once have you called him on his actions. You took the high road by choosing to show a united front, even when he did not." He patted Myles on the shoulder. "You're heading in the right direction." He started to walk off. "Oh, by the way, keep that Chrystina. Mitchell pulled a classic power move by taking her seat. She nailed it with class." He shrugged. "However, she needs a little work on handling her feelings for you."

"Feelings for me?" Myles shook his head. "Chrystina and I have worked together for years. We have a close professional camaraderie."

"Camaraderie?" Herb smiled. "If that's how you want to look at it. From my point of view your comrade wants to tear into Carrie for coming on to you." Herb chuckled then returned to his seat.

Myles understood what Chrystina had said earlier about Herb being the one who controlled the decision making. He was observant, insightful and plain spoken. However, he was off on that comment about Chrystina. They were a heck of a team, that's for sure, but there was nothing personal between them. He glanced her way to see her sharing that perfect smile with Cainan. Something primitive struck him. He did not like Chrystina smiling at the man, nor did he care for the way Herb's eyes followed her around. Myles shook the thought off then returned to his seat as he glanced at Mitch talking with Marty Wassermann.

"I hope you have an exit strategy in place, Mitchell," Marty laughed quietly. "You were masterfully out maneuvered here today."

"The boy doesn't have it in him to let me go. I'm too valuable."

"You're too dangerous and he knows it." Marty chuckled. "You played your hand too soon. I fear you underestimated your opponent. I'm rather impressed with the way young Dunning is handling himself, especially since you gave such a distressing impression of the state of affairs here."

"I've been doing this for over twenty years. This boy is no match for me. I can take this bank places."

"You have not succeeded in taking the leadership role you so desperately seek. You've lost this round. I suggest you tread lightly or you may not have another shot at it." He bit into the danish. "This is delicious, you should try one." Marty walked away.

Chrystina and Cainan watched the interaction between the partners from Hershel.

"I think this deal is done." Cainan turned from watching the men as he spoke.

"It's done when the signatures are on the dotted line." Chrystina's eyes narrowed as Carrie flirted with Myles. "Can I yank that blonde hair out of her head?"

Cainan looked over his shoulder. "Is she worth the multi-billion-dollar account we will lose if you do?"

She looked up at him. "You have a point. I miss AnnieMarie. She would have just let me do it."

"She would have helped you." He grinned.

The two smiled then returned to their seats to continue the presentation.

Twenty minutes later Herb turned to Myles. "I believe we have seen enough." He closed his booklet.

"I agree." Marty nodded as he stood and buttoned his suit jacket. He extended his hand to Myles. "We're on board."

Myles shook his hand. "Thank you, Mr. Wassermann. We look forward to Hershel joining our family." Applause echoed around the room.

William extended his hand out. "Herbert, welcome aboard."

Herb looked at Mitchell. "I tend not to shake hands with people who attempt to undermine their superiors. Make no mistake about it, Mr. Mitchell, Myles Dunning is your superior in every way. If I were you I would be questioning whether or not you still have a position with this financial institution." He started to walk away then stopped. "Oh by the way, the name is Herb." He then turned to Cainan. "Wonderful presentation, Mr. Scott." He extended his hand. "Your prediction indicates you are a progressive thinking young man. Exactly the type of man Myles is going to need to watch his back."

Cainan shook Herb's hand. "We are in transition mode. There will be trying times. It's my job to ensure Dunning's best interest is front and center."

"Tactful too." Herb smiled. "I like that."

William watched Cainan with Herb, then Myles with Wassermann. Yet he was standing there with no one. He was not going to be pushed out by Myles or anyone else. He turned to Chrystina's voice.

"Not to be presumptuous, but we prepared for this celebration in anticipation of an agreement," Chrystina said as Mrs. Vazquez walked in the door leading two gentlemen pushing carts of champagne with them. "I do believe this is now in order."

One of the servers popped the cork on the champagne and began filling the glasses.

Chrystina gave a glass to Myles, as others received theirs. Myles held it high. This was his first accomplishment as CEO and he owed it all to Chrystina's fast thinking.

"To the union of Dunning Bank & Trust and Hershel Automotive. May our bond demonstrate the power of loyalty as we pave the way for a lucrative and progressive future." He smiled at Chrystina as he downed the contents of the glass.

"Here, here," vibrated around the room with William's voice being heard over all others.

"Shall we take this celebration to my office?" William held a bottle of champagne in one hand and a glass in the other.

Myles shared a nod with Chrystina and Mrs. Vazquez.

"The celebration has been setup in Mr. Dunning's office," Mrs. Vazquez stated then held her hand out. "Ladies and gentlemen, if you would follow me."

As the people filed out of the conference room, Chrystina stepped in front of William, blocking his advancement.

"Mr. Mitchell, Mr. Dunning has asked to have a private moment of your time."

"We can talk after the celebration. Move out of my way." She took the glass from his hand, then reached for the bottle. William held it out of her reach.

"Actually, sir, Mr. Dunning feels the celebration would not be taking place if your plan had been successful."

"I have no idea what you are referring to."

Chrystina sighed. "Mr. Dunning is requesting you to wait in your office until the celebration, and subsequent announcement is made."

William held on to the bottle as he attempted to step around her. Two security guards appeared in the doorway.

The look William sent Chrystina could have lit a fireplace it was so fierce.

"What? We just landed a multi-billion-dollar contract. I have as much right to be included in this celebration as anyone else."

"I'm afraid Mr. Dunning doesn't see it that way."

"I do believe you are overstepping your bounds, Missy. I suggest you move out of my way before I speak to Myles about your insubordination," William demanded.

"I don't think you want to do that, Mr. Mitchell. Believe me when I say I am trying to save your job and your neck."

"Get out of my way." He attempted to push her aside.

A guard stepped up. "Ms. Price?" The guard raised an eyebrow.

"Ms. Price don't run things around here," William hissed. "I do."

"My apology, Mr. Mitchell. Mr. Dunning has requested us to assist you to your office, physically if it becomes necessary," the guard replied.

Chrystina took the champagne bottle from William. "Please escort Mr. Mitchell to his office. Remain with him. If he attempts to contact the outside world in any manner, stop him." She turned back to William. "A news conference is scheduled for three today. Please be sure to tune in, Mr. Mitchell." She walked towards the door. "I'm going to celebrate now." She smiled at the guards then left the room.

"How dare you treat me this way. I am the Vice-President of this bank. You cannot disrespect me in this manner."

Chrystina heard the man as she walked to the elevator.

"He seems pretty upset," Serena commented as she held the elevator door open for Chrystina.

"It does sound like he is having a bit of a fit," Holly added.

"He is," Chrystina replied as she pushed the button to the eighth floor. "Know where he is having it? Back there." The door closed as the two assistants laughed.

William stepped into his office to find Paulette, Nancy and two other employees he did not know there.

"Mr. Mitchell, we have been held here for the last three hours." Nancy jumped up first. "What is going on?"

"I don't even know why I'm here," the employee who handled facilities setup stated. "I only did what you asked me to do."

"William." Paulette elbowed her way to stand directly in front of him. "Were you in the meeting all this time?"

"Do we still have jobs?" Nancy shouted.

"How much do they know?" Paulette continued, ignoring the woman having a hissy fit.

William walked over to his bar and poured himself a drink as the questions flew at him. Paulette took the drink from him.

"Now is not the time to muddle your mind. What is going on?"

William looked around the room at the people staring back at him, took the glass back from Paulette and proceeded to drink his drink. "What does it look like? Our plans were discovered."

"What does that mean?" Nancy asked. "What's going to happen to us?"

"That is to be determined." William took a seat at his desk. "The good news is the meeting was successful."

"Successful in what way?" Paulette asked. "You convinced them to support your bid to become President of the bank by holding off on committing? Or did Myles get them to sign on the dotted line without supporting you?"

William took another drink without responding.

"Dunning got the account," Paulette summarized. "Without our help." She huffed. "That demonstrates they don't need us, William."

William stared at her knowing what she said was true. "It seems we played our hand a little too soon."

Paulette closed her eyes and walked away.

"What does that mean?" Nancy cried out.

"It means we all should start filling out our resumes," Paulette said as she slumped down into a chair.

# Chapter Nineteen

Walker Dunning Jr., with his tall, striking good looks, irresistible charm and the loyalty of a stray cat waited to be sure Myles had pulled out of the private road leading to the mansion. It was a good thing he was coming from the opposite direction or he would have had to hold a conversation with the man who had taken his place at the bank. "Don't get too comfortable, Myles. It won't be long now before I take over." He snickered then pulled into the driveway.

He stepped out of the vehicle, looked at the grand mansion that his brother built for his family and wondered if he wanted to take that too. The goal was to claim everything Hep held near and dear. Walker Jr. adjusted his jacket as he strutted towards the door. Before he could ring the doorbell it swung open revealing Winnie on the other side smiling.

"Hello, Jr.," her salutary voice rang out.

Ahh, the wife. I might take her too, he thought, as he pulled her into an embrace.

"Hello, Winnie." He held her at arms' length. "You look tired. How have you been holding up?"

Winnie stepped back. "Day by day, Jr. Day by day. Come on inside." She motioned with a tilt of her head.

"Hi, Uncle Walker." AnnieMarie walked into his embrace.

"AnnieMarie." He hugged her. "You look more and more like your mother every day. Hep was certainly a lucky man, surrounded with all this beauty."

Winnie smiled. "It was us who were lucky."

"That's true," Walker replied. She smiled at his remark, but he could tell she didn't like it. Good, he thought.

"Let's sit in the family room and talk."

The three turned and walked straight back to the open double French doors of the family room.

"Would you like a cup of tea?" Winnie asked.

Walker tilted his head to the side for a long minute as if in thought. "You know, I think I'll try a cup of coffee. Hep was always raving about Daisy's coffee."

"A cup of coffee it is."

"I'll get it, Mother." AnnieMarie nodded as she stepped out of the room.

"There were many lively conversations held in this room, I must say." Walker sat back and looked around. "Watching games with the boys. Laughing after scaring the girls' boyfriends half to death." He nodded. "Yes, this was a true family room in every sense of the word."

"It still is. I thought it would be the appropriate place for us to have this conversation. It may remind us that we are family. We are family, aren't we, Jr.?"

"Of course we are." Walker sat up. "Why would you question such a thing?"

"Here you are, Uncle Walker." AnnieMarie walked back in setting the coffee tray in front of him. "It could be Mother is questioning why the inquiries into Daddy's will," she said as she sat and crossed her legs.

"After all, she did just lose her husband. I would think it would be a time for the family to rally around to console her." She glanced at her mother. "At least those are my thoughts. I could be wrong. Mother?"

There was a flinch in Walker's eyes that he quickly concealed by bending to pick up the coffee cup.

"We are family. With Hep gone that leaves me the head of the family. As such I feel it is my responsibility to ensure you stay on top of things. In times like these important details could be missed." He sipped his coffee. "Humph, that's umm...rather strong."

"It's one of Daddy's favorites."

"Was..." Walker let the word linger for a moment as he glared at AnnieMarie.

"Well." Winnie patted AnnieMarie's hand. "Hep had very capable attorneys to handle his affairs." She sat back. "As for the head of this family that now goes to Myles."

"Let's not forget, Grace," AnnieMarie added. "She is handling everything with the attorneys. Would you like for me to give her a call? You can ask her where things stand."

"Yes, Jr., I'm certain Grace would be able to handle any legal situation that may arise." Winnie smiled.

Walker cleared his throat. He was still reeling from the last encounter with his spirited older niece over financial affairs.

"No. Myles is a bit young to take on the responsibility of the family and the bank too. Of course that could change once the will is read. When will that be, by the way?"

"I requested it be delayed."

"Delayed? Why?" Walker asked.

"I felt it was best to settle things at the bank before the reading."

"What things?"

"The appointment of the new CEO and President for one."

Walker nodded. "What about the shares?"

"What about them?" Winnie asked.

"Hep mentioned he would return my share of the bank's stocks. That would give me a say in who takes over the bank. Did he talk with you about that?"

"No."

"Not surprising." Walker smiled. "Hep always wanted to protect you from the day to day operations of the bank."

"Really?" AnnieMarie glanced at her mother. "We spoke daily about the bank."

"We did." Winnie smiled at AnnieMarie. "He kept me up on important matters."

"I can't imagine anything more important than returning shares of the bank to its rightful owner. The future of Dunning is at stake here, Winnie."

"Myles is the future of Dunning. As for the shares, it will be up to him to decide on how or if they are distributed."

"Myles?" There was a spike in his voice.

"You own 51% of the bank now that Hep is gone."

"That's true, however, as I am certain you know, yesterday Myles was voted as CEO and President. At that time I passed my proxy to him. He is in total control of Dunning."

"You did what?"

It was in that moment if AnnieMarie wasn't present, Walker would have grabbed Winnie.

He rose from the sofa as if he was a grizzly about to attack.

"Myles has no right to that control. I am the oldest son of my father. Hep should have never been next in line. The control should revert back to me. Not you and certainly not Myles."

AnnieMarie stood. "Lower your voice, Uncle Walker," she warned. "After all, we are family, are we not?"

Walker took a deep breath. Big picture, he thought, big picture.

"You are right." He retook his seat. "Winnie, forgive my outburst. I meant no disrespect, but I feel your actions may have locked me out of what is rightfully mine."

"I beg to differ with you, Uncle Walker. If I remember the story correctly, your father deemed you unfit to hold those shares. Due to your own actions he could not put the future of Dunning in your hands. My mother did not have anything to do with any of that."

"That was then, this is now," he said in a low, lethal sounding voice.

"What has changed, Jr.?" Winnie asked. "Have you stopped gambling? Or is the reason you are here because you owe a debt?"

Walker stood to his full height as a means of intimidation. "Hep's death was your opportunity to right the wrongs of this family. Any decent...person would have done what was right. I can see you believe you have accomplished your goal from the beginning. It wasn't enough that you wooed Hep with your feminine wiles to get him under your thumb. But you never fooled me, Winnie. I always knew it was about his money." He smirked. "Now your greed has expanded to wanting to control the bank." He walked towards the chair where Winnie remained seated. AnnieMarie stepped in front of him. He glared at his niece, then back to her mother. "Listen well, Winnieford. Until you return my shares to me, you and your children should be diligent in your movements and your affairs."

Winnie slowly stood, taking AnnieMarie's arm and pushing her behind her. She stared up at him. "Be careful, Jr. Your words sound like a threat against my children," she said in a deadly voice. "While I may seem down and wounded to you, make no mistake. You come after any one of my children and I will cut off your balls and stuff them down your throat."

"Mother!"

Walker snickered. "Well, I see the hood in you is coming to life with Hep gone."

"Uncle Walker!" AnnieMarie cried out as she stepped from behind her mother.

Winnie pushed her back. "People from the hood, as you call it, can be dangerous. We know how to take your ass out when you least expect it. I suggest you...watch your back."

"Mother!"

"Is there a problem in here?" Daisy stood in the doorway with a long handle cast iron frying pan in her hand.

Winnie shook her head. "No, Daisy. Everything is fine. Jr.... was just leaving."

Walker held Winnie's glare for a long moment then turned to walk from the room. "I don't think you want to take this stance against me, Winnie. Remember, I'm a Dunning by blood, you're not."

"Allow me to show you to the door." Daisy flipped the pan around in her hand.

Walker let out a menacing laugh. "This is just the beginning, Winnieford," Walker said as he walked towards the door. "Just the beginning." He opened the door then yelled back, "The kid gloves are off now, Winnie. I will have what is mine."

#

Daisy slammed the door behind him then stood in the foyer staring at Winnie and AnnieMarie. "Do you want me to call Myles?"

"No," Winnie argued. "Don't call anyone. I will handle Walker."

"Winnie, now I know you think you are ready for him, but Walker plays dirty, always has." Daisy walked back towards them.

"I was married to Hep for thirty-eight years. I know how dirty Jr. can go."

"Mother, let's take a minute here." AnnieMarie exhaled. "Uncle Walker is just upset right now. He will come to his senses."

"AnnieMarie, I know you love your uncle, and that is how it should be. However, to protect your father's, grandfathers' and all the Dunnings before legacy, I will fight Jr. to the death." The look she gave her daughter emphasized she meant every word she said. "And Daisy."

Daisy looked up at Winnie with a ready to kill look. "Yes."

"Thank you, my ride or die sister from another mother. Now put that frying pan back in the kitchen."

"Right after I fry his ass up in it," she huffed, then walked away.

Winnie and AnnieMarie laughed, then settled as the reality of what just happened hit them.

"Uncle Walker was quite intense." AnnieMarie took her mother's hand and began walking towards the kitchen. "I am glad I stayed with you. Is he right, Mother? Was he wronged by Grandfather?"

"In his mind he was. However, your grandfather did what he had to, in order to protect the bank. Unfortunately, Walker is still not prepared to handle the responsibility of millions of customers' finances. Power is a dangerous entity in the wrong hands. Your grandfather and many generations of Dunning men knew that. Before he made the decision to strip Walker of any controlling interest in DBT he consulted with the family. They all agreed Walker's gambling was a threat to his life and the sovereignty of the bank."

"Do you think Father reverted the shares back to uncle Walker in his will?"

"We will all find out soon enough, but I doubt it. In fact it was the attorney who told me I now own 51% of the bank. They suggested I speak with Grace to determine my next step," Winnie advised. "It was on her advice that I held the board meeting to solidify the leadership of the bank. It was the best way to keep DBT out of Jr.'s hands."

They walked into the kitchen holding hands.

"How did Uncle Walker know about Myles' appointment to CEO and President of Dunning? We did not issue a press release. Was he at the board meeting?"

Winnie stopped, turned and stared at her daughter. "I can't say for certain," she replied. "Walker always seems to be in the know when it comes to DBT."

"Well, I'm certain Grace will handle the legal end of things. Now, tell me, was it my imagination or did Uncle Walker sort of threaten us back there?"

"It wasn't your imagination and there was nothing sort of about it. He did threaten my children and for that he has declared war with me."

AnnieMarie sighed. "Yes, I was afraid of that." She nodded. "I'm not ready, but I think we better go talk to Daddy now. Cooler heads need to intervene here. I've seen you protecting your cubs before."

The cell phone in her pocket chimed. AnnieMarie pulled it out and saw the call was from Chrystina. "Hold on, Mother, it's the bank calling. Hello."

AnnieMarie listened intently. "That's wonderful, Chrystina." She listened more then glanced at her watch. "It's too close for me to make it into the office in time. I'll set it up from here. What room are you going to make the announcement from?" She nodded her head. "Good choice. Good choice. I'll start making calls right now." She hung up the telephone.

"What's going on?" Winnie looked on curiously as did Daisy.

"Myles just signed Hershel Automotive with Dunning. They are going to make the announcement from Daddy's office. I have to get the media in place." She looked at her mother. "Rain check on visiting Daddy?"

"Of course. Do what you have to do. I will be fine." Winnie watched as AnnieMarie ran off, then turned to Daisy. "That is quite a feat on his first day. Wouldn't you say so, Daisy?"

"Yes, I would." Daisy finally put the frying pan back on the rack. "Never had a doubt about his ability to take over right where his daddy left off."

"The only sad thing about the turn of events is that Myles' accomplishment today will put more money in Jr.'s pocket."

Winnie huffed. "He keeps coming after my children and I will have his financial support cut off completely." She continued talking as she was walking out the door. "The nerve of him to threaten me and mine. Jerome..."she called out. "Take me to see my husband. I need to feel his presence to calm me down."

The door closed.

AnnieMarie stood in the office doorway with the cell phone to her ear, staring at Daisy who was still in the kitchen. "I wonder if Uncle Walker knows he just walked into the eye of a storm?"

"Hell, girl, she's going to be a full-fledged hurricane by the time she finishes with him."

## Chapter Twenty

"She gave the controlling shares to Myles. Is that something you forgot to mention?"

"Only the proxy." Elaine attempted to control the raging Walker. "She can rescind it at any time. Tell me you did not lose your cool with her."

Walker huffed. "The very thought of one of Hep's privileged ass kids dictating my shares pissed me off."

"Big picture here, Walker. You have to keep the bigger picture in mind," Elaine gritted. "This is not just about a few million. This is about controlling the financial purse strings of Dunning. If we do this right every Dunning will have to come to you to get permission to breathe. Keep your temper in check or I will have no choice but to remove you from the final equation." She waited a moment. "Whatever you did, go back and undo it, now."

Walker sat in the car seething. It was not and never has been in his nature to bow to anyone. Particularly, his little brother or his wife. He did not care how smart she was, Winnieford Pitchfork was beneath their family.

When Hep first brought her home he thought of her as a nice piece of ass to keep his little brother occupied. Then the fool married her. What the hell? Walker thought at the time. Hep would get his share of the income from the bank and they will live their life. No sweat off his back. Until the day his father called the emergency meeting to declare upon his retirement the control of Dunning Bank & Trust would go to Hep. Walker could not, and to this day, over 20 years later, he still could not, accept the decision.

So what he bet the contents of one of the local bank vaults and lost. It was just one. It's not like he bet every vault at every branch. Hell they paid the debt and still had plenty left over. That was no reason to deem him unworthy of his birthright. And now to think it was in the control of Myles. That boy was just like his father. He would have had an easier chance with Grace taking over. They left no other choice than to align himself with people outside the bank to get what was rightfully his. There is no way in hell he was going to allow Winnie or her litter of bastards to control his fortune.

"Walker," Elaine called out. "Walker," she called out again.

"I'm here."

"Answer my question. Did you say something to upset Winnie?"

Walker closed his eyes. He did not need to hear a lecture at this moment. "I spoke my mind, that's all."

"At a time like this, Walker? The woman just buried her husband and we have a plan in play. This is not the time."

"She buried him a month ago; a month ago. What am I supposed to do, wait until she has disbursed my fortune to her children?"

"It is not your fortune, Walker. The bank does not and never did belong to any one family member. This is why you were removed as the next in line to control Dunning. You think of it as your personal ATM. Well it's not. Your family looks at Dunning as a part of history, as they should. Until you understand what they feel you will never gain control unless we see this plan through."

"I want what's mine."

"I want you to have what is rightfully yours as well. But right now, you sound like a spoiled child. You are old enough to understand what is at stake." Elaine sighed. "You get over 50 million dollars a year for doing nothing but sitting on your ass. If you stopped gambling you could have a pretty decent life."

"That's nothing compared to what Hep and his family take in."

"They work for a living, Walker. Every one of them come into this bank every day and work. You don't."

"You don't understand, Elaine. You didn't have your heritage stripped right from under you."

"Neither did you. You gambled your inheritance away. What did you think would happen when Hep died? Did you think that Winnie would just turn over the shares for you to lose them too?"

"It's not her place to make that decision. Hep was not supposed to control the bank. That was my birthright," he yelled into the phone.

"It was your father's right, and your grandfather's before him. They gave that right to Hep to prevent you from ruining the bank. Making you CEO would have amounted to giving a crack head the key to the room where the meth was being cooked." She took a deep breath. "Look, with the plans we have in place you can take over the bank in less than six days, Walker. That's it. Myles will be out, you will be in and I'll be gone. All you have to do is deliver at the right time. You get me, Walker? Everything is in place. Now chill the hell out and follow the plan." The call was disconnected.

Walker sat in his car sick to high heaven of dealing with bossy women and being broke. The plan would not be possible if it wasn't for his information. She talked to him as if this was all her brainchild. To be fair Walker could not take all the credit. It was William who had dropped the information in his lap. Now he knew what to do with it.

Timing could not have been better in Walker's assessment. Hep's death put the bank in turmoil. Everyone's guard was down while dealing with the loss. For him, he knew once Homeland Security got the anonymous tip, they would launch an investigation into Dunning. With the information that was planted, the authorities were sure to demand a new CEO be named. That was when he would step in. Elaine's job was to get William Mitchell out of the running. In return she would receive the BIT account to take to any competitor in exchange for an executive position with their organization. That would give him complete control of Dunning.

Walker grinned as he started the engine to pull out of the security gate of Hep's house. Six days, that was all he needed, he thought as a black SUV pulled in front of him blocking his progression. A low groan escaped as he recognized the driver. Interference was the last thing he needed today.

"Mr. Walker." The sightly accented voice of the man standing a good six-three came through the window. "Mr. Pavel would like a moment of your time."

Stephan Pavel, the son in Pavel & Sons Real Estate firm and the owner of several Gentlemen's clubs, is not the type of man you say no to. It would be considered an insult, which was usually met with physical trauma, if not death.

Walker looked at the man with the muscle bound arms filled with tattoos. This man was appearing in his life way too many times lately. He would never say much, only 'Mr Pavel would like a moment of your time.' Never any variation, just those exact words. As nerve wrecking as that was, Stephan Pavel being there in person was frightening.

Slipping into the backseat of the SUV, Walker looked around. The muscle man was now in the driver seat, another man dressed in a suit was in the passenger seat and Pavel was in the back sending messages on his phone.

"Mr. Dunning." A Russian accent more pronounced than Mr. Muscles', filled the air. "It seems your debt is increasing at a rate you can no longer afford. How do you intend on compensating me?"

Walker eyed each of the men sitting in the front, then looked back at Pavel. His steely blue eyes were now directly on him.

"I'm working on that."

"Am I to take your word for that?"

The men in the front seat chuckled.

"I have a substantial net worth," Walker grumbled.

"Yet, you could not meet your obligations when you came into my establishment. Perhaps you should have remained in the common area instead of insisting on entering the whalers' private poker game." Pavel smirked, then returned his attention to his phone.

The man in the passenger seat turned to Walker.

"You boasted of being one of the owners of Dunning Bank & Trust. It is for that reason you were extended the credit line of ten million dollars to participate in the whalers' poker game. At a rate of ten percent a day, your debt is now twenty million dollars. The terms were five days to pay the debt in full. Fifteen million dollars was not received by eleven-fifty-nine pm. At 12:01 am, on day six, you are notified of the delinquency and advised if twenty million dollars was not received in full by 12:01 am this morning an alternative repayment plan will be put in place."

"If your alternative plan is to kill me, you will never receive payment," the smug Walker hissed.

The men looked at each other and laughed.

Before Walker could understand the dangerous situation he was in, a knife slid across his throat. It missed major arteries, but the blood spatter and the pain was enough to shock a little reality into Walker.

Eyes bulging, with his hand attempting to hold the blood in, Walker cried out, "You cut me. I'm bleeding here. Get me to a hospital."

"Why would we do that?" Pavel taunted. "We are the ones who cut you." He looked at Walker as if he was crazy for thinking such a thing. "Men have lost their lives for speaking to me in a disrespectful manner. Do you think you can hold your tongue now?"

Walker nodded as he frantically attempted to stop the bleeding.

"Good. Fortunately for you, I am in need of your service."

Blood from Walker's neck dripped onto Pavel's hand. Muscles pulled a wet one from the mid console of the car and gave it to Pavel.

"Get him a towel will you," he said as he wiped his hand.

Muscle got out, grabbed a towel from the back of the SUV, threw it to Walker then returned to his seat.

Walker fumbled with the towel wrapping it around the front of his neck.

"Do I have your attention now, Mr. Dunning?" Pavel asked as Walker whimpered.

Walker nodded.

"Don't do that again," Pavel said. "You'll only lose more blood. Now, here is what you are going to do. You are going to work at your family's bank."

"Work?" Walker looked shocked.

"This is a time for you to listen, not speak," Pavel said then continued. "You will get a position as director of international affairs. You will hire my nephew Ivan as your assistant. Once this is done, you will receive further instructions."

"I can't do that," Walker choked out.

"You have thirty days to accomplish this."

"Did you not hear me? I can't do that."

"Very well." Pavel looked at Muscle man. "Finish the job."

Muscle man turned to Walker.

"Wait, wait." Walker scrambled to the edge of seat by the door. "I will pay you the money."

"We no longer wish to have your money. We want your services."

"For how long?" Walker asked.

"For as long as I desire them." Pavel glanced up with a nod. Muscle man stepped out then opened the back door.

Walker looked at the man, then back to Pavel. "Why?"

Pavel's attention was now back on his phone. "The cost to replace my suit and vehicle will be added to your debt. Make no mistake, Mr. Dunning, if you die before the debt is repaid" -he shrugged- "I will simply collect from your family. Good day, Mr. Dunning."

Walker stepped out of the vehicle and stood on the side of the road watching as the vehicle disappeared. He quickly got into his car and drove non-stop to the hospital.

#

The cut wasn't deep at all. It happened to be in a place where it bled like hell. While the resident at the emergency room worked on him, the provision made by the Russians began to take root in his mind. Letting the Russians into the bank may not be a bad move. In fact, it may expedite his plans. He began formalizing a new way to not only gain control of Dunning but to eliminate the Russians as well. He would have laughed at the genius of the plan if his neck didn't hurt like hell. Now all he had to do was figure out how he could convince Myles to let him work at the bank. His credibility with the family was shot. He had to get an intermediary to help and he knew just the person to use.

The emergency room resident had stopped the bleeding and bandaged the superficial wound by the time his sister, Vivian Dunning-Grey walked into the room. The stunningly dressed, middle-age woman with concern etched on her face, stood in the doorway assessing the situation. It was clear he had been injured in some way, however, she had fallen for his antics before. The warning received from her husband of twenty-two years, not to be taken in by her brother again echoed in her mind. This time, she decided to speak with the resident who treated him first, then she would see what Walker had to say.

Vivian stepped back from the doorway to find a nurse.

"Is there someone who can give me the status of Walker Dunning Jr.?"

The nurse pulled up the name from the computer. "Are you a relative?"

"Yes, I'm his sister."

"Do you have his code?"

"Code?" Vivian looked inquisitive.

"Yes. Each patient has a code that is given to relatives. That gives us permission to speak with them on the patient's condition."

"Oh, well no. I don't have that."

The nurse frowned. "I'm afraid I cannot speak with you without that code or Mr. Dunning's permission."

"Let's step inside his room. I'm certain he will give you permission to speak with me." Vivian stepped aside when her cell phone chimed. "Excuse me for a moment," she said to the nurse, then answered the call. "Hello."

"Hi, Aunt Viv. You called?" Grace asked.

"Yes, dear. It's your Uncle Walker. He's been hurt."

"Did my mother do it?"

Vivian was taken aback. "Your mother," she laughed. "Heaven's no. Why would you think that?"

"I got a call from AnnieMarie. She said he was at the house earlier giving Mother a hard time about Daddy's will. Things got a little heated and Mother said she would cut off his balls. Does he still have his balls, Aunt Viv?"

Laughter erupted before she could stop it. Vivian looked around at the people staring back at her. She stepped around the corner. "Well, I will check that when I see him."

"Yes, let me know. If she did not handle it, I'll see what I can do when I get home." Grace laughed. "What happened to him?"

"I'm trying to find out. It looks like he has a bandage around his throat."

"Maybe someone tried to choke some sense into him."

"Grace, that's your uncle you're talking about."

"I know, Aunt Viv. I'm sorry. I'm in New York, but if you need me to come home let me know."

"I'll try to get more information from the nurse. I'll call you back when I know more."

"Okay, Aunt Viv. Don't let Uncle Walker take you in again. Try to get the truth from him this time. In fact, there is a recording app on your phone. Push the button before you go into the room. Then send the recording to me."

"Is all of that necessary?"

"Yes, Aunt Viv. Remember what happened before. I love you, but I will not sit by and allow Uncle Walker to drain your bank accounts again. You have your husband and children to think about."

"You're right. I'll turn the recorder on now."

"Thank you. Call me when you leave his room."

Vivian disconnected the call, then found the recording application. She opened the app, hit record and placed the phone inside her purse.

She walked into the room to find the nurse adjusting the pillows behind Walker's head.

"Viv, oh, Viv," Walker cried out in a whispered voice. "I knew you would come. You are the only one who cares." He reached out for her hand.

"Of course I came, Walker. You're my brother. What happened?"

Walker closed his eyes squeezing them tight as if in pain. "Some thugs tried to rob me."

"Oh no." She squeezed his hand. "Walker, where did they hurt you?"

He swallowed then frowned from the pain. "They slit my throat, Viv," he cried. "They tried to kill me." He leaned on her shoulder and cried.

Viv hugged her brother. Okay, he was hurt. That part was true and she felt a little guilty for doubting him. "Where did this happen?"

"Where?"

The way he asked the question put her back on alert. "Yes, Walker. Where did it happen? What did the police say? Were they able to catch them?"

He lay back on the bed as if trying to catch his breath but held on to her hand. "I didn't call them."

"Well, how did you get to the hospital?"

"I drove myself, Viv. I had to get out of there before they came back."

Viv took a step back. "They cut your throat but you were able to drive to the hospital?"

"The people here patched me up. Look at this." He touched the bandage on his neck.

Vivian released his hand then sat on the side of the bed. "Tell me what happened."

"It was all my fault, Viv. I was upset."

"About what?"

He waved her off, shaking his head. "I should have known better."

He didn't say anything more. She knew this ploy. Walker would pull this on her and Hep all the time when they were younger. He wanted them to hang onto his every word.

"Known better about what?"

He sighed then looked directly in Vivian's eyes and lied. "I went to Hep's house to talk to Winnie about a job at the bank." He closed his eyes. "Of course, she turned me down. Now that Hep is gone Winnie is acting like she is the queen of the family."

"You...asked Winnie for a job?" Vivian was so close to laughter she was certain he had to hear the restraint in her voice.

"You don't believe me?" Walker said turning away from her.

"Well, Walker, it's just that..." She hesitated. "You haven't worked in a very long time. In fact I don't remember you ever working. Even when we were young and all three of us had jobs at the bank, you only showed up. You never worked. So, why would you ask her for a job now?"

"Because I'm broke and I need a job," he retorted angrily, then grabbed his throat in pain. "Is that what everyone wants...to see me begging for a job?"

"No, Walker. No one wants to see you begging." She shook her head, realizing she still has not gotten the whole story. "Why don't we let that go for now. What happened after you left Winnie's house?"

"I thought I told you."

"No, you didn't."

He huffed. "I drove around trying to calm my temper down after Winnie said those hateful things to me. You know she even has AnnieMarie hating me now. Sweet little AnnieMarie," he cried.

"Annie doesn't have a hateful bone in her body. Now, Grace, well she doesn't like you too much. Now, what happened after you left Winnie's house?"

"Hep's house," he countered on her. "She took the bank, my shares and now you're giving her the house too."

Vivian took a deep breath. "You know, Walker, you are my brother and I love you. But if you don't tell me what happened right now, I'm walking out that door and not coming back."

"Vivian," a well-placed simper came from Walker's throat.

"Right now, Walker."

"They mugged me, Vivian. Some thugs at a store mugged me. They took all the cash from my wallet, slit my throat and ran off to leave me for dead."

"Yet you were able to get in your car and drive to the hospital," she said in an unbelieving tone.

"You rather I laid in the street and bleed to death."

Vivian rose from the side of the bed. Losing her patience clearly etched on her face. She pulled a chair over then sat next to the bed with her legs crossed, then glared at her brother. "I'd rather you stop bullshitting me and tell me the truth."

## Chapter Twenty-One

The celebration was over and the announcement had been made. The financial world was whirling with the implication of the union between Herschel Automotive and DBT with BIT waiting on the sideline. The combination of the two would put Dunning Bank & Trust one step closer to taking the number two spot in the bank ratings.

Paulette sat still, arms folded over her chest watching the financial audits giving their take on the news. That condo in the sky she planned to purchase once Mitch became president of the bank was now gone bye-bye.

"The bonus is gone. I worked hard on that Hershel account. Putting all the right pieces together for months. And just like that" -she snapped her fingers in disgust- "it's gone."

"Your bonus isn't the only thing that's gone," Nancy hissed. "We are no longer employed."

Paulette rolled her eyes at the woman she considered clueless. "I have qualifications that will assure me another position."

"You think?" Nancy railed back. "You just attempted to sabotage your employer's acquisition of a major account. Do you really believe another financial institution will hire you?"

"It wasn't a sabotage," Paulette shot back. "It was a demonstration of strength and weakness. Loyalty should always be in the forefront in business. Where was Dunning's loyalty to William? He's been the second in command for years. He possesses the strength to take this bank to the next level. Myles doesn't."

"Really, well, we clearly see who has the strength and who the weaklings are now, don't we?"

"Dissention amongst friends?"

Everyone in the room turned towards the open connecting door between Hep and William's offices to find Myles and Chrystina standing there.

#

"Mr. Dunning, I have no idea why I'm here," one of the employees in the room ran to where they stood, pleading. "I simply set up the furniture in the room as I was instructed to do." Another employee stood behind him nodding.

"We had no idea what was happening. Hell, I still don't know what's going on."

Myles held up his hand. "Everyone, please, take a seat."

Paulette remained standing in defiance as the others sat back down. William, who sat behind his desk, never moved.

Chrystina walked over to Paulette then whispered, "I know what's in your bank account. You can't afford to piss me off." She patted the back of the chair in front of William's desk. "Have a seat."

Paulette hesitated, then slowly sat.

William continued to drink with a curious expression on his face.

Myles pulled out a chair from the wall, then took a seat. Mrs. Vazquez came through the door with folders in her arm and stood behind him.

Myles looked up at Chrystina, who was in his direct eyesight standing behind Paulette. "Well," he began, "it has been quite a day. Wouldn't you agree, Chrystina?"

"Yes, sir, I would."

"It is not every day we find executive officers attempting to discredit the highest ranking officer, is it, Chrystina?"

"No, sir, it isn't."

"Sir," one employee spoke up. "Again, I would like to reiterate I had no parts in that. In fact, umm, sir, I am not an executive officer, sir. And if this is how y'all act I don't want to be one."

Myles looked at the young man whom he found humorous. "What is your name?"

"Larry Taylor, sir. I work in the maintenance department downstairs. I don't even come up here unless there is a job I have to do. I mean I see y'all and everything, but I don't know y'all like that."

Mrs. Vazquez smiled as she handed a folder to Myles.

He glanced inside. "You were told to set up the room for a secret meeting with the Hershel group?"

"Yes, sir." The young man seemed eager to tell his story. "I asked for the written documentation, cause I know that's what you are going to ask next. But I did. I asked Ms. Nancy and she told me it was a direct request from Mr. Mitchell, the VP of the bank and it was a secret meeting. I was to do it and not tell anyone."

"Then you went against this policy procedure which has your signature on it?" He handed the piece of paper to Mr. Taylor.

Larry's face frowned. "Well...what happened was..." He moaned. "Yeah, yeah," he sighed. "I signed that and meant to follow every one of those procedures. But man, this was the VP of the bank making the request. I ain't know what he was up to and I didn't know the secret was from you. You know what I mean?"

"You could have refused to fill the request until the proper paperwork was completed."

"Man," Larry huffed. "Are you serious? I would have been fired."

"What do you think is happening now?" Myles raised an eyebrow.

Larry stared at Myles as if waiting for the next shoe to drop. He put his hands together as if in prayer. "Please, Mr. Dunning, I was just following orders. That is all I did."

Mrs. Vazquez discreetly touched Myles' shoulder.

Myles glanced at Chrystina, who gave him a sad face.

"Mr. Taylor, go home for the day. Report to work tomorrow at your normal time."

Before Myles finished the sentence, Larry was jumping out of his chair grabbing Myles' hand.

"Thank you, thank you, thank you, Mr. Dunning. It will not happen again." The sweat was on the man's brow as he bowed, grateful to still have a job. He glanced back at the smiling young lady who'd sat in the chair next to him all day. His smile faded.

"Umm, Mr. Dunning." He reached for the young lady's hand. "This is Pam. I don't know her last name, but we've been talking about this situation all day. She is really dedicated to this bank, sir. She has two little boys at home who depend on her. I believe she was pulled into this mess the same way I was. The only difference is she was told if she did not do what was asked she would lose her job."

Myles looked past Larry to the woman now standing next to him. He held up his hand and Mrs. Vazquez gave him another folder. He glanced through, then looked back at Pam.

"Pamela Green, is what Mr. Taylor said true? Was your job threatened? If so, by whom?"

Pamela Green did not seem to have the same nerves as Larry. She was a bit more reserved. "Mr. Dunning, as your event planner, I have to be honest. When I received the request, I knew what she requested was not protocol. I should have insisted she send the written request as required. I have no defense for that."

"You are taking responsibility for your actions." Myles nodded. "I can appreciate that. Was your position threatened by anyone in this room?"

Pam glanced up at Larry, who nodded, encouraging her to speak up.

"I was told my growth with this company would be severely limited if I did not comply with the order. I purposely kept the cost down so it did not have to be approved."

Myles waited. "You don't want to say by whom?"

Pam tilted her head. "I made the decision to place the order and charged it to the executive office as requested."

"Oh for goodness sakes. I was the one who told her to place the order for the meeting this morning. No need to act so chivalrous," Paulette complained.

Myles glared at Paulette as he spoke. "I admire your loyalty to your co-worker, Mrs. Green."

"You have two boys," Chrystina asked. "How old are they?"

"Three and five," Pam replied, somewhat confused by the question.

"Is the father in the home?"

"No."

"He was killed in the line of duty, two years ago," Larry stated. "He was stationed at Fort Lee and she decided to stay here in Virginia. She doesn't have any family here. Go ahead, finish telling them." He nodded to Pam.

She smiled at him. "I think they have the idea."

"They need to know the whole picture to make the right decision." He motioned with his hands.

Myles and Christina glanced at each other then back to the two employees.

Myles stood and reached into his pocket. He pulled out his wallet and gave Larry two, one hundred dollar bills.

"I imagine it's been a trying day for Ms. Green. I know you both missed lunch and Ms. Green may not feel like cooking dinner for the boys. I would consider it a favor if you would take her and the boys to dinner for me. I will expect to see both of you at your desks tomorrow, bright and early."

Pam looked from Larry to Myles. "I'm not being fired?"

"No." Myles sat back down. "Which is something I cannot say for your superiors." He looked directly at William who had not uttered a word.

"Myles!" Nancy jumped up.

"Mr. Dunning, to you," Chrystina corrected.

Myles put his hand up. "I'm coming to you, Nancy." He looked at Larry and Pam. "Larry, your actions today demonstrate what Dunning is all about. Family looking out for family. You could have left the minute you knew your job was safe, but you stayed to try to help a fellow employee. I'm proud to have you onboard."

"Give me a pound on that." Larry held his closed fist up.

Myles stared at him. "Not there yet, huh. Okay," Larry said then turned to Pam. "Let's go, Pam. Where do you and the boys like to eat?" he asked as the door closed behind them.

Myles remained standing as he braced himself for the next step.

"If you are going to fire me, be done with it," Paulette blurted out.

"I don't want to be fired," Nancy cried. "Chrystina, you know how I am. I act before I think sometimes."

"Stop begging," Paulette growled. "It's pathetic. Look, Myles, it wasn't anything personal. Change is a challenge for me. William is petty, but I know what it takes to get the job done the way he wants. You are a total mystery. To be honest I believe it was unfair to bypass William for the President's spot. He's been at Mr. Hep's side since I've been here. He deserves a chance to run things his way."

"Thank you for your frankness. I will be just as frank. Your reasons are unimportant. You attempted to sabotage a relationship with a major client. That is reason enough for termination in my book. However, Mrs. Vazquez and Ms. Price believe each of you has redeeming qualities."

Mrs. Vazquez gave him the two remaining folders. "You've each been demoted to the branch office closest to your home. Your salaries will be adjusted accordingly. Paulette, you worked on the Hershel account. The bonus designated for you will be in your next paycheck. You both will have reprimands on your record that will remain for five years. Each of you are free to seek employment elsewhere, if you choose to within that timeframe. If you decide to remain, all promotional opportunities will be limited to you for the next year. Until then one infraction of any kind and you will be relieved from your positions. Are there any questions?"

There was a shocked expression on Paulette's face. "You are giving me the bonus?"

"You worked on the project." Myles nodded.

"You are not firing us?"

"No," Myles answered.

"Why?"

"Loyalty and compassion flow from the top down." Myles nodded to Chrystina.

Chrystina turned to the security guards who were standing in the doorway.

"I suggest you take a little time to think on that one. Your offices and desks have been cleared. A guard is waiting to escort both of you out."

Nancy ran over and hugged Chrystina. "Thank you, I know you saved my job. I don't know why and I don't care. But thank you." She ran out the door.

Paulette walked slowly behind her as she glanced over her shoulder at William then to Myles. "Mr. Dunning." She gave a curt nod then disappeared out the door.

#

Myles took the seat directly in front of William's desk then glared at him.

The smirk on the man's face was condescending to say the least. Myles' hand was itching to knock it off William's face.

"You will never fire me, Myles." William grinned. "I know where all the proverbial bodies are buried. All the trade secrets as you will," he sneered.

"Is that so?" Myles sat back, stretched out his legs then crossed them at the ankle.

"It is a fact." William sat up, folding his hands on the desk as he held Myles' glare. "I've been around since before you were born, boy. Do you think your father got to this point doing what was right the entire time?" He shook his head. "Not even you can be that naive."

"Is that so?" Myles just sat there, glaring.

William sat back. "I don't know, maybe you are if you think I wouldn't have protection against this very thing." He laughed. "I knew once Hep was gone it would be a Dunning taking over this place. I prepared for the inevitable. You, Walker, it didn't matter who, I protected myself."

"Is that so?" Myles did not move a muscle other than his lips when he spoke. His eyes landed right on the man who had the audacity to attempt to smear his father's name.

"Do it. Say the words so I can shove them right back down your throat." He sat back and chuckled. "Yes, I can see it now. My first stop will be with the Federal Trade Commission. Yes, I have documents that show a little inside trading on your beloved father's behalf." He nodded his head up and down. "When I finish there, I think I'll have a press conference of my own to tell the world about Dunning's illegal hiring practices. I'm certain Homeland Security would get a kick out of that." William sat up again, this time snarling in Myles' face. "If that isn't enough, I'll expose all the sordid details of Walker's little escapades with female employees." He slammed his hand on the desk. "This is a man's game, boy. That's something your father never understood. All the social hand holding, and lifting this one up and helping your neighbor crap is for the weak. The strong capture and destroy." He glanced at Myles who kept his calm demeanor.

"Say something, boy," William shouted.

Myles did not reply.

William stood, puffing out his chest as if he had conquered something. "It's about time you people recognize who is superior."

"You people?" Chrystina questioned, but Myles raised his hand.

"Mitch deserves to have his say," Myles calmly spoke.

"Mitchell," the booming voice echoed in the room. William picked up the glass and threw it against the crest on the wall. "The name is William Mitchell. I've had it up to here with you people and this nickname crap. For thirty years I've had to deal with Mitch from Hepburn. Winnieford was the only one who ever understood my rank, my position in life."

Mrs. Vazquez and Chrystina glanced at each other.

"I've had to deal with you people and your righteous attitude about your rich history. Well, whippety damn do, your family can be traced back to 1806. We are now in the twenty-first century. It's time to do things my way."

"Is that so?" Myles still had not moved or reacted to William's rant.

William leaned across the desk. "Do you understand the kind of damage my documentation can cause your family? I will have you in a public relations nightmare of epic proportions. Now" -he stood and adjusted his suit jacket- "this is how things are going to work around here. You will retain the title, however, you will make no decisions without my approval. I will have final say on executive position appointments, and the president's bonuses on any future acquisitions." He grinned as if he had just conquered the world. "Once a reasonable amount of time has passed, you will step down and name me your successor."

There was complete silence in the room. Myles looked from Chrystina to Mrs. Vazquez.

Myles uncrossed his legs and stood. "Well, he let me keep the title."

Chrystina shrugged. "That's something."

"You don't seem to be taking me seriously."

"That's because we are not." Chrystina shook her head in disgust. "There is no way you can be that stupid. Do you really think we came in here unprepared?"

"You better rein in your hound dog, Myles. I may send a file out to a reporter out of spite."

"Did you just call me a dog?" Chrystina took a step towards him. "You little turd."

Myles put his hand out to stop her from moving forward. "Mitch," he began. "It seems you have the upper hand. Believe me it's a facade." He held out his hand to Chrystina.

She placed a folder in his hand.

He exhaled. "This is an exit contract. It includes a confidentiality agreement, precluding you from speaking to anyone regarding Dunning, its employees, past or present." He placed another document on the desk. "This document indicates you agree to the severance package." He pointed to the figure on the page. "That totals your annual salary for each of the thirty-four years you have been with the bank. This document." The last sheet of paper was put in front of William. "This document is important so pay attention. This document only needs the signature of the CEO to file embezzlement charges against you for creating fraudulent credit cards to cover personal debt. Over the years you have stolen over 25.7 million dollars from Dunning."

William's face was turning shades of pink, then red as Chrystina began to speak.

"Our investigation shows four of those cards are still in existence. One in each of your brothers' and sisters' names. Due to the nature of the crime, you and they are looking at up to twenty years in prison."

"In case that is not enough to convince you to leave quietly." Mrs. Vazquez stepped forward placing a folder in front of him. "These are still pictures of you over the years with women in rather...interesting positions."

William opened the folder. Color drained from his face as he looked at picture, after picture.

"To say you have a particular type would be an understatement, wouldn't you say so, Mr. Mitchell?"

Chrystina stepped forward. "Wow, Mr. Mitchell, I must say I'm shocked. I thought you were prejudiced. I can see that I was mistaken."

"A mistake," William mumbled.

"It seems you have a few secrets of your own," Myles added. "I can't help but notice, each of the women in the pictures resembles my mother."

William stood, his face so flushed it seemed as if blood was draining from his face in front of them.

"How long have you had these?"

"For years," Mrs. Vazquez replied. "Mr. Dunning had you followed and watched for years."

William looked at them, stunned. "Why?"

"He knew you were conspiring to take over his family's bank."

"Hep knew? All these years, he knew?"

"Yes," she replied.

"Then why...?"

"You introduced him to the love of his life," Myles stated. "He never forgot that."

William just stared at him, unbelieving.

"Tell me, William." Myles stepped forward. "When did you fall in love with my mother? Was it before she met my father or after?"

"Winnie was mine...mine," he yelled. "Then your father stole her from me. From me." He poked himself in the chest. "I found her. I made her popular on that campus...me. And what did I get for it? The moment she found someone with more money she left me."

"Was she ever with you, Mitch?" Myles asked.

"That's not the point. I found her," he cried out. "I did. Not Hep...Me."

Tears were brimming in his eyes.

Myles looked from Mrs. Vazquez to Chrystina. "Mitch, I don't want to see you in jail. Sign the papers and go on with your life."

Chrystina stepped forward. "Mr. Mitchell, over the years you have conspired in one way or another to interfere with the growth of Dunning. That Mr. Hep kept you on board as long as he did was a sign of his loyalty towards you. However, you did not return that loyalty. In addition your first reaction to Myles being named the new CEO was to undermine his first major acquisition." She stepped closer to the desk. "In my opinion you are not trustworthy to the family or the bank, which I find unforgiving. You never married. You have no children that we know of. Dunning was your life. Yet you spent the last 30 years constantly trying to destroy the man who has provided your livelihood." She turned to Myles. "I hate for anyone to lose their job, but I have to support the decision for termination. He is not trustworthy. In this instance continuing to employ this man is a mistake."

Myles turned to Mrs. Vazquez.

"I concur, sir." She looked sadly at William. "I believe it would be a mistake to keep him on."

"A mistake," William hissed. "Thirty years of my life and you call it a mistake," he spit out.

Before anyone could stop him, he grabbed Chrystina around the neck and threw her to the floor. He banged her head once and was pulling her up to do it again when Myles' two hundred pound body flew across the desk, taking William to the floor. He began punching the man with no remorse.

Mrs. Vazquez called for security as she helped Chrystina from the floor. It took three security guards to pull Myles off William.

"Take him out," Myles snarled.

"Take me out!" William yelled. "I own this bank." He pulled against the hold of the guards. "Thirty years...thirty years I carried Hepburn on my back. He would have never accomplished any of this without me. Me..." he yelled. "Get Winnieford on the phone. Call her now. She would never...never allow this."

Myles walked over to where the guards held him. "I was going to allow you to leave with your dignity intact."

"Allow....allow?" William was kicking and screaming. "Boy, you don't have the right to walk in the same light as me. You don't know your place, Hepburn...Don't you know you are to walk two steps behind me at all time...all times. That's how this world is. It was I...yes I, who allowed you to be in my presence. Doors opened because I was in front of you...Don't you think for one moment that I would let you take Winnieford and the bank too, boy...I built this...I built it all...Hepburn...do you hear me, boy?"

Myles and Chrystina glanced at each other as they realized William was losing it. His mind seemed to go back in time.

"Mr. Mitchell," Chrystina spoke softly as she approached him.

"Chrys," Mrs. Vazquez stopped her. "Let me."

"I'll call for an ambulance," Chrystina said.

"William." Mrs. Vazquez stepped forward.

"Marie, you tell them." William seemed to recognize her. "Tell them who I am." He spoke quietly. "That I am the Vice-president of this bank. I am to be treated with respect."

"I will tell them, William. You know Mr. Dunning listens when you are calm. Remember the breathing exercises we used to do?" She began to breathe deep, then let it out. "Let's do them now," she encouraged William.

"Tell Hepburn what is happening. He will right this atrocity."

"I will," Mrs. Vazquez said as the guards escorted William out the office.

# Chapter Twenty-Two

"What a freaking day," Chrystina sighed as she dropped to the chair in front of Myles' desk.

It was well after eight o'clock that night by the time William was taken away and things began to settle down. They had used the back entrance for the ambulance and the employees' elevator to take William away. Mrs. Vazquez went with William as Chrystina spoke with the police. Instead of having William arrested or sent home alone, Chrystina had him admitted to the hospital under what was once referred to as a green warrant. It was used when one believed a person is in danger of harming him or herself or others. Myles was too pissed to care one way or another what happened to Mr. Mitchell. However, Chrystina convinced him that protecting Mr. Mitchell was not only smart for Dunning, it was the humane thing to do. With the different office shootings taking place around the country, no one hesitated to have him hospitalized and checked out. Once Mrs. Vazquez updated them on William's condition, she was told to go home.

"Put this on your neck." Myles walked over with an icepack then literally dropped it on her lap.

Chrystina picked up the cold pack and placed it on the edge of his desk. "You know, I don't think I have ever seen you lose your cool."

"What are you talking about?" Myles asked as he walked back over to the bar and poured himself a double vodka, straight, no ice.

"I've seen you seriously concerned, deeply hurt by your father's death. But I don't think I have ever seen you ready to kill. What on earth was going through your mind when you came flying across that desk like a rocket out of hell?"

"He put his hands on you," Myles stated as he walked and sat behind the desk with a thump.

"So? I'm a big girl, Myles, I can take care of myself."

"Well you weren't doing a good job of it, Chrystina." He slammed the glass on the desk. "The man left marks on your neck for goodness sakes. You are a brown skinned sister. Red marks on your skin let me know he had a damn good grip on your neck."

She watched in awe as the vein in his throat pumped viciously. Something had to be done to calm him down. "Well, the important thing is Mr. Mitchell is in the hospital now. I hope his care will include a mental evaluation. He may be suicidal. Losing your father and his position with the bank all within the same month made him somewhat shaky. It sounded as if he was confusing you with your father."

He yelled, "You don't administer first aid to the enemy, Chrystina. They will only rise to come back at you again. I don't care what his problems may be. He threatened the bank and he put his hands on you."

"What is with you?" Chrystina yelled back as she glared at him. "You were the one who wanted to find a way to keep him on board. Now, all of a sudden you see him as the enemy. You sound like you want the man dead."

He slammed his hand on his desk. "He put bruises on you," he yelled again.

"So you said loud enough for the people standing in the line at the pearly gates to hear." She stood with her hands on her hips. "There is no way you can believe for one minute Mr. Mitchell would have harmed me or you for that matter. He was distraught, Myles. That's all." She glared at him.

"He slammed your head in the floor." He jumped from his chair. "What in the hell do you think I am? This damn day started with my youngest sister crying on my shoulder about a man I can't seem to find a damn thing out about. My mother stuffing a plate of waffles in her mouth, nearly choking just to prove to me it's okay to leave the house, Michael calling with some mystery revolving around one of our executive board members. Then I get to read about how inadequate I am as the president of this bank, Mitch trying to undermine a major commercial customer. Then having to meet with that customer with little or no prep time. Not to mention, releasing valuable employees from their positions." He then hit the desk with his fist again, causing Chrystina to jump. "Then to deal with the audacity of that man defaming my father's reputation, putting his hands around your neck. I'm a man, Chrystina. I don't have super powers that allow me to not feel some kind of way about this crap."

Before speaking Chrystina calmed her spirit, counted to ten, took a deep breath.

"I know you are a man, Myles," she spoke softly. "And you are right, it has been one hell of a day. I have to say I am honestly more than a little concerned about you. As president and CEO, this is what your days are going to consist of from now on. Not all will be this crazy, but they will be interesting. Once everyone settles in with the changes, the concept of your days will improve. But for now, during this time of change, it is what it is." She looked directly into his eyes. "Myles, the question you need to ask yourself is do you have the mental capacity to continue as CEO?"

"You planning on issuing a green warrant for me too?"

"Is your ass going crazy? Cause if you are, yes, I'm going to have to take you out in a straight jacket too. Where would that leave Dunning?"

The two held each other's glare for a long few minutes. It was a standoff.

"Grace Heather," Myles sighed.

"Which one? Grace I can handle. Heather..." Chrystina shook her head from side to side. "I don't know. I think I'd rather have to answer to your uncle Walker."

The look of disgust on Myles's face caused Chrystina to holler out loud in laughter.

"You cannot be serious," Myles laughed. "You would take Walker over Grace Heather?" He gave Chrystina a side eye.

"I would prefer to have the man I trust, Myles Dunning. However, I will take Walker over Heather. Have you seen the other side of your sister in action?"

"I have."

"No, I don't think you have. Not to the extent of us girls who have gone out to clubs with her."

Myles smiled. "I know she can get a little wild."

Pleased to see him returning to the even tempered man she loved, Chrystina decided to keep his mood change going in the right direction.

"A little wild? Let me tell you something." She crossed her legs, her thick brown thighs peeking from the side of her skirt. "We're in a club. There is a long bar, at least twenty feet of drinks lined up from one end to the next. There is a man at the opposite end of the bar drinking, with a woman mind you. Grace-Heather decides that's who she wants for the night. AnnieMarie and I are used to her antics, but this particular night she went all out."

Chrystina decided to demonstrate his sister's actions, as Myles retook his seat to hear the story.

"Now mind you we are at the beginning of the bar. Grace-Heather kicks off her heels, then used the stool to climb onto the bar. She yells, 'Make way. This woman is after that man.' She points at the man who is at the bar with another woman. The sister sitting next to him glares at Grace-Heather. AnnieMarie and I are removing our jewelry because we know we are going to have to fight this woman. Did any of that stop her? Nooooo."

Chrystina kicks her heels off allowing them to fling backwards, stood then walked to the side of Myles' desk. She sat his laptop on the floor. In one step she climbed onto the top of the desk. With hands on her hips she continues with the story as she acts it out.

"Your sister struts down the bar, bare feet, walking over people's drinks until she reaches the man of her desires, for the night. She then kneels on the bar in front of him, cleavage all in the man's face and says" - Chrystina's lips were a mere breath away from Myles'- "have you ever felt the power of a Lamborghini going 200 miles per hour? The woman sitting next to the man goes, well I never. She turns to look at the woman and says I believe you. She then turns back to the man and asks.." -Chrystina looks directly in Myles' eyes, then pursed her lips- "do you want to ride?"

#

It wasn't planned. He had no thoughts of doing it. Myles found his hand cupping her face then took Chrystina's lips with a voracity he did not know existed.

The moment their lips touched his world exploded. A possessiveness he could not explain took control. Every muscle in his body tensed as his heart rate spiked. His lips locked with hers. He pressed further causing her lips to part. His tongue plunged in between her lips. Exploring every corner, seeking all the sweetness she had to give. The world around him stopped. Frozen in the moment. The only thing existing was her. The way she laughed, the way she walked, the way she took care of him. It all flooded his mind as he took his fill of her sweetness. It wasn't enough, not for the day he'd had. Not for the lifetime of searching for this feeling. Not enough to relieve his testicles that were filling with need. Just not enough. He pulled her closer causing his chair to roll backwards.

What in the name of sweet Jesus was happening here? Chrystina's mind asked when it finally registered what she was doing. She was kissing Myles...again. Who made the first move she did not know, nor at the moment did she care. When his hand touched her face, the vessels in her body began humming. The sensations she felt a month ago were surfacing all over again. Then his lips touched hers and she could feel her nipples harden. It was the tongue exploring, touching every corner that caused her inner lips to moisten. She had no idea if this was right or wrong, but like before, she'd be damned if she would let this feeling go.

Her body matched the rhythm of his tongue. Before she could think about what she was doing her hands grabbed his arms and she moved forward, closer to his body.

His chair moved back, tipping with the additional weight. The crash landing on the floor shook them apart.

Myles braced her fall with his body, as the chair rolled from under them to the other side of the room. The rip of her skirt was heard as if it was the only sound in a library. He rolled to her side. "Are you hurt?" His hands checking everywhere.

Chrystina had not recovered from the kiss and could not answer.

"Chrystina." Myles' voice was laced with concern. "Are you hurt anywhere?" he asked again as he looked down at her.

She laid there with her eyes closed and a smile on her face. Then she realized she was hurt.

"You bit my tongue."

"What?" Myles stared down at her.

Chrystina opened her eyes then touched her tongue with her finger. "You bit my tongue. See." She held her tongue out and pointed to the spot.

"Let me see." Myles moved her hand away. He searched her mouth for any bruise or bite. "Turn your head to the side."

She did as he asked thinking he was still looking for the bite. He wasn't.

He kissed the side of her neck, then her cheek, then captured the sweetness of her mouth again. This time with the full understanding of what he was doing and intended.

He rolled on top of her then kissed the crest of her breasts. His fingers began unbuttoning her blouse. "I suggest you speak now or forever hold your piece, because I plan to have you, Chrystina Price."

He unclipped the front hook of her bra. "Chrys," he moaned as he took one nipple into his mouth. His tongue smoothly circling one while his thumb rolled over the opposite nipple.

"Myles." Chrystina cupped the back of his head as she fell back, taking in the sensual motion, allowing it to flow through her body like a dam running free. She wanted this, needed to know their first time at her place wasn't a mistake. Needed to know the ecstasy she felt that night wasn't a dream. She needed him. Following his lead, she unbuttoned his shirt, pushed it over his broad shoulders and down his back. Her hands touched his naked flesh, feeling the muscles expanding under it.

He sat up. Yanked the shirt off, then pulled her skirt up. "Chrystina, stop me," he pleaded.

She shook her head as he pulled her skirt up her thighs.

He spread her thighs, admiring the smooth thickness with his lips, gliding up one then the other. He kissed her center, right where the moisture was building. He licked his tongue, then gently stroked her to the core. Tasting every bit of the juices flowing from his touch. Plunging inside over and over, as her body rose to his. He felt like a butterfly inside her cocoon, with the warmth from her thighs surrounding his head, her fingers now massaging his scalp, her sweetness filling him as he heard her breath catch, her muscles contract, and her body jerk.

He came up smiling as he crawled back to her lips, leaving her wet and throbbing for more of his touch. He kissed her, then looked down into her eyes. "That's the taste of you wanting me."

"Ahrrgh," she moaned. "Then give me what I want," she said breathlessly. "Give it to me now,

Myles," she ordered as she unzipped his pants, pushed them over his hips.

He did not hesitate. He entered her with a slow, deliberate motion. The feel of being between her thighs was one thing. The heat of her inner lips caused an animalistic need to submerge himself deep inside of her and never come out. He plunged deeper as he pulled out and re-entered her. Deeper still when he did it again and again, loving the sound of his flesh hitting hers. He put her legs on his shoulders, then filled his hands with her behind, to get even deeper inside of her. He squeezed, and pumped, squeezed and pumped until he couldn't stand the building up of his seed ready to explode. The moment he felt her contractions, smothering, demanding, pulling what had built up inside of him, he let go. He just let go.

One gasped at the release, the other growled at the sweetness; neither moved. He stayed on his knees, between her legs, rubbing them, first fast matching the pace of his heart, then easing up as the fierceness of his veins pumping through his body slowed. He eased her thighs off his shoulder, bent over and kissed her with a gentleness that brought tears to her eyes.

Myles rolled over gathering her in his arms and exhaled.

"Are you all right, Chrys?"

She started laughing. There was no rhyme or reason to the sound, but it was the only thing she could do. She finally stopped and exhaled.

"Myles Dunning, whew.... you are too damn funny."

He looked over at her lying in his arms, breast against his chest, thigh over his leg, then laughed along with her.

"I don't believe we just did that in the office."

"We have broken every HR rule there is," Myles laughed. "Man, if Grace saw us right now...."

Chrystina laughed. "I don't even want to think about it."

They were both silent, neither wanting to let the moment go.

"This isn't like the last time, Chrys." Myles rubbed her back. "We both know what we are doing. Before it was emotions, need. This was different. We could have stopped it, but I didn't want to stop. Did you?"

Chrystina kissed his chest as her hands roamed over it. "No."

Myles took a deep breath and exhaled. "There's something I need to say to you. You don't have to respond. Just listen."

Chrystina nodded, then continued to trace his chest with her finger.

"Anytime a man puts his hands on the woman I care about, his life is in danger." His hands continued to stroke her shoulder. "I'm in love with you, Chrys. There's no time frame I can give you as to when it happened, but there it is. We can try to ignore it for another ten years, or we can embrace it, cherish it and move forward with our lives together. I don't know where you are on this. And there is no pressure. If you don't feel the same, we'll close this night out as if it did not happen."

Chrystina stopped her hand motion, then held her head up on his shoulder. "I can't do that, Myles. No more than I could forget the night a month ago. There is nothing forgettable about you. I don't sleep around and I certainly don't sleep with my boss. At least I didn't until now."

He smiled up at her. "You know what I always wondered?"

Chrystina frowned. "Really, you're going to interrupt me when I'm about to tell you I'm in love with you too? You're going to do that?"

Myles smiled. "I knew that," he bragged then laid his head back down on his hand.

She playfully smacked his chest. "You did not know."

He took her hand into his then kissed it. "No, I did not, but I am damn happy to hear it."

"I can't believe you feel that way about me. My heart is racing, my stomach is flipping and I just feel like laughing." And she did just that.

"You know a less secure brother could get a complex from this."

"You need me to reassure you?" She kissed his neck. "I can show you how much just the thought of you turns me the hell on." She bit his nipple.

It was his turn to laugh. "Show me what you got."

She spread her legs across him, then bit his other nipple, as his hands roamed over the curve of her back. Her hand slid between their bodies until she reached her desired object. The tip of her finger swirled around the head of his penis as her tongue followed the motion on his nipple. Myles groaned as he jerked at her touch.

Her tongue trailed across his chest, down his abs, while her fingers circled him fully. She laid him flat between her inner lips; she did not take him inside, no, she placed him in the warmth of those lips, allowing the moisture dripping from her arousal to lubricate him. She slid up and down him as her tongue circled his navel and her thumbs circled his nipples. She could feel him growing between her lips. She moaned at the feel, the thought of his thickness entering her.

"Chrys," he moaned, ready to drive inside of her.

"Can you feel how much I want you inside of me? How wet I am? The heat waiting for you?"

His hand tightened around her waist. "Chrys." This time he growled.

"Yes, Myles," she chuckled. "Are you ready to take a ride?"

That was it. He lifted her by the waist and plunged inside. They both growled.

Her hands balanced on his abs, his moving from her waist to her breasts. She moved up, then down him slowly, measuring each stroke for the ultimate pleasure. The pressure building with each stroke pushed her to get more, faster.

Myles sat up, placing one nipple into his mouth, as his hand circled her waist. He guided her, pumping up and down. Both of their hearts racing to get to the anticipated release, him sucking, her pumping, neither missing a stroke. Then her womb contracted, his penis exploded and the world turned upside down.

They sat in that position. His head resting between her breasts, hers on his powerful shoulder, both waiting for their hearts to settle.

Myles raised his head, taking her face into his hands, then kissed her with a thoroughness of claiming what is now his.

"You know what just occurred to me?"

"What?"

He held her eyes. "History is repeating itself."

"How?" Chrystina frowned.

"I'm going to have to free Mitch and take care of him."

"Why?"

Myles closed his eyes against his thoughts, then sighed. He placed his head on her forehead. "He is responsible for this whole day ending up with you and

I at this point. Just like with my parents, he brought us together."

## Chapter Twenty-Three

The moment Chrystina closed the office door behind her she fell, literally fell into her desk chair. Her legs were weak. Her body was tingling and her mind was swirling.

"What did I just do?" She sat there in a daze. There was never a time she felt prohibited around Myles, but she had never gone that far. She shook herself. She had to get out of there before he tried to take her home. That was a bad idea. No one should ever see them together in that way. They had to stay professional while in the office.

She picked up her cell phone and noticed her mother had called several times in addition to sending text messages. She immediately sent a message back.

"This is why I need to drive myself," she fussed. Gathering her sneaker bag and uneaten lunch she made her way to the elevator. She had to get out of the building before her body betrayed her by going back to his office, his arms, his..... "Come on!" She anxiously pushed the button again. She needed to get away from Myles so she could think. Lord the man

was good....no, he was more than good....he was
sensational. Nothing in her dreams prepared her for
the feel of his hands, the touch of his lips or the
thickness that filled her....nothing. She leaned her
forehead against the wall. Was it possible to get wet
from a memory? Of course it was while your body is
still tingling from the reality.

The elevator swished open. "Thank goodness,"
Chrystina said as she stepped inside. Just as the door
was about to close a hand slipped inside.

"I just can't..." she started to say thinking it was
Myles.

She looked up. "AnnieMarie." She looked shell-
shocked. "What are you doing here?"

"I decided to come in to wrap up the aftermath of
the interview."

"Oh," Chrystina said wondering if...no, her office is
on the other side of the building. They hadn't been
that loud, had they? "We've missed you. Are you ready
to come back to work?"

"I don't see where I have much of a choice.
Interview requests are coming in for Myles like crazy.
We have to make some decisions on which ones he
should do."

"Send me a list. I'll take a look at them." The
elevator door opened at the lobby. "We can talk about
which ones to accept."

"Sounds good." AnnieMarie looked around. "Are
you okay?"

"Yes," Chrystina almost yelled, then caught herself.
"Why?"

"I don't know. You look a little flustered. Almost
blushing."

"No...no, um... I'm good."

"Okay," a speculative AnnieMarie replied. She looked around the main lobby. "Why are you getting off here?"

"I rode in with my mother this morning. She's going to pick me up out front."

"Oh, I'm going on down to the garage."

"I'll ride with you."

"No," she replied a little too fast.

Chrystina nodded. "Someone waiting for you?"

"No." AnnieMarie was insistent, then sighed. "I don't know." She slumped back. "Most nights when I stayed late he would be waiting for me in the parking lot."

Chrystina nodded. "When are you going to give that man a break? I hate seeing both of you so miserable."

"I'll give him a break when you let Myles in."

"What? What do you mean?" a stunned Chrystina asked.

"You have been in love with my brother for as long as I have known you. When are you going to tell him?"

Chrystina looked away, shook her head and laughed. She looked back at her friend with glee in her eyes. "I did, tonight."

AnnieMarie's eyes grew large as she stepped out of the elevator. "What? Oh my goodness. It's about time."

Chrystina blushed. "I don't know where it's going to lead or if I should let it go any further."

"Are you crazy? You don't let love wait. When you find it, grab it, hold on and cherish it. You don't just throw it away, Chrystina."

"Then stop throwing Cainan away. See you tomorrow, AnnieMarie." Chrystina waved and walked out the lobby door.

#

"Do you work this late every night?" Beverly asked as Chrystina threw her bags in the back and climbed into the passenger seat.

"Not every night, but most, especially now."

Beverly pulled off. " I called you at least five times." Her cell phone buzzed.

"Gina, this is not a good time." She listened to her daughter then looked at Chrystina. "Did you pay Gina's water bill?"

Chrystina frowned. "I forgot all about it." She could hear Gina's reaction through the phone. "I wasn't being selfish," she yelled back. "It's been a hell of a day and I forgot." She slumped back in the seat with a sigh.

Beverly put the phone back up to her ear. "Gina, stop yelling and listen. I will take care of it tomorrow. But you better have a plan in place to pay me back." She hung up the phone then glanced sideways at Chrystina.

"I need a drink."

The car stopped. Beverly turned to her daughter. "It's a Wednesday night." She looked at the dashboard. "Damn near ten o'clock and you want a drink?"

"Yes. I need a drink."

"Okay," Beverly said as she looked around. "A drink it is."

Ten minutes later the two were at a bar with a double shot of Hennessy in front of them.

Chrystina downed the drink, motioned for another.

Beverly raised an eyebrow at the daughter who usually nursed a margarita with sugar around the rim, frozen not shaken, all night.

"We made love." She downed the second glass. The bartender immediately poured another.

"Who made love?" Beverly held a hand over the glass signaling that was enough. The bartender nodded, then walked away.

Chrystina put her head down into her hands and silently screamed into them. She then propped an elbow on the bar, resting her head in her hand then looked up at her mother.

"Myles," she said. "Myles and I made love tonight."

"Myles Dunning...your boss?"

She pointed a finger at her mother. "That's the one."

"Was it good?"

Chrystina gave her a look then laughed.

Beverly crossed her legs. "Well, it's about damn time."

Chrystina gave her the side eye.

"Don't look at me like that. You've been lusting after that man since you were nineteen years old. Everybody can see it, except you two."

"He's my boss, Mother."

"Don't have nothing to do with a good dick. You find it where you can. Yours happens to be in the office. So be it."

"Mother!" Chrystina turned to pick up her glass.

Beverly took it from her. "Look." Beverly waited. "Chrystina, look at me." She closed her eyes to gather her patience, then looked at her daughter. "You are a beautiful, intelligent woman. Any man would be crazy not to recognize that. Myles saw it early on and gave you up. You don't realize it, hell I don't think he does, but in my eyes he has been grooming you to be a permanent part of his life for the last ten years. I've seen you read other boyfriends up one side of a wall and down another with no problem. My guess is you didn't feel for them the way you do for Myles. You have an opportunity here to get the happiness you deserve. He has opened the door. Don't be stupid and close it in his face. Grab that happiness and tell anyone who don't like it to kiss your behind." She stood. "Now, let's get out of this bar cause drunk ain't pretty."

An hour later Chrystina had showered and was laying in her bed, one arm over her forehead, her eyes wide open. Her body was still vibrating from Myles' touch. Even after brushing her teeth, his taste still lingered on her lips. And her heart was bursting with joy. So why did her sixth sense keep telling her to beware?

Her cell phone chimed, bringing her thoughts to the present. The name appeared on the caller ID. She sat up then rushed in when she answered the phone.

"Making love to you tonight wasn't my intention. I was trying to ease your anger by imitating your sister's crazy antics..."

"Chrys, stop." The voice soothed her immediately. "I knew you would be stressing over this. Let me ease your mind. Tonight wasn't a mistake. I love you. Get some rest. We're starting our morning together in the gym."

Chrystina hung up the phone and closed her eyes. She didn't need the voice message. Tonight she had the real thing.

## Chapter Twenty-Four

Myles entered his parents' home through the kitchen entrance. Placing his briefcase on the floor, he stripped out of his suit jacket then rolled up his sleeves. He opened the refrigerator to grab some items to make a sandwich. He had not had a chance to eat all day, then used up all his strength making love to Chrystina. God she was amazing. He smiled at the memory as he put the bread on the breakfast bar. He turned to the sound of the door from the basement opening.

"Good evening, Mr. Dunning."

Myles began to chuckle as he put the cold cuts on the counter. "Not you too." He reached into the cabinet to pull down two plates. "Have a sandwich with me?"

Jerome nodded as he took a seat. "You don't like being called Mr. Dunning?"

"Not when you have called me Myles for the last ten years."

"You are now the head of the bank and this family," Jerome said as he caught a beer bottle Myles threw his way. "That comes with a certain amount of respect."

"Well, I appreciate that, Jerome," Myles said as he continued making the sandwiches. "We had somewhat of a trying day."

Jerome took a swig of his beer. "Your father and I would hash through how his days went nightly. I'm here if you want to talk about the office."

Myles slid a sandwich over to Jerome. "What did you talk about with Dad?"

"Everything from Mitchell, the board, public fascination, but most of all the security of the grounds."

It was clear to all members of the family that Jerome was never just a driver. There was some military, security, and dangerous aspects to the man's demeanor and the way he handled certain situations. No one questioned why he was brought into the family, until now.

Myles took a seat on the opposite side of the breakfast bar. "Why did Dad hire you? Please...be frank." Biting into his sandwich, Jerome knew what Myles was asking.

"Your father was a wealthy man and president of an international bank. Over the course of time he received a number of viable threats to his person and his family. He wanted to ensure you all were safe at all times."

"Who were the threats from?"

"In addition to expected kidnapping attempts, there were...closer threats from Walker. But that wasn't what concerned your father the most. It was the people Walker continued to associate with."

"Walker himself was not a threat." Myles nodded his understanding. "What are your duties?"

"To protect his wife and children from possible retaliation from anyone connected to Walker or seeking to use them against him for extortion."

"Have there been any incidents that fueled his concerns?"

"One or two that was handled outside of the public knowledge." Jerome nodded.

"And you do this alone? Just you?"

"There are times when you only need one person; however, when the full family needs coverage I have friends."

Myles gave him an inquisitive glance.

"Yes. I'm damn good." Jerome smirked. "Let's take the beer down to the security room. There's some activity from earlier today that should be brought to your attention."

The two men grabbed their plates and beer, then walked down the back staircase to the basement. They walked past the theater room, the recreation room, Daisy's living quarters and Jerome's rooms until they reached the last door in the hallway.

Inside the security room there was a small office, then an open area with a conference table that seated eight and a wall with three monitors.

"Have a seat," Jerome said as he turned on the lights.

Myles sat at the conference table facing the wall of monitors. As they each came on he scanned them to determine what they displayed.

"You've changed it around a little since the last time I was here."

"We added another monitor with a little more security."

"Is there a reason for the enhancement?"

"Yes." Jerome pulled a chair out from the table, sat then turned to face Myles. "Someday soon I'm going to tell you more than you may want to know. For now, let's look at today's footage." Jerome zoomed in on the center monitor.

Myles sat forward to take in what was happening on the monitor.

"Who are the men in the SUV?" he asked as the scene with his uncle unfolded.

"His name is Sergi Koslov. He is the enforcer for Stephan Pavel."

"I don't know the mane," Myles stated.

"You would have no reason to, until now."

Myles raised an eyebrow. "Who is he?"

"Let me fast forward to when your uncle leaves the vehicle." Jerome did what he indicated.

Myles sat up. "Is that blood?"

"It is."

Myles looked at Jerome then back at the screen. "What happened? Is Walker all right?"

Jerome turned off the monitor. "I don't give a damn about Walker's well-being at this moment. He brought the Russian Mafia to your parents' home. I am very uncomfortable with that. When I get uncomfortable people die."

"The Russian Mafia?" a stunned Myles questioned. "What in the hell are you talking about?"

"Stephan Pavel and his family are the branch of the Russian mafia located here in Virginia. They are into prostitution, guns, and gambling. It seems Walker is indebted to them. How deep my sources do not know. They are still working on gathering that information. There were three people in the vehicle with Walker. I have been able to identify Koslov because we had a clear view of him. The other two men never stepped out of the vehicle. However." He clicked a button on the remote. "We were able to get a partial on this man. Stephan Pavel. I can only guess that Walker is in deep to qualify for a personal visit from Pavel. Or it could be that Walker has access to something that Pavel wants."

"Such as?"

"We'll get to that. Did it ever occur to you to have an autopsy performed on your father?"

Myles' head snapped around to look at Jerome. "Should it have?"

Jerome shrugged. "There were things, small incidents that concerned me at the time of Mr. Dunning's death."

"Such as?" The man now had Myles' undivided attention.

"For one, your father was healthy as a pure-bred horse. He worked out daily. Of course he ate pretty much what he wanted to. However I was with him during his last physical. There was nothing abnormal." He took a swig of his beer. "If it was my father I would have a conversation with his physician. If he gave him a clean bill of health, and in light of the people Walker is involved with, I'd want to know what sent my father to his grave."

Jerome sat back staring poignantly at Myles.

Myles held the man's glare. "You are insinuating that someone may have contributed to his death."

"I could be completely off base with this, Myles."

"You don't think that you are. You would not have mentioned it otherwise. Do you think Walker had something to do with my father's death?"

"That would be a yes. It may be inadvertent on his part. However, people may want him to have control of the bank or possibly control of the family. What better way than to eliminate the head of both."

The vein in Myles' neck was throbbing.

"I want to be clear here, Jerome. You believe it is possible my father did not die of natural causes?" Myles leaned forward.

Jerome nodded. "There is something else I need you to consider. You are now the head of the family and the bank; in my estimation that now makes you and anyone close to you a target."

## Chapter Twenty-Five

Vivian sat in the room with her husband and three children as they shared movie night. Her mind wasn't on the family drama on the projector screen. You see there were rules in their house. No one in the family missed Sunday dinner, movie night, or game night in their household without cause. It was their way of having family time together. In all honesty she was present, but her mind was actually 15 miles away at her brother Walker's house.

There were two things that she knew for a fact. First, there was no way she was going to allow Russian thugs into her family's bank. Second, Walker was going to go away for a long time, either to prison or rehab, and at the moment she did not care which.

"Are you okay?" her husband Ken asked as he put his arms around her shoulders.

"No." She snuggled up to him in the seat. "I was just thinking about Winnie. Her and Hep will never have moments like this again." She told the white lie to cover her true concern.

Ken kissed her cheek, then pulled her a little closer. "I know. Why don't you give her a call?"

Vivian looked up at him with eagerness in her eyes. "Really? You don't mind?"

"Well, I will miss the warmth of my wife in my arms. But you go ahead, give her a call. I will consider this with cause."

She smiled up at the love of her life then snuggled a little closer. "I'll call her later when the movie is over."

An hour later Vivian picked up the phone, uncertain what she would do. Should she help Walker get the position and save his miserable life or tell Winnie the truth and let Grace deal with the problem?

"Winnie, hi, this is Vivian. Did I catch you at bad time?"

"No. I was doing some reading. How are you, Viv?"

"I miss him," Vivian declared. "Miss his calm presence. His wit. Hep was always doing something to get under Walker's skin to keep us laughing." She hesitated. "How are you?"

"Ha," Winnie sniffed. "A shell of a woman right now. But don't you dare tell my children I said that."

Vivian smiled. "Your secret is safe with me. You know I'm only a phone call away any time you want to talk."

"I know. Thank you, Viv. I'll take you up on that one day. But right now I don't want to burden anyone with my sadness."

"Please do, Winnie. I have strong shoulders. I miss him too and sometimes I just want to talk about him." She hesitated. "Winnie, I understand you had a visit from Walker this morning."

"Hmmm," she laughed. "Yes, I did."

"He said he spoke with you about a job."

"No, he asked me to return the controlling shares of the bank back to him. He feels they were stolen by Hep. In fact he stated I was wrong for not turning them over to him when Hep died."

"Are you kidding me?" Vivian sighed.

"I'm afraid not. In fact he threatened my children when I told him I gave all my shares to Myles."

"He did not," Vivian said as she sat in her private sitting room. Walker was more desperate than she originally thought. He had done so many crazy things in the past it's hard to believe what he told her today.

"Winnie, Walker is in trouble. Will you have lunch with me tomorrow and let me tell you what I know?"

"I can do that," Winnie agreed.

Vivian exhaled. "Thank you, Winnie. I think it's time we get Walker in line."

After disconnecting the call, Vivian dialed the number to her closest ally. That person, who asked no questions, just did whatever she could to help.

"Grace, where are you?" The music could be heard through the phone.

"Aunt Vivian?"

"Yes."

"Hold on. Let me step outside."

Vivian heard movement on the other end of the line. Then she heard a door close. The loud background music stopped.

"Aunt Viv, are you still there?"

"Yes, I'm here. Where are you?"

"I'm in DC doing some things for the bank."

"I thought you were in New York."

"Yes, I was earlier today. Do you need something? Are you okay?"

"I'm fine, Grace. Don't worry about me."

"I try not to, but I worry about all of you. I can't help it."

"There is something. I need you to check on a person by the name of Stephan Pavel. He is the owner of a real estate company called Pavel and Sons."

"Is he the father or the son?"

"I don't know. However, before I get involved with these people I would like to know who I'm dealing with."

"Okay. Do you want to know about him or the company?"

"Both. I need to know about any illegal connections he has."

"Okay..." There was some hesitation. "I'll find out what I can and get back with you in the morning."

"Thank you, Grace." Vivian smiled then disconnected the call. She was going to sleep well knowing she would have some answers in the morning before she met with Winnie. At this point she had no idea if Walker was pulling a fast one or was seriously in trouble.

#

Grace hung up the phone with her gut telling her something wasn't right. Aunt Vivian rarely called her when she was away working. They had a loving relationship and tended to talk about anything and everything. She was the aunt who let her try on make up at 14, which her mother had forbid. The aunt who covered for her whenever she went somewhere her parents told her not to go. Vivian was the one who broke down all the barriers about sex to her. Yes, she was the one who told her not to be afraid of her own sexuality and life had never been the same. So when this aunt calls and Grace hears concern in her voice she pays attention. Grace looked at the name she put in her phone and knew what she had to do. She walked back into the club, said good night and goodbye to the man she had just hit on then walked out the front door. Twenty minutes later she was knocking on the door of another man.

"Roark, open the door. I know you are in there and you better not have another woman in there with you." She banged on the door trying to contain her laughter. "Roark," she yelled and was about to say more when the door flung open.

"Grace...are you crazy?"

She started past the half-dressed man standing in the doorway then walked straight back to the closed bedroom door.

"Grace, don't..."

It was too late. She had kicked the bedroom door in, then turned to him and yelled, "Who in the hell is this?"

The half-dressed woman jumped out of bed and began picking up her discarded clothes. "I think a better question should be who are you?" the woman yelled back.

"Who am I?" Grace yelled. "You are in here with my husband and you want to know who I am?" She turned to the man. "Really, Roark?"

"Husband?" the woman and FBI Special Agent Byron Roark asked at the same time.

Grace turned on him. "You conveniently forgot you have a wife and children at home?" Then she turned on the woman who was trying desperately to put her clothes on. "And you. Did it matter at all that he was married with three children?"

"Children?" The woman stopped buttoning her blouse then quickly put on her shoes. "I had no idea."

"You expect me to believe that?" Grace charged at the woman who wasn't moving fast enough for her liking. "How long has this been going on?" She looked between Byron and the woman.

"Look." He stood between the two women. "It may be best for you to leave. I will handle this."

"You are going to handle me, Roark, really?" Grace railed on as the woman rushed into the living room with Roark in tow. "You're going to handle me? This I have got to see."

"I will call you," Byron said to the woman as she ran by him.

"Don't bother," she screamed back as the door slammed behind her.

Grace walked into the living room, then took a seat at the breakfast bar that separated the living room and kitchen. "I've never seen that one before. Is she new?"

Byron knew not to say anything. He had seen this side of Grace before. Until she got what she wanted, which seemed to be his attention, this tirade was going to continue. He leaned against the wall that led to the kitchen in nothing but a robe staring at the crazy woman whom he called a friend. He had no idea why he put up with her other than the fact that she was the one woman who seemed to be immune to his charm. "Why are you here?"

"I need you to check something out for me." She jumped up and walked over to the refrigerator. "Do you want a beer?"

Byron shook his head. "Sure, let me get dressed." He walked into the bedroom. "How is your family doing?"

"We are all dealing with things. Myles was named CEO of the bank. That's why I'm here in DC. He has some things he wanted me to check out."

"How have you been?"

"Okay," Grace admitted as she pulled two beers out then sat back down. "So, who was she?" she asked loud enough for him to hear her in the bedroom.

"Just someone I met at a bar."

"And you brought her to your home? Isn't that one thing you told me to never do?"

"You are a female," he replied as he walked out of the bedroom in sweats, pulling a tee shirt over his head. "I am a highly trained killing machine." He kissed her on the cheek, then picked up his beer.

"What is so important that you had to pull the angry wife act?"

Grace smiled. "I like doing that one to you."

"Yes, well, the next time you will replace whoever you chase from my bed."

"That's not going to happen," she argued as she crossed her legs.

"Why do you treat me so bad? Am I that unappealing to you?"

"No, and you know you are too good looking for your own good." She shrugged. "You're my friend and I want to keep you."

"Sleeping with me is a sure way to accomplish that." He slumped onto the sofa next to her.

"No, then I'd have to discard you."

"Did you discard Michael?"

Grace sent him a warning look. "You know how I feel about Jonathan. So don't go there." She saw the hurt look on his face. "Oh, Byron." She punched him. "Let's not have the same fight again. Jonathan....well, he's that one for me."

"Yeah, well, where is he? He went back to London to work for your competitor."

"Hell, you would have too with the offer they made him."

Byron didn't say anything for a moment, then conceded, "You have a point there." They both laughed. "He's got to be one of the richest of our classmates to date, excluding you."

"Oh, I don't know about that. But he is doing well."

Byron exhaled. "Well, I certainly don't want to spend my time with you talking about the man who stole your heart from me." He sat up. "What do you need?"

"I need you to do a search on a name for me. And if he has any illegal ties I should know about."

"What's his name?"

Grace clicked on her phone as Byron opened his laptop that was on the table.

"Stephan Pavel. He owns a real estate business, I'm told."

Byron logged into the FBI database, then keyed in the name. "Let's see what we have."

The silence that followed made Grace uneasy. "What's wrong?" she asked seeing the expression on his face.

"Grace, where did you get this name?"

"My Aunt Vivian."

He stood to get his office cell phone and dialed a number. "Pete, it's Roark. Log onto the system for me and key in this name, Stephan Pavel." He listened to his partner as he keyed in the name and began sharing the information. Finally, he nodded. "I'll see you in fifteen minutes."

He disconnected the call, then turned back to Grace.

"What is it?" she asked.

"Why are you searching the name of a member of the Russian Mafia?"

## Chapter Twenty-Six

**"Y**ou're late."

"Yes, well I wasn't sure...I mean, I didn't know if or how....."

"Are you confused about last night?"

"Yes," she sighed out loud. "Aren't you?" She dropped her bag with her clothes for work to the floor then walked towards him. "Don't get it twisted, it was a hell of a night. I just don't know how to act around you now. I mean, you are my boss. We work together and as much as I enjoyed last night, we...us is new. You know what I mean?"

Myles smiled as he looked down at her. It was amazing how youthful she looked with her hair in a ponytail rather than that French roll and no makeup on her face. Had he missed that too? Wait, how old was she? He remembered when they first met he made a mental note to keep his distance because she was nineteen at the time, he was twenty-five. She was an intern working in his department. He felt it was inappropriate to think of her in a sexual way. It probably still was, however age wasn't an issue at this point. She should be twenty-eight now.

"Myles?" Chrystina called out.

Clearing his mind, he stared at her, not sure what she had just said. "Do you know you are short?"

Chrystina raised one eyebrow. "Excuse you?"

He laughed. "You are short."

She looked to the side then back at him. "Yes, well, I don't have my heels on. I have on sneakers, which I just bought, along with the clothes this morning so I could workout with you."

"You did that for me?"

She gave him a slow once over. "I did it for me. You just happen to be a bonus."

They stood there staring at each other for a long moment.

"Why don't you put your clothes in the locker room. When you come back let's take a run on the treadmill. We can analyze while we run."

Chrystina took a step back. "All right, I can do that." She picked up her bag then looked around. "Umm...where is the locker room?"

Myles frowned. "You don't know your way around?"

"No."

"You've never been up here?"

With her bag in one hand, the other went to her hip. "Myles, look around." He did. "Now look at me. Does it look like I been on any of this equipment?"

Myles laughed then walked towards her. "It sure felt like it last night." He grabbed her ponytail. "Follow me, short stuff. Allow me to show you around."

Ten minutes later they were on the treadmills on the balcony of the gym.

"I had no idea all of this was up here," Chrystina said as she looked around. "I love the view of the skyline."

On the balcony of the gym were a row of bikes, treadmills, and elliptical machines. There were also weight benches and two battle rope stations, literally a mini version of the indoor equipment with the exception of the circuit machines.

"My dad liked working out on the inside with the air conditioning. I like the natural elements when I work out."

"I have a feeling natural elements is going to sweat my hair out."

"A little sweat never hurt anyone." Myles pushed a few buttons on one of the treadmills. "Here, I'll set this one to no incline and the speed to gradually increase every 2 minutes for 20 minutes. That's very low impact so we can talk as we walk."

"Low impact?" She sent him a questioning gaze before stepping onto the machine.

"Low." He grinned as he stepped on to the treadmill next to her.

She watched as he began. "You are running. What is yours set on?"

"High impact, mountains."

"Un huh...you can run and talk?"

"I've been at it for a while." He grinned at her. "A hell of a night, wouldn't you say. Which part did you enjoy the most, the missionary or the ride?"

Chrystina stumbled, grabbing the handles to catch herself before falling.

"Are you okay over there?" Myles smiled down at her as he continued to run.

"Ha ha, Myles. You are trying to distract me on my first day of working out. You got jokes."

"No, I'm curious on your likes and dislikes."

"My sister said I wouldn't know what a good ride was if it slapped me in the face. I beg to differ with her now. I can assess the impact of a good ride." She grinned at him. "That was a ride."

He nodded his head as he ran. "That was a ride." He laughed. "You have a sister?"

Chrystina gave him a side-glance. "Yes, I do. Her name is Gina."

"I did not know that."

"You had no reason to."

"You've worked for me in one capacity or another for almost ten years. I should know something about you. You know everything about me."

"It's my job to know everything about you, Myles. I have to assess your every need. Not vice-versa."

"You are very good at your job, Ms. Price." He winked.

"Thank you," she said as she glanced at him.

They held the look for a long moment until Myles turned away. "Is she younger or older?"

"Who?"

"Your sister." Myles smiled.

"Oh, Gina is younger, thinner, more beautiful, but not smarter than me. It's the one thing I have over her."

"I doubt that. You are a very beautiful woman."

"Yeah, yeah, cute but chubby. I've heard it all before."

"I felt every inch of you. You are curvy, but not chubby," Myles corrected. "Now that you've started working out your body will slim down, if that's what you want it to do."

"Well, I've never attempted to workout before. It may be too late to slim down. How much longer do we have to do this?"

"It's never too late. It's all in what you put into it."
He glanced at his watch and grinned. "Another fifteen
minutes."

He laughed at the look she gave him. "So.... do you
have other brothers and sisters?"

"No, just my mom and us."

"What about your father?"

"Oh, he's around." She shrugged. "My parents
divorced when we were very young. But both of them
have been an intricate part of our lives. Keith never
married again. I think they still have a thing for each
other."

"My mother always says once you find real love the
artificial is easily recognized. Your heart yearns for the
authentic."

Chrystina looked over at him. "Is that why you and
Savannah did not work out?"

Myles smirked then looked towards the blue sky
with the white puffy clouds in the distance. "Savannah
may fit the outward expectation a man would seek,
however, the deeper you explore the less value there is
until you literally see nothing. A black hole is all that's
there."

"I can believe that."

Myles laughed.

"Sorry," Chrystina laughed. "I didn't mean it quite
that way."

"Yes, you did." He glanced at her. "You're
beginning to slow down. Walk it through. I'll grab us
some water before we start the next exercise."

"What?" Chrystina glared at him. "What
next...What?"

Myles grinned as he pulled two bottles of water
from the refrigerator in the corner and threw one to
her. "That was just a warm up to get you started." He

walked over to the weight bench. "Let's do a few sit ups."

"Who is going to do sit ups? Where?" she asked after drinking half a bottle of water.

Myles pointed to the bench. "You. Right here."

Chrystina laughed. "Myles, you don't understand. I have never done a sit up in my life."

"There is always a first time. Have a seat."

She shook her head. "Myles...."

"Sit," he said. "I'll spot you."

"Spot me? What does that mean?"

He reached out and took her hand. "Come on. Lie down on the bench."

With a wary look, she unzipped her jacket, threw it on the treadmill handle. She put her hands on her hips. Then she looked up at Myles and exhaled. "Okay," she said then sat on the bench.

Myles wished she had kept the jacket on. With the V-neck tee he could see the swell of her breasts. He vividly remembered the feel of them in his hands, the taste of them between his lips. How the hell was he supposed to concentrate on her breathing and not on her breasts?

"Alright," he said. "Lie back and cross your hands over your breasts."

She complied.

"Good. Now bring your feet up."

She did as he instructed.

"Be careful how you arch your back. The idea is to feel the crunch right here." He touched her stomach. "We are going to start off with a low count, like 10 reps."

Chrystina spread her legs wide then looked between them at him. "Ten? That low?"

Myles groaned and wished she hadn't done that. He remembered how those thick thighs felt around him last night. Whew, he could do this, he thought. This is for her. "Yes, ten is low."

"And you want my feet up like this?"

"Yes, I'll anchor them as you pull up to your knees."

"Up to my knees?"

"Yes." Myles laughed at the bemused look on her face. "I believe in you. You can do this."

"Okay." Chrystina settled in to concentrate on getting her body to do as Myles commanded. If he wasn't so damn fine and could bang her brains out with such force, she would get up and say the heck with it. But the truth of the matter is she appreciated him taking time to work out with her. It was seven in the morning. They both had a mountain of work on their plate today in addition to moving. Yet, he was there with her. Yep she was going to do this for him, but mostly for herself. "You start with one and go from there, right?"

Myles bent at the end of the bench and placed his hands around her ankles. "That's right. Let's get this first one out of the way."

Chrystina pulled up half way on the first one.

"That was good. This time come all the way up to your knees. Bring it to me, Chrystina."

She did another, bringing her closer to where he stood over her. The next one caused a problem. The vision of him standing between her legs caused her stomach to flutter. Three more came easily as she used reaching his lips as her goal. When she reached nine, her body began to tell her to stop.

"I'm not feeling this, Myles, so this is only for you."

"Come on, Chrys. You can give me one more, just one more."

She gave it her all. Holding her abdomen in, she pulled up and let it rip.

The fart that escaped was loud. Myles fell backwards onto the deck. Chrystina jumped up from the bench and ran to stand over Myles.

"Myles, oh my God, Myles. I am so sorry." Her hands flew to the face that was red with embarrassment. "Myles, Myles. Oh my God. I can't believe that happened. I didn't know it was coming. I am so sorry."

Myles was rolling onto his back. His body was shaking as this weird sound escaped him.

Chrystina stopped apologizing and stared down at him. "Are you laughing at me?"

He did not respond. It seemed he was too consumed with laughter. Her hands flew to her hips.

"Myles Dunning, you get yourself up right now. Stop laughing at me," she protested.

"Chrys." He looked at her then he burst into laughter again. "I'm trying." He put his hand up. "I swear I'm trying." He laughed, then took in several deep breaths to contain himself. "Whew." He sat up with his arms around his knees taking in deep breaths. "Baby, that last one blew me away." He fell backwards laughing again.

"Myles, I can't believe you are laughing at me."

"I can't believe you farted on me." He laughed out loud then. He stood then bent over this time, sniffed, then stood straight. "Okay." He turned to her. "I'm sorry I laughed at you."

With her arms wrapped around her waist and him calmed down, Chrystina whispered, "I'm sorry I farted on you."

Myles laughed again. Chrystina turned away in dismay. "Oh, come on, Chrys. Don't be mad at me for laughing. It was funny. Passing gas is natural." He pulled her in an embrace. "It goes to show how natural we can be with each other." He put a finger under her chin and brought her eyes to his. "Just like kissing someone whose very presence puts a smile on your face."

Chrystina bashfully looked up at him. "It wasn't just a thing?"

"The fart?"

She hit his chest as he laughed.

"I'm sorry." Myles thought for a second. "No. Want to know why?"

"Why?"

"Because I want to make love to you again. But for now I'll settle for a kiss." He lowered his lips to hers then gently caressed the thickness of them.

What in the hell was happening? She was losing her mind. Chrystina knew pulling away was the smart thing to do, but it felt too good. Her dreams never went this deep, never burned like this. She never knew a touch, a kiss, could burn so deep and she had a feeling he wasn't done yet. Throwing all caution to the wind Chrystina plunged in, meeting him stroke by stroke until a sound from inside the gym broke through.

Myles slowly pulled away. "Keep kissing like that and I will let you fart on me every day." He grabbed her jacket and walked towards the entrance of the gym.

It slowly dawned on her what he said. "Myles Dunning, no you didn't."

Myles held the door open. "No, I did not...you did," he said as she snatched her jacket. "AnnieMarie is going to get a kick out of this," he laughed.

"Don't you dare tell her."

"It's the only way to air this situation out."

Chrystina was so embarrassed she tried to walk faster to get away from him.

"Did you think I would let you walk away without telling? Oh no. I'm telling everyone I know about the pressure release you just had."

Chrystina turned to face him. "I cannot believe you would take advantage of me during a vulnerable time such as this."

His laughter was contagious. Chrystina had to join in.

"Now that was a stretch. There is nothing vulnerable about you, Chrystina Price. It's a part of your charm."

Hearing laughter come from Myles filled her in an unexplainable way. She had heard his laughter before, but this was different. The new pressures on him would cause a lesser man to be filled with anger. This was the sound of a man who was enjoying this moment in his life. The thought of being a part of making that happen for him made Chrystina smile.

He leaned forward and whispered in her ear, "If you keep looking at me like that, Chrystina, this thing between us is going to move a lot faster than either of us is prepared for."

The ding from the elevator arriving interrupted the moment. And not a minute too soon, Chrystina thought, as a few employees walked in ready for their morning workout.

Myles' attention turned to the employees entering the room. Christina saw the carefree Myles disappear.

"Myles?" Chrystina called out. "Is everything all right?"

The expression on his face clearly indicated something was amiss.

"There are some things that came to light last night I need to share with you. Let's shower and change. I'll meet you in the office."

The change in his mood was instantaneous. She wondered what caused the sudden concern. "All right."

She continued to watch as he walked towards the male shower rooms. Was it something she said, she wondered, as she looked around at the employees now working out on various equipment? Taking a few steps toward the female shower rooms it dawned on her. Myles was fine, free, open before the employees came in. Could it be he did not want to be open with her around the employees? Is it possible he did not want to be seen in public with her? She glanced around the room self-consciously. Just as sudden as the thought occurred to her she wiped it from her mind. She refused to believe that of Myles.

## Chapter Twenty-Seven

It is time, AnnieMarie thought, as she pulled into the parking garage. She was going to have to face Cainan sooner or later. The last time they talked was a month ago. The night before her father's death to be exact. That was the night they realized what was happening between them was more than a mere flirtation. The feelings were real. The night had replayed in her mind several times until she realized Cainan was keeping something from her. She wanted to make love to him that night, and knew, could feel it deep inside that he wanted her just as much. But he pulled away. He insisted that she speak with her father first. It was imperative to him, that her father gave his blessing before they went any further.

It wasn't until now that she came to the conclusion that Cainan knew the reason her father did not want her to be involved with him. What was the reason and why wouldn't he tell her? The unanswered questions would not go away. Whatever her father's reason it did not explain why Cainan would not confide in her. She would give him one chance to tell her and pray it was something she could live with.

AnnieMarie parked her car, then used the employee entrance to access the elevators. She stopped in her office first and was not at all surprised to see her assistant, Phillip Haynes at his desk.

"Well it's about time you decided to rejoin the land of the living. I noticed some of the documents that were on your desk now have your signature. Did you come into the office last night?"

All of this was asked as they walked from the entrance of the Public Relations suite to her office, and subsequent desk.

"I did," AnnieMarie replied. "I have a lot to catch up on."

"I'll say." Phillip gave her a document. "These are the requests for interviews for Mr. Dunning, along with my notes on who is significant and who is not. You also have a number of international ad agencies wondering if we would like to increase our print ads with their publications."

AnnieMarie looked over the document as she stood behind her desk. "Return calls to these," she said as she used a red pen to mark the call sheet accordingly. "Send apologies to these." She glanced at the bottom of the sheet. "I need to do a little more research on the results from previous ads before making a decision on increased space." She dropped her purse in the bottom drawer, then grabbed her coffee cup.

"You're leaving?"

"Just to the cafe to get some coffee. I'll be right back." She walked towards the door.

"He hasn't been there in the last few weeks," Phillip called over his shoulder.

AnnieMarie stopped then turned back to Phillip.

"You will probably find him in his office," he said as he stood to face her. "No response to text messages, no returned phone calls. Nothing from you in weeks has pushed him off his game. I suggest you go to his turf."

She held his glare for a long moment. "You're upset with me."

"Yes, and he should be too. However, he is more worried about you than upset." Phillip walked to the door where she stood. "He's a decent guy. You are usually a pretty nice person. If you weren't my boss I'd take you for myself."

She smiled at him. "It would never work. You are too arrogant."

"True. Cainan on the other hand is confident and gives a damn one way or another when it comes to you. I don't know what happened with you two, but I think he is the type you keep."

AnnieMarie took a deep breath then sighed. "I wish things were that simple."

"The degree of difficulty is what you allow it to be." He walked by her and returned to his desk. "We will cover the rest of this when you get back from your coffee break."

"I know you don't want me to share this with other people, but you really are a good guy."

"Lies you tell. Now man up and make the first move." Phillip smiled as she walked away.

AnnieMarie walked around the corner and down the hallway with the empty coffee cup in her hand determined to get this first contact out of the way. She tossed the cup around, not certain why she was so nervous about seeing Cainan again. That wasn't true, she knew exactly why. She had not returned his calls or messages and did not have the decency to tell him why. Her pace slowed, as she got closer to the point of no return. She smoothed her skirt down, then ran her hand over her hair.

She took the next step that gave an eagle view into Cainan's office. Her heart sank.

He looked tired. He was on the telephone talking to what sounded like a client. The strain in his voice let her know he was struggling to keep his temper in tow. She watched his hand go up to smooth out his brow. It was his tell move to keep him from going off on the person on the other end of the call. She stopped tossing the cup and smiled.

The moment he looked up, their eyes met and held. Time stood still as Cainan slowly rose from his seat.

The person on the other end of the call must have said something."Mr. Peters, I will have to call you back." He nodded without taking his eyes from hers. "I understand, Mr. Peters. I will call you back." He hung up the phone as she walked in and closed the door.

"How are you?" Cainan asked in a voice laced with concern.

A small smile touched her lips. "Wishing I could tell my father I love him one last time."

Cainan nodded. "I know."

They held each other's gaze, neither willing to look away, both longing to touch.

"I read your messages. Thank you for the flowers and the strawberries. That was very sweet."

"Did you eat them? I know you love them covered in chocolate, so I thought...." He shrugged.

"Each one reminded me of you," she replied with a tear at the brim of falling. "I can't see you romantically." The tear fell.

Cainan held out a hand motioning for her to have a seat. "Your father disapproved?" he asked as he sat behind his desk.

"Yes." AnnieMarie wiped at the tear. "Can you tell me why, Cainan?" Her voice was whisper soft. "I believe you have the answer to my question. Can you tell me why?"

His eyes fell from hers. She could see he was struggling with something internal.

"Your father was a very wise man. He was good to me in ways I can't say at this time. If he had given any indication he was uncomfortable with me seeing you I would have honored his wishes." He looked up at her. "We were friends before the kiss. Is it possible to keep that intact?"

AnnieMarie closed her eyes, prayed he would someday trust her enough tell her what he was keeping from her. But today was not that day. She stood.

"Okay, friend. I'm going to the cafe to get my morning coffee. Will you join me?"

Cainan opened the cabinet behind him, pulled out his Barack Obama coffee cup that matched her Michelle cup. "Okay, Michelle, what veggies are you making me eat today?" he asked, smiling as he stepped from behind his desk.

Relieved laughter filled the air as AnnieMarie opened the door. "Well, Barack and Michelle are gone. May their love live on forever."

"Let's drink our coffee in their honor today." They clicked their president and first lady cups together.

"I'm going to miss them," Cainan said. "You know what I am not going to miss?"

"What?" AnnieMarie looked up at him as they walked.

Cainan stopped and frowned down at her. "Squash. I'm telling you as beautiful as Michelle is, that vegetable garden was killing me. I bet Barack is sneaking out eating a good steak or burger somewhere."

AnnieMarie's laugher rang out. Her heart filled with sadness and love. Sadness because she knew, for now, she could not tell him how much love she had in her heart for him.

The two walked into the cafe and took a seat. "Mitch is gone?" Cainan asked.

"I'm afraid so. I feel bad about it. He's been around since I can remember."

"What he tried to do was pretty low." Cainan shook his head. "Myles handled it well and was able to pull the contract despite Mitch's action. He is going to be a good leader."

"I understand you had a hand in making it happen."

"After learning the part I played in the deception it was the very least I could do."

"AnnieMarie."

She turned to her brother's voice. "Myles, good morning." She saw the surprised look in his eyes. "What?"

"Nothing." Myles looked at Cainan. "Would you excuse us for a moment?"

Cainan nodded. "Of course," he said as he started to stand.

"No, don't get up. We'll just step over here."

Cainan watched as the two talked. He was a little relieved when he saw the confused expression on AnnieMarie's face then heard the laughter from the two. The conversation was not about him and her, he thought as they both returned to the table.

Myles hit him on the shoulder. "Please accept my apology for interrupting." He then turned to AnnieMarie. "You got it?"

"I have it." She waved him off. "I'll take care of it right now."

Myles nodded then walked off.

Cainan looked at her with a raised eyebrow.

AnnieMarie smiled shaking her head. "You don't want to know."

# Chapter Twenty-Eight

"It looks like a war zone out there," AnnieMarie said as she entered Myles' office.

"Did you get it?"

She had seen that look many times before on her big brother, but it had been years.

"Yes, I have it. It took going to a number of novelty stores, but your promise for lunch at Maggiano's more than compensates for my time. Besides, I am curious why you wanted one of these of all things."

Myles took the bag from her. "You'll see. Was Chrystina at her desk?"

"No," AnnieMarie replied as she watched her brother. "I see all the boxes. Did you decide to move into your new office today?"

"Yes, Chrystina and Mrs. Vazquez are packing up both offices." Myles shrugged. "With all that happened with Mitch yesterday, I feel the move is necessary."

"I set up the press conference. We need to be in front of this story before it hits the media."

Myles nodded as he continued working on the device. "I want Cainan Scott with me during the announcement."

"Cainan?" The sound of concern resonated. "Why?"

Myles looked over at her. "He's a good man. What he did for us yesterday was nothing short of brilliant. I want to do more with him."

"But Myles-"

He held up his hand. "No argument here, AnnieMarie. I want Cainan there. I expect you to make it happen." They heard a sound outside the door. "That's Chrystina." Myles grinned, then ran over and placed the device where he wanted it. "Stay there," he instructed his sister, then sat behind his desk as if he had been concentrating on a document. He pushed the intercom on his desk. "Chrystina, would you step in here for a minute and bring your tablet?"

"Be right in," the response came back.

AnnieMarie started to walk towards one of the chairs in front of his desk.

"No, no." He waved her off. "Stay there." Then returned to the document.

She stared with mild curiosity at her bother, who seldom displayed childlike tendencies. It was great to see him like this again.

Chrystina walked in, opening the door in a way that blocked AnnieMarie from view.

"I want to work on the announcement to the staff today," he said without raising his head to look at her.

"Yes, sir, this is going to be a delicate situation," Chrystina said as she walked over and took her regular seat.

The loud sound of a human passing gas filled the room.

Chrystina jumped up with an expression of pure shock on her face.

"Flatulence again, Chrystina? I mean really!"

She looked down into the seat and screamed, "Myles Dunning, I'm going to kill you."

Myles was falling over in the chair laughing as she took the whoopee cushion from the chair and ran around the desk hitting him with it. "I can't believe you'd do something so childish. Shame on you," she yelled.

He grabbed her around her waist and pulled her onto his lap. "I got you on that one." He then proceeded to kiss her until she was no longer angry.

They both jumped when they heard the door slam.

Chrystina's expression was priceless and AnnieMarie had to struggle to keep her laugher from escaping. She stood there with hands on hips, tapping her foot, frowning at the two of them.

"So, this is what you two do behind closed doors all day long."

"No, of course not," Chrystina declared.

"We will now." Myles continued to laugh. "You have to admit that was funny," he said as he looked at the blushing Chrystina.

"AnnieMarie, I promise you this is the first time. Well not the first time we have kissed, but certainly the first time he's ever pulled something like this."

AnnieMarie stood there with a raised eyebrow and a furious expression on her face. "Is that so?"

"Yes." Chrystina looked from her to Myles who was not helping the situation by sitting there grinning. "Say something, Myles."

"I never knew a sister's blush could be so red."

The look she gave Myles caused AnnieMarie to laugh out loud.

Chrystina turned on her. "Oh, don't encourage him." She glanced back at Myles trying to give him the evil eye.

"I have no idea what is going on with you two, but I like it." AnnieMarie laughed. "I cannot believe you are acting like a teenage boy experiencing his first crush. I love it."

"Me too." Myles smiled at Chrystina.

"Don't you two get too carried away." Chrystina walked back to her seat and sat, throwing the whoopee cushion on Myles' desk. "I have no idea how I feel about all of this."

"Oh you love it." AnnieMarie sat in the chair next to her. "I want to hear details." She smirked at Myles. "For now we have to get this announcement together."

Myles sat up. "What do you think the best course of action would be?"

"What are the doctors saying about Mr. Mitchell's condition?" AnnieMarie asked.

"They will hold him for forty-eight hours to ensure he is not a danger to himself. I contacted his family. His sister will be flying in on tomorrow. She will meet with us after she checks in on him."

"That gives us a little time to draft a statement for the press." AnnieMarie nodded. "Let's make sure we put Mitch in the best light possible. I don't want his reputation damaged by us."

Chrystina smiled. "That is our best path."

Myles nodded in agreement. "Include Mrs. Vazquez in the announcement. She was closer to him than any of us."

"This would be a good time for you to address your appointment as CEO. Give the employees a vision of where you see Dunning going under your leadership," AnnieMarie added. "The financial world is still reeling from yesterday's announcement. We'll play Mr.

Mitchell's retirement as an advancement of your agenda."

"The question on the table now, Myles, is who are you going to replace him with?" Chrystina asked. "You are going to need a number two."

"You're my number two."

"Me? No." She was adamant. "I am your executive assistant. You need a number two who has a global view of the financial world."

"She's right," AnnieMarie acknowledged. "With the new direction of Dunning it's time to bring someone on board who knows and understands banking on a global level. We stumbled onto this status. It's not where we set out to be at all. Yet, here we are."

"We now owe it to our customers to accept our new status and move forward," Myles commented. "I think we should look in house first. What about Preston?"

"He is good, but a little wishy washy to me." AnnieMarie shook her head. "His loyalty can be bought."

"What about Elaine Jacobson?" Chrystina offered.

"Don't trust her," AnnieMarie stated then looked at Myles. "If you had your choice of anyone, anyone in the world outside of family, who would be the name at the top of your list?"

Myles sat back, as if giving her question serious consideration. "Anyone?"

"Yes, anyone."

"Jonathan Michael."

"Whoa," Chrystina exclaimed. "You went straight to the top."

Myles nodded. "The man has proven himself in the world of Phase International. That could not have been easy for a man of color. It shows his intelligence, stamina and the patience it takes to work in an environment where he was the only one who looks like him."

AnnieMarie nodded in agreement. "I think he would make a great second in command."

"Hell if I thought for one moment he was available and interested, I'd step aside and let him have at it."

"No, you would not, simply because I would not let you," Chrystina advised. "You are still coming to terms with your new position. You are the only one. Your employees, your customers, along with your family see their future in you. Like it or not, you are the face of Dunning Bank & Trust. The financial world is looking to you as the new trend setter in banking."

"My first responsibility is to my family. The bank is second. If there is someone who I believe can take DBT to the next level, I would have no problem giving them the lead."

AnnieMarie watched Myles' eyes as he listened to Chrystina talk. It was clear to her that Chrystina was Myles' strength. Her belief in him is key to him being the great man he was meant to be. How fortunate are they, she thought.

"I think we should give Grace a call."

The two turned to AnnieMarie. "Why?" Myles asked.

AnnieMarie smiled. "Grace Heather is the key to getting Jonathan Michael."

"How so?" Chrystina asked.

"You two really need to get out of the office more," AnnieMarie said with a giggle as she stood. "I have work to catch up on. If you want Jonathan Michael talk to Grace." She left the office.

Chrystina looked at Myles. "Do you want me to reach out to Grace?"

"No," Myles stated. "I want people who are committed to Dunning, not to Grace. Reach out directly to Michael."

Chrystina made a note. "What position?"

"Chief Financial Officer."

A stunned Chrystina stared at him. "Some people may take offense to you offering that position to an outsider."

Myles nodded. "I'm sure some will. As the CEO of Dunning, they will need to trust my instincts. Get me everything you can find on Michael. All interviews, any quotes, writing memos...anything you can find on him. Have Mrs. Vazquez and, what was the young lady's name from yesterday?"

"Pamela Green." Chrystina looked up at him.

"Yes, I like her. Recruit her to assist. Set up a call with Michael. I want to see where his mind is on the future of the banking industry. Set up one on ones with Elaine Jacobson, Cainan and Preston Long. I'll meet with the family board members together."

"Yes, sir." Chrystina continued taking notes as he spoke. She was so proud of him in this moment. The instruction she was receiving was from a leader who has accepted his role and was steam rolling ahead.

## Chapter Twenty-Nine

It was nine fifteen in the morning, when Vivian kissed her husband goodbye, showered, then walked downstairs to start her day.

"Good morning."

Vivian was startled as she turned to see Grace sitting at her kitchen table.

"I figured I would alert you to my presence so you wouldn't shoot me." Grace walked over to the island and placed her cup in front of her aunt as she sat on a stool.

"Uncle Ken let me in. He said you were taking a shower and would be down soon. You want to tell me why you are dealing with the Russian Mafia?"

Vivian was filling Grace's cup up with coffee and froze at question.

"The who?" Vivian laughed.

"Russian mafia, Aunt Viv. That's who you asked me to check into." Grace sipped her coffee. "Cream and sugar, please."

Vivian pulled the container from the refrigerator and placed it in front of her very serious niece.

"It's not often you call me late at night with a request. My curiosity was peaked to say the least. I don't mean to be disrespectful, however, I am certain this has nothing to do with you, Uncle Ken or the children. That leaves Uncle Walker. What has he done and how deep is he in with these people?"

Vivian was thinking the entire time Grace was talking. Walker never said these people were part of the Russian mafia. He had to have known. Why didn't he warn her? She poured herself a cup of coffee and sat on the stool next to Grace. "I don't know the whole story and only believe half of what Walker told me." She sighed. "Well a little more than half with what you just told me."

"So he is involved with these people?"

"Not exactly."

"That's too close for comfort." Grace picked up the phone sitting on the island and held it out to her. "The first thing you are going to do is call Uncle Ken and ask him to return home."

"Why would I do that?"

"Because Uncle Walker may very well lose his life behind this antic. That I can take. I cannot take losing you. Not this close to losing Daddy." She put the phone on the counter and pushed it towards her. "Call him now."

As Vivian made the call, Grace picked up her cell phone and dialed. "I made contact. I don't know all the details yet. However, I will call you as soon as I know more facts."

"Grace, these people are dangerous. They have connections all over the world. What is your aunt doing involved with them?"

"As I said last night, I don't believe it's her. I am certain it's my Uncle Walker."

"The only way to beat the Russians is to be two steps ahead of them. Get protection for her, her family and your uncle," Byron ordered.

"I need to know all the facts before I put my family through this," Grace declared.

"You want some facts? Here they are. That search into that name could have triggered an alert. These people are smart. It would not surprise me or anyone at the agency if they had a program in place to detect any search of their key people. If this Stephan Pavel is one of their top people they already know the FBI search was done. Grace, these people leave body parts, not bodies. They don't just shoot you. They cut you up then distribute different pieces of your body in different countries so no one will ever be able to identify what they cannot find which would be your body. Do you get my meaning?"

"Thanks for scaring the living crap out of me."

"That's exactly what I am trying to do."

"Look, thanks for the help. I have no idea how deep this goes. For now I need to make sure my aunt is straight. I will keep you updated." She disconnected the call as she heard Byron call out to her.

"He is on his way home," Vivian said to Grace as she turned to her. "Is all of this necessary?"

"Yes, Aunt Viv, it is."

"Ken is going to be upset with me when he hears about this."

"You didn't tell him? Why not?"

"Because," she sighed. "Walker has lied to us on several occasions. Remember the last time he took the account number off a check I gave him and all but cleared us out."

"Uncle Ken told you to stay away from Uncle Walker for a reason."

"I know, but he's my brother. I just lost Hep. I don't want to lose Walker too."

"I'm afraid Uncle Walker may have taken that out of our hands." Grace walked over and hugged her aunt. "I know you love him. As much as he drives me crazy I don't really want anything to happen to him. But Uncle Ken is right. You are going to have to stay away from him."

"What has Walker done this time?"

The two looked up to see Ken standing in the kitchen entrance. "I thought you were at the office." Vivian walked over and hugged her husband.

"No, I stopped to get coffee when it dawned on me that Grace was in DC last night. I asked myself why would she be in our house this early in the morning? She must have driven through the night. If she did what was the urgency?"

"That's what happens when you marry a lawyer. Their minds are always thinking conspiracy," Vivian joked.

"I think we all better take a seat," Grace suggested. "Now, Aunt Viv, tell me, how did you get Stephan Pavel's name?"

Vivian told Grace and Ken the story Walker had told her. When she finished, the two simply stared at her without mumbling a word. After a very long moment, Grace and Ken glanced at each other, then sat back.

"This is one time I can attest Uncle Walker is in trouble." Grace exhaled. "One thing is for certain we cannot give him access to the bank."

"He said they will kill him if he does not comply."

Ken shook his head. "If they wanted him dead they would not have cut his throat. They would have simply killed him."

"If he doesn't do what they ask they will kill him, Uncle Ken," Grace assured him. "That will be his cross to bear. The key is controlling the collateral damage around him." Grace stood. "I do not want to see you, your family, my family, or peoples' lives at the bank destroyed because of Uncle Walker. I am going to make another phone call. Uncle Ken, contact the security team. I think they should be put on high alert," she said over her shoulder as she left the room.

"Ken." Vivian looked sadly up at her husband.

He shook his head. "Don't, Vivian. Your brother has brought his troubles into this house for the last time."

"Ken, he's my brother."

"A brother who does nothing but use you to his own advantage. Why do you think he chose to call you and tell his story. I will bet you he made it seem like he didn't want to tell you what happened. That is how he gets to you. He makes you think you had to drag it out of him. When you do, you feel like you have to fix it for him. Walker is your older brother. He should be protecting you, not the other way around, Viv." Ken stopped and exhaled. "You and the children are my life. I will be damned if Walker is going to take you away from me." He pulled out his phone. "Hell, it would not surprise me one bit if it came out that Walker had something to do with Hep's death."

"Ken," Vivian scolded.

"Don't Ken me. You know how angry he was about Hep taking over the bank. It's been years and every time he comes into this house he has something to say about it. He was obsessed with schemes to take control away from Hep. You know that. He even said it, right here in this house."

"He did not mean that," Vivian protested. "You know he had been drinking and was very angry."

"Yes, but what if he did mean it? I'm sorry, Vivian, I worked out with Hep at least twice a week. I know how healthy he was. As I said before, I can't accept the heart attack as a cause of death. Out of respect to you I haven't voiced my concerns to anyone. But so help me, if I find out Walker had anything to do with Hep's death I'm going to tell everything I know."

Grace heard the comment as she walked back towards the room. It stung her, causing her to take a step back. Was it possible that Daddy didn't die of a heart attack? she thought. No. An autopsy would have shown if there was foul play. Wait. She stopped herself before walking back to the room. Did they perform an autopsy? She thought back. No. There was no reason to once the doctor indicated it was a heart attack. Everyone just accepted it. She made a mental note to discuss this with Myles. If her father's death was caused by anything other than natural causes it could mean her mother, the other members of her family, may be in danger. She took a deep breath, exhaled then continued into the kitchen.

"My friend is going to fly down on the next flight out of DC. We need to assess the situation a little deeper before he arrives."

"I better call your mother."

"Mommy?" Grace glanced at her aunt. "What does she have to do with this?"

"We were going to have lunch today. My intention was to tell her about the situation with Walker."

Grace smiled, a bit relieved. "I am happy to hear that. For a minute I thought you were going to try and deal with this on your own. I will call her and tell her to meet us here."

"That's fine, dear. However, I will ask you one favor. Please don't tell Myles. It will ruin any chance Walker has of getting back into the bank."

"Aunt Viv." Grace held her glare steady. "Believe me when I say, Uncle Walker has no shot at returning to the bank in any capacity."

Ken walked back into the room. "A security team will be here within the hour."

Grace nodded. "My friend with the FBI will be here soon. We are going to have to make a decision on how to proceed. From the little he has shared with me, this branch of the mafia family is dangerous and not afraid of the law."

"I think we should advise Myles," Ken stated.

"No," Vivian objected. "That would just cause more problems for Walker."

"On this point I have to agree with Aunt Viv," Grace cautioned with a stern look at Vivian. "Myles has enough to deal with. We'll advise him on a need to know basis. Let's try to get this handled without involving Myles or the bank."

"Plausible deniability?" Ken asked.

"Exactly. Until we know the legalities of what we are dealing with there is an outside possibility that one, or all of us may get called into court. If Myles is called, as CEO, he would be able to say he has not been privy to the situation without perjuring himself."

"Do you think that will happen?" Aunt Viv asked.

"Until we know more I can't say. However, it is my responsibility to protect Myles and Dunning."

"Don't tell me you are trying to protect Walker now too?" Ken smirked.

"In this instance protecting him is a benefit to insuring family members I love are safe. Aunt Viv, how much money did Uncle Walker tell you he owed these people?"

"He said he borrowed 10 million but with the interest it's now 30 million. They gave him the option of paying the money by the end of the week or he had to get a job with the bank."

"But he receives at least 50 million a year from bank profits. Why would he need to borrow 10 million?"

"Walker is broke," Ken stated. "He has been broke for years. The only reason he still has the house is because it is in the bank's name. He could not borrow against it. Have you been to his house lately?"

"No," Grace replied to Ken as he sat at the kitchen table with a cup of coffee.

"Well it's pretty empty, at least downstairs. Anything he has that had a value to it he sold."

"Is his gambling that bad?"

"It is not the gambling alone," Vivian added. "It is his over-the-top lifestyle. Everything has to be flashy - the car, the women. Everything is over-the-top."

"And now he has no way to pay for it, so he gambles and takes from those who love him." Ken glared at his wife as he spoke.

Grace saw the look on Ken's face when he spoke of Uncle Walker. If the Russians did not kill him first she was pretty sure Uncle Ken would.

"What I do not understand is how would Walker working at the bank benefits these people? I mean he will make a salary but that would be nowhere near what he owes them."

"They want access to something within the bank's grasp," Grace suggested. "Or it could be a way to get their money cleaned."

"What does that mean?" Vivian asked.

"It is a way to turn your illegal gains into legal assets," Ken explained.

They all turned at the sound of the back door opening.

Winnie walked in. She took one look at the long faces at the table and asked, "So?" She sat next to Grace. "What did Jr. do this time?"

Grace kissed her mother on the cheek. "Did Jerome bring you or did you drive?"

"Hello, sweetheart. I thought you were in DC."

"I'm sorry." Grace smiled. "Hello, Mother. I was, however this situation came up and I was needed here more. Did you drive over?"

"Yes. I drove over. Why?"

"Excuse me." Grace stood. "I need to make a call." She stepped out the room.

"Does this have anything to do with the call you made to me last night?" she asked Vivian.

"I'm afraid so," Vivian replied. "Walker has gotten himself into a hot mess and it seems he has dragged me into the fire...again."

Winnie glanced at Ken who shared a knowing glance her way as well.

"What else is new?" Winnie smirked.

"Jerome will be here to drive you home. My friend Byron Roark is flying in. He should be here in less than an hour. We hope he can shed a little more light on this situation."

"The FBI agent?"

Grace nodded. "Yes, ma'am."

"He's a nice young man, but you know he is not the one for you."

"Thank you, Mother." Grace glanced at her aunt and smiled. "Do you see what I have to deal with?"

Vivian smiled. "Your mother knows best."

"That's a good thing, Grace, for your aunt's judgment isn't very good these days."

"Ken." Winnie reached out and touched his hand. "I don't know what we are dealing with, but whatever it is, do not allow Walker Jr. to come between the two of you. Life is too short."

Ken sat back and exhaled. "You're right, Winnie." He reached out and took Vivian's hand. "I'm angry because I love you too much to watch your brother continue to use you in this way."

Vivian covered his hand with hers. "I know. This is my fault for rushing to his side every time he calls. I have to be the one to put a stop to him."

"Grace." Her mother glanced her way. "Why is your friend coming here? Does it have anything to do with the bank?"

"We aren't sure of all the details. We are only going on what Uncle Walker told Aunt Viv. However, the people involved have requested access to the bank through Uncle Walker."

"What people?"

"Bad people, Mother, very bad people."

# Chapter Thirty

"Mr. Dunning." Mrs. Vazquez stood in the doorway of his new office. "I am sorry to disturb you, however, you have a visitor who is insisting on seeing you."

Myles looked up to see a not too happy secretary staring at him. "Who is it?"

"Ms. Savannah Whitfield. I explained you were in the office, however you were not free for visitors. She on the other hand insists you will want to see her."

He noticed Mrs. Vazquez had taken a seat and gotten a bit comfortable. "I take it, you want to make her wait?"

"That is the ideal thing to do. It pleases me to no end to have her removed from the building, if it pleases you."

Myles smiled. "It may be time to get this visit done and over. Would you mind sending her in?"

"Yes," Mrs. Vazquez replied as she stood. "I don't like her."

"I know others who feel the same way. However, her father is a client and a business partner. It would be prudent to treat her nice."

"I got her nice," Mrs. Vazquez muttered as she opened the door. "But if you insist I not demonstrate it at this time, I'll show her in."

Myles closed the folder on his desk and stood as Savannah walked into the office. She looked around then turned to him. "Impressive, Myles. Very impressive." She walked towards him. He held his hand out. She walked right up and kissed him on the lips.

He stepped back. "Hello, Savannah. You look nice."

"I have to when I'm coming to see you."

Myles pointed to a chair in front of his desk. "Have a seat. What can I do for you?" He sat in his chair and waited.

"I thought I would drop in to say hello since I was in the area. Elaine mentioned you moved into your new office today. So, I thought you would need a few decorating points. But it seems whoever you used knows you very well. This office fits you."

"Thank you. Chrystina worked with Mrs. Vazquez to get it ready."

"Oh." The response was flat. "Well, I can see Mrs. Vazquez's touch."

"Yes," Myles agreed then waited.

When he did not continue Savannah cleared her throat. "We saw the announcement yesterday on Hershel. What a catch on your first day as CEO. Congratulations, Myles. I can see we are going to get big things from you. Have you done anything to celebrate?"

"No, I'm afraid it's been a little busy."

"Oh, Myles, you have to throw a party. This is a great accomplishment. You need to celebrate not only becoming CEO but the new account. Let me plan it for you. I can see it now. We could rent out the Jefferson Ballrooms, invite the movers and shakers of the city and do it up right. What do you say? Let me do it, please."

Myles sat forward. "You think it would be a good idea for me to celebrate becoming CEO due to my father's death? I don't think that would go over too well."

"It could be looked down on," she sighed. "Well, let me at least take you to dinner to celebrate. I don't want your moment to go unrecognized. You work hard, Myles, but you never celebrate your moments."

"The time isn't right. We have a number of board positions to fill and personnel to replace, not to mention some reorganization. It's a pretty busy time."

She got the message. "I understand." She uncrossed her legs and stood. Myles did as well. "Why don't I get out of your...."

"Myles, I have the information you requested on Jonathan..." Chrystina walked in from her new office with documents in her hand but stopped talking the moment she looked up and saw Savannah in the room. She glanced at Myles as she slowly walked over to his desk. "Excuse the interruption. I did not know you had a visitor." She pulled a tissue from the box on the desk then gave it to him. "You have lipstick on your mouth."

"Oh." Savannah smiled brightly. "That was from me." She winked an eye at Myles. "There are more where that came from."

"Hmm." Chrystina smirked.

"Savannah stopped in to say hello," Myles explained.

"I see," was Chrystina's short reply.

"Yes, Mrs. Vazquez brings a much needed touch of professionalism to the office." She looked in the direction Chrystina had come from. "Where is your office, Chrystina?"

She pointed to the door on the other side of the room. "Right through that door." Chrystina smiled.

"Moving her next door to me was the best solution for everyone. I need her more now than I ever did before." Myles smiled at Chrystina.

Savannah looked between the two. "I see," she said in a flat voice.

"It's going to be a very busy time for us," Chrystina added.

"Is that so?" Savannah nodded. "Well, Myles, I do hope you will take me up on that offer for dinner before things get too busy. In fact." She turned back to him. "You should know my father will be in town next week. It's my understanding he will be negotiating the deal for BIT with Elaine. Perhaps a dinner at my place will give you two an opportunity to talk without interruptions." She glared at Chrystina then turned back to Myles.

"Yes, it would be. However, we have a number of meetings on the calendar for the next few weeks."

"Oh, I'm sure you can squeeze in one little dinner." Savannah smiled. "I'll reach out to Mrs. Vazquez to set it all up. With that, I must be on my way." She smirked over her shoulder at Chrystina as she strutted out the office.

"Do I need to explain what that was all about?" Myles glanced at Chrystina.

"Her being here? No, that was her attempting to get back into your bed. Is that something I need to be concerned with?"

"Savannah back in my bed? No. She doesn't fart on me." Myles laughed as Chrystina punched him in the chest.

"You cannot hold that over my head forever." She pushed as he pulled her in his arms.

He kissed her forehead. "I don't plan to, but it is funny right now."

"We are not doing this in the office." She slowly pushed away. "Did you assign the BIT account to Elaine?"

"No," Myles replied.

"Hmm, then why is Mr. Whitfield meeting with her on BIT?"

Myles stared at her. "Good question."

"Yes, one we need an answer to. But that's not why I came in here." She sat in front of his desk.

"What do you have on Jonathan?" Myles asked as they got back to business.

"These are the articles Pam has pulled together so far."

"Really?" Myles looked at the stack of documents, impressed with the results in such a short period of time.

"She's good and thorough. I like that. But there is more I need to tell you before you start digging in."

Myles looked up. "What do you have?" He was curious because of the excitement in Chrystina's voice.

"I called Mr. Michael's personal assistant. I love her accent. Anyway, it seems he will be state side next week."

Myles sat up. "Really?"

"Yes, that's not all." Chrystina smiled. "He is taking a leave of absence from Phase effective Monday morning."

"Did she say why?"

"No, only that it would be a smashing idea."

Myles stared at her, blinking. "Smashing?"

Chrystina laughed. "Yes. 'It would be a smashing idea, mate,' were her exact words. So, you know me. I looked it up. It means a conversation would be a wonderful idea, friend."

"Interesting," Myles said as he sat back.

"I'm hoping it happens just so I can hear the accents and other phrases they use."

"This looks promising. But I don't need you getting giddy over Michael."

Chrystina was shocked. "Myles Dunning...is that a bit of jealousy I hear coming from you?"

"No. I know what I have and how to keep it."

Chrystina smiled. "Do you now?"

"I do," Myles replied as he held her gaze. "Have dinner with me tonight?"

"Yes."

"Good. Now stop looking at me like that if you want me to keep my word not to jump you in the office."

Chrystina blushed and looked away. "Okay. Work. I've scheduled Elaine Jacobson, Cainan Scott and Preston Long's meetings for this afternoon. I've allowed an hour for each. First up is Cainan." She checked her watch. "He should be here shortly. I've sent you a list of accomplishments over the last five years on each, with the exception of Cainan. He hasn't been here that long."

Myles opened his laptop. "I'll review those now. Give Mike a call. See if he can do an investigation on Jonathan Michael's personal life."

"Will do." Chrystina stood. "I'm liking what I see from Pamela Green. What do you think of promoting her to my position in Risk Management?"

"Her personnel file indicates she is qualified. See if she would be interested." He shrugged and began reading the information on the computer.

## Chapter Thirty-One

Chrystina loved giving good news to employees. Her mood was almost giddy when she walked out of her office to see Pam. She passed Cainan in the hallway on his way to see Myles. "Hey, good luck in the meeting."

"Thanks," Cainan replied. "Any idea what it's about?"

"He's working on board members. You should be fine." She continued around the hallway to the elevator focused on how she would give Pam the news. The doors opened and she stepped inside. Right before they were about to close, Savannah stepped in with a wicked grin on her face.

"Hello again, Chrystina."

"Savannah," she groaned.

Savannah hit the close door button, folded her arms across her chest and took the one leg out pose.

Chrystina had to keep herself from laughing.

"You seemed to have positioned yourself as useful to Myles. But I know what your game is and let me tell you something. Myles likes the finer things in life. And

you, my dear" -she looked Chrystina up and down-
"are far from it. Oh, I see the hair is in a ponytail. A
little childish, but I get what you are trying to do. But
try as you may, you will never look like this." She
fanned her hand over her body.

The elevator stopped on the sixth floor. An
employee started to step in.

"Take the next one," Chrystina said then pushed
the close door button. "You are a scheming,
egotistical, trashy excuse of a little ho who I am sure is
intelligent enough to know when a man is done with
you. Myles has moved on. I suggest you do the same."
Chrystina stepped back, folded her arms across her
chest and took the same pose.

"Moved on to what?" Savannah took a step
towards her. "You? I think not. Have you looked at
yourself in a mirror? You are not a threat to me or
anyone else. What are you, a good two-fifty? Now,
take a good look at me." She stepped around in a
circle. "Slim, petite, just the right size to lift, bend, or
carry." She did the motions as she spoke. "You see, it's
easy to flip up and rub it down." She smacked her own
butt in Chrystina's face. "You know what I know to be
a fact? Myles is a very active lover." She smiled.
"Variety of positions takes flexibility." She looked
Chrystina up and down with a smirk. "Can you even
open those things you call thighs?" She grinned. "I
can...wide." She held her arms wide open.

"Hmmm...all of that and he still walked away."
Chrystina took a step closer to Savannah. "Could it be
you spread those legs wide for one too many men?"
She put a finger up to her chin as if thinking. "Or
could it be what's between those things could not
compensate for what is missing in your brain?" She
placed a hand on her hip. "I could be wrong, but after
the spreading of legs, you need something else to keep

a man interested. Your depth of conversation is as shallow as you are. A man needs a before and after to stimulate and entice his mind." She turned her back on Savannah and smacked her behind. "Every now and then a little more meat on the bones don't hurt either."

Savannah stepped back. "So...you finally came clean on your feelings for Myles. Good for you. The question you need to answer is does he feel the same way about you. I doubt it, but let's say he does. Why the sudden interest on his part? You have worked together for years. Could it be he simply needs a shoulder to cry on? With all he's been through in the last few months, it is conceivable. Don't you think? Here is something else for you to consider. Now that he has full control of the bank, where does that put you?" She used her fingers to demonstrate a quote. "'Family First and Foremost.' Are you somewhere in there? I think not." The elevator stopped on the third floor. Savannah stepped out, then held her hand out to keep the door from closing. "Oh, and you might be right, Chrystina, men do want a little meat to hold on to. What they don't want is a whole hog." She smiled then let the door close.

That stung, Chrystina thought. She was thick, too thick, that was no lie. She had to take steps to change that. Working out with Myles was just a start. She realized she needed to be more serious about her weight. "Okay, Savannah, you may have unwittingly given me the push I needed." Her resolve was in place. The next time she saw Savannah Whitfield, she was going to smack that ass right in her face. Chrystina huffed to herself. The elevator stopped on the first floor, but her spirit wasn't right to give Pamela the news. She pushed the button to go back to the eighth floor. Why now, hit her mind. The question Savannah asked. Why was Myles all of a sudden attracted to her? There was a lot of turmoil in his life. His father's death, the emotional drain from helping his family cope, now all the pressure of the bank. The incident with Mr. Mitchell couldn't have been easy to deal with. Like it or not Savannah may have a point. This could all come down to having a shoulder to cry on. What happens after the scars heal, and things settle down? Will there be anything more than her wishful thinking left to hold onto? Will his kisses, his touch last or is this a temporary reprieve for him? The elevator ding interrupted her thoughts.

The door opened and to her surprise Myles was standing there.

"A meeting in the elevator?" He raised an eyebrow.

"Not exactly." Chrystina exhaled then started to walk away.

Myles reached out taking her arm, then pulled her into the executive elevator. He waited until the door closed then hit the stop button. "Cainan mentioned Savannah rushing to get on the elevator with you. I am certain he is wondering why I left the office suddenly. So I am going to have to make this quick. I'm certain words were spoken between you and Savannah. Do you want to share?"

Chrystina thought for a moment. The two of them had always been open and honest with each other, almost to a fault. She had no intentions of changing jobs, which meant if this attraction between them led to something more or not, they still have to have a working relationship that had to be maintained. "I need honesty here."

"Always." Myles frowned as he took a step back.

She exhaled. "Why the sudden attraction? I mean we've been working together for almost ten years.

Never once did you even look at me the way a man looks at a woman. So why now?"

"Honestly, I don't know. It could be you never crawled across my desk in a seductive manner before."

"That one act - and that is what it was, an act - doesn't take you from boss to...lover?"

"You may have a point there." He bowed his head, then looked back up at her. "All I can say is for ten years I've come to depend on your counsel, your blatant honesty and that radiant smile you bring into my life every day. I don't know why now. I do know that I want that in all aspects of my life. In the office and when I go home at night. It's not an attraction, Chrys. I'm in love with you. Your mind, your body, all of you. Life is short, I don't want to spend time questioning why."

"Savannah suggested I'm the shoulder you need to sink your sorrows into. At least that was my take on what she said."

"In other words I'm using you to hold me together right now." The anger in his voice was evident. "I'm not strong enough to deal with my father's death or take over the leadership role in the bank or with my family. Is that what you think, Chrys?"

"No," she replied with a bit of an attitude. "I know what you are capable of, Myles Dunning, and I don't appreciate you trying to turn this back on me. I'm telling you what your ex........thinks."

"It could be your unyielding belief in me that is causing this sudden attraction."

He took a step closer. The anger had dissipated. It was replaced with a softness. Her stomach was fluttering. He nudged her chin up with his thumb, then gazed into her eyes. The confusion there disturbed him. It was something he never wanted to see there again. He held her gaze then slowly lowered his mouth to hers. He brushed her lips with the gentleness of a summer's breeze at first, but that taste. Her taste enticed him far more than it had the night before. He cupped her face with his hands then possessively delivered a thorough kiss with more passion than he knew he possessed. The he pulled back. "I'm invested in you and me. Are you?"

Chrystina smiled then put her arms around his neck, nudging his lips back to hers. "Invested. I like your play on words." Her mouth captured his, matching the passion he shared so freely.

Myles took complete control at that point, pushing her body against the back wall, raising her hands above her head. Their bodies flush. A fire, so intense emerged from deep inside of him. He wanted her. Needed to be inside of her. The elevator next to them dinged. The sound made him realize they were in a public elevator. He had to pull away. Stepping back his lips parted from hers. But he held her arms in place. "No doubts, Chrys?"

The weakness in her knees did not deter her from acknowledging his words. "I'm all in."

Myles smiled. "Thank you. No more elevator meetings. We are going to take our time at this. More than anything, outside interference will not be allowed. Clear?"

"Clear."

He pushed the open door button, and they stepped out, together.

# Chapter Thirty-Two

The sedative had worn off. William looked around the room horrified at where he had landed. His father's words from years ago came back to haunt him. 'You follow that colored boy and he's going to lead you to a place of despair.' Well, here you are, he thought.

It was always his plan to take over the bank. To show his father he was a leader, not a follower. Yes, he would control the bank and have Winnieford as his mistress. The realization that he could never marry her only now apparent to him. After all the years that had passed, the truth was so clear now. Winnieford could never love him because he was a white man. The memories of her smiles when they were in the library studying was, what? Just her being nice? He sighed and turned over on his side to clear the undesired thought from his mind. No, that was impossible for him to believe. All the time they spoke together. The talks they had about a better future. The laughs they shared. Was it all in his imagination? It could not have been. Winnieford loved him until Hepburn came into the picture.

"William?"

That wasn't Winnieford's voice.

"William? I've been here for almost two hours. Now wake up. Open your eyes."

The harshness of the voice warned him to dig back into the recesses of his mind. Don't do it. Keep your eyes closed.

"William, open your damn eyes."

William opened his eyes and looked over his shoulder. He knew those legs. But that voice, the anger. It couldn't be.

"William."

He looked up. "Elaine."

"What in the hell happened yesterday? Did you talk to Myles about the BIT account?"

"What?"

"The BIT account, William. Did you talk to Myles about putting me on the account?"

William turned back over and closed his eyes. "I was fired yesterday, Elaine. Fired. After giving them thirty years of my life. He fired me just like I was nothing."

"William." Elaine walked over to the other side of the bed and shook William until his eyes opened. "Tell me what happened? Everything."

"I don't want to go through that, Elaine." He turned over.

She yanked him back to her. "You are going to have to, William. I've been called into a one on one meeting with Myles and I need to know what you told him."

William jerked back to the other side.

Elaine walked around in a circle, frustrated. She stopped, closed her eyes and exhaled. She did it again. When she felt she was ready, she walked around to face him again. She pulled up her chair and sat next to the bed.

"William," she spoke softly. "You know I have always been here for you. Nothing has changed."

"Yes it has. My life is ruined," he cried out. "Ruined."

She wanted to slap him, but she knew to get her answers she had to stay cool. "Tell me, what did he say to you?" she asked in the most concerned voice she could pull together. "It couldn't have been much. Why, he doesn't know half of what you do about running Dunning. Whatever he said, you and I know he was wrong. There is no way Dunning is going to function without you."

"That's what I said."

Elaine almost jumped out of the chair with relief. "What did he say when you told him that?

"They pulled out files." William frowned. "Files from years ago. Marie had them. Had been keeping them for years."

Elaine sat closer to his bed. "What files?" Her mind was whirling.

"They had everything. They had people following us. Following us, can you believe that? They know everything."

"I will get them for you."

William's eyes opened wide. "You will?"

Elaine smiled and spoke, almost crooning. "Yes, William, I will get those files for you and destroy them."

"They had files on everyone in the room. They probably have them on you too."

"Really, on me? I haven't done anything."

He sat up. "Oh yeah, remember when you tried to seduce Hepburn? Remember that night Marie walked in on you in Hepburn's office with no clothes on? I bet they have that. You have to get it. And get those files on me too. If we get rid of those pic.... I mean files we can make things right again."

"Yes, William, we can. Now, tell me this. Where do they keep the files?"

"How would I know that?"

"Think, William. Who told you about the files?"

"Myles and Chrystina, but Marie had them."

"Okay, okay, that's good. I'll check for them. Now tell me one more thing. Did you talk to Myles about BIT?"

"No-no, I never got a chance to. They found out about the meeting with Hershel."

"What meeting with Hershel?"

"The one I set up to force Myles to make me President of the bank."

"You did what?"

"Oh, I had it all planned out. I was going to meet with the Hershel reps to show them how incompetent Myles was to take over as President," he said, eagerly telling her about his failed plan.

Elaine was livid. "You stupid son of a bitch. I had everything we needed to bring them down in place and you ruined it with a stupid scheme that had no chance at succeeding. All you had to do was follow instructions, William.  What is it with you stupid ass men? Of course you got caught. Who in the hell said you were smart enough to pull off any side jobs?

"The plan was simple. Get Homeland Security to do an investigation. Have BIT pulled from under them. With the investigation looming, Hershel would have walked."

"Elaine." William sounded like a wounded child confused by his mother's anger.

"Everything was in play, William. All you had to do was lay low and you would have had what you have wanted all these years. You would have had the bank, the money, and Winnieford. Now look at you. You have nothing."

"I still have Winnieford," he whimpered.

"No, you don't and you will never have her. You want to know why? Because you are white. Her husband was black. You are stupid. Hepburn was smart."

"That doesn't mean she can't love me."

Elaine all but screamed, "Oh my lord, please save me from stupid ass men." She grabbed her purse and stormed out of the room.

"She loved me before Hepburn," he yelled at her back. "When I leave here I'm going to prove it."

"Mr. Mitchell, do you need anything?" the nurse asked from the doorway.

He slid back under the comfort of the sheets then turned his back. His eyes closed and his mind drifted back. Hepburn was supposed to be his friend. He knew how William felt about Winnieford. The conversation they had after William introduced Winnieford to Hepburn was clear.

*"She's beautiful, isn't she? Those bright brown eyes and that wonderful laughter. She is always like that, you know, Always cheerful and happy. I'm going to have her," William said. "When she is ready, I'm going to make my move. She is poetry in motion and I'm ready to ride her like a stallion." William laughed. "I'm telling you, Dunning, she is going to be mine."*

William's mind dug back deeper trying to recall Hepburn's reaction to his declaration. Somewhere along the way he missed it. It was the following week, when Hepburn walked Winnieford to the library. That was when William saw what was happening. The two walked hand in hand smiling at each other. William was so angry he snarled out his hello to them. He waited until Hepburn was gone before saying anything to Winnieford.

*"What are you doing with Dunning?"*

*Smiling, Winnieford placed her books on the table and looked at him. "Thank you for introducing us, William. You are a wonderful friend." She touched his hand. He was so taken by her touch that all William could do was nod in agreement. The next day in the locker room William approached Hepburn. He whispered to keep others from hearing. "You knew Winnieford was mine. I told you so. Why would you go after my girl?"*

*"Winnie isn't a piece of property, Mitch. She doesn't belong to anyone." Hepburn stopped what he was doing then stood to his full height over William. He stared at the man and said, "A woman is not an animal for you to ride. She is a gift from God for you to love and cherish."*

*"What in the hell is that supposed to mean?" William asked.*

*"Winnie is a woman, not a horse. She is to be loved, treasured as if she was the most precious gift a man could have. If you don't understand the difference in your observation of Winnie and mine, you are a lost soul."*

Opening his eyes, he noticed the drapes in the room were open. The light poured through. Looking out the window, the weather seemed to be as cloudy as his spirit. He was a lost soul. He had lost the bank, Winnieford and his dignity. What in the hell was there to live for?

He closed his eyes as the last forty-eight hours of his life replayed in his mind. The company he had worked for over thirty years voted in a boy younger than some of his shoes over him. He should be President now. That boy humiliated him, had him escorted out by security all in front of employees who were beneath him. That was not the way he should have been treated. Adding insult, Myles exposed his darkest secret. If his family ever saw those pictures they would disown him.

There was a knock on the door. "Mr. Mitchell, this gentleman has some documents for you," the nurse said then stepped out.

"William Mitchell, you have been served." The man put the document down then walked out.

William picked up the document the man placed on the bed. He opened it and read. It was an injunction. He was not to enter headquarters or any branch offices of Dunning Bank & Trust.

Maybe it was time, William thought as he lay back down. Hepburn and the bank were gone. The only thing that was left was Winnieford. His Winnieford. After all the years he had loved her, he could not believe she would just stand by and let this happen to him. She would come to him. He knew in his heart Winnieford would not let Myles do this to him. She would come. He knew it. He would give her a day or two. If she doesn't well then he would have to show them all what he was made of. Yes, they believed he was down and out, but they had no idea he had just begun. How dare Hepburn die and leave him at the mercy of his son. The more he thought about it the more he realized his problems began and ended with Winnieford Pitchfork-Dunning. No worries. They will fall. The mighty Dunnings will all fall.

#

Elaine got into her car then screamed into the steering wheel. "Two years of planning. Getting everything lined up just right and these dumb ass men. The leaders of the world could not get it right. Damn."

She sat there trying to collect her emotions. "What now?" she said. "How can I save this?" Scenarios ran through her mind. She planned to use William to lock in the BIT account, Walker to setup the investigation with Homeland Security and Jonathan to secure a new position. So far none of them had come through.

She picked up her phone and dialed Walker.

The phone rang, but he did not pick up. She left a message. "Walker, call me as soon as you get this. William has been fired from the bank."

Her head fell back. "William is MIA." She screamed again as she watched her carefully timed scheme begin to unravel. She exhaled. "Phase." She dialed the international number. "Jonathan Michael, please."

"Mr. Michael has taken a leave of absence. May I connect you with another party?"

"A leave of absence? Where to? How long will he be gone?"

"We are not able to give out that information. May I connect you-" She hung up the phone. "What in the hell is happening?"

Her cell phone buzzed in her hand. It was her office. "Hello."

"Hello, Ms. Jacobson, this is Chrystina Price calling with a reminder of your meeting with Mr. Dunning at 3:00 pm."

"Thank you, Chrystina."

What in the hell was the meeting about? That concerned her. And these files William mentioned. Could they have one on her? Have they been following her too as William said?

Her cell phone buzzed again. She saw the number and cringed. She did not want this call...not now. But she knew it could not be ignored.

"Things seem to be a bit off track."

"Yes, well, that's what happens when men are involved."

"How do you plan to deliver what you promised?"

"All is not lost, I have another play."

"Good. I would hate to think we are throwing in the towel when we are so close to winning. Remember, the bottom line is simple. It's time for the Dunning men to pay for their sins."

## Chapter Thirty-Three

"Elaine, thank you for agreeing to meet with me."
"Agreeing? Myles, you are the CEO. You request our presence and we make it happen. Is someone giving you concern in that area?"

"No, not at all," he replied. "The transition has had a bump or two, but overall I believe we are in a good place." He did not let it show, but he wondered if Elaine had just given him a little shade when she called him Myles instead of Mr. Dunning and again when she insinuated he did not have control of his staff. "I thought it would be good to speak with the board members one-on-one to see where your thoughts are on the future of Dunning."

"My thoughts aren't important, Myles. Dunning is now in your hands. It's up to you to determine if we are in a position to push for the number two ranking by bringing in more high level corporate business or to continue to grow on the loyalty of our personal customers. We've been exemplary on one, and okay on the other."

"Do you believe one has to be sacrificed for the other?"

"No. To my knowledge we haven't sacrificed either so far."

"I hear a bit of hesitation in that response. Do you have a concern?"

"Not a concern." She shrugged. "I think we have an opportunity here. With the acquisition of Hershel, which will surely raise our standing in the banking industry, another immediate corporation acquisition would set the industry on fire with Dunning's name."

Myles could see her excitement at the possibility, he just wasn't sure if it was genuine.

"What steps would you take to secure additional corporate accounts while keeping our base customers happy?"

"You sound like you are interviewing me for a job," she laughed. Myles didn't. "Okay."

He watched the emotions crossing her face.

She cleared her throat. "We have great customer service on both fronts. I think we could improve incentives on the corporate side. Let's use BIT for example. I think we should take the current package off the table and enhance the incentive to lock up that acquisition."

Myles nodded his head. "We have a number of corporate packages on the table. Is it your intention to enhance those packages also?"

"None of them will bring in as much attention to the industry as BIT. Don't you agree?"

"I believe all customers, corporate or personal, deserve to receive equal incentives in accordance to the size of the account they bring to us indifferent to what attention the acquisition brings to Dunning." Myles closed the folder, stood and extended his hand. "Thank you for your time, Elaine."

She stood. "Of course." She nodded. "I have the feeling you were not pleased by my response."

"This was a conversation where you have an open forum to discuss the future of Dunning. Your thoughts are just that, your thoughts. It's not my place as the CEO to say they are right or wrong. I'm here to listen to all then make the best decision for the direction of Dunning."

"Will you answer a question for me?"

"Of course."

"What happened with William?"

"You are a board member and will receive details in the next meeting. It came down to this, Mr. Mitchell attempted to sabotage the acquisition of the Hershel account. Any employee who takes such action to harm the reputation or bottom line of Dunning will be dealt with swiftly and severely."

There was something in her eyes when he made the statement. Myles didn't understand her reaction. She was a board member. Their job was to promote and protect the sovereignty of the bank.

"Well, thank you for the meeting."

"We will talk again soon." He watched as she walked out the door. "Mrs. Vazquez, will you come in for a moment?"

"Yes, sir."

There was something about Elaine he had never been able to put his hand on. There were times when it felt she was with Dunning all the way. But, there were more times he had the impression that there was a certain hate just under the surface with her.

"Yes, sir?"

"Please have a seat."

"Hmmm, I don't like the sound of that." She chuckled then took a seat.

"What can you tell me about Elaine?" He held his hand out. "Please don't tell me what's in the file. Tell me what is not."

Mrs. Vazquez dropped her head. "I knew this day would eventually come." She shook her head, then looked up at him. "Let me ask you this before I answer. You've been on the board with her for nine years. What does your gut tell you?"

"She's a time bomb. There is something boiling right under the surface." He sat forward folding his hands on the desk. "Until I was named CEO I took it as just the way she was. The last few days there has been something different."

"Okay." Mrs. Vazquez sat back. "What is not in the file is the reason Elaine took a leave of absence and returned to a lower position. Elaine believed herself to be in love with your father. Your mother took exception to this."

Myles raised an eyebrow.

"However, she dealt with it as she does everything, with grace. Until, we walked into Hepburn's office one night to bring him dinner and we found Elaine stretched out naked on his sofa."

Myles cleared his throat. "With Dad?"

"No. However your mother and I did not know that at the time. Needless to say, Winnie was more than a little upset and proceeded to force feed the dinner she brought for Hep to Elaine." She stopped talking and coughed to cover the laugh. "Hep came in while I was attempting to pull Winnie off Elaine. He was with a client." She laughed. "I'm sorry. It was a funny scene. Hep walked in the door, grabbed Winnie by the waist and put her over his shoulder. She was kicking and swinging until Hep swatted her on the behind. The client kindly took off his suit jacket and put it around Elaine. Your wildcat of a mother kicked

Hep in the balls and he let her fall to the floor. She then started to give Hep a piece of her mind as he was bent over clutching his balls."

Myles had tried to hold it in, but he laughed. "This is not a funny story." He stopped laughing. "But the visual is funny as hell."

"It was funnier in the moment. It took a moment for her to calm down enough to look around, but when she did she noticed the client. Winnie looked up and asked, 'Who in the hell are you?' The client said I was with Hep at dinner. Winnie gave him a look, then she looked at Hep. Then she turned to Elaine and asked 'Who in the hell were you in here with?' Hep asked the same question. Come to find out Elaine was waiting to seduce Hep. He was clueless on how she felt about him. Winnie felt bad for the way she force-fed Elaine. She begged Hep for Elaine's job. They compromised. Winnie found her someone to help deal with her feelings for Hep. In return Elaine agreed to a demotion and never to approach Hep again."

Myles nodded. "Thank you for that information. Do you believe she has a grudge over the incident?"

"Yes."

"Enough to sabotage our accounts?"

"Yes."

"Okay, thanks for the blow by blow," he laughed as she turned to walk out the door.

"You have no idea."

#

Myles checked his watch. There were so many things he needed to tackle. But for some reason the conversation with Elaine had him rattled. He walked over to Chrystina's office. He walked through the door and thought she wasn't there for a minute until he saw her feet. He walked over to the desk and looked under it. She was spread out under the desk pulling up carpet.

"Chrystina, why are you under the desk?"

She looked up. "Oh, hey, Myles. I'm trying to figure out where this wire goes."

"It did not occur to you to call the tech people to check it out?"

She looked from under the desk. "Why would I do that when I can figure it out myself." She sat up on her elbow. "Tell me something."

"Sure." He sat in her chair.

"Did you hear the contempt in Elaine's voice as she spoke?"

"You heard that?"

"I did. I walked in to tell you about this wire, but turned when I heard her talking. I never noticed it in her before."

"Same here."

"Do you think it's resentment for what happened with Mr. Mitchell or you being named CEO?"

"It may be a little of both, I'm afraid."

"Excuse me, Mr. Dunning."

They both looked up to see Mrs. Vazquez in the doorway. "Yes?"

"You have visitors in your office. I've had refreshments brought up. I think you are going to be a while."

"Any idea what I'm walking into?"

"None. I will say neither Grace nor your mother look very happy."

Myles stood straight up. "My mother is here?"

Mrs. Vazquez nodded as she opened the door for him.

"I'm going to figure out what this wire is to. Yell if you need me."

#

Walking back into his office, Myles was surprised to see his mother sitting in front of his desk. Next to her was a young man who looked vaguely familiar. Grace was standing by the window. She turned when he walked in.

"Myles." Grace walked towards him. "You remember my friend Byron Roark from college."

Myles kissed his mother on the cheek then extended his hand. "I do. It's good to see you again."

Byron glanced from Myles to Grace as he shook Myles' hand. "You may not feel that way in a moment."

Myles raised an eyebrow as he glanced at Grace. "Why is that?" he asked as he pointed to a seat in front of his desk.

"Why don't we sit at the conference table." Grace glanced at Myles, then Byron. "That will give us more room."

"All right." A confused Myles nodded in agreement.

"It's important, son, or you know I would not have bothered you," Winnieford explained as she stood and walked over to the conference area of the huge office.

"Are you okay with me being here?" Myles leaned close to her ear.

"In the office?" his mother questioned. "It's where you belong."

Myles smiled as he pulled out the chair for her to sit.

"I'm happy to see you moved into this office," Grace said while taking a seat at the table. "We are going to need your guidance."

Myles sat at the head of the table. "You want to tell me what this is about?"

"I'll explain as soon as AnnieMarie arrives."

"I wasn't aware she was joining us."

Grace exhaled. "I think all the family members of the board need to be in on this decision. I sent a message to Michael and Gary as well."

"This is..." Myles questioned as he took a seat.

"A mess," Grace responded just as the door to the office opened.

"Hi." AnnieMarie rushed in. "I went to your old office only to discover you are now here." She walked over to the conference table. "Where is Chrystina?"

"Organizing things in her office, tearing up carpet, fielding calls, handling the transfer of files."

She nodded to Myles' reply then looked at Grace. "You look tired. Did you get any sleep last night?"

"Not really," Grace replied. "Why don't we all take a seat and let me tell you what is happening."

"That would be welcomed." Myles exhaled.

"You all know Byron. What you may not know is he is now with the FBI."

"The FBI?" AnnieMarie smiled then glanced at Myles.

Myles sat up, concerned. "Is there a problem?"

Byron reached into his jacket pocket and pulled out a business card. "First, I want you to have this, Mr. Dunning. It is my contact information as well as my superior's name and phone number. This is a fast moving situation. He has given me the authority to act on behalf of the agency. I am with the DC FBI office and will coordinate our actions with the local office here, if you agree to cooperate with us."

"Cooperate with you on what?" Myles asked.

"Uncle Walker," Grace scoffed.

Myles closed his eyes and sighed.

"What about Uncle Walker?" AnnieMarie asked.

"Mr. Dunning, I'm trained to read people. You don't seem surprised that Walker Dunning is the topic of this meeting. May I ask why?"

"Uncle Walker has a history of doing things family members would frown upon," Myles answered. "What are we talking about here?"

"It seems Uncle Walker has some dealings with a member of the Russian mafia," Grace stated.

"Do they exist?" AnnieMarie frowned.

"Yes," was the reply from Byron, Grace and Myles.

"Okay, so what does that have to do with us?" she asked.

Byron spoke, "It seems Walker Dunning Jr. is in debt to this organization to the tune of twenty million dollars."

"That sounds like Uncle Walker's problem," Myles retorted.

"It seems that amount changes depending on who you speak to," Grace added. "Uncle Walker told Aunt Vivian he owed thirty million. That's why this is our problem. Uncle Walker involved Aunt Vivian."

"Aunt Vivian?" Myles questioned. "What does she have to do with this?"

Grace sighed. "She called me last night to check out a name that Uncle Walker gave her. He indicated the man cut his throat then demanded he infiltrate the bank with one of their people."

"What?" Myles sat up, stunned. "To what end?"

"It's our belief Pavel wants to use the bank to launder money," Roark added.

Gary walked in then quietly took a seat as he nodded to Grace.

"Money laundering?" Myles sighed, then turned to Grace. "Hold that thought." He pushed the intercom that was in the center of the table. "Mrs. Vazquez, find my brother Michael and conference him in on this meeting." Myles turned back to Grace. "Start from the beginning."

Grace told Myles what was told to her in a chronological manner. Throughout the conversation tension built inside him as the scene from the security camera Jerome showed him last night played in his mind. This rendition of events from Grace seemed to correspond with what he saw on the tape. Mrs. Vazquez interrupted his thoughts when she walked in, pushed a few buttons on the intercom system, then walked back out.

"Mike, are you with us?" Myles asked.

"Yes, I'm on the highway. Grace did not give a lot of details."

"She's giving them to us now. Grace, Gary, AnnieMarie, Mother and special Agent Roark from the FBI are in the room with us. Continue, Grace."

"As I was saying, we put security in place for Aunt Viv and her family. The question is how much do we believe of Uncle Walker's story to Aunt Viv? What exactly does this Stephan Pavel want from him? More important how do we want to proceed?"

Gary chimed in. "We want to stay away from this, Myles. Any whispers of money laundering would have us under investigation."

"I'm concerned about this mafia connection," AnnieMarie added. "From the human resources point of view I am concerned how this may impact our employees' safety."

"If we are seriously talking the Russians," Michael chimed in, "once you get in bed with them there is no escape. Now, I don't know all the details. From what I've heard so far, I would have to say Uncle Walker is on his own."

Myles watched his mother as the conversations swirled around the subject. Her expression was impassive. He wasn't sure where she stood. What he did know was she entrusted him to protect the bank and their family. There was no way he would let her down.

"Special Agent Roark, what exactly is the FBI asking of us?" Myles sat back.

"We have two options. One, we could allow Mr. Dunning to believe he is fulfilling his obligation with Pavel. Let him come to work at the bank with Pavel's person. Track their transactions then take them down at the opportune time. The agency would be able to swoop in and take out the entire organization."

"At what cost?" Myles asked. "I have never known any criminal organization to go down without a fight. Someone, employees, family members or even your men would end up as a casualty. That is not an option."

"I understand your concern, Mr. Dunning. However, I need you to understand, Russians believe that the debts one is owed is owed by the family as well. They will collect what they feel's owed to them one way or another," Byron stated.

Myles sat forward. "Special Agent Roark, this is a bank. We will never jeopardize the trust our customers have in us or the reputation my family has enjoyed over the years to assist the agency in doing their job. What is your second option?"

Byron cleared his throat. "The second option would be to allow Mr. Dunning to embezzle funds and we will arrest him in hopes he will turn evidence over on Pavel. However, the likelihood of Mr. Dunning testifying at the trial is quite low."

"And?" Michael's voice came loud and clear through the speakers.

Myles turned. "Special Agent Roark, would you give us a few minutes."

Byron nodded, stood then stepped outside the office.

"We can't allow this," Grace said as she stood to get a drink.

"Allow Uncle Walker to take responsibility for the consequences of his actions?" Gary asked. "Why not? This isn't the first, second or third time he has gotten mixed up with illegal activity. Why should we keep bailing him out?"

"Because he is family," AnnieMarie replied. "We don't leave family out to dry."

Grace came back to the table. "I don't know. There has to be a way we can keep these people out of the bank and try to save Uncle Walker too."

Myles' gaze went to his mother. "Mother?"

"No, son." Winnieford met Myles's eyes. "This is your call. You do what you have to."

"Before I make a decision I want to talk to Uncle Walker and this Stephan Pavel."

"No," Michael, Gary and Grace's voices echoed around the room.

"You can't be seen meeting with a member of the Russian mob," Grace declared.

"She's right," Gary protested. "The visual implications alone would kill the bank's reputation."

"That's if you make it out of there alive," Michael added.

Winnieford stood, pushed her chair under the table then smiled at her son. "That is exactly how your father would have handled this. You don't need me here. I'll see you all at Sunday dinner."

"Is Jerome waiting for you downstairs?" Myles asked.

"Yes." Winnie nodded then left the office.

"Have a good evening, Mother." Myles turned to his siblings. "We are going to have a conversation with Uncle Walker tonight."

"I'm with you," Mike echoed. "I should be pulling in within the hour."

"I want in," Grace stated. "I think we should include Byron."

Myles nodded. "He is welcome as long as he understands our first priority is not to the FBI."

"Understood." Grace left the office to speak with Byron.

"I'm with you," Gary stated. "I think all of us should know what Uncle Walker is up to."

"I'm staying home with Mother," AnnieMarie proclaimed. "One of us has to be left standing to tell the authorities where to find your bodies."

#

"Chrystina?" Myles called out.

"Yes?" She came from behind the console near the conference table.

"Still following the wire?"

"It's weird, Myles. I've followed it over here and it disappears behind this wall. But it doesn't seem to be connected to anything."

He dismissed her concern. "Babe, I have to cancel dinner tonight. We have a situation with Walker."

"Your uncle?" She stopped what she was doing then walked towards him. "Is he all right?"

"I think he is at the moment. He may not be when I finish with him."

"That doesn't sound good, Myles. What do you need me to do?"

"Family stuff. I'll call you later." He kissed her forehead then walked out of the office.

Family first and foremost, Chrystina thought as she watched him walk away.

## Chapter Thirty-Four

Two vehicles pulled up to a closed gate that surrounded the home of Walker Dunning Jr. He had inherited his parents' home some years back. As far as they knew he lived in the mansion alone.

Mike was driving the first vehicle with Myles and Gary as passengers. Grace rode with Byron to show him the way.

"There are no lights on," Gary observed. "Do you think he is home?"

"Yes, I do," Myles replied. "I think he is hiding out. From who I'm not sure."

"You wouldn't happen to know the combination to the gate, would you?" Mike asked Myles.

"No. But it's easy enough to get." Myles pulled out his cell and dialed the number. "This is Myles Dunning. I would like the gate opened and alarm deactivated for the property on W. Dunning Rd. My pin number is 809." Myles waited a moment and then replied, "Thank you."

A second or two later the gate opened.

"You are the man." Mike grinned as he pulled onto the property.

They all stepped out of the vehicle and walked up to the front door. Myles opened the door and walked in. They were all surprised at the virtually empty rooms downstairs.

"I'll check upstairs," Mike said as he took the stairway to the right.

"What in the hell happened here?" Grace asked, stunned by the sight.

"Where is all of the furniture, the art?" Gary asked in disbelief.

"Uncle Ken mentioned this to me earlier today," Grace said as she walked from room to room downstairs. "He said that Uncle Walker has sold just about everything."

"It does not seem that was an exaggeration," Byron stated as he took in the lack of contents in the rooms.

"The art alone is worth a fortune," Gary stated. "How much debt can Uncle Walker be in if he sold everything that was here?"

"I'm sure he did not sell it for market value," Byron stated.

"No, he sold it for whatever his greedy little hands could get," an agitated Grace replied.

Myles looked around but did not comment. He was not concerned with Walker's living conditions. His only concern at that moment was to determine how Walker's actions impacted the bank and his family.

"He's up here," Mike called down the stairs.

They all walked up the spiral staircase and stopped at the entrance. A few covered their nose.

The master bedroom looked like a train wreck occurred and the disaster team never cleared it up. Amongst the discarded clothes, empty food containers and whiskey bottles was a king size bed in the center of the room with Walker spread eagle in the middle.

"I cannot talk to him in here." Myles shook his head. "Get him up, bring his ass downstairs."

"You got it." Mike and Byron picked Walker up as the others walked out of the room.

Ten minutes later they were all in the kitchen which did still have tables and chairs. Mike sat Walker at the table dressed in a robe.

"What happened to your neck, Walker?"

Walker held up his hand then squinted his eyes to try to see who was talking. "Hep, is that you?"

Myles took an angry step towards the man. Mike blocked his way.

"We are not going to get any answers that way. Why don't you let me take this one?"

Myles threw up his hands then stepped back next to Grace.

"Uncle Walker, this is Mike."

"Hey, Mike." Walker grinned. "Have a drink." His voice was raspy.

"No thanks. Uncle Walker, who is Stephan Pavel?"

"Whoa..." Walker shook his head. "Bad man. Dangerous. You stay away from him."

"Do you owe the mob money?"

"Sssshhhh, don't tell Hep."

"Uncle Myles, Daddy is dead." Grace was losing her patience.

"I know." He grinned.

Grace stepped forward. "Did you kill him?"

Everyone in the room stared at her, shocked by her question.

"I can't tell you." He frowned. "But he is dead." He began to cry.

"We're not going to get any answers tonight," Myles stated. "Mike, take him somewhere and get him cleaned up. See if you can find any hospital records on his injuries. Grace, take possession of this house. Have a cleaning crew to come in."

Gary nodded. "I'll have an assessment of what's left done by one of my people."

Myles nodded as he looked around. His grandparents were probably turning over in their graves over the state of this house. "I'm glad AnnieMarie did not come."

"She would have cried," Grace said as she looked around.

Myles took her and Byron aside. "Grace, why did you ask about Dad's death?"

"Uncle Ken said something today that made me wonder. He believes Walker had something to do with Daddy's death."

Myles exhaled. "Jerome believes it too. We need to know."

"We can have the body exhumed and have tox screens ran. But your mother will have to give her permission," Bryon offered.

Myles sighed then shook his head. "I'll talk with her about it."

"If he is involved with Pavel, he knows this is where Walker lives. They could be watching the house. For his own safety, you have to move him."

Myles and Grace glared at Walker. "I want him somewhere he cannot talk to anyone until he talks to us," Myles ordered.

"I have a place and people to keep him company until he sobers up," Mike said.

"Take him there. Get a team of people around him. We need answers."

# Chapter Thirty-Five

It was well after nine p.m. by the time they got Walker settled in, the house locked up and Myles had returned to the office. Calling it a day he got into his car and drove straight to Chrystina's apartment. When she opened the door, just the sight of her calmed his raging spirit. He stepped inside the open door and fell into her arms.

"This has been a trying day, babe." He kissed the side of her neck. "I needed this, the feel of your warmth around me."

"Sometimes changes in life aren't easy. That's when family and friends step in to help you through. You want to talk about it?"

"No." He picked her up and carried her down the hall to her bedroom. "I just want to hold you. Make love to you and leave the office and family behind, just for tonight."

He laid her on the bed, then opened her robe. She was wearing a night shirt that read, 'you staying for breakfast?' He smiled down at her, then removed his jacket, his shirt and kicked off his shoes. He unbuckled his belt, unzipped his pants and let them drop to the floor. He dropped to his knees. "You have beautiful thighs." He ran his hands up them. "They are so smooth, so soft." He pulled her panties down, then put her legs up on the edge of the bed. "I want to see you." He pushed her gown up.

"Myles," she moaned.

"Sssssshh. I need this tonight." He leaned forward, kissing her thighs from her knees to her center. He inhaled her scent. "You smell like peaches and cream," then licked her lips open. He heard her sigh. "You taste so sweet." His tongue traveled down the other thigh until he reached her knee. "I need you now, Chrys. I need you now." He pushed her thighs open and back, then entered her with a tenderness that made her cry out.

His strokes were smooth and easy, as he stood between her legs watching the play of emotions cross her face. He could stand there, pumping inside her for the rest of his life. Seeing the pleasure he was giving her tired his need as he began to pump harder, faster, stroke by stroke. Then when her hands covered his on top of her knees he lost all sense of control. All of the day's frustrations began to leave his mind, his body. He pumped fiercely, now wiping out all the doubts and trouble from the day, clearing the clouds away with each stroke until her inner lips began to close around him, pulling the need to a head and finally exploding with her, freeing his soul for her to conquer. He fell on top of her, exhausted in triumph. Her lips met his and the bliss of their love filled them, then induced them to sleep.

Sometime during the night her robe and night shirt came completely off and they made love again. Afterwards they laid awake in each other's arms gathering the strength for another day.

"Walker is involved with the Russian Mafia."

The statement shocked Chrystina in the quiet of the night, but she did not say anything. She just listened. "The bank seems to have some part in the deal." His head rested on hers. "I don't know why but I have a feeling Elaine Jacobson is up to something. Jerome thinks Walker had something to do with my father's death."

That sent a jolt through her. She sat up and looked at him. "Your father had a heart attack."

He put his hand behind his head. "That's what we were told."

"Why does he think there is something more to it?"

"It's not just him. My Uncle Ken believes it too."

"What do you believe?"

He shook his head. "I don't know, but I'm damn sure going to find out."

This was just the first week of his leadership. There had been many ups and downs. "The personal things you have to handle. There is no way you can let anyone know about Walker. I'll work on things in the office like getting the second in command you want. He will be able to handle Elaine." She looked at the clock. "You know, there is no time like the present." She picked up her phone, found what she was looking for then pushed the button.

"Mr. Michael, please hold for a call from the President and CEO of Dunning Bank & Trust, Mr. Myles Dunning." She put the call on hold, then held the phone out to Myles. "You're on."

He took the phone.

"I'll fix some coffee." She jumped out the bed just as Myles spoke.

"Mr. Michael, Myles Dunning. I would like to know your views on the global state of the banking industry."

## Chapter Thirty-Six

There came a time in every man's life when you just have to stand up for yourself. That's the reason we have the stand your ground law. It's time to take a stand. He had waited two days and nothing, not one word from Winnieford. Well, he wasn't waiting any longer. William nodded and exhaled as he stepped out of his vehicle. This was his time.

With that in mind he walked into the executive elevator, took it up to the eighth floor. He wasn't concerned about running into anyone for he had taken the elevator just about every day of his life for the last 30 years.

#

Myles and Chrystina had completed their workout. He was in his office working on notes for his 9a.m. meeting with Jonathan Michael. The possibility of bringing such a brilliant mind onboard energized him.

Chrystina was full steam ahead on filling positions, and settling things in the office. It was time to get back to the day-to-day operations. Clearing out her old office to make way for Pamela Green to take over her old position. She decided to make a trip to the basement to get boxes. In her mind the wire in her new office was still bugging her.

#

Stepping off the elevator on the eighth floor William nodded to one of the employees walking in the hallway. On this day at 8:45 am he took a different route. He was not headed to his office. No, on this day he had another task in mind. He turned right into the hallway that lead to the risk management suite. He walked to the opening where the sign read Myles Dunning, Director of Risk Management.

"Who are you?" he asked as he stared at a young woman unpacking boxes.

The woman turned to him. "Oh, hello, Mr. Mitchell. Pamela Green, remember me from the other day?"

A little confused, William watched as she dropped an empty box on the floor. She picked up another box and began removing items.

"What are you doing here?"

"Mr. Dunning promoted me." Pamela smiled at him. "Can you believe that, Mr. Mitchell?" She shrugged her shoulders. "I mean the other day I was certain that I was going to be fired. Instead he promoted me to the assistant to the director's position. He is such a considerate, forgiving man. Why, he could have fired us for what we did. But that's not what happened. He listened and gave us a second chance. I will tell you, Mr. Mitchell, Myles Dunning has a loyal employee for life." She smiled brightly at the man. That smile slowly faded as the vision of a gun came into focus.

William fired one shot, turned and walked away.

Employees running by him did not stop William's progress. He simply kept walking to his next destination. Another employee passed him, running in the direction of the sound.

"Mr. Mitchell, was that a gunshot I heard?"

William did not answer the question. He simply raised his weapon and fired it again.

Employees were now in the hallway looking out their office doors. At the sound of the second shot they got back in their doors and closed them quickly. William continued on his journey.

#

The quiet afternoon was shattered with a single gunshot. Elaine sat stone-faced at her desk as a second shot rang out. Then she calmly picked up the phone and dialed 911.

"Gunshots have been fired in the executive offices of Dunning Bank and Trust headquarters. Get the police here now. Please hurry before he kills someone," she shouted and slammed the phone down. Smiling at her performance, for she knew the 911 tape would be played in every news cycle for the next two days, she took her tablet in her hand and waited for what she knew would happened next.

#

Myles jumped from his desk at the sound of the first shot. Before he made it to the door, Mrs. Vasquez burst through.

"Emergency measures have been put in place," she stated as she walked past him to the desk. "Security has been notified," she said then she pushed the button under the desk.

"Was that a gunshot?"

The bookcase on the far wall slid open. Behind it was a safe room. "I believe it was, sir. I need you to step into the safe room."

Still stunned by the sound, Myles did not hear what she had said. "Where did it come from?"

"The other side of the foyer."

The other side of the foyer is where Risk management was located. "Where is Chrystina?"

"I don't know, sir. I need you inside the room, Mr. Dunning."

"I need to find Chrystina." He rushed towards the doors.

"Myles, I need you to stay inside of the safe room," Mrs. Vasquez insisted.

"You go inside the room and stay there. I'm going to find Chrystina and check on the employees," Myles argued as he ran out the door.

Two security guards stopped his progress by each taking an arm and placing him back inside the office.

"We cannot allow you to go out there, sir, until the situation is in hand," one security officer stated. "If you will remain here, we will ascertain what course of action needs to be taken."

A second shot rang out. The officers pushed Myles back then pulled their weapons. One crouched down behind the opening, the other standing behind the doorframe, both sweeping their weapons in a wide arc around the reception area.

Myles ran to the connecting door of Chrystina's office and burst through. She wasn't there. He then ran to her door that led to the receptionist area.

The security officers swung their weapons in his direction.

"Mr. Dunning, please, sir, get back."

Myles saw the employees who worked in the area and waved to them. "Come in here. Now."

Lynn, Sean, Sonya and Annatasha all ran to him.

Cainan appeared. "Myles, you okay?"

"Yes. AnnieMarie?"

"I don't know."

"What's going on?" Cainan asked as the others ran into the room.

"I don't know," Myles repeated. "I can't get past the guards to see." He glanced at his employees. "I want all of you to go into my office and stay in the safe room with Mrs. Vasquez until we can figure out what's going on."

"Here." Sonya ran over to the conference room table. "This should help."

She pushed a button on the intercom panel. The doors on the wall cabinet opened to reveal six computer monitors. Myles' eyes widened. Where in the hell did that system come from? Then it hit him, the wires Chrystina was talking about. But why was this security system in Mitch's office? he wondered.

Sonya pushed another button to activate the monitors. The monitors all came to life.

"This is the reception area in the lobby," she said, then pushed another button. The picture from another monitor came into view. "This is the hallway by the elevator on this floor."

"Is that Mr. Mitchell?" Annatasha asked.

They all stared at the monitor as the man holding the gun turned towards the camera.

"That is Mr. Mitchell," Sean confirmed.

"Everyone in the safe room," Myles ordered.

"I'm staying with you," Cainan declared.

"I'll take the women," Sean offered, then walked through the adjoining door to Myles' office.

"What is he doing?" Cainan asked.

Myles watched as Cainan quickly glanced from one monitor to another as if assessing every detail.

"I have no idea," Myles replied as he followed Cainan's moves. "Look that's Chrystina standing in front of the elevator. What floor is that?"

"That's the basement," Cainan replied.

Myles looked to see where Mitch was now. He was standing right by the elevator.

"The executive elevator is an express," Cainan stated. "If she gets on it, she will walk right into Mitchell."

"We have to stop her," Myles said as he reached into his pocket for his cell phone. He dialed her number. To his surprise it rang in the room. He turned to see her cell phone was on her desk. "Oh hell."

"Call the maintenance department," Cainan suggested.

Myles grabbed the phone and pushed the button for maintenance. It rung once, twice....

"Maintenance, Larry Taylor speaking."

"Larry, this is Myles Dunning. I need you to go to the elevator and stop Ms. Price from getting on it."

"Excuse me, sir?" Larry asked, somewhat confused.

"Larry, stop Ms. Price from getting on the elevator, now!" Myles insisted.

"Yes, sir, yes, sir, I got you."

Myles watched as Chrystina stood there positioning the boxes on the floor and balancing the ones in her hands. Another gunshot rang out. Both Myles and Cainan turned towards the sound. It was a lot closer this time. When Myles turned back, Chrystina was gone and Larry was running towards the elevator doors, which were now closed.

"Damnit," Myles declared. "We have to stop that elevator. If she steps off she will be directly in his line of fire."

"We can stop it," Cainan declared. "There is an elevator service room at the end of the hallway. If we can get security to pull Mitchell in this direction, we can use the hallway exit from this office to get to the service room."

"Isn't that door locked? Only maintenance would have a key to it."

"Or someone who knows how to pick a lock." Cainan smiled.

#

Chrystina had kicked the last box into the elevator and pushed the button when she thought she saw someone running towards it. With boxes in her hand she couldn't push the button to hold the door open.

"Oh no, sorry," she called out not sure if the person could hear her. She leaned against the back panel. What a day it had been. It felt good giving Pam Green the news about her promotion. The look on the woman's face was priceless. Chrystina smiled at the memory. What a way to start her new position. She was going to have to find a way to thank Myles for allowing her to be the one to break the news. With the positions coming open, it would be great to start each day giving someone great news.

"That's it," she said out loud to herself, then searched her pockets for her phone. She didn't have it.

"Oh, man." She was disappointed. "Okay, we will start a 'good news' trend at the office. Hmm." She smiled. "That will be fun."

Suddenly the elevator jerked. Chrystina fell backwards, spreading her arms to brace herself until the elevator was motionless.

"Okay," she said slowly as she stood straight. She kicked the boxes out of her way and pushed the button to the eighth floor. Nothing happened. She looked up at the floor number.

"We came this close," she chuckled as she saw the number seven. She reached for the elevator phone and pushed the emergency button. The phone rang once, twice, three times. Nothing.

"Okay," she said, patience still in check but about to go haywire. She pushed the emergency button again. Nothing. Then she heard a thump and felt the elevator move.

She looked up, nerves getting a little shaky. Then there was another thump. Maybe someone was up there.

"Okay," she said. "They know the elevator is stuck and someone from maintenance is there to open it. Yes, that's it."

The panel, in the top of the elevator, was pushed to the side. She looked up, not believing what or whom she was seeing.

"Myles? What in the hell are you doing on top of the elevator?"

"Babe, I'll explain later," he said as he jumped down into the car beside her. "Right now we have to get you out of here." He bent down. "Climb on my shoulders so I can lift you up."

"What?" she laughed. "I'm not climbing on your shoulders."

She had barely finished getting the words out of her mouth before Myles wrapped his arms securely around her thighs and hauled her upwards.

Chrystina let out a scream while holding on to Myles' shoulders. "Maybe you can carry me wherever you want," she laughed.

"Chrystina, give me your hands."

She then looked up to see Cainan. She looked into Myles' eyes. That's when she saw something wasn't right. "What's going on?" she asked in a serious tone.

"Let's get you out of here and then we'll talk about it." He pushed her further up until she could reach Cainan.

Cainan pulled her straight up through the opening. "It's a good thing I started exercising," she joked.

Cainan laid flat on top of the elevator car then reached down for Myles. Pulling him up was more of a struggle. Chrystina held his legs down to keep him from being pulled inside the car as Myles climbed along the walls of the elevator car until he was able to haul himself up by his elbows.

They closed the emergency door on the elevator.

Myles pulled her into his arms, kissed her temple and just held her.

"It's okay." She rubbed his back to comfort him. It wasn't clear to her why he needed that, but she knew for a fact Myles needed her comfort.

"We need to climb back up," Cainan said after clearing his throat.

Myles pulled away. "Yes, let's go."

"Umm, excuse me?" Chrystina looked around. "We're climbing where?"

"Back up the shaft." Cainan pointed. "It's a half of a floor, Ms. Price. We can make it."

"I'm going to be behind you, babe. No worries. I got your back."

"I know there is a good...really good explanation for all of this."

The fear was clear in her eyes now, as she looked down the side of the elevator car. The pulley wires and nothing. Seven floors of nothing were between them and the basement.

"Don't," Myles said as she started to bend further to see over the side. "Let's just move up."

Cainan grabbed the mounted steel ladder then climbed up until he reached the service room door. Chrystina followed, with Myles trailing behind her.

#

William turned to the sound of the scream from inside the elevator. The security officer's walkie talkie sounded.

"Live shooter. I repeat, live shooter. Follow emergency 2 procedures. We have two down in Risk Management. Get medical assistance up here right away."

"Police are on site. On their way up now," the security officer responded back.

"Mr. Mitchell, sir," the chief security officer called out. "Please put your weapon down, sir."

"We do not want to harm you, sir," another guard called out.

William looked around a bit flustered.

"Wait." Elaine stepped out of her office. "Please let me talk to him."

"Ms. Jacobson, please go back into your office, ma'am."

"William." Elaine stepped towards him, placing herself between him and one of the security guards. With her hands up she looked at William, pleading. "Please, William, will you give me the gun. I don't want anything to happen to you."

"Elaine?" William was confused.

She continued to walk towards him as the guards called out for her to move out of the line of fire. Elaine knew some of the employees were watching. She had to make it look good for them. Yes, she wanted to be the heroine in this scene. Wanted the employees to tell Myles how she brought down William. Let him be beholden to her for saving his employees. As for William, she knew he would never shoot her.

"William, I want you to give me the gun."

"I haven't killed Myles yet," William explained. "You know what I have to do."

"William," she called out before he could say more. "I'm going to protect you. I will not let any of them hurt you. I'm going to be your shield."

It took him a minute, but then he understood. William reached out and grabbed Elaine. He put the gun to her head. "Any one of you comes closer and I will shoot." He began backing up towards the hallway entrance to the stairwell. He kicked the door open then closed it.

"Hit me on the head, William, then take your private exit."

"I don't want to hit you, Elaine."

"Do it now, William, and go. Get out of here. Don't go to your house. You understand?"

William brought the butt of the gun up then slammed it on her temple. She fell to the floor blocking the door. He turned and ran down the stairs.

# Chapter Thirty-Seven

"**W**hat do you mean he got away?" Myles yelled as security officers surrounded the office.

"Everything was happening so fast. The minute he pulled Ms. Jacobson into the stairwell, we tried to get in. Her body was blocking the door."

"Surround the building," the police officers who had just arrived ordered. "Mr. Dunning, what can you tell us about this man?"

Chrystina and Cainan ran down the hallway checking employee offices one by one. Cainan stopped where Elaine was with an officer.

Screams and loud chatter erupted as Chrystina made her way to the Risk Management area.

One male employee was sitting on the floor leaning against the wall with blood running down his arm. An officer was working to stop the bleeding.

"Jacob," Chrystina called out as she walked by. "You're going to be okay?"

"Yes, ma'am." The pain was clear in his response.

She then ran towards the crowd of employees standing in the entrance to her old office.

"Please let me get through."

The crowd made way and Chrystina's knees all but buckled.

"Oh my God," Chrystina cried out. "It's Pam." She ran and kneeled beside the officer who was working on the woman who had just taken her place.

"This should have been me," she said to the officer. "Not her. Please don't let her die. Please don't."

"We're going to do all we can, ma'am. If you can give my partner her information that would be helpful," the officer said without stopping his movements to help Pam.

The officer spoke into his walkie talkie. "Female, approximately late twenties. Gunshot wound to the left shoulder. Unresponsive. Slow pulse. Substantial blood loss."

"EMTs on site," a response came back.

"Her name is Pamela Green. She's twenty-nine, with two boys. Her husband died in Iraq a year ago." Chrystina spoke softly. "Her boys need her. Do you understand me? You will not let her die."

The officer looked at Chrystina. "No, ma'am, we will not."

Chrystina nodded her head, certain the officer got her meaning.

#

Myles pushed through the crowd. He immediately ran to Chrystina's side.

"Myles," Chrystina cried up at him. "It's Pam. Myles, it's Pam."

"I know." He picked her up so the officer could work.

"How is she?" Myles asked

"She's losing a lot of blood. We need to transport her to the hospital," the officer replied.

The EMTs entered the room taking over the care for Pam.

"We have to go with her," Chrystina cried as tears streamed down her face.

Myles turned to one of the employees. "Call Larry Taylor in maintenance. Have him to meet us in the front."

"Yes, sir." The employee ran off.

The EMTs were moving Pam out towards the foyer, with Chrystina and Myles following behind.

"Everyone, please listen up," a British accented voice called out. "What has happened here today, is shocking to say the least. You are shaken. I will ask that you check on your co-workers to assure everyone is accounted for. Anyone who needs medical attention, let's make certain they get it expeditiously. Tellie your loved ones. They will hear of this on the news. Assure them you are fine. Any employee who feels they need to go home, you are free to do so. Mr. Dunning is granting liberal leave. Those who are in vital positions, you know who you are, please man your stations."

Myles recognized Jonathan Michael when he turned the corner. He held his hand out. "Myles Dunning."

"Jonathan Michael. What in the bloody hell kind of operations are you running here, Mate?" the calm, but alert man asked.

"A hectic one at the moment. That's a hell of an impression you made. Taking charge of a volatile situation wasn't in the negotiations."

"All in a day's work." Jonathan nodded. "How many injured?"

"Three, from what I can tell." Myles exhaled. "Two shot, one hit in the head."

"That would be Elaine Jacobson?" Jonathan raised an eyebrow.

"Yes." Myles noticed the look in Jonathan's eyes. "Do you know her?"

"We've spoken. Let's get the employees settled down. We can chat later."

Myles turned to Cainan. "AnnieMarie?"

"She was out of the building. She's on her way back now."

Myles nodded. "Have security do an office by office check on employees as we secure the building. I want every employee accounted for within the hour."

# Chapter Thirty-Eight

"Darling, life is not the same without you." Winnie sat on the bench next to Hep's grave, the mound of dirt from the burial still evident. The headstone had just been set that morning, finalizing the tragedy of his passing.

"The children are coming along-AnnieMarie a little slower than the others. I don't know what the issue was you had with Cainan Scott, but AnnieMarie loves him the way I love you. Please find a way to send her a sign. She is hurting inside. I don't want to see her shrink away from being all she can. You know like I do, without that special love in her life, she will dwindle away. I've watched Cainan and I believe his love for her is just as deep." She sighed. "This is hard without you," she said as she looked out over the grounds.

"It seems Walker has gotten into some trouble. Gary and Michael are handling him, for now. It's the only way to keep Myles from killing him." She smiled. "He doesn't have your calm exterior when it comes to Walker. If it were up to him, Myles would let Grace's

FBI friend lock Walker up and throw away the key. Speaking of Grace..." She inhaled then continued. "I don't know if you remember the young man Grace introduced us to during college. His name is Jonathan Michael. He is from London, England. Well, it seems the two are meeting up in New York. Grace Heather isn't saying much, but she is excited about seeing him. I think he may be the one to settle her wild behind down." She sat forward resting her arms on her thighs.

"Speaking of settling down. Myles and Chrystina, finally, are together." She laughed. "How many nights did you and I fall asleep laughing at those two. I wish you could see Myles with her. It's as if the sunlight made an emergence through the fog. I see nothing but bright days and loving nights ahead for them. All I have to do is find a way to let Myles know it's okay for him to move back out of the house. He works all day at the bank then rushes home to check on me. I know it's that darn Daisy making him think he needs to be in the house with me." She shook her head. "Between Daisy, Jerome and AnnieMarie, I'm not alone in the house. I'll find a way to convince Myles to find a home with Chrystina and start a family. Now, that would make me happy." She smiled. "Of all the ways we thought it would happen between those two, you will never guess what finally did it. This thing with Mitchell at the bank." She sat back and exhaled.

"I might as well get it out. First, I will say Myles has been causing quite a stir at the bank and in the financial world. You would be so very proud of him, Hep. It's as if you are channeling your spirit into him. The employees love him for making the transition easy on them. Each issue thrown at him, he has met the challenge with the kind of grace you always used with the employees." She shrugged her shoulder.

"Well, with the exception of William. I'm afraid he had to let William go. As you know William always pulled behind the back deals with clients along the years. Well, he did it with Myles. This is the one area you and Myles certainly differ. While you handled the situation and kept documentation, Myles took action. It's clear he does not feel the same loyalty towards William as you did. I know." She smiled. "William was responsible for giving you the greatest joy of your life." She giggled like a young schoolgirl. "You said that thirty years ago when you hired him. It still warms my heart to know you put up with so much from him because of me. Anyway..." She shook off the melancholy feeling that was about to take over. "About Myles and Chrystina. It seems William attempted to sway the executives from Hershel Automotive from connecting with Myles. Some way Chrystina found out about it and was able to get Myles and the Hershel execs together. You will be happy to know they signed with Dunning. After the deal was made public, Myles' plan was to demote William, allow him to retain his title; however strip him of any executive power. Of course Chrystina did not agree with his decision and she let Myles know it. Apparently William did not appreciate Chrystina's take on things and attacked her in front of Myles." Winnie laughed. "Hep, you really need Marie to tell you the story. But, she said Myles went across that desk like a linebacker after a fumbled football. He grabbed William by the throat and would not let go. Said it took her, Chrystina and two security officers to get him off William." She laughed out loud until tears were falling from her eyes.

"I tell you." She wiped the tears. "That was something I would have loved to have witnessed." She sniffed, then settled down again. "Anyway, as far as

Myles was concerned, William sealed his fate by putting his hands on Chrystina. He was let go with an attractive severance package, so I'm told. But I don't think he will ever work at the bank again." She sighed. "Another part of our history coming to an end."

A breeze shifted through the trees behind her causing the leaves to rustle. "The night air is changing," she said as she pulled her sweater around her shoulders. "I miss your warmth, Hep. Your laughter, those eyes." She wrapped her arms around her shoulders, tilting her head to the side. "I miss your arms, your kisses. I miss your spirit so much, Hep. I know you are still with me in my heart. Am I being selfish to want you back here, with me, in the flesh?" She heard the rustle of the leaves again.

"Well, my darling, it's getting late. Jerome, Daisy or both will be out here looking for me soon." She looked up at the sky. "My bed is cold and I blame you, Hepburn Dunning. I am angry at you and will never forgive you for leaving me so soon," she yelled then wiped the tears that fell away. "But I still love you, Hep, and will love you until the day I join you again."

#

Winnie was about to stand when she felt the weight of hands on her shoulders. There was something in the touch that sent chills through her. She looked at the brown hands on her shoulders. They were short and stubby. Then he spoke.

"Do you know how many years I've waited to hear you say those words to me?"

She glanced at the hands again. That was William's voice, but those hands were brown, not the pale color she was used to seeing.

"William?"

"Yes, darling. It's me. I've come to you just the way you have always wanted." He put pressure on her shoulders when she tried to stand. "There is nothing to stand between us being together now. Year after year I tried to understand why you chose him over me. We were both athletic, handsome, charming. While Hep's family was wealthier than mine, I don't think you felt it was a significant difference. No, I know it was never about money with you, Winnieford."

"William, what are you doing here?" Winnie asked in the calmest voice she could gather.

"I'm here for you, Winnieford. I'm here to warm that cold bed. With Hep gone, the job ending at the bank and now the changes I've made, why there is nothing, nothing to keep us apart."

"Changes?" Winnie looked around.

His hands clamped down harder on her shoulders, digging in.

"William, you are hurting me."

His hands loosened. "I would never hurt you, Winnieford." He walked around the side of the bench and knelt in front of her.

Winnieford gasped. "William, what did you do?"

"I did it for you." He smiled. "Don't you see, Winnieford? It was the only thing keeping us apart. This is how much I love you." He touched her knee. "It was a process, let me tell you. But it is all worth it."

Winnie looked into his blue eyes; there was something different. She could see he wasn't himself...in many ways. Moving her knee slightly to remove his hand, she slid to the end of the bench. The wrought iron railing stopped her from moving further.

"William, tell me what you did?"

He stood proudly. "I changed my skin color, Winnieford." He nodded with a sense of accomplishment. "I became a man of color, just for you. I used a spray gun. Yes, it wasn't difficult at all. I heard you talking to Hep and I have to say I was angry with Myles for dismissing me the way he did. I wanted to kill him. I tried, but I couldn't find him. But to be honest, it would have never been the same without you." He glared at her. "You were never coming back to the bank, were you? I understand. With Hep gone, coming to the bank would only bring bad memories." He fell to his knees and took her hand into his. "For thirty-eight years, Hep has been between us. But now, he's gone and look." He leaned back and held out his arms. "I made myself over so you will have no fear of being with me. And yes" -he nodded and smiled widely- "it's all over my body. Every inch of me is now brown. Just like you. I could go as dark as Hep, but depth of the color of my skin isn't what's important. No, this is only a demonstration to show the depth of my love for you. I will walk through the depths of hell for you, Winnieford." He jerked back towards her, grabbing her hand, kissing her fingers.

Winnie stood quickly, pulling her hand away. The action caused William to tilt forward, bracing himself on the bench to stop his fall.

"William, this isn't right." Winnie looked around, no one was in sight. Walking backwards, away from him, she shook her head. "I love Hepburn. You know that. I don't love you."

He moved so fast it caused her to lose her balance when he grabbed her by the shoulders.

"Don't say that." He shook her. "Don't you ever say that." His anger shined through his eyes at her, causing her to whimper. Then suddenly, like a snap of a finger, his anger was gone, his eyes softened. "Winnieford, don't look at me like that." He pulled her to him and hugged her, tight. "I would never, never hurt you." He then pushed her back and held her at arms' length. "You should know that I've saved my heart for you all these years. Waiting for you to finally realize you married the wrong man. It should have been me, Winnieford. Of course we would have had to keep it a secret from my family, but that would have only been for a while, until they got used to you."

"Oh, William," Winnie cried. "I am sorry." She nodded. "Very sorry. You have been a friend, William. All these years you have been a friend."

"I know, I know." He smiled, cupping her face with his hands...his brown hands. "But now, we can be so much more. Don't you see? There are no obstacles between us now. We're free. Yes, we are free. Free to love." He pulled her face close to his. His tongue moistened his lips, his eyes closing as he brought her lips closer to his. "Finally, we are free, Winnieford, free," he said as his lips were a breath away from hers.

Winnie pushed him away, the momentum causing her to fall over the heap of soil on Hepburn's grave.

"William, no. I don't feel that way about you. I don't love you," she cried out as she crawled to the other side of the grave.

William grabbed for her leg. She kicked at him as she continued to crawl on the ground to get away from him.

"No," he shouted. "I have waited all these years. I became a Black man for you...A Black man," he yelled. "I will have you." He caught her ankle as she kicked out.

Winnie screamed loud enough to wake the dead.

William stomped across the mounted dirt, causing the earth to disappear under his feet. Both hands grabbed Winnie's feet as the grave beneath him opened more, causing his body to fall deeper into the ground.

Winnie gasped at what she was seeing. It was as if William was being pulled into the grave...Hep's grave.

She screamed, and grabbed at anything she could find on the ground to keep his momentum from pulling her under with him. She kicked at his hands, still reaching around for something, anything to loosen the grasp he had on her ankles.

"Jerome," she screamed out. "Jerome."

Seconds later, she heard a thump. The grip on her ankles was gone. She turned back to see Jerome standing on the other side of the grave with a bat in his hand. William could not be seen from her angle on the ground. She pulled her legs from the opening in the ground, then crawled towards it.

Looking over the side of the hole in the ground, there was William, lying at least three feet under the ground, where in her mind, she imagined Hep's hands would be in the coffin.

"Do you want me to go ahead and throw the dirt in on top of him?"

Winnie looked up at Jerome with a bemused expression. She wasn't sure whether to laugh or cry at the situation.

"Do you think...." She let that statement drop. "No." She shook her head. "Never mind."

"Is that a no to burying him where he lay?" Jerome asked as if he was unaffected by the scene.

Winnie looked down into the hole again. With dirt everywhere, from her nose to her hair, and all over her clothes she began to laugh. "I will not put my husband through an eternity of having William on top of him." She stood and began to brush the dirt from her clothes.

"You want me to pull him out?"

The way Jerome asked the question was as if he was disappointed. "Yes, if you don't mind. Pull him out."

"What if I do mind?"

This time when she looked at Jerome there was a curve to his lips. Funny, she never noticed just how charming a man he was.

"Pull him out anyway." She cracked a smile.

"Hell, all right." Jerome reached down, grabbing William's arm and pulled the man from the hole. "How do you suppose the ground gave way like that?"

Winnie knew what she was thinking but there was no way in hell she was going to tell anyone Hep reached up from the grave to pull William's ass in.

"I don't know," she replied instead.

"Well, I'm calling the authorities on him and the funeral director for Mr. Hep." He looked up at Winnie. "You go on up to the house."

Winnie swiped at her pants, then brushed her hair back. "Yes, I must look a mess," she said as she glanced back at William on the ground.

"You never looked a mess a day in your life."

She gazed at Jerome, then looked towards the house. "Yes, well. You okay taking care of this?"

"I'll have this taken care of in no time. Mr. Hep would be upset if he thought for one minute I wasn't taking care of you right. I'll clean up this pile of crap."

Winnie smiled. "All right." She turned and started walking the path back to the house. Glancing back once or twice she wondered what Jerome meant by taking care of her.

#

"You will not believe what just happened down at the park." She was still trying to clean herself up when she walked into the kitchen. "I was talking to Hepburn and that darn William walked up behind me." She stopped, thought then spoke more to herself than to Daisy. "How did he get onto the property?" She shook her head. "Not important, Jerome has him now."

When no question came back to her, Winnie finally looked up to see Daisy's eyes glued to the television.

"Are you seeing this?" Daisy asked without turning towards her. "There is APB or a warrant or whatever they call it out on William Mitchell."

"What?" Winnie walked over to stand next to Daisy to get a better view of the news report.

"Again," the reporter spoke, "There has been reports of gunfire in the Dunning Bank & Trust Headquarters. Police have named the shooter as Ex-Vice-President, William Mitchell. We've learned just about a week ago, Myles Dunning was named the new CEO and President of Dunning Bank & Trust, taking over the seat of his deceased father, Hepburn Dunning. We've also learned, a few days ago William Mitchell was relieved of his position by Myles Dunning." The reporter grabbed her earpiece. "Hold on, Chip, I believe a spokesperson for Dunning Bank and Trust is coming out to make a statement."

Winnie gasped, "William?"

"Shhhh," Daisy hushed her.

"Oh, thank goodness." Winnie grabbed her chest. "There's AnnieMarie coming out of the building. Was anyone hurt? Is there any word on Myles?"

"Shhhh," Daisy said as she turned up the volume.

"Good morning, my name is Annie Dunning. I am the Public Relations Director for Dunning Bank and Trust. At approximately 9:05 am this morning an ex-employee entered the building and opened fire. Three employees were injured; two from gunshots and one with a head wound. They have been transferred to local hospitals. There is no update on their condition. Their names will not be released until relatives can be notified. The shooter is no longer on the premises; however, security measures have been put in place until the person is captured. CEO Myles Dunning is currently securing the building to ensure the remaining employees are safe. That's all for now."

Winnie picked up the phone and dialed a number. Her expression visibly relaxed when the call was answered.

"I only needed to hear your voice. But I have to tell you, William is here." She held the phone from her ear at Myles' booming voice. "Jerome has him and has called the police."

Sirens could now be heard.

"I'm putting the alarm system on." Daisy rushed from the room as Winnie nodded.

"We're fine, Myles. You handle what you need to at the office." She nodded her head to what he was saying on the other end. "I'll have Jerome to call you. Myles, was anyone seriously hurt?" She closed her eyes to say a silent prayer as she listened. She looked up when Daisy walked back into the room. "Go ahead, son, I'll talk with you later."

"What did he say?" Daisy asked.

"One young woman was seriously injured. She's in surgery. Chrystina is with her."

"My Lord, Mitchell finally lost it." Daisy stood with her hands on her hips as she shook her head and sighed.

Winnie watched as Daisy gave her a once over.

"What in the hell happened to you?"

## Chapter Thirty-Nine

"Where are you?"

"Leaving the hospital," Chrystina told him. "How are things in the office? Is everyone accounted for?"

"Yes," Myles replied. "Every employee has been verified. The building is closed for the remainder of the day. Essential personnel are on duty."

"Any word on Mr. Mitchell?"

"He showed up at my parents' home. Jerome apprehended him and called the police. He is now in custody. How are you?"

"Shaken. I can't stop thinking that should have been me."

"If it should have been, it would have been. God don't make mistakes. So get that out of your head. How is Ms. Green?"

"Out of surgery. Doctors believe she will make a full recovery."

"Let's send someone to check on her children."

"Larry has them. I will coordinate things with him and make sure he has everything he needs for them.

I'll make a quick run home to change clothes then will return to the office."

"Take care, I'll see you soon."

Myles hung up the telephone then turned back to Jonathan. "All is well with Ms. Green."

"Splendid news. There was a bit of chaos but the storm is not over."

Myles sat back. "Why do you say that?"

"You are about to enter into the realm of petty you would never imagine."

Myles almost laughed. "How so?"

"Well, mate, you are now the number one enemy of Phase International and America's Bank, two of the most influential financial and political organizations in the world."

"With that knowledge, explain to me why you are here, Jonathan. Your pedigree is superb. You are the number two man at Phase. You should be looking at starting your own financial institution. Why are you taking a meeting with me knowing at best you would be second in command."

"I was fourth at best at Phase." Jonathan crossed his legs. "It's all relative." He smiled. "Would you believe I'm here talking with you out of a sense of duty."

"No." Myles walked over to his bar. "Would you like a drink?"

"Aye, I think a spot of tea would do well."

"Tea?" Myles frowned.

"Yes, tea."

"Tea it is." Myles sat his drink on the desk then buzzed Mrs. Vazquez. Who walked in with a cup of tea.

Myles frowned.

"No mystery," she responded to Myles' expression. "Sydney indicated he would want an afternoon tea."

"Spot on." Jonathan smiled at her.

Mrs. Vazquez blushed at his response then retreated from the room.

"Can you do anything about that accent?" Myles rolled his eyes. "You will be charming half of my staff before the day is out."

"Sorry, mate," Jonathan laughed. "The accent comes with the man."

"Does that mean you are considering our offer?"

"My purpose in coming here is to save your bank."

Myles placed his glass on his desk. "I wasn't aware we needed to be saved."

"The precise reason why I am here." He sipped his tea then looked at Myles. "You have a traitor in your midst and I am here to help you sort out the bloody mess."

"Why?"

"Well if you don't believe the duty to my race, will you believe it's because I'm madly in love with Grace? At some point in my life I plan to make her my wife. For that reason it is my duty to protect her at all cost."

"What happens if Grace does not feel the same?"

"She does." Jonathan shrugged.

"What if she doesn't?"

Jonathan sat his cup of tea down then glared at Myles. "Have you ever been in love, Myles?"

Myles thought about Chrystina and smiled.

"Ahh, you are in love."

He nodded his head. "Yes, I am."

"Was there ever a time where you doubted her love for you?"

"No."

"Then you know how I know Grace is in love with me. I've had many women in my life, but have only loved one. She is challenging, intelligent and one of the most graceful women I know. When a man loves a woman the way I love Grace, it's because that woman loves him just as fiercely. I've put Grace off to allow her to build her career, me to build mine. It's now time for us to balance our worlds."

Myles' cell phone buzzed. He checked the caller ID then answered the call. "I'll be right out, AnnieMarie." He hung up then stood, adjusting his suit coat. "Dunning wants you on board. Our motto is Family First and Foremost. It's the same whether you are family or not. We can probably match your salary with Phase and add a few incentives. If you choose to accept our offer, I expect you to eliminate the traitors, then protect us from it happening again. I have to meet with the press."

"Go, man, we will chat soon."

#

Jonathan followed Myles out of the office. He stopped in the reception area and looked around.

"How may I help you, Mr. Michael?" Mrs. Vazquez asked.

"I was seeking my assistant."

"Sydney, she is right in this office." She took him to the office next to Myles'. "If you decide to stay this will be your space."

He looked around. "This will do nicely. I will need a tea tray at some point."

"You have a wonderful voice." She smiled.

He tilted his head. "Pleased to delight you. I am rather charming."

"That you are." She closed the door.

"What a bloody day," Sydney said from behind the desk.

"It was."

"Are we staying? If so, I'll need to acquire a flat, and transportation. It doesn't seem this place has trolleys."

Jonathan looked out the windows to the downtown area. "I have to stay," he stated. "Unfortunately, I don't think the drama is over. In fact, I'm certain it's only the beginning."

Sydney stood, then walked around to the front of the desk. She took a seat in the chair, pulled out her tablet then stared up at him. "Where do you want me to start?"

With a smile, he took a seat. "Find a flat for you and a home for me. One that a family can grow to love."

"Shall I begin to search for engagement rings?" She smiled up at him.

#

Later that night, standing in the doorway of Elaine Jacobson's hospital room, a man watched her, riveted by the news report on the shooting at the bank. The reporter spoke of the bravery of Elaine Jacobson. Literally putting her body between other employees and the shooter. He clapped three times slowly to get her attention. She turned towards the door, the smile of glee on her face slowly dissipated.

"What a performance, Elaine."

"Jonathan Michael. What in the hell are you doing here?"

#

Across town, in a one-bedroom apartment in a run down section of town, Shawn Bolton sat up as he watched the news. He could not believe his eyes. He pulled his cell phone out and snapped a picture of the scene playing out on the screen. Staring at the picture a wide grin began to form on his face.

He scanned through the contacts on his phone until he came to the number he needed. He pushed the call button, sat back on the ragged sofa and crossed his legs.

"Hey, long time."

"What do you want, Bolt?"

"I'll say a half-million for starters."

"I'm hanging up."

"Doing that is going to cause Johnnie to slit your throat for not sharing the news I have for him."

"What in the hell are you talking about?"

"I'm talking about the man you have spent three years requesting delayed court appearances, to give you time to locate and eliminate him."

There was silence on the other end of the phone.

Shawn nodded his head up and down. "I see I have your attention."

"I'm listening."

"I'm texting you a picture. If you find this information worthwhile, you have my number. Call back with a figure in mind." He disconnected the call, then sent a picture of Cainan Scott to the number.

#

The family gathered to give thanks that everyone was safe. Before the meeting began, they said a prayer for Pam Green for a full recovery.

Myles, Grace, Gary, Michael and AnnieMarie sat in the family room with all eyes on Winnie.

"You want to take your father from his resting place because you think there was foul play?"

"Yes," Myles replied.

"Who do you think would have wanted Hepburn dead?"

Myles hesitated. "We can't say. We've been told there are certain noninvasive tests the FBI can run to determine if what we suspect is true."

Winnie closed her eyes.

Grace glanced at Myles, then stepped over and kneeled before her mother. Taking her hands, she squeezed. "What we are asking is one of the hardest decisions we've had to make without Daddy's guidance. He would say Family First & Foremost. If someone did this to him, it is our duty to find out who and why."

Myles spoke. "He would want me to lead that search. Before I can I have to be certain if someone had a hand in taking my father from us."

AnnieMarie walked over and kneeled on the other side of her mother. The men looked on. "I think you, Grace and I should go to New York. Let Myles handle all that needs to be done."

# Epilogue

"One problem settled, a hundred more to go," Myles said as he climbed into bed next to Chrystina. "Walker is under lock and key. The FBI is opening a case against the Russians. Cainan really proved his loyalty to Dunning today." Myles shook his head. "There is something about him that makes you trust him with your life. I can't put my finger on it, but there is more to that man than meets the eye."

"AnnieMarie will agree with you on that. She thinks he is keeping something from her."

"Believe me. There are layers to that brother. Dad trusted him, so why did he have a problem with Cainan and AnnieMarie dating?"

"Well, that's the mystery. Did you talk to your mother about Jerome's theory?"

"I felt we had to. All of us sat down with her about exhuming Dad's body. She agrees, if he did not die of a heart attack we need to know how and why."

Chrystina nodded her head in agreement. "With Mr. Mitchell gone, the employees are safe. What happened today exposed a weakness in our security at headquarters. We have to look at every entrance, install a new camera system."

"Oh, that reminds me." Myles pulled her into his arms. "I know where the wire goes to in your office."

"Where?" Chrystina sat up on her elbow.

"You have security monitors that cover the entire building. Sonya showed it to us. That's how I knew you were in the elevator."

"Who installed it?"

"I take it Mitch did."

"Why?"

"That I don't know. But I think we should go through the tapes to see what has been captured. Who knows what people are doing in the building."

"You mean like making love in your boss's office?"

Myles sat up. "We have to check that."

"Yes, we do." Chrystina sighed as she settled back down. "How is your mother?"

"She was a little shaken, but Jerome has her covered."

"Can you believe Mr. Mitchell was that far gone?"

"I think he had help. I think someone was influencing him. The whole scenario with Elaine was off."

"Do you want me to look into it?"

"Jonathan is going to handle it."

"He agreed to come on board?"

"He agreed to take a look at our operations. He believes we have a traitor in our midst."

"Who?"

"He didn't say, but I have a feeling it's Elaine. The problem is he doesn't think she is working alone. He wants to find out who is spearheading the whole thing."

"The thing being?"

"We don't know. Whatever it is he felt it was important enough to leave Phase to help us."

"Are we sure he is not a plant from Phase?"

"Pretty sure."

"Why?"

Myles pulled her under him and settled in on top of her. "His reason for helping is because he is in love with Grace. I have come to understand the depths a man will go for the woman he loves."

"You mean like climbing down an elevator shaft and picking up a heavy set woman."

"Light weight." He smiled down at her. "I would do that and more for you, Chrystina Price."

"Know what you can do for me right now?" She wrapped her legs around him.

"It's yours, just name it."

"I think I need a workout."

"Let's work it out."

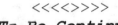

**To Be Continued**

Coming July 25, 2017

Final Book of The Protectors Series

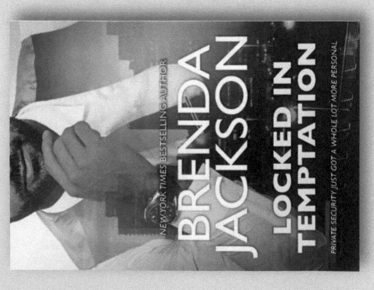

**His job is to protect her...no matter the cost**

Police detective Joy Ingram's connection to elite security expert Stonewall Courson is instant. Undeniable. Electric. But her commitment to protect and serve has always come first. Everything else is secondary—especially when she uncovers an underground surrogate baby-making ring. Joy can't risk a distraction during the most important case of her career, not even one as sexy as reformed ex-con Stonewall.

There are few things Stonewall values more than a strong woman. But when Joy's investigation draws her into a deadly conspiracy that goes deeper than she ever imagined, he must convince her that he's the best man to protect her. And while he puts his life on the line to save hers, the insatiable attraction between them becomes the one danger neither of them can escape.

## INVESTED

Myles Dunning, the thirty-five-year-old CEO of Dunning Bank and Trust, is fighting off one takeover attempt after another to save his family's historical bank. Recently ranked the third largest bank in the world, the leaders in the financial industry conspire to prevent further growth by any means necessary.

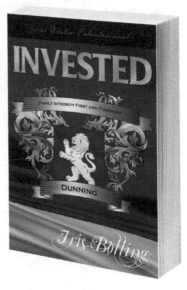

Chrystina Price is a voluptuous, lovable, powerhouse, whose sole purpose in life is to uplift and protect the man she has loved from the first day they met...Myles Dunning. Discovering enemies, close and afar, Chrystina throws everything she has into uncovering and blocking each attempt to bring Myles down.

After a boardroom victory raised the bank closer to the number two ranking, Myles and Chrystina share a victory kiss that unleashes an unstoppable flow of love that no dam could control. The bliss of love is short lived when Miles learns a tragic truth.

When the integrity of the family always comes first is it worth Investing in love.

### Sparrow's Song
Piper Huguley
In the hot summer of '68, recent graduate Sparrow Jones takes a job running the summer program at her family's church hoping to save enough money to attend music school. Despite her mother's objections, music is Sparrow's ministry.

### Lark's Lyrics
Deborah Mello
Devastated by the death of her mother, Lark St. Clair must mend more than a broken heart.

### Dove" Dream
Iris Bolling
Life should be a song worth singing. That's what Dove Warren's grandmother always instilled in her. Anthony Perry, a strong, caring man who lost his brothers to violence, vowed to give his mother at least one child who turned his back on the street life.

Three Voices-Three Generations-One Dream

CPSIA information can be obtained
at www.ICGtesting.com
Printed in the USA
LVHW05s0316270718
585041LV00013B/965/P

9